ANNA BURKE

IN THE
ROSES
OF
PIERIA

THE BLOOD FILES
BOOK ONE

Bywater
BOOKS

2023

Bywater Books

Copyright © 2023 Anna Burke

Print ISBN: 978-1-61294-273-5

Bywater Books First Edition: August 2023

Printed in the United States of America on acid-free paper.

Cover designer: TreeHouse Studio

Bywater Books
PO Box 3671
Ann Arbor MI 48106-3671

www.bywaterbooks.com

*for the academic at heart
and Tiffany, as always*

EPIGRAPH

κατθάνοισα δὲ κείσῃ οὐδέ ποτα
μναμοσύνα σέθν
ἔσσετ᾽ οὐδὲ †ποκ᾽†ὔστερεον· οὐ
γὰρ πεδέχῃς βρόδων
τῶν ἐκ Πιερίας· ἀλλ᾽ ἀφάνης
κἦν Ἀίδα δόμῳ
φοιτάσεις πεδ᾽ ἀμαύρων νεκύων
ἐκπεποταμένα

—Sappho, Fragment 55

CHAPTER ONE
Someone Sends an Unexpected Email

History was a product I packaged and sold to students staring down the barrel of the future. Spores of pollen floated in the thick rays of May sunshine penetrating the antique glass of the classroom, obscuring the faces of my pupils behind a sparkling curtain. Unfortunately, it didn't conceal the fact that several had drifted off to sleep, chins propped up on their hands, mouths slightly agape, as if they could absorb the exam review lecture orally. I imagined the pollen filling their lungs with allergens. The spring breeze wafted in with the sound of luckier students laughing on the quad, along with the sharp scent of cut grass.

"Can anyone tell me when the Nektopolis city-state was founded?" I asked, fighting the urge to toss a piece of chalk at the nearest somnolent student. The sound of the chalk clinking off her teeth would have been satisfying.

"Anyone. This *will* be on the final." At that, a few of my undergrads consulted their notes. I called on the first to raise their hand, a kid with hair cut stylishly short and an earnest expression.

"328 BCE," they said.

"And who founded it?" I prompted.

"Nektarios."

"Good. Does anyone remember the conditions around the founding?" I tapped the map behind me, though the projected image was weakened by the intense brightness outside. I could have pulled the blinds; I didn't. Nektopolis, nestled between Epirus, Macedonia,

1

and the Roman Protectorates, their modern-day counterparts Albania, North Macedonia, and Greece, wavered in the resulting sway of the projector screen.

Another student raised her hand. Light flashed off her glasses, hiding her eyes.

"Nektarios was one of Alexander the Great's generals."

"Yes. And why is that relevant?"

"Because when Alexander died, some of his generals took over their parts of the empire?"

"Precisely. Nektarios saw an opportunity. What are some of the defining features of Nektopolian culture?"

"Women's rights," said a boy I hadn't called on. I nodded, indicating he should continue. "And . . . uh . . ."

"Poetry?" guessed another girl.

"Yes. We have several Nektopolian epics, which is unusual, considering the dearth of surviving material from that era compared to what we know existed thanks to the work of Greek scholars. Anything else about Nektopolis you think might be on the final?"

One of my brighter students raised her hand. "Nektarios's gender."

"What about it?"

"There's speculation Nektarios might have been a woman."

"Or trans," said another.

"Some sources," I began in a tone that I hoped implied all their answers were possible, "suggest Nektarios was actually Nektaria. There were women in Alexander the Great's army. His half sister, Cynane, is known to have commanded some of his forces, and Thracian-Scythian women fought for and against the Greeks."

"The Amazons," a student interjected.

"Yes. Tyras, for instance, a Greek colony in what is now Ukraine, is known to contain burial mounds with battle-scarred female skeletons. It is possible that Nektarios is a translation error by modern scholars, whose biases might have informed their research. With so few primary sources, it is hard to be certain."

I had their attention, now. My Ancient Mediterranean and Near-East History survey course usually enjoyed this bit of history. Probably because it was my favorite, too, and my enthusiasm still overrode my cynicism.

"Nektopolis didn't last very long, though," said the boy who had spoken out of turn. I encouraged my students to speak up, so I couldn't exactly fault him for it, but I had to stifle an urge to chide him as he redirected the conversation back to our exam review. Knowledge for knowledge's sake went only so far this time of year.

"True. What are the dates of its existence?"

"Um." He glanced at his notes.

"We're not entirely sure," said the girl in the flashing glasses. "Macedonia began encroaching on its territory around 200 BCE from one direction and Rome from the other. We know Macedon surrendered in 148 BCE, and ..." She scanned her notes. "The Achaean League surrendered to Rome in 146 BCE, so we think Nektopolis fell around that time. Will the final want an exact date?"

"Since we don't have an exact date, the final will ask for a range," I said.

"Will it be multiple choice?"

I answered their questions, which were less concerned with the material and more concerned with how it would be represented on their exam. Trying not to dwell on how this was part of the problem with the American educational system, I pasted a smile on my face and went over the details, wishing I'd assigned papers, then remembering that I would have had to read and grade those papers and congratulating myself on the wisdom of my decision.

"Any other questions?" I asked as the clock ticked toward the end of the lesson. A student who rarely spoke up raised his hand.

"Is it true there were women charioteers?"

"Great question. Anyone? What sources do we have suggesting this?"

"Pottery?" someone guessed.

"And textile art," said another.

They *had* paid attention. A flush of warmth transformed my pasted smile into something genuine. This was why I couldn't just quit my job and leave academia for something more lucrative and less time-consuming—for example, literally any other career.

"What about the textile art?"

At my prompting, eyes flew to their screens as my class scoured their notes for the information.

"'Not only does Nektopolian textile art depict women in roles generally believed to be masculine,'" one read off her screen, quoting a text we'd read, "'but the weaving pattern contains what some scholars suggest is poetic meter, implying there was an epic tradition of women celebrating other women in those typically masculine roles.'"

"Thank you."

I shut off the projector, and at the cue, my class rushed to pack up. "I'll see you at the final, and if I don't get a chance to tell you then, have a great summer."

I slid my lecture notes into my satchel, noting the warning signs of wear at the seams and calculating the cost of replacing it versus the effort of manually reinforcing the canvas myself. Patches might be unprofessional, but if the university wanted me to look professional, I thought with a bitterness that would probably age me before my time, then they should pay me a living wage.

My classroom emptied slowly. A few students lingered to thank me for the semester or to ask more questions about the final exam before they, too, left. I slumped against the long table at the front of the room. The wood-paneled walls glowed with the light, and the tops of the desks threw dazzling rays into my vision, oiled from student hands. Another semester nearly finished. Another year as an adjunct, with no end in sight. I'd applied for a slew of full-time positions, as I did every few months. Three interviews. One job talk. All it had amounted to was a failed search and rejections. The failed search, as usual, hurt the most: it meant the program would rather have *nobody* than me.

I checked my email on my phone out of masochistic habit. Student questions. Departmental meeting notes. An update about my course evaluation response rates. A thank you for donating plasma earlier in the day, and a reminder about taking care of myself afterward. And an email from an unfamiliar address, with the subject line: Nektopolian Archivist Needed for Private Collection.

I clicked it.

Dear Clara Eden,

We hope this email finds you well. Your research interests have come to the attention of the estate of Agatha Montague, holder of the largest private collection of Nektopolian artifacts in the U.S. We've been conducting a discreet search for the ideal candidate over the last few years and believe you to be a potential fit for our needs.

The Classics department of Brixton University speaks highly of your dedication. On behalf of Ms. Montague, we would like to extend a conditional offer of private employment. Please see the attached terms, proposed salary, and summary of benefits.

We look forward to hearing from you.

Sincerely,
Fiadh Halloran

I read the email twice more before clicking the first attachment to be sure it wasn't a scam, then shook off my suspicions. This was too specifically tailored to me to be a scam, and anyone who went through the effort to do this much research on me would also know I had nothing worthwhile to offer potential scammers. Outside, someone shrieked with laughter. The sound barely penetrated the shock I experienced as I saw the figure proposed for my starting salary. I counted again. Six figures. And benefits.

Even more interesting, however, was the section on the collection itself. Over seventy preserved written documents. Textiles. Pottery. Sculpture. Burial goods. A wealth of primary sources, more than I'd ever hoped to see in one place in my life, and none of which had been publicly studied. A chance to confirm, perhaps, theories of Nektaria once and for all, establishing myself as a leading expert in the field. I could further the work of Gretchen Smith and Emmet Vokse, whose scholarship had informed my dissertation, reshaping views of women in antiquity across the field. My pet theory aside, who knew what avenues of research would open up to me with access to such a trove?

Sweat pricked my armpits as my nervous excitement peaked. This couldn't be happening. I stared around the room, but the sounds of the next class gathering in the hall assured me this wasn't an exhaustion-induced hallucination. I grabbed my things with numb fingers, still clutching my phone with the open email in one hand, and fumbled my way out the door. The next class poured into the empty classroom.

I crossed the green outside the academic buildings, dodging the mushrooms that had sprung up after yesterday's rain as well as the students sprawled with their laptops, and slid into my car.

5

A job offer. After six years of working as an adjunct—though I knew plenty of adjunct professors who had been working longer—an opportunity had finally come my way. I hadn't even had to apply.

Who *had* they spoken to in my department? My former PhD advisor hadn't mentioned anything to me, nor had my direct supervisor. I worried my lower lip between my teeth. Surely there were better options out there. Emmet Vokse, for instance, was still publishing. I knew Nektopolis's relatively short history and scarcity of artifacts meant there wasn't an abundance of scholars eager to enter the field. I'd come to Brixton because it was one of the few universities in the world with faculty who had actually published on the subject, but even so—why me?

"Always looking a gift horse in the mouth," I said to myself in imitation of my mother. My voice sounded loud in the car, even with the windows down and the sounds of the campus filtering in. I was qualified. I was on the job market. Why shouldn't they reach out? No doubt they had connections in the academy. Perhaps one of the jobs that had turned me down had passed my curriculum vitae along.

I opened the second attachment. A PDF labeled Montague Estate Archivist Housing popped up, and I shaded my phone with my hand to better see the photos.

The first image showed the lawns and gardens of what had to be the estate. I noted a pond surrounded by landscaping manicured to look artfully wild before I noticed the cottage in the background. That had to be the housing in question.

The next photo zoomed in on the cottage, and I exhaled with longing. Built from the same reddish-gray stone and blue slate roof as the manor house featured in the letterhead, the small house was nestled between an oak tree and the pond. Flowering clematis vined up around the shutters with an open, welcoming feel to the arrangement of windows and doors, as if the architect intended to welcome the viewer home, drawing the eye up the path, through the garden, and to the blue front door.

The remaining photos showed the interior. I scanned them one by one, my longing growing as I catalogued the stone fireplace and cozy couch; the copper pots and pans hanging over the kitchen window; the small bedroom, which would have looked right at home in any upscale country bed-and-breakfast; a breakfast nook with a view of the pond; and a home office, complete with antique desk and shelves.

Nine hundred square feet of perfection. Too small for a large family, perhaps, but perfect for a single woman and her cat. Would the cat be a dealbreaker? Nothing on the PDF said, "No Pets," and I chose to interpret that as a good sign.

This place alone was worth it. Still chewing on my lip, I tapped out a reply expressing my interest, and hit send before I could somehow talk myself out of it.

⚊ ⚊ ⚊

A week and a half later, I stared, eyes wide enough to burn, at the contract resting on the smooth mahogany desk before me and skimmed the fine print of the impenetrable legalese for the catch. Offers like this didn't happen to academics. Reasonable pay? Healthcare? Paid time off? My salivary glands acted up like they'd just caught a whiff of free pizza in the faculty lounge.

The job couldn't have been more tailored to my tastes if I'd designed it myself: translate, catalogue, and digitalize the private collection of Agatha Montague, one of the only other people alive who cared about works written in the long-dead language of the equally long-dead city-state of Nektopolis.

"The salient points are at the top."

The lawyer, an older man with a nose sharp enough to file graphite, pointed at the sheet of paper I had cast aside. On it, in carefully lettered bullet points, were the conditions of the contract deemed most important by my employer: In addition to the archival work, under no circumstances, ever, was I to speak, write, or communicate in any manner the contents of the material in the collection to anyone besides Agatha without her express written permission, which would require additional contracts. I could not publish work derived from my study of the material. I could not share even so much as a joke about the material over a drink with a friend. Duplicating the material for my own purposes would render me dead, legally speaking, and while the sum I was being offered for the work was more than I'd make as a tenured professor—a prospect as distant as the sun—it was nothing compared to the legal fees I'd accrue when Agatha's lawyers came after me for breach of contract.

7

It all seemed a bit over the top, and admittedly piqued my curiosity in a way I was certain wasn't healthy.

"What is *in* these documents?" I asked him, unable to contain myself.

"I do not know, nor would I tell you if I did," he said, examining me with displeasure. "As I would have signed this very same NDA."

Nondisclosure, or a gag order? I wasn't sure of the difference, but I knew what I was looking at meant trouble. Still, it didn't necessarily mean *bad* trouble. The salary printed at the top of the contract made thinking difficult. Perhaps the collection contained previously unknown Nektopolian pornography or something.

It was the "or something" that concerned me.

"What if the material is criminal? Aren't I obligated to report it? Wouldn't that make me an accessory?"

He linked his fingers on the desk between us and did not reply.

Right. That was clear enough. If I was willing to sign an agreement to never speak of this work, then I would be an idiot not to realize there was a reason. Besides. The only crime that made sense was theft; perhaps Agatha had come by these materials on the black market. She wouldn't be the first. Technically speaking, the majority of artifacts I'd studied were the result of nineteenth-century plundering by Western archaeologists. I could take this job or walk away. No one was forcing me.

But if I couldn't publish any of my research . . . I wiped sweating palms on my slacks. *Knowledge for knowledge's sake.* Would that be enough for me? I'd managed to spin myself fairy tales in the time between receiving the email and now. In them, I accepted prestigious awards for scholarship, broke new research ground, spoke at conferences, and corresponded with my scholarly idols.

"I need a moment," I told him.

"Take your time." His tone suggested the offer had an expiration.

I considered my options. I either continued working as an underpaid adjunct with no time to work on my own research, donating blood plasma now and then to earn a few extra bucks for groceries, or entered the private sector with its attending moral quandaries and enjoyed reliable health insurance, a salary large enough to start thinking about things like retirement funds and home ownership, and the alluring promise of secret Nektopolis documents. Could I live with myself if I turned the latter down? I could always publish on existing material, letting the private collection inform my interpretations.

The lawyer's pen felt cool in my hand. Like his desk, it was carved from richly oiled wood, and my signature flowed from the tip.

I paused. "It's red ink."

"Yes."

"I thought legal documents—"

"Not this one. Don't worry. It's just as binding."

Shrugging, I finished signing with a flourish to mask my sudden discomfort. My name, Clara Eden, glared wetly up at me from the cream-colored paper, red as blood.

Agatha Montague, according to the deep dives I'd performed on various online databases, was a ghost. She existed, but in the way only the truly powerful could exist: behind a carefully constructed public image, more barricade than façade. Whoever she paid to scrub her presence from the internet was good. I couldn't find even a photograph. No whiff of scandal or anything remotely personal existed anywhere. Not online, and not in print newspapers in the library archives. Most notable, however, was the absence of any links between Agatha and Nektopolis. The closest I came was a series of donations to the university from an anonymous benefactor that might have fit her profile.

Eventually, I gave up. I'd signed the contract and given my notice to the university. I'd find out the details soon enough.

My apartment in what passed for downtown Brixton overlooked a back alley. I gazed out the window on the morning of my first day of my new job, ignoring the shabby vinyl siding of the building opposite and focusing instead on the sunlight breaking through the clouds. A bird flitted past, swooping like my stomach. I'd be out of the apartment at the end of the month and on the grounds of the estate, which, in a twist of fate, was located within driving distance of my current lodgings. I fed the cat on autopilot. He meowed at me reproachfully as I gave him a cursory scratch. Then, I opened my closet.

The narrow recess, more cupboard than proper closet, contained the few nice items of clothing I could afford. I chose a blue wool blazer, white blouse, and dark-washed chinos. It was that or my only suit, but a suit seemed excessively formal. I would be translating old documents, not giving a lecture. Still, I wanted to impress, so I put my hair up in a French twist, hoping it conveyed the elegance my clothing did not, and ran a lint roller over the entire outfit to remove evidence of Mr. Muffin and my own hair, which shed just as copiously. Eating wasn't an option. Nerves squirmed in place of appetite, so I packed a breakfast bar in my bag for later, topped off my coffee thermos, and prayed my old Volvo would start.

Agatha lived beyond the city limits. Ramshackle manufacturing plants faded into farm fields as I drove the thirty minutes to the address provided by her assistant. Eventually, a winding country road leading into the blue morning hills delivered me to a private drive lined with sentinel oak trees, each at least a century old, and on to an estate overlooking a pond I recognized from the photos of the archivist's cottage. Sprawling gardens flush with spring growth surrounded the Tudor-style brick mansion. I turned off the car with a surge of excitement. Would I be allowed to take my lunch on the grounds in warm weather? I pictured sitting by the pond, smelling honeysuckle and water lilies, perhaps with a novel in hand. It didn't get much more bucolic. The engine clicked and pinged to itself as it cooled, and I snapped a photo of the ivy climbing several of the walls, framing the large manor windows, before remembering the NDA agreement. Did that include the house itself? Deleting the photo and leaving my phone in the car seemed safer. I liked to avoid avoidable mistakes, preferring to make unexpected ones instead. I hoped this job wasn't one of them.

Yet despite its size, the house and attending grounds radiated a friendly charm. My reservations faded. Anyone who let their roses grow in such wild abundance had my favor.

Thus buoyed, I crossed the gravel drive to the front door, took a deep breath, and knocked. The noise echoed. Footsteps sounded from the other side just as my nervous system decided sweating was the clear solution to the delay, dampening my armpits uncomfortably. The door opened to reveal a young woman with shockingly dark eyebrows in a severe brown dress.

"Clara Eden?" she asked.

I nodded and extended my hand. She looked down at it, then up at me, and then took a step back to let me into the house. My hand fell limply to my side. Perhaps she didn't like germs and her refusal to shake my hand wasn't the snub it seemed. I clung to that delusion and added more paste to the smile slipping from my lips.

"I am Ms. Montague's private secretary, Fiadh. We spoke over email. Please come in."

So that was how her name was pronounced: *Fee-ah*.

The foyer was spacious and bright, adorned with citrus trees in large ceramic pots chosen to complement the floor tiles. I forgot about Fiadh and my slighted handshake as I examined them. Modern manufacturing, but Nektopolian in style, hints of Grecian influence evident in the meander patterns. The contrast with the Tudor exterior worked, despite the inherent contradictions. My pulse galloped ahead of me and I longed to sketch the pattern into a notebook since I couldn't take a photograph. All personal inside photography was forbidden by my contract. Rich people and their paranoia. My gaze roamed the rest of the room. Huge windows. High ceilings. And Fiadh, gesturing at me impatiently to follow her.

Tile floor transitioned to hardwood and carpet as we entered the house proper. We passed sitting rooms painted bright, light colors, a small art gallery complete with statuary, and an open area large enough to accommodate a wedding party. A ballroom, maybe. I wanted to slow down and explore, but Fiadh's quick tread necessitated I nearly jog to keep up. Her petite form had deceived me. She moved with the brisk efficiency of a cat. I felt awkward and gangly lumbering after her.

At the top of a flight of stairs, she paused before a large, oak-paneled door.

"This is the library. There is a bathroom down the hall, and a kitchenette. There will be no need for you to leave this area."

Translation: the rest of the house was off-limits.

"I understand," I said. Loath though I was to miss out on the opportunity to wander, offending my new employer was not an option.

Thoughts of trespassing died the moment she opened the door. Beyond lay a scholar's dream. Shelves upon shelves of books filled the space, and glass cases contained scrolls, bound vellum manuscripts, and even hides, if my quick appraisal was any judge, with drawers beneath the shelves that I assumed held items too fragile to be exposed to light. An arched window overlooked the pond and grounds below, framed by reading chairs and a window seat, and a long wooden table perfect for spreading out documents dominated the center of the room. A green reading lamp and a conspicuously out of place ergonomic chair completed the tableau. My back hummed with anticipatory gratitude.

"You'll be provided with a camera for digitalizing the files, and a work laptop connected to our private internet. We have top-of-the-line security, and a closed, local network you'll use for uploading the files to our digital server. We take security very seriously."

"I understand."

"The first thing Ms. Montague would like you to do is catalogue the collection."

"The complete collection?" I said, gesturing at the library.

"In stages, yes. Some of the work has already been completed by your predecessor, but you may wish to double-check."

Something about the way she said "may wish" implied "absolutely should."

"You'll begin with the Nektopolian. Most is here, though there are some pieces in the gallery, which have already been catalogued. You may update those entries as you see fit. Once you've catalogued the work, Ms. Montague will select the pieces she wishes given priority for digitalization and translation. Only the Nektopolian will require translation in this first stage, given your specialties, but your CV states you are also fluent in Greek and Latin, and competent in several early Indo-European dialects."

"That is correct." I modulated the excitement in my voice. The need for such knowledge suggested the breadth of material in this room.

"Some translation will have to take place in order to determine the nature of the artifact for the catalogue," I said.

Fiadh waved away my implied concern about the order of operations. "As you see fit. Each day, you will collect the keys from me. The work computer will remain in the library until you have moved onto the estate. This is part of our standard security protocols," she added, perhaps sensing from my expression that I was feeling villainized.

"You'll find supplies, as well as the Nektopolian collection, in here."

She removed a key from a chain around her neck and opened a drawer beneath one of the glass cabinets. Viewing cloths; an assortment of magnifying glasses: handheld, stand, and ocular; microscopes; gloves; book-binding materials; and more.

"There is a light table available for your use as well." She pointed toward a closet. I opened it, and found a state-of-the-art conservation station neatly tucked inside. I knew from my follow-up email conversations with Fiadh that some conservation work would be required of me as necessary. With these supplies, I'd be well equipped.

"I was hoping to speak with Ms. Montague—" I began.

"Why on earth would you need to do that?" Fiadh contracted her impossibly dark brows as if I'd asked her where I might take a public leak. I noticed her eyes for the first time. Green—the clear, turquoise green of a lagoon.

"I had a few questions—"

"Ms. Montague is a very busy woman. I will answer your questions."

"With translation," I said, wondering how much Fiadh understood about the process, "especially with works dating from Nektopolis, it can be difficult to preserve original sentiment. Does she have an audience in mind? Shall I provide context?"

"Feedback will be provided to you as needed. The audience is Ms. Montague. No one else."

"I see." I didn't see, but that was fine.

"I'll leave you to it then. Oh, and Clara?"

I met Fiadh's eyes. Her pupils were two sharp points. "Yes?"

"Your discretion is of the utmost importance."

I gave her my most reassuring nod. She left, her sensible low heels shushing across the carpet as she exited the library. When the door shut, I let the grin I'd been suppressing spread across my face. This place was incredible. I felt the history sink into my pores as I breathed in the musty fragrance of old paper, leather, and ink. No dust marred the shelves. The room was meticulously maintained, and I paced it, counting the shelves while my fingers itched to stroke the spines of the books behind their UV-protectant casings. Some were embossed, but most were clothed in archival-grade replacement covers with handwritten labels.

I paused before a volume with a handwritten Greek title, unlocking the case with the key Fiadh had left me, and taking it down with gloved hands. The pages were thin, almost transparently so, and I could see the fibers of the plant that had made them when I held it briefly up to the light. Vowing I'd start work in just a moment, I started reading.

"She has an entire book of Sappho. A previously unknown *book*. Not just fragments. Of Sappho. In the original Greek."

Fiadh didn't so much as blink in surprise, shutting the door quietly behind her in the wake of my outburst.

"I can talk about the collection with you, right?" I paced back and forth, all the hairs on my arms standing on end. Fiadh had returned to check on me after several hours, during which time I'd had my mind effectively blown.

"Of course."

"I'd have to authenticate the poems. It's clearly a copy of an older work. I'd have to date the parchment, too, but the minuscule script and similarities in the calligraphy to other extant works suggests tenth century, which—"

"All things for the catalogue entry," said Fiadh.

"That's not—this changes everything we know about Greek poetics."

"There are some remarkable verses, it's true."

"You've *read them*?" I was nearly shouting in my excitement.

"Well of course. Agatha keeps a second copy on her personal shelves, which you'll no doubt find shortly, if you haven't already. You may borrow from them for your own reading, though the books cannot leave the property, and she'd prefer them digitalized before you remove them from the library."

"Right. But—"

"She also has some Greek plays you'll no doubt find interesting."

"But—" I tried again, sputtering like a dying engine. "Posterity! Scholarship! This could change—"

"Nothing. Every work in this library belongs to Agatha Montague and Agatha Montague alone. You'd do well to remember that."

Her trim brown dress with its austere collar made her look like an angry schoolteacher, and I quieted even though we had to be near the same age—early thirties—and she might have even been a few years younger. A lifetime of brown-nosing the academic establishment, however, had left its mark on my psyche. The need to please temporarily surpassed my shock.

"I do understand. It's just . . . a lot to take in."

14

She gave me a look I couldn't interpret. Pity, maybe.

"Yes. I forgot to tell you that you're free to help yourself to the kitchenette. It will be stocked with whatever you need. Make me a list. Ms. Montague wants you to be productive, and she understands that scholars . . ." Here she paused as if swallowing her own judgment regarding scholars as a group., ". . . can forget to take care of themselves."

The gesture unsettled me with its thoughtfulness. I felt seen, exposed almost, as if Agatha herself had just patted me on the shoulder. I swallowed further protests about Sappho.

"Thank you."

Fiadh nodded, searched my face once as if she wanted to say more, then exited without another word.

I took as many deep breaths as my lungs could handle. What else lay undiscovered in this library?

The architect had shaped the reading room of the library in the Greek letter Ω. A turret, which I'd seen from the parking lot, housed the curving window seat and Agatha's personal shelves. I sat on one of the plush cushions and pressed my cheek to the warm glass. This was so much more than I'd dared hope for. My heartbeat thrummed in my ears as I tried to slow my breathing. There was enough work here to last a lifetime—work I yearned to complete on a cellular level. I wanted to study everything at once, and I was also paralyzed by the sheer number of artifacts suddenly at my disposal. I didn't know where to begin.

The quiet of the room gradually calmed me. I did, actually, know where to begin: with a list. I moved to the table and pulled a notebook and pencil out of my bag. First, I needed to wander the library as I had been doing, but with purpose, figuring out the general organizational strategy, if there was one, and noting any major works that seemed like they might be relevant to Nektopolis, provided I didn't get too distracted. Then, I'd begin the process of cataloguing and digitalizing, starting with the Nektopolis collection and working outward from there.

Sunlight shifted across the room as I strolled the shelves and carefully opened drawers. Fiadh hadn't lied about the Greek plays. As I pulled books at random, I discovered copies of ancient commentaries on Classical texts, some of which I'd heard of or read, and some that were entirely new to me. Tragedies and satires were bound together, almost haphazardly in some places. In one drawer, I discovered an illuminated manuscript with a scribbled catalogue card, dating it

15

roughly twelfth century from a nunnery I hadn't realized produced illuminated manuscripts. When I opened it, I discovered not, as I'd originally thought, a traditional book of hours, but a collection of psalms interspersed with erotic drawings, many of which featured nuns performing a different kind of devotional act. The occasional demon surfaced, which was traditional in medieval eroticism, but there was a tenderness in some of the scenes that exhibited real artistry, despite the prevailing tendency to represent human anatomy in the general shape and color of a parsnip.

Other drawers contained incredibly preserved papyri; still more revealed small carved figures, knives, and textiles. I recognized a Celtic fertility figurine, but not a misshapen bronze figure weathered past recognition by age. One drawer held a jeweled cat skull. I shut it gently, not loving the way the emeralds set in the eye sockets seemed to watch me.

The next cabinet I opened was the one Fiadh had waved at first: Nektopolis. Pottery lined the top shelves, along with fragments of what had once been a mosaic. Reddish brown mosaic tiles depicted part of a flower, but the rest of the scene was missing. I pulled a drawer open at random to find a collection of papyri pressed between preservation-quality sleeves. Adrenaline tasted metallic on my tongue.

So little writing had survived the collapse of the kingdom. And here were sheaves of it.

I'd start my cataloguing here. Pulling the light table out of its closet, I prepared the surface and gently laid the first fragment on the glass.

The alphabet was Greek; the words were not. I snapped a photo of the fragment with the camera and then selected one of the magnifying glasses. Agatha had clearly called in a professional conservationist at some point, for the document was as pristine as it was possible to be. It must have come from a tomb in an arid location, kept out of the light and away from moisture.

Slowly, mouthing the syllables with reverence, I read.

Collection: Nektopolis
Title: Letter 1
Description: Correspondence; Gata and Natek
Date: TBD
Cataloguer: Clara Eden

From[1] Natek to her dearest and sharpest of knives,
You burn me[2]. Or rather I think you long to, for it
is twice, now, that my words have found you. They
have found you. If you thought to fool me with
your silence, you're not the adversary I know you
to be. What did you do with that letter? That curl of
papyrus? Did you burn it in effigy?

I felt the shift when I entered your awareness: a
silence past sound, a stillness beyond death. The
immensity of you is what intrigues me most. My own
influence is vast, but this is as it should be. Yours is
vaster, which is not.

If I am wrong, tell me. You know where to send your
reply. You've known, I think, for quite some time.

Natek

I read it again, wondering if I'd misunderstood. The word "burn" in Greek figuratively meant "love," but this meaning hadn't been established in Nektarian. I needed more context, and time to sit with the possible variations. Still, the pure thrill of reading words that had been written a thousand years before erased all else. It could have been a grocery list, for all I cared.

---

1   Translator's note: The merging of Greek with the existing population's native tongue, an Indo-European language thought to be similar to Greek but with enough structural differences to make it unintelligible to the uninitiated, led to the development of the Nektopolian language. Prior to conquest, there had been no written form.

2   Translator's note: Initially I thought this to be a passing comment, but upon further reading, I believe it is a reference to Sappho Fragment 38: ὄπταις ἄμμε, which translates approximately as 'you burn me'. This dates this correspondence to a time after Sappho, which helps confirm the dates for Nektopolis. Sappho (615-570 BCE) died 234 years before Alexander the Great (356-323 BCE), and Nektopolis was founded shortly after his death, though the precise date remains speculation. The close linguistic links to Nektarian Greek (a blend of Greek and the Thracian language) and Greek are also evident in this line.

Checking first that the photographs were the necessary quality, I placed the sleeve back in its folder and reverently removed the next papyri, making a note of the location.

Birdsong floated in through the glass. The quietude enveloped me, saturating the very air with peace. I wanted to stay in this room forever. No stress hormones wafting off passing students. No noxious cleaning chemicals. No criminally uncomfortable library chairs. Tension I hadn't realized I'd been carrying slipped off my shoulders.

I scribbled out rough translations of the first documents I planned to catalogue in my notebook, along with the materials used and my best guess at the date. I'd talk to Agatha—or Fiadh—eventually about the style of translation and alternative approaches. Without knowing her context awareness of ancient Nektopolian culture, I'd have to compensate, replacing ancient phrases with phrases more familiar to the modern reader, instead of remaining completely faithful to the text—not that complete faith was possible in any translation, especially where there were words and meanings without direct counterparts in English.

The next complete document looked like a response to the sender of the first. My hand shook on the camera. I took a steadying breath.

Collection: Nektopolis
Title: Letter 2
Description: Correspondence; Gata and Natek
Date: TBD
Cataloguer: Clara Eden

Natek[3],

If I wished you to burn, you would be ash. Is this how you begin all your wars?

Gata

---

3   Translator's note: For context, the formal address adhered to in the genre of letter writing from this time is standard, whereas this more casual opening is arguably intentionally insulting.

18

I stared at the words I'd transcribed. It was a letter, to be sure, but what did it mean? Could this be Nektopolis's equivalent to Queen Atossa of Persia, who had written the first preserved letter known to scholarship? To hold this missive in my hand—

Giddy, I began working on the following page, which seemed to be another direct reply. The handwriting differed: this one sloped, where the other stalked upright across the page. Checking the camera, I confirmed it resembled the handwriting in the first. I jotted notes and possible interpretations, slowly compiling a text that made sense.

Collection: Nektopolis
Title: Letter 3
Description: Correspondence; Gata and Natek
Date: TBD
Cataloguer: Clara Eden

From Natek to Gata,

You surprise me. You always do. I did not think you would respond without further coaxing, let alone give me your name. I am beginning to think you do not fear me at all.

This is no declaration of war. We've been working at cross purposes since I first came to this land. It took me time to see: an undisturbed hillside where I'd planned the death of cavalry, or famine when I needed plenty. I see your work, but I do not see you at work. I do not know how you are possible. Will you tell me?

Yours,

Natek

The soft clearing of a throat interrupted my perusal of the translation. I looked up to see Fiadh standing on the far side of the table, chin tilted high. Her cheekbones reflected the evening light.

"Ms. Montague thanks you."

The dismissal was clear. I gathered my things, returned the archival materials to their homes, and realized I was starving. Yes. Home to the apartment I still had four months of a lease on before I could vacate, a quick meal, and then I could process the turn my life had taken.

CHAPTER TWO
Will the Rich Ever Understand?

"Ms. Montague is pleased with your work," Fiadh said the moment she opened the door.

I smoothed the front of my shirt where the strap of my briefcase had rumpled the cotton and tried not to look as relieved as I felt by her words, though what work, precisely, she was referring to, I wasn't sure. The translation notes, or the photographs?

How her employer's pleasure made Fiadh feel was anyone's guess. Her back was to me as she led the way down the hall, and the smart line of her shoulders, encased in a dress of sensible forest green, gave nothing away. I took the opportunity to gaze around me. Whoever maintained this place did so with loving care. No paint peeled in the corners, and the floors were waxed to a shine that brightened up even the shadows in the halls.

"Do you live around here?" I asked Fiadh, hoping to establish friendlier relations. If she was to be my point of contact, I might as well get to know her, and perhaps scrape some of the frost off the surface.

"I live on the property."

"Oh." What was I supposed to say to that? *I will soon, too?* She already knew. Did she live here, in this house? "A place like this must require a large staff."

"Not really. It's just me and my mother, and Agatha, of course. Oh, and the groundskeeper, though Ms. Montague does most of the gardening herself, and he doesn't live on the property. His wife and son do the cleaning."

"Well, it must be nice living here."

"Very."

The conversation died, and Fiadh made no move to revive it.

I picked up where I'd left off, settling into the desk chair with the laptop open. Yesterday's photographed files awaited. I left the originals on their shelf. If I needed them, I knew where to find them, but there was no need to expose them to potential damage without cause, miraculous preservation notwithstanding.

Before I continued photographing the artifacts, I sat down to compile a list of the words less familiar to me. Tracing the etymology of dead languages whiled away the morning, and eventually the grumble of my stomach alerted me to the afternoon's arrival. I paused my work and wandered down the hall toward the kitchenette. Along the way, I snooped.

This floor of the house contained only the library, a series of guest rooms, and the kitchenette. The guest rooms were lavishly appointed as best I could tell; sheets covered the furniture in all the rooms save one.

This room, with its light blue wallpaper and elegant four-poster bed, looked like a photograph from a luxury English hotel, but told me nothing save that Agatha did not frequently host more than one person or couple on this floor at a time. The room definitely didn't belong to Fiadh. For one thing, it didn't smell like her perfume, which I'd noticed lingered in the air behind her. The scent wasn't overwhelming, a hint of something floral maybe. This room smelled like Pine-Sol.

My stomach grumbled again, and I abandoned my curiosity in favor of food.

The kitchenette's window overlooked a small, walled garden. Wisteria climbed a trellis, framing the windowpanes, and I thought I recognized one or two of the other bushes growing below. Over the wall, a bird circled the glass dome of a greenhouse. Its reflection chased after, white against the blue of the reflected sky.

The kitchenette itself was modern: a small counter cut from black, gold-shot stone, sleek cupboards, and new appliances. I felt oddly disappointed not to discover a cozy little cast iron stove with an antique kettle. Instead, the stove and microwave gleamed with stainless steel. Fiadh hadn't lied about keeping it stocked, however. Tea and coffee—good coffee—filled one cupboard, and a bowl of assorted fruits graced the small table. A note lay beside it:

Please let me know what refreshments to provide.—F

Refreshments. I didn't want Agatha thinking I was taking advantage of her generosity. On the other hand, I'd certainly scavenged far worse from faculty lounges. Perhaps it was time to embrace an existence other than that of resident trash panda.

Another cupboard revealed my favorite brand of ginger tea cookies. I shoved one into my mouth and savored the spicy crunch. I'd gotten hooked on them thanks to an ex-girlfriend, but could never justify spending money on expensive British imports. I wouldn't object to a work stash, however. I pulled a pencil from behind my ear and scribbled a *thank you* beneath Fiadh's *F*, along with the brand of biscuits and a request for fruit. It seemed like a reasonable compromise between her blanket request and my own sensibilities.

Fueled by a quick lunch—a lackluster sandwich scraped together hastily this morning from the dregs of my peanut butter jar and a friend's homemade jam—and a cup of coffee, I returned to the library, listening to the quiet of the house. The slow amble of a silver cat caught my eye as I passed the landing down to the first floor. It paused to inspect a patch of sunlight on the ground, then sauntered on.

I grew used to my routine after a week. Arrive by eight thirty, greet a glacial Fiadh with forced cheer, and settle into Nektopolis. My list of words continued to grow as I performed the rough translation of the first folio of documents for cataloguing, and as I read, I checked my work against what was known about Nektopolian history and culture. Some of it matched; still more didn't. I read over my most recent translation with my lower lip between my teeth, worrying a bit of dry skin.

Collection: Nektopolis
Title: Letter 4
Description: Correspondence; Gata and Natek
Date: TBD
Cataloguer: Clara Eden

> Names mean nothing. I've worn many, as have you.
> There is nothing permanent about one's own name.

Only the names of others are indelible.

I do fear you. I fear what you represent, and who. I fear the change you seek to bring. Herophilos[4] says the intellect resides in the brain, not the heart. I struggle to believe this when fear lives in every part of me.

Your mistake is perceiving fear as a weakness. I am possible precisely because I fear.

Gata, writing to Natek

Each time I read over my notes, the magnitude of the artifacts struck me anew. Few complete personal accounts, if any, survived of the average Nektopolian citizen. Yet here were two correspondents writing of their lives. Much of the text didn't make sense to me in a larger context, but perhaps it would in time.

Collection: Nektopolis
Title: Letter 5
Description: Correspondence; Gata and Natek
Date: TBD
Cataloguer: Clara Eden

Natek, to her dear knife's edge,

I appreciate the effort you went through on my behalf. The organization required to pull off that little trick suggests I know even less about you than I thought, and Gata, I've been digging. I cannot resist an enigma. Some would—and have—called it a character flaw.

But how did you bring down half the garrison? It will take me time to recruit and rebuild, irreparably throwing off the campaign season for the year. If you wished to dissuade me, you've erred—without a campaign to run,

---

4   Translator's note: Herophilos was a physician and anatomist, notable for believing the soul resided in the *calamus scriptorius*, along with founding the modern concept of anatomy.

you have my full attention. This is not a threat. Merely an observation. You, like I, are a keen observer, and the arrogant side of my nature wonders if this was your intent all along. Why else would you have left that corpse on my doorstep? Though conventionally it is considered impolite to gift an empty wine sack.

Here is what I do know: you cannot destroy me as easily as I once thought, or you would have done so already. I will not entertain the other option, which is your mercy. If I live by your sufferance, end it now, Gata, for that alone I could not bear.

I think of you as rooted. I've been working on this metaphor[5] since my last letter, and you cradle this black earth to you as you spread beneath my feet; but there is only so far even the deepest root can run. Your power, no matter how immense it seems, has limits. I shall have to learn them.

Yours, Natek

—m— —m— —m—

The next sheaf of preserved papyri was not correspondence. Instead, I photographed a series of early legal documents, granting ownership of several establishments to a woman named Galatea. Following these was a will for the same woman. This excited me so much I almost overlooked the beneficiary: a niece named Gatalina. Legal documents revealed so much about a culture, from gender and social norms to perceived existential threats. The sound of my fingers on the keys and the click of the camera matched the quiet rhythm of the afternoon.

---

5   Translator's note: A concept discussed in Book Three of Aristotle's *Rhetoric* and an established literary device by this time. The reference here suggests the correspondents were well educated, either formally or through their own research.

The end of the day once again arrived too soon. I packed up, returned the key to Fiadh, collected my phone from the lockbox by the door, and drove on autopilot, my mind still back in Agatha's library.

I made myself a quick dinner of slightly wilted salad and some hard-boiled eggs. When I received my first paycheck, I vowed, I'd spoil myself by replenishing my larder. As it was, I didn't see much point stocking up since I was moving in two weeks. My apartment felt particularly dingy as I compared it in my mind to my future living quarters.

Settling on the couch with my laptop, I checked my email. Nothing pressing. Someone wanted to buy my bed set, which would earn me a quick $75, money I could put toward gas.

On a whim, and because the university hadn't yet revoked my access, I logged onto the academic search databases and typed in "Natek" and "Nektopolis."

Nothing popped up. I hadn't expected it to. I tried Gata, Galatea, and Gatalina. One hit, but outside of Greek mythology, Galatea was the name of the author of the Nektarian article, not the subject. Then, I tried searching for some of the artifacts, wondering if I was about to discover they'd gone missing from museums years ago. More nothing. I supposed that was a relief.

I tried a few more search variations before giving up.

—m— —m— —m—

My new routine consisted of wandering the shelves for the first half hour, randomly examining the contents. I hoped this would gradually get me familiar with the scope of the collection. Also, I was secretly hoping for another racy illuminated manuscript. I didn't find another quite so explicit, but, in a small volume of gorgeously rendered biblical illustrations, I did find some delightfully inappropriate marginalia.

In a climate-controlled drawer—the cabinets were all state-of-the-art artifact storage units—I found something that made the hair on my arms rise straight up. Approaching the light table, I laid the papyri down, picked up a magnifying lens, and confirmed my suspicions.

The library of Alexandria, fabled and mourned, hadn't been

destroyed in one single fire. Rather, it had been destroyed and rebuilt multiple times, and other libraries had sprung up across antiquity in its image. To keep track of the fluctuating catalogue would have been a tall order, but there were those who made the attempt, including Callimachus, who, in his *Pinakes*, catalogued the contents of the library during his tenure. Like much of the work from that era, the *Pinakes* had been lost, and scholars knew about it only from references in other work.

Which did not explain why I now held a large portion of a scroll that looked to be part of that very catalog. I scanned the lists of titles and authors, my eyes bulging. This papyri was worth millions. Maybe more. And its worth to the academic establishment was priceless. It was a crime to withhold this from the public. My hands shook as I put the papyri back in its drawer. *What the actual fuck.* I crouched on my heels and rested my head in my hands, staring at the red library carpet.

Private collectors, I thought as blood beat angrily in my ears, should be forced to report the contents of their collections. It wasn't right that one woman should stand between scholarship and such artifacts just because she was rich. How many hands had that catalogue passed through? How many individuals had decided, again and again, to keep that sacred knowledge to themselves?

I should steal it. I should bring it straight to the nearest museum— or fly it to Alexandria myself, where it belonged—my contract be damned.

"Clara?"

I started. How long had I sat there, fuming? Long enough that when I stood, the rush of blood to my head sent sparks around my vision. I swayed as the sparks were replaced by a growing darkness. Fiadh was across the room and clutching my elbow before I could fall.

"Are you all right?"

"Yeah." My vision cleared as my bodily equilibrium restored itself. "Blood rush."

"You were on the floor." She stepped back from me, leaving a lingering hint of perfume. It made me feel dizzy in a new way.

I hesitated. We'd already had this argument about Sappho. I wasn't keen to repeat it, but I also still vibrated with anger, and Fiadh's uncharacteristic concern was disorienting. Or maybe that was still the blood rush.

"Well, I just stopped by to see if you needed any more archival supplies. It's been some time since the last archivist left us, and Ms. Montague wanted to make sure you were fully stocked."

"What happened to the last archivist?" I wondered if they'd quit in protest.

"She retired. She'd been with the estate for years."

A loyalist, then.

"And she never had any issues with . . ."

"With what?" Fiadh's brows lowered in warning.

"Do you have any idea what some of these things are worth?"

"Perhaps you can note it in the catalogue entry."

"Not just monetary worth. I just found a record from the library of Alexandria. It should be in a museum, not here."

"Why?"

"Because knowledge should be available to everyone!"

She crossed her arms over her chest. "I disagree."

"This collection could revolutionize previously held conceptions—"

"We've discussed this already."

"Yes, and *I* still disagree."

"It isn't your decision. Shall I tell Ms. Montague you've reconsidered the position?"

That shut me up. I didn't want that. Nor did I want Fiadh to report on my outburst to her employer, who would no doubt be glad to fire me.

"No," I said.

"If you cannot handle—"

"I can handle it."

"Are you quite sure? Because this is the second time you've brought this up."

"I just . . ." I softened my tone in the interest of job security. "I know what it would mean to my colleagues to have access to this material. I know what it means to me. Wealthy collectors shouldn't have the right to hoard this information."

"And knowledge distribution should be egalitarian?" She tilted her head to one side, studying me.

"Well ideally, yes. What if something happens to her collection, and everything is lost?"

"She's employing you to digitalize it to prevent that very possibility."

"And it should be authenticated by experts—"

"There is no doubt of the authenticity."

"Some of these artifacts are over a thousand years old. She can't have clear provenance. In fact, there are no records of provenance here."

"Because those records are not kept in the library. At any rate, I am not here to argue ethics with you. You are being paid to do a job, not insult your employer's morality. I'll have to let Ms. Montague know of this outburst. I do not advise a third."

She spun on her heel and marched toward the door. Panic nipped at my throat. I lunged after her, snatching at her sleeve. She scowled up at me. I dropped her arm, feeling huge and ungainly compared to her petite frame.

"Sorry," I said, gesturing at her sleeve. "I understand if you have to tell Ms. Montague. But I'm not sure you understand how shocking it is to touch something you've been told all your life is lost to history. She has some of my field's holy grails in here. I know I'm acting unprofessionally. I don't mean to. It's just a lot, and I wasn't expecting it. I was trying to calm myself down when you came in but clearly hadn't succeeded yet."

Her eyes, this close, were shockingly turquoise. Maybe she wore colored contacts. I took a step back as I realized I was crowding her, horrified at the boorishness of my actions.

"There is a provision in Ms. Montague's will to leave her private collection to the American Academy of Arts and Sciences, with instructions to return the artifacts to their home regions. Does that satisfy your ethical dilemma?" Her tone carried a mocking edge, but the words were, in fact, a comfort.

"Yes. This won't happen again."

"It certainly won't happen a third time."

My mind was still occupied with my disastrous outburst when I returned home that evening. Mr. Muffin's yowling carried down the flight of stairs leading up to my small one-bedroom apartment, and the note of consternation and betrayal in his tone shattered my reflective state. I took the stairs three at a time, fumbled my keys from my pocket, and then stumbled into my apartment as the door swung open beneath my hand before I could put the key in the lock.

"No." The word emerged from my chest in a groan. Mr. Muffin

hurled himself at me, still yowling. I scooped him into my arms as I surveyed the damage. My crappy TV was gone, as was the nice set of speakers my parents had gotten me for the holidays two years ago, and gone, too, was the gaming system I'd gifted myself when I received my doctorate. No more Ancient Roman RPGs for me.

The thieves had thoroughly tossed the living room, though not irreparably, and I stepped over a couch cushion on my way to the bedroom. Drawers stood open like crooked teeth. Since I owned very little jewelry, however, and none of it valuable, the damage here was mitigated. My mattress lay half off the bed with a rent slashed along the seams. I'd been planning on tossing it when I moved anyway, but the sight of the exposed stuffing, and the way my quilt had crumpled on the ground beside a tumbled stack of books, tightened my throat. Mr. Muffin's yowl settled to a growl, then a purr. I, meanwhile, felt a yowl of my own rising in my chest.

Someone, or multiple someones, had broken into my home. Almost, I imagined I could smell them, their presence lingering like acrid smoke, staining the walls. I began to shiver. What was I supposed to do now?

Call the police, said my voice of reason.

Instead, I called my friend Mark.

"Slow down," he said as I blurted out what had happened.

I repeated myself more slowly. "Someone broke into my house and stole my stuff."

He swore, and I heard him yell at his girlfriend over his shoulder to turn off the TV. "Have you called the police?"

"Not yet."

"Here's what you need to do. Call the police and get a report filed. Then call your landlord. Tomorrow, contact your insurance, or see if they're open now. You do have renter's insurance, right?"

"Yes."

"And stay with us tonight."

"Okay."

"I want you to hang up, call the police, then call me back, okay?"

I murmured something unintelligible and hung up. My mouth tasted like bile. My skin itched. I wanted to grab Muffin and run far, far away from this apartment, where the miasma of violation stained every surface, and which no longer felt like mine.

"Good mor—" Fiadh broke off her chilly greeting and frowned as she scanned my face. I knew what she saw: purple circles beneath my eyes, hair still-damp from my seventh shower of the last twelve hours, rumpled clothing. "Clara?"

I gave her a wan smile. I'd considered calling in sick, but knew that wasn't an option after how she and I had parted ways the day before. I also didn't want to be home, or at my friend Mark's, where I'd spent the night before, repaying him for his kindness by abusing his hot water heater.

"I'm fine. I just didn't sleep well." It wasn't a total lie. I hadn't slept well. Nor would I ever sleep well again.

Fiadh regained her composure and began leading me to the library.

"I can probably find my own way now," I said, needing to be alone before my own composure cracked.

"It's protocol."

"Oh. I just didn't want to inconvenience you."

"You're not an inconvenience." I cringed, waiting for her to comment on my behavior yesterday. Instead, she said, "There are strawberries from the gardens in the kitchenette. Please help yourself."

I burst into tears. We'd only gotten as far as the formal sitting room. Fiadh winced, looked around, then ushered me inside the room and to a winged armchair. I slumped into it, sniffling. She stood awkwardly several feet away and wrung her small hands. I'd braced myself for her cool displeasure, not courtesy.

"I'm so sorry," I said when I could breathe again. "My apartment was broken into yesterday and I didn't sleep. I'm a bit of a mess."

"Oh." Fiadh let out a sigh, and her voice warmed above freezing for the first time since I'd met her. "Oh, you poor thing."

I looked up. Her green eyes had softened with sympathy, and she crouched before me, chafing my hands between hers. The skin of her palms was warm and dry. She withdrew the touch after a moment. Her black hair, which was cut just above her shoulders in a severe line, swayed with the motion.

"I'm normally not this unprofessional two days in a row," I said.

"Please, don't worry about it. Home invasions are major violations. I'm sure Ms. Montague will understand if you need to take—"

"I'd like to work."

"If you're sure . . ." Her eyes searched mine with an intensity that made me look away.

"Yes." Work would distract me, and I needed that distraction if I was going to keep it together for the rest of the day. She stood, and I followed suit. We walked in silence the rest of the way to the library, the halls of the house surrounding me with protective familiarity, but she paused at the door and looked up at me once more.

"Will you be moving in sooner now?"

I hadn't thought about it, but at the suggestion, my heart leapt. The idea of returning to those tainted rooms overwhelmed me, and Fiadh had offered me a way out. My mind conjured images of mold creeping over the furniture, floor, and walls, leaving slick black swirls everywhere the intruders had touched.

"Is that an option?"

"Of course. The house is empty. We were just waiting for the end of your lease, per your request. You could move in as soon as tonight. I will check with Agatha, of course, but I see no reason why not."

—⁓— —⁓— —⁓—

Burying myself in Nektopolian history temporarily smoothed the frightened hairs on the back of my neck. The morning passed in a sheaf of more correspondence, and an invoice, this time between Gatalina and a merchant. She'd taken over her aunt's shipping business, it seemed, and while a plague had recently decimated the city, business remained steady. The lists of goods fascinated me. Textiles, mostly, but there were also spices I hadn't thought had made it that far west, yet, and the notes scribbled in the margins, though largely indecipherable, made references to the character of the merchant in question, which she compared to that of a carnivorous snail.

Beneath the invoice lay another letter from Natek. I stared at it for a long time before deciding today was not the day for cryptic missives.

Fiadh came for me after my lunch break.

"Come with me."

Summer afternoon air softened the green of the ivy on the walls and soothed some of my anxiety as we left the manor house. I couldn't name more than a fraction of the flowers and shrubs. Roses, wisteria, hydrangea, butterfly bush . . . I let my hand brush the foliage as we passed through a hedge. Ahead, dew sparkled on an expansive lawn shaded by vast oaks. The carriage house bordered one side, and on the other, tucked between two of the trees, sat the small cottage that would soon be mine. Fiadh waved me on, and the gravel transitioned to mossy flagstones, punctuated here and there by large, brown mushrooms as the path wound past the pond and toward the cottage. Speckled ivy climbed the trellised walls, and the place looked entirely too cozy to be real. The photographs hadn't done it justice.

"Oh, wow," I said softly, taking it in. She smiled at me in faint amusement.

"Would you like to see the inside?"

Pale green walls and white trim greeted me as I set foot in the cottage. The ceilings were lower than the main house, but still higher than where I lived now, and Agra rugs graced the wood floors. The furnishings were antique and—thankfully—less obviously expensive than the furnishings in the main house, but looked comfortable, and the little stone fireplace in the living room took my breath away with its quaint, weathered charm. I pictured Mr. Muffin curled up on one of the wide gray fieldstones and almost smiled. He'd love it here. As for me, long windows looked out over the pond and the lawn, giving me a view of the main house, yet it was set far enough back to be private—a world of difference from my current bleak alley view. Somehow, despite how much I'd been looking forward to moving here, I hadn't fully allowed myself to accept that this place was real.

I drifted into the kitchen in a dream. Slate countertops. A gas stove with warm, red trimmings. Hanging pot rack, complete with copper pots, as promised. I tried not to visibly swoon.

"The security is state of the art. There are no cameras here, though we can certainly add some, but the perimeter is monitored closely and there are sensors on your doors tied into the main alarm system."

My mind spun out all the possibilities for this space. My pitifully wilting houseplants would appreciate the increased sunlight, and the small patio off the back door would make a perfect spot for an evening glass of wine.

"It's perfect," I said, longing evident in my tone.

"I'll have the keys ready for you at the end of the day. There is just one thing you should know: The main house remains accessible only during work hours without explicit permission."

"Of course. I will respect Ms. Montague's privacy."

"Wonderful. Now that you'll be on-site, you are welcome to borrow books from the reading shelves. Not the main collection, of course, as many are too fragile, but I highly recommend browsing. You may also take the laptop home with you, should you prefer. Let me give you a more detailed tour of the grounds so that you know what is shared property and what is private. I live in the carriage house with my mother, and Ms. Montague's head of security works out of an office off the back of the carriage house if you have an emergency."

I listened as she listed the daily routine of the estate. Living here would be something out of a fever dream, or an answered prayer—if I ever prayed, which I didn't. No more broken pipes, loud neighbors, and high rents. I'd have my own space. Perhaps a small garden. Fires in the winter. My heart filled with warmth at the thought, and I nodded along as Fiadh explained how I'd pay utilities, which is all that would be expected of me for the privilege of living in a home out of a fairy tale, and all the other details I'd need to know to make this place my own.

—※— —※— —※—

Mr. Muffin emerged from his carrier with an expression of utmost betrayal. He'd yowled on the car ride over, and then I'd had to leave him locked up while I made successive trips to gather the rest of my belongings. Initially, I'd decided to bring over only the essentials for a sleepover, but I couldn't bear the thought of leaving anything I cared about in that violated space. I'd get it cleaned up later, or pay someone else to do it. Mark, who was the only academic I knew who bench-pressed regularly, had been an incredible help with my books. My back thanked him. I'd invited him to stay for a beer, but he'd declined with a, "Sorry, Clara. I've got a hot date with a deadline."

I collapsed on the couch, noting the time—midnight—only to be reminded of my treachery by a pitiful yowl.

"Welcome to your new home," I said to Mr. Muffin as he sniffed the air. His hair slowly settled back to its normal position, and after a moment's hesitation, he stalked away from me to explore.

I watched him for a few minutes. He'd never marked before, but I didn't want this to be the first time. Had the last tenant owned a cat?

I settled by my boxes of books once I was mostly convinced he would behave and began unloading them onto the shelves, exhausted

34

but too buzzed from the move to sleep. Academic texts, novels, large art books, more novels, and language dictionaries gradually lined the bookcases built into the walls. I stroked familiar spines and reserved a favorite novel for a reread, setting it on the arm of the couch. I knew I wouldn't feel truly at home until the books were all unpacked. Clothes could wait, as could my other possessions—books were the stuff of life.

Too exhausted to cook, I slathered peanut butter on a slice of bread and chewed slowly. The night was warm and heavy with the scent of flowers. I opened the front door, careful not to let Mr. Muffin outside, and leaned against the doorjamb. Moonlight dripped over the lush foliage of the cottage garden and spilled mercury across the lawn. I soaked up the peace. Crickets and peepers joined in a riotous chorus, and a light breeze raised a susurrus from the nearby oak tree. Peanut butter coated my tongue as I breathed in the clean air. No cigarette smoke or car exhaust. No dumpster fumes. No lingering whiff of hot asphalt. I could get used to this.

Something moved on the far side of the lawn. I froze. My first thought, panicky and irrational, was that whoever had broken into my apartment had followed me here. I was still waiting on my renter's insurance to reimburse me, so it wasn't like I had anything to steal, but cold sweat sprang up all over my body at the remembrance. I squinted. The person was pushing a wheelbarrow toward the greenhouse.

Who the fuck gardened at midnight? A light flicked on in the greenhouse as I contemplated investigating, and I could see the silhouette of the woman as she paused to lean over tables of plants. Fiadh's words from my first week came back to me. "Ms. Montague does most of the gardening herself."

Was this Agatha? If she worked long hours, then it made sense she might putter around her greenhouse to unwind at the end of a long day. I smiled. There was something appealing about the thought. It made me like her. I watched her shadow for a few minutes longer, trying to suck peanut butter from my teeth, then went back inside and shut the door.

I fell asleep in my new bed with a chair lodged against my bedroom door. My dreams were full of running. I fled unknown pursuers in the dark, their laughter sinister and haunting.

"You're lucky to be a cat," I murmured to Mr. Muffin as I woke up from one such dream in a clammy sweat. Dawn lit the sky in gray streaks. Giving up on sleep, I turned on my work computer, which I'd brought home, now that I could, and began translating the letters I'd photographed earlier.

Collection: Nektopolis
Title: Letter 6
Description: Correspondence; Gata and Natek
Date: TBD
Cataloguer: Clara Eden

Natek,

You are persistent—nettles along the road. I used to gather them with my daughter, showing her how to harvest without touching the small stinging hairs on the leaves and stem. Now you burn my ankles as I pass. Well, nettle, I am not about to tell you my secrets no matter how flattering the metaphor.

Now that I have your full attention, a thing I have avoided since you founded[6] this city with your drawn kopis and your sweat-dark mare, heed my warning: there are no lengths to which I would not go. How far can you reach, Greek?

Gata

Collection: Nektopolis
Title: Letter 7
Description: Correspondence; Gata and Natek
Date: TBD
Cataloguer: Clara Eden

Natek, writing to Gata,

Far enough to reach you. And you presume—my father was Greek, but my mother was Illyrian. It was

_____

6   Translator's note: "Founded" implies governance, raising interesting questions.

36

one of the things that first drew me to Cynane[7], though my father was not a king. And I've told you what I want: an enigma, solved. It's so rare for me to feel surprise.

I give you roots, and am given nettles in return. Yes, we foraged for them often while on campaign, as has every hungry child in this world. Cooked, they lose their sting. What do you mean to imply? And why break your cover now? That was no careless slip. I've speculated a great deal, and your actions are reactions—rarely do you strike unprovoked, and never so blatantly. I think, and forgive the assumption, you wished to be discovered. It is the only explanation that rings true.

Let us speak of more pleasant things. On the back of this letter you will find a map. Follow it until you find the place where the water holds the heavens. This is not a trap. Tell me what you think.

Your Nettle

Collection: Nektopolis
Title: Letter 8
Description: Correspondence; Gata and Natek
Date: TBD
Cataloguer: Clara Eden

Gata, writing to Natek on the fifth day of Pellaiios[8],

"This is not a trap"[9] is precisely what someone

---

7   Translator's note: The name used here in the original was not Cynane, but rather a nickname for Cynane, half-sister to Alexander the Great, and specific enough that it can refer to none other, despite the lack of context. I am happy to provide you with supplementary reading if this history intrigues you, Agatha.

8   Translator's note: The Greek calendar month corresponding with November.

9   Translator's note: I have used quotation marks instead of the diplé, borrowed from Greek, which was used to indicate speech, among other textual devices.

would say if it was, in fact, a trap. I waited a year to be sure, and yes, I did receive your gift. The wine sack was appreciated, even if the humor was not.

The beach is as you said: the waters here hold oceans of stars, the surface so still I felt in danger of falling into the heavens. Yet as much as I appreciate the suggestion—I would not have found the location, nor the hospitality of its locals[10] without you—I keep thinking of your first letter. The one I burned.

It is the burning that troubles me. I had no cause to condemn it to the flames. I report to no one but myself. And yet I tore it into pieces and watched those pieces turn to ash in my brazier. I've shown more mercy to meals than I showed your letter.

I was wrong—you are no nettle. Your words are a hunter's snare around my ankle, and I cannot trust you, no matter how vulnerable you pretend to be.

There is a garden in the capitol, past the ruined shrine to Athena, with a mosaic I think you'll enjoy. Let me know if you find it.

Gata

PS.[11] Do not think your attempts to cultivate me have gone unnoticed. "Your Nettle" and all your little endearments. They will not work.

Collection: Nektopolis
Title: Letter 9
Description: Correspondence; Gata and Natek

---

10 Translator's note: A substitute. The original text is damaged, here, and the word it most closely resembles, "witches," does not make sense in context.

11 Translator's note: Postscripts as we know them did not exist until the 1500s, but for the sake of clarity, I have added them here to organize the addendums to the letters.

Guileless Natek, writing to suspicious Gata,

I am glad you found the beach, though it is not the sea. I walked by the Aegean often as a child in my father's house. The taste of the brine lingers still, caught in the back of my throat like the beginning of a cough. When I think of it, I find myself craving sailors. Salt runs in their veins.

You say you do not trust me. I am glad to hear it. Caution serves us well, but so does boldness, and if you can accuse me of false vulnerability, I can accuse you of false timidity. You are bold, Gata. Deceptively so.

I did find the mosaic. Such intricate tilework is a dwindling art form, and the red bears a striking resemblance to old blood. Clever, and consider your warning heeded. Do you have thorns, Gata? Or are you all petal and supple stem?

Trust. I don't think there can be trust. Not for us. Do you wish to hear I will never hurt you? No creature can promise such. Do you wish to know I won't betray you? I'd like to say I wouldn't, but how do I know what betrayal tastes like on your tongue?

I can promise you this: Curiosity drove that first letter. Nothing more.

You did not ask how I first found you.

I'd like to hear you guess.

Fondly,

Natek

PS. We shall see.

CHAPTER THREE
Remember the Rules, Clara

Dear Ms. Eden,

I was sorry to hear about the difficulties with your lodgings. I hope you find the cottage to your liking. Don't hesitate to come to Fiadh with any concerns.

Your Nektopolian is wonderful.

Agatha Montague

The handwritten note lay on the library table. I traced Agatha's looping signature, admiring the controlled swoop of the *g*s, and felt warmth spread through me. Praise was hard to come by in the academy. Even my PhD advisor, whom I got along with, rarely offered anything besides criticism. The urge to pin this on my fridge, as my mother had done with my report cards growing up, took longer to suppress than it should have. The compliment also suggested Fiadh hadn't gone to Agatha with complaints about my outburst. Relief pulsed through me.

My eyes burned with lack of sleep, and my muscles burned with the strain of lifting boxes the previous evening, but the lure of history burned strongest of all. I'd read plenty of intriguing exchanges during my studies, some hostile, some romantic, but nothing like this. I wanted more. These people, dead for hundreds of years, had pulled me into their world and left me reeling.

Today, I'd decided to pause my rough translations in favor of following up on some etymological leads. This would help triangulate the time period as well as clarify any potential errors. I set to work, compiling lists of the words I needed to investigate and cross-checking them against my dictionaries.

"How was your first night on the grounds?" Fiadh asked at the end of the day when she came to collect the keys. I thought of the letters, and of the person I'd seen in the greenhouse.

"Peaceful. I had a little trouble sleeping," I admitted, "but . . ."

Did I tell her about the correspondence? I wasn't sure I liked her very much, but I had no one else to share this with. I couldn't send the translation on to any of my university friends. The need to discuss, to process, to have someone else understand the spell of these words hammered at my temples. The subtle flush of her perfume in my lungs added its own rhythm.

"But? Is something not to your liking?" She frowned, and in my exhaustion, I nearly reached out to smooth the V-shaped furrow between her brows.

"No, it's not that. It's . . ."

Fuck it.

"Would you like to read some of the things I've been cataloguing?"

"What?" Surprise cleared her expression. Her lips remained slightly parted, revealing a glimpse of her neat, white teeth.

"There is this letter exchange in the collection. I can't describe it, but it's fascinating, and . . ." I trailed off and rubbed my jaw to free up some of the tension I'd been carrying. Uncertainty appeared to gnaw at her. Was she not allowed to read the material I'd been working on? That seemed unlikely, considering her access to the library. Did she not *want* to read it? I didn't think so—there was a gleam of curiosity in her eyes I recognized. That left me with no reasonable explanation, save that she didn't want to engage with *me* specifically. I began adding more bricks to the wall between us in preparation for rejection.

"I'd like that."

"Oh." I stared at her like an idiot. "Oh, okay, good. I have some rough translations, which could be entirely wrong. I'm not sure how to get it to you, though."

"Are the translations on the laptop?"

"Yes."

41

She sat beside me in one of the non-ergonomic chairs, smoothing her dress beneath her. Our arms brushed as she reached for the computer and pulled it toward her. She didn't appear to notice. I, however, became uncomfortably aware of our proximity.

Since I already had the exchange pulled up on the screen, I didn't protest her commandeering of the laptop; instead, I turned to a page of my notes and pretended to work as she read. The light from the monitor cast a luminescent glow across her irises. Her posture remained straight, though she did lean forward the longer she read, and again I saw the glint of teeth beneath her parted lips as the work absorbed her attention.

She shouldn't have absorbed mine. I knew this, just as I knew how foolish it would be to let myself continue down that path. But her lips were a dusky rose, bitten red in the same spot I chewed my own lip, and there was a softness to her mouth that contradicted her rigid formality. I'd always been overly fond of contradictions.

"Well," she said when she'd finished reading. It couldn't have taken her more than twenty minutes to get through the correspondence, but the staccato pounding of my heart made the minutes stretch.

"What do you think?"

"What do *you* think?" She folded her hands and didn't meet my eyes right away. A faint pink tinted her cheeks.

"There are obviously some translation errors, and I'm not entirely sure of the context—so much gets lost in translation."

"They're compelling," said Fiadh. She hesitated, then added, "I haven't read anything like it. Not . . . between women."

"This is the first preserved evidence of same-sex relationships between women in Nektopolis. Obviously, we can't be entirely sure of gender, but—"

"Are you sure they're in a relationship?"

"They're clearly romantically inclined."

She chewed the red spot on her lower lip. "How many more are there?"

"I'm still cataloguing the Nektopolian documents. It's remarkable that Agatha has these letters at all."

"Your dissertation was on Nektarios," she said.

"Yes." Fiadh had been actively involved in my hiring. There was no other reason for her to know my academic background, and I shoved aside the flush of pleasure.

"I read it."

The air in the library turned briefly solid. "You read my dissertation?"

"It was interesting."

I stared at her, too stunned to speak. Her lips curved in a slight smile. "You seem surprised."

"I—" I broke off. "Yes."

"You shouldn't be." She leaned back, tilting her chin up and gazing at me out of half-lidded eyes. That small smile still clung to her lips, part amusement, part mockery. "I enjoyed it."

"You . . . enjoyed it?" People outside of academia rarely used that word to describe academic texts, but I supposed Fiadh wasn't exactly an average example of the populace. Look at where she worked. For all I knew, she was also an academic.

"You argue for and against your central thesis well, and even though it is clear that you want to believe the circumstantial evidence, if it can even be called evidence, your use of rhetorical strategy brings the reader to your conclusion through the use of counterargument. Which is more impressive now that I know you."

A subtle dig, but I'd still take the compliment.

"A classics scholar who *hasn't* read up on rhetoric wouldn't be worth her salt."

"A phrase particularly apt for the era. Will you tell me when you translate more of these?" she asked.

"If you want, sure."

"Thank you." She stood, her hair swaying with the motion. Her shampoo filled the air. I didn't recognize the scent, which probably meant it was expensive. I watched her leave with the growing awareness that if I wasn't careful, I'd start finding her attractive.

Which made sense, I justified to myself as the door shut behind her, since she was the only person I saw these days. I needed to make an effort to see my friends.

First, though, I needed to clean my apartment and get the rest of my stuff out. Returning to my violated sanctuary filled me with unease. However, before I could wipe it from memory, I needed to satisfy the terms of my lease, and so I headed over after work to haul the furniture and furnishings I wasn't keeping to a donation center or the curb, clean up the shattered glass, wipe things down, and pack up. I blasted Swedish pop music while I worked to banish the sensation I was being watched. It almost helped, but I still felt the miasma of

43

invasion clinging to the walls.

—ᴟ— —ᴟ— —ᴟ—

I unlocked a small drawer in one of the library cabinets a few days later to discover a metal box tucked in the back. When I opened it, nestled amid packets of silica within a smaller plastic container lay three coins. A magnifying lens revealed the images printed on the precious metals. One, a small gold disc, showed a bull. Another a shield. The third, however, looked more Roman in style, and depicted a woman's helmeted head. Athena, I thought, but the magnifying lens picked up the letters embossed behind the woman. Age hadn't obscured them: Nektaria.

"Holy fuck," I said to the empty library. Incontrovertible evidence winked up at me in silver. On the obverse was the unmistakable horse head of Nektopolis.

I had to find Fiadh, and not just because she'd made that comment about "wanting to believe circumstantial evidence." With the thought came the conviction I was right—this wasn't the kind of revelation I could handle alone. My entire body felt tight and buoyant, like one of the soap bubbles that had floated over the stone sink and into the pink light of the setting sun as I'd washed a copper pot the evening before, the sound of crickets just barely audible over the scrub of brush on metal and the gush of the faucet.

The manor house hummed to itself as I peered around the library door. Like all old houses, it creaked periodically, but beneath the rumbles and clicks of modern technology and the distant roar of an airplane, I heard the house itself. The hum was cheerful, as inviting as an old friend, and I experienced none of the disquiet I usually associated with large estates.

"Fiadh?" I called down the hallway.

Nothing.

She'd essentially forbidden me from wandering on my first day, but since she had my phone locked in a box in the foyer, leaving me no way to contact her, I felt I was owed one exception. Especially for this. My feet made almost no sound as I trod on the carpets running the center of the hallways. I passed the familiar dustcloth-shrouded rooms on the library level, and then descended to the first floor.

"Fiadh?" I called again.

44

More silence. I slipped through the sitting room where I'd broken down in tears, and then into the art gallery. I hesitated. One glance informed me Fiadh wasn't in here, either, but I'd be remiss if I didn't take this opportunity to at least glance at Agatha's collection. What else might she have from Nektopolis? Looking over my shoulder, I edged into the gallery.

I wasn't sure what I'd expected. More priceless lost artifacts, perhaps. Renoir. Monet. A few Modernists. Instead, a motley assortment of art from around the world met my gaze. Chinese landscapes. Grecian vases. Portraits dating from antiquity to the last century. A damn medieval tapestry fragment with a constipated-looking unicorn. No curator would ever place these pieces in the same room, but private collectors did as they pleased.

I peered at one of the portraits. A woman stared back. Age had faded and cracked the paint, but those eyes—my god. The intelligence in them, even rendered in oil, disconcerted me. She had high cheekbones, and while the painter had adhered to the style of the times—early 1100s, if I wasn't mistaken—there was something almost contemporary in the way the woman had been captured. Cloth covered her hair, obscuring the color, and her lips were stylistically small, but if she had walked into the room right now, I felt as if I'd recognize her. No plaque gave her name or the painter's. I tore my gaze away from her painted one and reminded myself why I'd come downstairs.

Fiadh wasn't in the kitchens, which sparkled with stainless steel cleanliness, nor was she in the office on the first floor. I chewed on my lip. There were several more flights of stairs leading to the house's upper levels, as well as the carriage house. Perhaps she'd gone home. Could I call on her for something like this? My excitement, which had borne me out the door on its cresting wave, faltered. Yes, she'd read my dissertation, but that didn't mean she was as invested in Nektopolian history as I, nor might she appreciate the interruption.

But I needed to share this with someone. I set off down the main hallway on the first level, figuring I'd eventually come to the backdoor.

Birdsong floated through an open window. My shoes were silent on the carpet runner. A flawless early summer day coated the grounds with honeyed light, and each window framed a different view: honeysuckle growing by a stone wall, a small weeping willow by a fountain, roses, more roses, the sweep of the lawn.

A door tucked in an alcove beside two large potted ferns caught my eye. Dark wood paneling gleamed in the shadows, and it sat slightly ajar. Perhaps Fiadh was in there. I put my hand on the cool brass of the handle; it swung open on silent hinges. Beyond lay a twisting flight of stairs. Wine cellar, maybe?

"Fiadh?" My voice echoed off the stone steps.

Light footsteps answered. Fiadh lit up the stairs like an undergrad late for an exam and pulled me forcefully out of the small landing and back into the main house. Her green eyes were wide with shock.

"Um," I began.

"What are you doing?"

"Looking for you."

Her hand dug painfully into my wrist despite her diminutive frame. I tried to withdraw from her grip as she shut the door behind her with one foot. The wild look in her eyes abated only when she glanced at her hand where it clawed my arm. She dropped me, expression changing to guarded suspicion.

"I thought I was clear—"

"Yes, but I needed to find you, and how else am I supposed to contact you? You have my phone."

"I—that doesn't matter." Her scowl brought her brows together, emphasizing her slightly pointed chin.

"I'm sorry. I did a little shouting, but . . ."

"Well, I'm here now. What is it?"

"Is that the wine cellar? I'm not about to steal." I didn't mean to sound defensive, but the harshness in her tone raised my hackles. I'd thought she was warming up to me. I'd thought wrong, apparently.

"It has nothing to do with that. Ms. Montague is a private woman. What did you need from me?"

"I found something."

"Oh." Her face smoothed, and she visibly gathered her composure. "Very well."

She locked the door before turning to stride away from me, short legs nearly blurring.

"Please slow down," I said as she sped away.

She obliged, though the look she shot back over her shoulder begrudged me every wasted second. I had to jog a few steps to catch up.

Today's outfit brought butler chic into this century. Her green jacket flared into tails in the back, which, I couldn't help noticing, framed her hips rather nicely, and the starched white collar of her shirt rose high around her neck before plunging toward her sternum. Her pale skin was flushed from her jog up the stairs. I averted my eyes, staring once more straight ahead. Being tall meant I had to be careful about where I let my eyes rest. I prided myself on respect. I didn't like my cleavage being ogled, and I wasn't about to make someone else feel that same discomfort.

"I'm sorry," I said, stifling my annoyance.

"As am I," she said without looking at me. "I did not mean to leave you with no way to contact me. As for the cellars, they're not safe. This is an old house."

I hardly saw how that added up, but I didn't question her. The apology was too surprising. "I won't go near them again."

"Thank you." I saw the flash of her eye as she glanced at me sidelong. "I will get you a work phone."

"I could just use—"

"On our protected plan."

"I'd appreciate that," I said, deciding not to question her.

"And there is a direct line to the carriage and the main house from the cottage phone."

A pause.

"I truly did not mean to snap at you." Fiadh's voice was softer this time, and I slid my eyes in her direction. She was back to staring furiously ahead, as if angry at herself. Maybe it breached protocol for her to show emotion.

"It's fine."

She made a noncommittal noise in the back of her throat, and we lapsed into tense silence until we reached the library. I wanted to tell her about the coin, the silver image of Nektaria floating in my vision, but her curt greeting had curbed some of my enthusiasm.

"What did you find?" she asked as she opened the door.

My heart rate accelerated with excitement. "It's incredible."

"So you say." That slight smile graced her lips again, as if my passion amused her. The expression might have bothered me on someone else, but it wasn't condescending. More . . . intrigued.

I slipped past her into the library and hovered over the coin case. She joined me at a slower pace, which, seeing as I knew how quickly she could move, seemed almost teasing. I gestured at the lens I'd left beside the box. She picked it up delicately and leaned over the table, her hair obscuring her expression. I waited. Seconds passed. The soft overhead lighting fell along the curve of her spine, revealing the floral pattern inlaid into the dark green cloth of her coat: vines and small budding flowers. Subtle. Elegant. Distracting.

"Does that say—"

"Nektaria? Yes."

She set the magnifying lens down and straightened. Her lips were parted slightly in the expression I was coming to associate with her unwilling enthusiasm.

"Nektopolis, like many countries, imprinted the names of its rulers—or occasionally past rulers—on its coinage."

"And you think this means she really was a she?"

"It's the most concrete evidence I've found. There are pieces of pottery and a few surviving vessels with images of Nektaria, but like the Greeks and Romans, Nektopolians painted their heroes in their drinking cups and amphorae. Doesn't mean those heroes were real. The Greeks were obsessed with the women they called Amazons. Nektaria fits that mold."

"She'd be compelling at the bottom of a cup."

"It's worth looking up online. You'll see."

"I will," she said as she stroked the curve of the magnifier. I realized I didn't have any follow-up statements. I'd shown her the coin—that had been as far ahead as I'd planned this encounter. Fiadh wasn't a fellow academic. I couldn't expect her to wax poetic with me about the significance of this finding for hours, as one of my university friends would.

"Anyway," I said to save face. "I thought Agatha might want to know the significance of this piece."

Fiadh's hand lingered on the box a moment longer. "History has always mattered to Agatha. I'll be sure to let her know."

"That, um, was all I needed to talk to you about."

At my lame conclusion, her eyes snapped up to mine, searching them. Whatever she saw shuttered the comparatively open expression she'd worn earlier; her professional mask returned.

"I'll let you get back to work." She gave one last glance at the coin before leaving, however, and in that glance, I recognized a curiosity as burning as my own.

Collection: Nektopolis
Title: Letter 10
Description: Correspondence; Gata and Natek
Date: TBD
Cataloguer: Clara Eden

Cautious Gata, writing to Natek in Xandikos[12],

Trust is the only lasting currency. Its rarity gives it its value, and by this standard, we're both impoverished. Yet you want me to guess how you found me. Do you seek my praise? Well done, Nettle. You've flushed me out. Or do you hope to trick me into giving more away?

Romans to the east, Macedonians to the north. There are some who thrive in such uncertain times. I[13] am not one of them.

Without some sort of guarantee of, if not mutual trust, then understanding, I think it time our correspondence comes to an end.

Gata

Collection: Nektopolis
Title: Letter 11
Description: Correspondence; Gata and Natek
Date: circa 200 BCE
Cataloguer: Clara Eden

---

12 Translator's note: March in the Macedonian calendar. Why the switch in this letter from Greek to Macedonian (essentially the Babylonian calendar) is unclear. Perhaps this indicates location? A temporary shift in power or influence? Macedon began encroaching on Nektopolis around 200 BCE, which gives a possible date for this letter.

13 Translator's note: I must raise the possibility that this correspondence is an example of *pseudonymoi*, the Classical Greek tradition of anonymous authors impersonating commoners, famous figures, and personalities in letters for popular entertainment.

Untrustworthy Natek writing to her dear friend Gata,

Why on earth should we break off correspondence over something as trivial as trust? Have you ever trusted? Truly trusted? The only place for trust is the battlefield, where if you do not—cannot—trust the man beside you, you are dead. He either has your back or you spend too much time checking your peripherals. The rest of the time trust is a luxury not afforded those who play the long game. Time is on betrayal's side.

You mentioned mercy several exchanges past. Do you still feel for them[14]? I find this almost as intriguing as your isolation. I thought we learned to harden ourselves out of necessity, but perhaps this is just what I was taught. Did you have a teacher, Gata? Did someone guide your hand to the vein, or were you left to face the dawn alone?

The Poetess[15] says the most beautiful thing on the black earth is what you love, and I love the blade. There is beauty in conflict. Every strike has its twin, every parry its counterpart. I've had many teachers. Alexander. Cynane. And the one who made me what I am, who is more beloved and terrible than both. They all shared this love with me, and so I pour blood into the black earth in libation. Perhaps you've tasted it, as you've made your rounds.

Mercy, though— Do you wield it tenderly, or with the swift, brutal efficiency of the flood? I use mercy as I use everything—as needed, on a carefully deliberated basis. But that is work. I will not lie to you and say my motives are pure. So long as we are at cross purposes, what little I glean, I will use, yet

---

14 Translator's note: It is unclear who the "them" in question is, here, though the root word, *demos*, suggests the general population.

15 Translator's note: Sappho, though I suspect you already know this, given the extent of your collection of her work.

you do not strike me as an asset easily groomed.

In place of trust, I've sent you a collection of poems from my homeland, copied in my own hand. You'll know the author.

Fondly,

Natek, writing to Gata

I finished my rough translation and sat listening to the staccato race of my heart. Sappho. Alexander. Cynane. The references confirmed the influence of Greek culture on Nektopolis, which made sense given its founding. I recognized the line of poetry from Sappho Fragment Sixteen, which, considering the *complete fucking volume* I'd discovered in the library, was sheer luck. Natek could have easily referenced a line I didn't know. As for Natek, I wasn't sure of their gender. This bothered me, because the reference to blades suggested a fighter, and if Natek was a woman, that would add further credence to theories surrounding relative gender equality. Much more likely that they were a man, however, especially considering the tone, which was almost flirtatious. I checked my internal biases; I knew I wanted Natek to be a woman for this reason, too. But such want had no place in research. Linguistic clues might come in time, or they might not.

I was still thinking about feminine, masculine, and neuter articles in the Nektarian language when I joined Mark and several of our other friends from the university for dinner.

"What, you really can't talk about it?" asked Patrice, raising a pierced eyebrow over her beer. "Come on."

"I can't. I'm sorry."

"Well, can you at least give us some hints?" She leaned her elbows on Mark's kitchen table, where we'd gathered for drinks and some of Patrice's girlfriend's sinfully delicious guacamole, and gave me a beseeching look.

I hesitated. "It's in my field of study, but that's really all I can say. It sounds much more mysterious than it is, I swear."

A lie, but I wanted them off my back before I breached my contract under the influence of beer, food, and friends.

"It sounds *very* mysterious, just saying."

"As if you haven't done your fair share of weird."

"True." Patrice studied race in medieval Europe, and she'd scoured royal British library collections while working with her advisor, one of the most lauded specialists in the field. I was positive she'd seen things the rest of us peasants weren't allowed to know existed.

"Do you like it?" Mark, bless him, steered the subject into safer territory.

"Yeah. It's fascinating."

"And you're living on the Montague estate. What's that like?" Patrice's girlfriend, Daphne, worked in food service, and she'd catered events at estates like Agatha's, so she knew better than most what I'd gotten into.

"I love it. I'll have you all over soon, once I'm settled."

"You better," said Patrice.

"Do you have much contact with the rest of the staff?" asked Daphne.

"Just Agatha's assistant. She's . . ."

They waited.

". . . hard to read," I finished.

"Stuck-up?" Daphne suggested with a sympathetic grimace.

"A little." Bitching about Fiadh made the beer slosh unpleasantly in my stomach. It felt disloyal, especially when I remembered how she'd comforted me when I'd broken down in tears, going so far as to help me move out sooner. Had I properly thanked her for that?

"*Vive la révolution*," said Patrice. "Tell her we won the class war."

"Did we, though?" Mark said.

Mark and Patrice devolved into a political rant. Daphne and I listened, interjecting when appropriate. My mind, however, remained snagged on Fiadh. *Should* I thank her? Or would that just make things more uncomfortable? I didn't need her to be my friend, but if I was being honest with myself, I did want her to at least like me. I pictured her severe wardrobe, stiff spine, and verdant eyes. Briefly, I considered inviting her over for a coffee or a glass of wine, then scrapped the idea. It would be too awkward if she declined, and besides—I had other friends. Friends who deserved my full attention. I joined the debate with an acerbic comment about public transit and put Fiadh and Nektopolis out of my mind.

Midnight approached by the time my rideshare pulled into the estate. I thanked the driver and set off across the grounds, appreciating the warm summer night. Moonlight glazed the buildings and gravel paths. Beer still warmed my system, and I hummed as I walked, thinking of my bed and what I'd do with my day off.

The path wound near the greenhouse. No lights lit the panes this time, and while I strained my eyes for signs of Agatha, nothing moved within or around the building. Figured. Anyone sane was tucked in bed, as I would be in a matter of minutes. I shook myself. Stalking my employer was in bad taste.

Instead, I veered to follow a path along the pond. Night creatures warbled and burbled to each other, silencing as I approached and resuming as soon as I'd passed. Bats swooped in the hunt, and a small mammal scurried away from the water's edge ahead of me. It was so peaceful here. The damp air smelled of water and honeysuckle. Not wishing to relinquish the sensation of calm just yet, I sat on a stone bench and faced the water. Moonlight chased itself in ripples over the surface. An owl called, low and mournful.

"Lovely evening," said a voice from behind me.

I startled hard enough to nearly unseat myself, then scrambled to maintain my composure as I turned around—and saw no one. Insects continued their chorus. The breeze wafted softly off the water. Had I dozed off? I blinked, eyes straining in the darkness. Nothing.

The imagined encounter unsettled me enough to spur me on my way back to the cottage. I beheaded a few mushroom caps in my haste, and they lay, gills exposed to the moonlight, in the path my feet had cut through the dew.

—〰— —〰— —〰—

Collection: Nektopolis
Title: Letter 12
Description: Correspondence; Gata and Natek
Date: TBD
Cataloguer: Clara Eden

Gata, addressing Natek,

Why do I tell you these things? It can hardly matter.

Some days I don't even remember my mother's name. Yet you speak of Cynane and Alexander as if they were still alive. How many years since his empire fell? He turned the whole earth red, and you speak of poetry.

Your false transparencies do not amuse me. You would have me lower my guard. I do not share your love of risk, Natek, and do not forget who began this. You sent the letter; I set the board.

I did have a teacher, but we parted ways and ideologies long ago—I have not missed the company. I do not seek out our kind, as you seem to. Tell me, am I your only correspondent, or does your papyrus fly to many? I will not be jealous. Your name precedes you, Nektaria: the woman whose tongue dripped such nectar even Alexander bent his ear to listen. Did he raise you to general so that he didn't have to stoop to hear you from his horse? Some say he won his battles on his own brilliance. I did not know him. But I do know you. Coincidence rarely wears the same face quite as often as she has worn yours.

As you love the blade, I love my garden. What memories I retain are of growing things: the smell of sap and decay, the passage of sunlight over leaf. My garden is small, but it serves its purpose. I've grown fascinated with a new variety of tuber. If I am correct, it could solve some of the current shortages. Keeping the populace fed is self-serving, but I feel great satisfaction in the work. Far more so than I do thwarting you. Wear your player's mask if it suits you. I will not spill your secrets.

Gata

PS. I would rather have faced the dawn alone.

Nektaria. I was wide awake, now. I paced through the dark cottage and fumbled with the kettle, putting water on for coffee while the name rang down my spine. Not *the* Nektaria, surely. Probably the writer had been named for the general, just as she had studied the legacy of Alexander and Cynane. This Nektaria was at least a hundred years too old to be the general herself, but at least I knew she was a she now. The kettle whistled. I poured it over the grounds in my French press and took the press and a cup back to bed, remembering to barricade the door just in case someone decided to rob my new home as well as the old.

Collection: Nektopolis
Title: Letter 13
Description: Correspondence; Gata and Natek
Date: TBD
Cataloguer: Clara Eden

Gata,

I speak of poetry because it is the language of war as well as longing. You know I grew up in Alexander's court, and I told you my mother was Illyrian. She died when I was eleven. Childbirth, as ever. It was Cynane who taught me the sword instead, as she'd been taught by her mother, and her mother before that, as is the way of Illyrians. That is, when Cynane wasn't courting Olympias[16]. She also sang to me. I worshipped the oiled soles of her feet like any child worships one far older, and thank the gods, for nothing fixes memory like idolatry. There is one song in particular of Sappho's that reminds me of you in its later verses. I still hear it in Cynane's sweet, rough voice; I wish you could, too.

---

16 Translator's note: Alexander's mother? Cynane was perhaps the only potential rival Olympias didn't attempt to eliminate, but there is little else to back up this claim. This could also just as easily refer to another Olympias.

For if she flees, soon she will pursue.
If she refuses gifts, rather will she give them.
If she does not love, soon she will love
even unwilling.

Or perhaps I presume. Tell me, what else do you grow? I can't help picturing things with thorns. I'm fond of cutting edges. A kopis. A reed. A soldier's smile. But while you grow tubers, I write. I've become something of a scholar over the years. Perhaps one day you'll read my work. I imagine you in some distant future, browsing the great library of Alexandria and coming across one of my scrolls. You'll know my name, whichever one I'm using, just as I'll know yours.

My flocks of papyrus do indeed traverse the roads and waterways, but my other correspondents are not you. Some are poets, for I've cultivated an interest in the art among my court. My teacher—of this second life, not my first—writes me often with news, and so do my blood Sisters, letters from the whole world over. You are the only one I like to think of growing jealous waiting for my reply. Do not ruin this for me with your protestations of impartiality.

It is not easy to linger in the shadow of my past. Sometimes I wish I could forget the woman I was, but the sculptors come too close in their approximation, and the poets and philosophers won't shut up. Bless them for their dedication. They sing of Nektarios, thanks to a necessary cover. The change to the historical record was unsurprisingly easy to engender. Some men will never accept the truth. I don't even entirely blame them. Is there anything more terrifying than a woman confident in her own power?

You, though. My gardener. You must miss the sun, great and terrible though I know you to be. You are entirely too quiet. It is remarkable, how few ripples

56

you've left in your wake. The flat stillness before the wave. I look for patterns in the weave, you see—patterns are the heart of strategy—and there is an absence around you that cannot be coincidence.

Will you take a walk with me, one of these years? I like to draw up truces face to face.

Yours,

Natek

PS. Just this month I received a long letter from my teacher about a horse. I breed them—a line from Bucephalus and my own mare. Fast, fearless, and sturdy. The filly I sent her was particularly fine, and I was especially pleased to hear her night vision is unparalleled. I have another filly from that pairing I'm hoping carries the same traits. You've mentioned breeding tubers. While I am proficient, I am not above humility. I'd love to see your notes. Perhaps there are applications for animals as well as plants.

PPS. Another word for absence first came to mind, but I did not write it. Your wariness of me has not abated, even if I no longer believe you sit up nights sharpening your blades in preparation for my breast. But I cannot seem to close this letter without writing it, though I've been trying. That word, Gata, was loneliness.

As Alice would say, curiouser and curiouser, I reflected the following day as I stared at my work. The silence in the library contained its usual peacefulness, perfumed with the scents of old books and expensive, book-safe cleaning products. If I was given to flights of fancy in my translations, which I was not, I would have hazarded a macabre guess at the nature of these women, but unless this was some sort of elaborate hoax . . . I contemplated the prospect for a moment before discarding it. Hoaxes weren't played on nobodies like me. Besides—the pay was real enough. My bank account had never registered such a high balance.

Reality TV show?

I glanced as surreptitiously as I could around the library, searching for cameras. Nothing jumped out at me. Then again, hidden cameras wouldn't, would they? But didn't reality TV shows usually have larger casts?

No. Much more logical that I was mistranslating something, than that Gata and Natek were . . . I couldn't even frame the word in the privacy of my mind. It sounded too ridiculous. Still, I was unsettled enough that I put off translating further letters between Gata and Natek for several days, focusing instead on cataloguing documents I hoped would bring their correspondence into greater context.

"Fiadh," I said at the end of another day spent avoiding Gata and Natek, "may I ask you something?"

"I believe you just did."

"About the work."

Fiadh paused in the hall and turned expectantly. "Yes?"

"Not . . . not here. Do you want to come over for a glass of wine?" I blurted the sentence out so quickly it sounded like one long word, but I couldn't voice my doubts in the friendly hallway with its comfortable creaks.

Fiadh blinked five full times before responding, her eyebrows contracting in guarded puzzlement. "I'd prefer—"

I nodded, resigning myself to the rejection.

"Oh, I suppose we're neighbors, after all. Give me a moment to grab my things."

I hoped I'd managed to hide my surprise. She escorted me to the foyer, then walked briskly back into the house, emerging a few minutes later with her bag while I fingered the sleek leaves of a potted orange tree.

"Shall we?" she said.

I followed her out the door, standing aside so she could lock up, and let the early evening sunshine reassure me. That assurance faded as we approached my cottage and I realized the only wine in my house came from a box, and no matter how many awards said boxed wine had accumulated, I suspected someone like Fiadh would still turn up her nose. Also, I was worried I'd forgotten to scoop the cat box this morning, and for all I remembered, I'd left clothes scattered about the place—though this wasn't my usual habit. Still. I erred on the side of caution and gestured for her to sit on the pleasantly cool patio while I ducked inside and sloshed wine into two glasses, sniffed the room for unpleasant odors, and established that the cottage looked like it was inhabited by a responsible adult before joining her on the patio. Mr. Muffin watched through a pane of glass in the door and meowed plaintively. The sound was silenced by the glass, which made it all the more pathetic. I wasn't about to let him get snapped up by a nighttime predator, however.

"Thanks for coming," I said as I sat. Fiadh's prim posture hadn't stayed behind in the house. She might have been a painting of a woman rather than flesh and blood: back straight, legs crossed primly beneath yet another sensible dress. This one also had a high collar despite the summer heat, though at least it was sleeveless.

"What's bothering you?" she asked.

No small talk, then.

"I've made some errors in translation."

"What kind of errors?" She took a sip of the wine, and a drop clung to her lip.

"There are a few words that I clearly haven't translated correctly, despite checking and rechecking my sources. But in context—"

"Are these errors in any particular documents, or all of them?"

"Selected correspondence."

"Gata and Natek," Fiadh guessed.

"Yes." She'd read all but the few most recent.

"I've been thinking about those. The footnote you left for Agatha about—"

"Pseudonymoi. The Greeks had a tradition of epistolary correspondence written in the voice and style of commoners or famous people. It would make sense that it made it over." I drank my wine, feeling significantly better about the world.

"Blood cults are also not unheard of, if that is what is troubling you."

I didn't like how close her words came to my suspicions. Then again, hearing them verbalized was validating. "This would be the first known record of blood cultists in Nektopolis."

"You said yourself that much of that era's history is lost."

"True." Warming to my subject, I continued. "I could check the archives at the university for more information on Nektopolian cults.

And no, I won't mention anything to anyone."

"Not twice."

"What—oh. That's a threat."

Fiadh shrugged and unpinned her hair from the bun she'd started wearing with the arrival of summer's heat. It didn't fall into its usual sweep above her shoulders, but instead clung to its pinned shape until she forcibly shook it out with her fingers. I pictured her spraying her hair into submission with hairspray each morning and suppressed a grin. I liked the idea of her hair defying her.

"Where did you go to school?" I asked, steering the subject away from blood.

"Brixton. But I stopped with my master's degree."

"In what?"

"Hotel management."

"I would have pegged you as a literature major," I said, trying not to sound too arch.

"I have a bachelor's in museum studies, actually."

"You should have led with that."

"Oh?" she asked.

"I'm a scholar. Museums are more my wheelhouse."

"Hotels are museums of a sort."

"How? Aren't they the exact opposite? People come and go and never stay?"

"They're a monument to impermanence."

"You just proved my point," I said.

"You're thinking too linearly." She leaned forward and fixed me with those impenetrably green irises. "Museums are monuments to impermanence, too. Artifacts are tangible proof of the march of time. Hotels are just more honest about it. Museums give us the illusion the past can be preserved."

"It can," I said.

"It can't. Not purely. We only have a fraction of the picture. It's like holding a few pieces of a jigsaw and claiming you can see the whole puzzle."

This was, admittedly, a good point, and tied into our earlier discussion. It also made me love her, just a little. "But hotels are so . . . corporate."

"Not all of them. Like here. Agatha doesn't use it as a hotel anymore, but it was for years, and there are many estates like it that rely on tourism for their upkeep. Plus, there are considerably more hotels than there are museums."

"Job security," I said, raising my glass to toast her. She didn't mimic the gesture.

"That was never a concern. I knew I was going to work for Agatha before I left for college."

"Then why go to school at all?"

"Because Agatha insisted, and because the position has certain educational requirements."

"What is it that you do, exactly?" I asked. "Besides making sure I don't get into trouble."

"Estate management. PR. She has other assistants for her business pursuits, but I oversee the physical estate, curate her gallery, and make sure no one bothers her."

So Fiadh was to blame for displaying the constipated unicorn tapestry.

"Do people frequently bother her?"

"Not twice."

It was the second time she'd made that comment, but this time, I wondered if it had been a joke. She was still leaning toward me, and I struggled to meet her eyes. They really were unsettlingly green, and the aura of schoolteacher hadn't quite left her. Part of me squirmed, eager for her approval.

"Do you ever read her collection?" I asked, wanting to change the subject. I knew the answer—she'd mentioned the shelves for borrowing books—but I wanted to draw her out.

"Oh, definitely. Not as much as I'd like, though. For instance, I haven't gotten around to Sappho."

"What have you read, then?"

Fiadh opened her mouth, then closed it and pursed her lips. "I prefer novels to poetry. Surely you've noticed Agatha's fiction selection?"

I hadn't, truthfully. Or rather, I'd skimmed over it in favor of more classical texts. "What kind of novels?"

Fiadh gave me a look that dared me to mock her. "Romance."

I stared at her, then into my wine, then back at her. "Like, bodice ripper romance, or *Pride and Prejudice*?"

"I read widely," she said primly.

"Bodice rippers, then." I couldn't help my grin, and I leaned back in my chair, enjoying the faint blush coloring her cheeks. Fiadh letting her guard down was new, and I didn't hate it.

"The romance novel is the oldest kind of novel. Did you know that, Professor Eden?"

"I might have heard it." My earlier assumption that she'd studied English hadn't been far off, then, though the studying seemed to have been done on her own time. "Do you have a favorite?"

"What do you read when you're not translating?" she asked, ignoring my question.

"Translations." My grin remained, and I could tell it was irritating her. "And Agatha? Does she read?"

"My employer's reading tastes are not in your purview, nor in my interest to disclose."

And just like that, she buttoned herself back up.

"So, you live with your mom?" I tried, hoping to continue the conversation, if only because I didn't want to be left alone with thoughts of Natek and Gata and blood cults.

"Yes."

"Living with parents can be hard."

"Perhaps for others," she said with a disdainful sniff.

"Well, aren't you special."

"The carriage house is large. Mother and I have our own apartments."

And she called her mother "mother." I couldn't with this woman.

"How many cats do you have?" I asked, because if Fiadh wasn't a cat lady in the making, I would eat my left foot.

"Several." Her voice lost some of its edge again. "Agatha has a soft spot. You'll see them around the estate."

"That's Mr. Muffin yowling at the door." I pointed at my miserable baby boy. "He doesn't like not being allowed out, as if he's ever been allowed on anything besides a balcony in his entire life."

"He's very handsome."

Mr. Handsome currently looked like I fed him moldy milk on the daily, his eyes wide with betrayal and his tail twitching.

"I got him one of those backpacks that look like little submarines, but he didn't like it."

Now I sounded like the cat lady.

"Those are adorable." Fiadh's smile transformed her sharp features into something soft and nearly approachable, and I felt a twinge behind my breastbone I recognized as a Problem with a capital P.

"Lend me one of your favorite novels," I said, inspiration striking at the same time as the certainty that for a moment, at least, I'd found Fiadh attractive.

She looked up at me through her lashes as if weighing whether or not I intended to mock her further; then, finishing her wine with a long swallow, she nodded. "I'll leave it for you in the library."

—☞— —☞— —☞—

That night I dreamed of blood. It ran down my neck and pooled between my breasts, and no matter how tightly I gripped my throat the blood kept running from a wound I couldn't feel. Meanwhile, the sounds of my apartment being ransacked punctuated my desperate gasps.

I woke tangled in my bedsheets in the cottage to the feel of sticky liquid on my skin. Panicked, I fumbled for the bedside lamp, only to discover that the liquid was just tears. I'd been weeping, not bleeding. Mr. Muffin hulked on the back of the bedroom chair. His expression stated plainly that I was making far too much noise for his beauty sleep. I waited for the sound of breaking glass to announce intruders: nothing. The cottage was quiet, save for the humming of appliances, and outside crickets chorused. Just another nightmare.

I was getting tired of them. The blood was a new addition, and one I didn't relish, but I supposed it made sense. I'd gone to sleep thinking about blood cults. Naturally blood had permeated the usual dreams of home invasion. I knew from recent experience sleep would elude me for a while longer, so I powered up the computer provided by Agatha, considered making myself a cup of tea—then decided against it, as venturing into the kitchen didn't seem like the best idea even with the return of logic—and began translating.

Collection: Nektopolis
Title: Letter 14
Description: Correspondence; Gata and Natek
Date: TBD
Cataloguer: Clara Eden

Natek,

I should send you a knife instead of this letter. Nettle, if you know—If all this time you've been pretending that particular ignorance—Solitude does not come naturally, to me. It was something learned, and the lesson was one of those cutting edges you admire. There was no poetry to it. Loneliness is an amputation. All these years later I still flex ghostly fingers, reaching out for what I've lost. Did you ever have a child?

You live in the shadow of your own legacy. I live in the absence of mine. The work I do instead is a counter-narrative. Roots, not waves. Reaction. As you said. But a truce will only be possible if you are willing to bend. Be a rose, Nettle. Lovely, fragrant, and sharp. Hold fiercely to what you claim is yours, but bend beneath the storm. What I ask is simple: do not disturb the soil. Do not raze the forests for your war machine.

I've tasted poetry. Or rather, poets. Complex, like good wine. I dwell far from the roses of Pieria[17], here in the countryside, though the night birds provide a pleasant chorus of their own. Your collection keeps me company.

I do miss the sun.

Gata

Collection: Nektopolis
Title: Letter 15
Description: Correspondence; Gata and Natek

---

17 Translator's note: The roses of Pieria were believed to grow in the home of the Muses on Mount Olympus and represent the highest flowering of art. In some stories, they crown the Muses.

Date: TBD
Cataloguer: Clara Eden

Dearest Gata,

Such rains we've had. The streets run with filthy water, and farmers complain incessantly while produce rots in the fields. Pestilence will no doubt follow. In times like these I am glad my womb never quickened. I cannot pretend to understand that particular grief, but I have known enough grieving mothers to understand it is a pain that never fades, never dulls, never heals. Perhaps one day you'll tell me of your child.

There is a particular poet I've grown fond of. Her work is divine but underappreciated. I'll send a volume the usual way. She was in desperate need of a patron. So desperate, in fact, that I've invited her to live with me and my husband. He's quite taken with her, poor man. I'm half tempted to let him have her, for while he has his uses, he is tiresome. It was a much more straightforward thing to be a queen. I shall dispose of him soon. You should dine with me then.

I do not believe the Muses have abandoned you. There is poetry in growth, and I confess I've written of you often.

Yours,

Natek

PS. Thank you for your copied notes, my golden one[18]. I could not help but observe from them that it is not only tubers you grow. Send me a rose to solidify the lesson.

---

18 Translator's note: A term of endearment.

Collection: Nektopolis
Title: Letter 16
Description: Correspondence; Gata and Natek
Date: TBD
Cataloguer: Clara Eden

Gata writing to Natek in the rain,

We've had the same rains, here: drenching, cosmic almost, and the temples are full of the fearful devoted. They are right to be afraid. Crops drown the same as children. And yet, despite this, your Nektopolis prospers. You asked me once if I let you live on sufferance. It isn't as simple as that. You are a good steward when you are not seeding chaos. To remove you from behind the curtains of power would cause the kind of damage I strive to avoid, and would take an effort from which I might not recover. Rome has withdrawn, though I don't believe any of us hope for more than a temporary reprieve. Too much foot rot in her soldiers. The legions will return when the rains dry up and you will meet them at the border and defend us. I've only ever had one enemy, Nektaria, and you are not she.

Your invitations taunt me. How much do you really know of me? You claim ignorance, but I cannot trust it. I cannot trust you. Even admitting this uncertainty is dangerous. You know—you have to know, for your mind is far more cunning than you let on— that there is a reason I prefer to go unnoticed. And yet you taunt me with implicit promises of kinship, of something more than the scraps I've made my meals from all these years. Rationing; I could teach your country all there is to learn of the art. And you. You are a feast, and I am starving.

But do not take me for a fool. Your suggestion of affection plays on what you perceive to be my weakness, but it is also my strength: I have been lonely too long to be anything else. Poetry is

[fire-damaged document]

"Damn." Smoke damage eclipsed the remainder of the letter. I made a note of the file. Later on, once the work of the initial rough translation was complete, I could return to it. Perhaps Agatha would allow me to bring it to the university, where I could use their facilities to chemically revive lost words, though if whoever had done the conservation work on these letters hadn't been able to bring them back, I doubted my university's conservation department would have any better luck.

Had the damage really needed to obscure Gata's thoughts on poetry? My eyes grew heavier the more I pored over the words, my brain filling up with Greek characters. At last, my body succumbing to its natural rhythms, I shut my computer and drifted back into sleep.

CHAPTER FOUR
Us versus Them and All Their Ghosts

Collection: Nektopolis
Title: Letter 17
Description: Correspondence; Gata and Natek
Date: TBD
Cataloguer: Clara Eden

Natek, writing to her beloved gardener,

I have planted the rose in the courtyard of our villa. "Villa." Such a dirty, Roman word, but few enough remember a time before the occupation now, and if we do not adapt…well. Enough to say I have a villa in the country, and your rose thrives. The flowers are the most peculiar shade of red. Almost black, like blood in the moonlight, save for the edges of the petals. And so full! The heads bend the stems, which are all thorn. I am flattered beyond words it reminds you of me.

Did my poet arrive? I apologize for the lengthy silence on my end. Things grew heated on campaign and the roads too dangerous for messengers. I hope you've avoided the worst of the riots. My town house was thoroughly ransacked. Can't say I blame them. Mobs rarely arise without reason, even if the reason is not what they believe.

The nights here are peerless. Truly, will you not come stay? I understand your hesitation, but I do not play games with you, Gata. Sometimes I try to remember what it was like before I first wrote to you. Your letters live with me in the daylight hours, as incendiary as my flesh. There can be no return. You hide behind your loneliness, but it is not a shield wall, dear one, it is a plague. Would you deny me medicine?

Yours,

Natek

Collection: Nektopolis
Title: Letter 18
Description: Correspondence; Gata and Natek
Date: TBD
Cataloguer: Clara Eden

Gata, writing to Natek,

Your poet sang sweetly and tasted sweeter. I made her sing of you, and how the sun once flashed from the bronze of your helm and even the horsewomen of Scythia feared your war cry. She sang me the poems you wrote, too. How long did it take her lips and tongue to learn them? I do not wonder at your talent. Years have their advantage. I listened many times, until the ache grew too great and I had to save myself from the temptation. The thought of you teaching her slices even as it thrills. Your hand on her lips. Her lips on your hands. She was delirious with it, all poetic ecstasy and eyes wine-dark with longing.

You accuse me of contagion. You, who sent me this.

Gata

[A series of indecipherable fragments, some damaged by fire, others, age]

I scoured Agatha's collection over the next few days and turned up nothing to explain the oddities, though I did come across a surprisingly large collection of botany texts in various languages, and a subsection of ancient fairy tales and folklore, compiled in handwritten journals. I opened one, and an exceptionally friable page with the words *Edax Animae* penned at the top released a puff of age. I put the book back quickly and made a mental note to recommend climate-controlled storage for that section. The only thing that remotely alleviated my frustration, as I dutifully returned to cataloguing, was a novel.

It appeared on the table the second day after my impromptu glass of wine with Fiadh, bound in nondescript leather. The title, *The Honey Gatherers*, intrigued me, as did the author: ANonymous. The circle around the N was stylized in gilt, the only color on the otherwise plain, faded brown cover. *Throughout most of history, Anonymous was a woman*, Virginia Woolf had famously said, and I tucked it into my bag for later reading.

I had cause to be glad I hadn't opened it in the library. While the text was archaic, and the prose wrapped in euphemisms, there was no denying that the acts described were carnal as hell. The story followed a widow with a taste for pretty maidservants, and anything and everything that could be done between two people took place between those pages. I would have called it erotica, except that the central thread was hauntingly romantic, almost elegiac, and written with the force of a symphony. I'd never read anything like it in my life. When I turned the last page to the bittersweet ending, I realized I was crying.

"What even *was* that?" I said to Fiadh the following week, after reading the book a second and then a third time, my fingers careful on the brittle pages.

"I have no idea. It defies categorization. The only copy I've ever heard of is in Agatha's library. I've been searching for more information on it for years. There's not even a record of that printer."

The name of the printer, Pieria Press, appeared in faded ink on the first page. There was no date.

"Have you tried text-based archival—"

"Yes, I have exhausted the reaches of the internet," said Fiadh.

"I have access to scholarly sources you might not, though. I could look."

Fiadh paused in the act of running her finger down the book's spine—a gesture that carried an intimacy I promised myself I would try not to think about later—as if she might snap at me, but she seemed to think better of it. Instead, she said, "Thank you, but Agatha has access to every archive on the planet, even ones unfriendly to Western scholarship. If those cannot find it, then it simply isn't there to be found. It is possible that the original copy was destroyed, very likely in the Second World War, and that there was only one print run made. Understandable, considering the content is a touch . . . risqué."

"No kidding." I was uncomfortably aware of how much reading the book had altered my perceptions of Fiadh herself. I was familiar with the stereotype of the prudish woman with a penchant for steamy romances, but this was different. Fiadh was right: the book was impossible to categorize, and I couldn't help wondering which aspects Fiadh found appealing.

"Did you enjoy it?" she asked. Her eyes were innocent, as was her tone of voice, but I squirmed regardless. You didn't just come out and admit to liking a book that spent ten pages comparing cunnilingus to a girl eating honeycomb by a summer stream.

"It was . . . compelling," I managed.

Fiadh laughed, actually *laughed*, at my discomfited expression. The sound was surprisingly light. Then she turned to leave.

"Wait," I said, remembering she'd asked to read further translations of Gata and Natek's correspondence. "I have another letter, if you wanted to read it."

"Those are also . . . compelling," she said, her tone that same, carefully neutral tone I suspected concealed her amusement.

"In a very different way."

"Maybe." She tilted her head and examined me with a slight crease in her brow. "But then again, there is something haunting, too, don't you think? Even if it is all just a game."

A game. I nodded my agreement, even as I wondered.

71

> While current scholarship surrounding the founder of
> Nektopolis, Nektarios, suggests previous historians
> may have been influenced by cultural biases,
> recent findings lend further credence to theories
> that Nektarios was in fact Nektaria, one of several
> influential women in Alexander the Great's court. The
> discovery of Nektopolian coinage with Nektaria's
> profile and name, along with correspondence—

I stopped typing. This was stupid. I couldn't use any of the artifacts in my research, and I certainly couldn't publish whatever it was I thought I was writing.

A book, my brain informed me, *incorporating my dissertation with updated findings, which would refute the blatantly sexist work of Antonio Bertucci, my least favorite Nektopolian scholar, once and for all.* My fingers tapped the keyboard in frustration. I could write this, knowing I couldn't do anything with it until Agatha died. At least then I'd have the satisfaction of being the first to the proverbial punch. But Agatha could live a long, long life. I could die before she did. This was a waste of my time. I should focus on scholarship surrounding artifacts I could actually *use*.

I knew I was going to write it anyway. Settling deeper into the surprisingly comfortable chair in the cottage's office, I took a sip of tea and considered how I'd incorporate the letters. The coin was concrete, conventional evidence, and therefore much harder to misinterpret. I could compare it to the thousands of extant examples of coinage from that era. Translations, however, were trickier, and I'd need to verify that these documents were indeed Nektopolian and not some bizarre forgery, not to mention checking and triple-checking my translations. Warm light from the desk lamp illuminated my scribbled notes and the smudged keys of my laptop. I glanced at the notepad.

A rose, then. Something with thorns.

I'd written the words idly in the margins. Lines from the correspondence dogged me like song lyrics. What did they mean?

Why pretend to write across such a vast expanse of time? I'd ruled out the impossible explanation—that Gata and Natek were somehow immortal, and that Natek was Nektaria—but an alternative hadn't presented itself. Forgery still seemed most likely. Papyri and other paper mediums surviving from antiquity were exceedingly rare; complete correspondences were almost unheard of.

I scrolled down to one of the chapter headings I'd inserted into the document and reread my notes, then began typing.

> Greek views on female homosexuality may have extended to Nektopolis through Nektaria's influence. Native cultures were generally allowed to thrive under Greek occupation, but analysis of Nektopolian pottery and textiles suggests either closer links to their Achaean neighbors than previously believed, or a direct result of Nektaria's influence. An examination of Nektopolian law, which codified rights for women more similar to northern Thracian-Scythian societies than the hegemonic laws of Greece, and the body of evidence of Greek artistic styles in Nektopolian art, indicates a heterogeneous culture that accepted, at least nominally, basic rights for women, as well as granting them some sexual autonomy.

Rough, but a start. Crickets chirped outside my window as night fell. I crossed my legs beneath me and sank into the work, taking comfort from the familiarity of ordering my thoughts into prose.

—⁓— —⁓— —⁓—

Days passed, and summer bathed the grounds in soporific heat. When I wasn't in the library or writing, I drowsed on the emerald lawn on a blanket or sat in the shade of the willow by the pond. Fiadh periodically joined me. The overture toward friendship felt tenuous, and I held myself back from the exuberance I might have shown someone else. I couldn't risk this going sour from a professional standpoint, and from a personal one, she was the only other person I could talk to about my work.

"You're developing a bit of an obsession," said Fiadh one languid August afternoon as I speculated on Natek's relationship to Nektaria. The library heat had been so stifling even with the air conditioning she'd suggested I leave an hour early while she put in a request to the maintenance team about fixing the temperature. I'd changed into shorts and a swim top, though I had no intention of bathing in the pond, having seen the resident snapping turtle earlier that summer. Instead, I'd brought a spray bottle of water, which I periodically spritzed over my torso in a vain attempt to cool my skin.

Fiadh joined me soon after, still dressed in her skirt and blouse. She wiped a hand across her forehead as she sat.

"You'll melt in that," I said through the slits of eyelids, which were all I had the energy to open.

She unbuttoned her blouse in response. I stilled, momentarily panic-stricken, until I realized she had on a camisole beneath. Dappled shade fell over us both and turned her skin alternating shades of green and gold. Her freckles seemed to dance in the shadows.

"Have you translated any more?"

"No," I said, twisting a blade of grass between my fingers. "I'm trying to catalogue the rest of the Nektopolis collection. Maybe it will help things make sense."

"Does it bother you when things don't make sense?" she asked. I couldn't tell if she was teasing.

"More than you can possibly imagine."

I studied her as she leaned back on her elbows and lifted her face skyward. She had a curvier figure than I'd realized. Her austerity suggested a spare frame, but her shoulders, chest, and hips were gently rounded, and in my heat-dazed state, I decided she probably had the kind of lap that made a perfect pillow. Not that I'd dare. I continued to study her in silence as sweat beaded on her upper lip from the oppressive air.

One of the shadows on her neck didn't move with the shifting leaves. A bruise, maybe. Perhaps she had a significant other. It wasn't like I knew anything about her personal life except that she lived with her mother—in separate apartments. I didn't even know how old she was.

"How old are you?" I asked.

"Thirty-four."

Three years my senior, then.

"And you've worked here since you got your master's?"

"And during. The only time I was really away was when I was at undergraduate."

"I bet you lived it up," I said, letting my sarcasm show.

"You'd be surprised."

"Yes, I would. What, did you stop alphabetizing your socks by color?"

"Unnecessary. My socks are always black."

Currently, her feet were bare, and she'd painted her toes a shade of coral that veered from red to pink then back to red in the light. My own toes hadn't received paint in years, as I didn't have the patience to let nail polish dry, and they looked rather bleak and neglected in comparison.

"Black socks never get dirty," I began in a sing-song voice, "the longer you wear them, the stronger they get."

She arched a brow in my direction. "Did you just make that up?"

"No. It's the 'Black Socks' song. My college roommate taught it to me."

"It manages to be both charming and revolting at the same time."

"Much like socks."

"Fair enough."

She closed her eyes, but the corners of her lips remained tilted in a faint smile.

"The last letter . . ." I began, unsure how to frame what I wanted to say, or even what I wanted to say at all.

"What about it?"

"Well, aside from the fact that it doesn't make much sense, the underlying tone is . . . erotic. But they don't talk about ever meeting in person. Gata doesn't want to. I don't understand why."

Fiadh was silent for a moment as she considered this, then said, "I think I understand."

"Really?"

"If they really were just correspondents, then there was so much to lose by meeting in person. Like meeting a date you've only spoken with online. You have no way of knowing if the person is really the person you think they are. Perhaps Gata was afraid. Or perhaps she wasn't who she pretended to be."

This hadn't occurred to me. "God, people have always sucked, haven't they?"

75

"Since we came down from the trees. Probably before that, too. Monkeys throw their own shit."

I'd never heard her swear before. It sounded incongruous.

"I ship them anyway," I said.

"Of course you do."

"Though . . ." I trailed off.

"Hmm?"

"Nothing." The sun was too bright and the day was too warm. Perhaps if we'd had a few drinks, and a stormy night was knocking branches against the windowpanes, I'd have the courage to put my doubts into words. I didn't think she'd take me seriously, however, if I explained I thought someone was deliberately fucking with me.

"It's so hot." The words dragged in her voice, almost a groan. I inched toward the far edge of the blanket and patted the empty space I'd left behind. She eyed it, then lay gingerly down beside me. When I offered her the spray bottle, she accepted. At least a foot separated us. There was nothing inappropriate about sharing a picnic blanket on a day like this. And yet, her willingness to lie beside me, eyes closed and mist sparkling on her bare skin, suggested a level of comfort I hadn't expected from her. I listened to the sound of her breathing in the companionable quiet, interspersed with the trill of a bird or the drone of insects. The estate was far enough away from the main road and any other neighboring properties that we couldn't hear the sounds of cars or lawn mowers. I didn't think I'd ever been in a place this peaceful.

I must have drifted off at some point because when I woke up it was twilight, Fiadh was gone, and I had become a buffet for mosquitos.

I stayed outside on the patio late that evening, much to Mr. Muffin's dismay. It was too hot to be indoors, and the cottage did not have air conditioning. A jar of iced tea kept me company as I watched the stars peek out through the trees and crown the estate.

At ten o'clock, a light came on in the greenhouse. Agatha Montague's silhouette moved about, and I saw her carry a flat of some sort of plants out onto the grounds. I stood without allowing myself to dwell on my decisions, scratching at my mosquito-assaulted stomach, and ambled across the lawn as if I was out for an evening stroll.

Agatha looked up from the moonlit patch of carefully mulched flowerbed where she knelt, planting something spiky and dark green. Or at least I assumed it was dark green; night leached color from the foliage and painted everything in shades of indigo and gray.

"Ah, Clara, I presume?" She had a low, husky voice, and a face I couldn't decide to categorize as plain or gorgeous or something in between. I settled on the word *compelling*, thinking of Fiadh, and then realized I couldn't even place Agatha's ethnicity. Her age was equally unclear. Thirties? Forties?

"Ms. Montague?"

"Call me Agatha, please."

"I didn't mean to disturb you."

"Not at all." She stood and dusted off her hands. At her fullest height, she came to my chin, but I had the sensation I was the one looking up at her. Her eyes had gravity, though they were as colorless as the leaves. "It's a lovely night for a stroll."

"And too hot to sleep," I added.

"Indeed. That's one of the reasons I prefer gardening at night."

Her hair was up in a business-like bun, but a few tendrils curled around her ears and neck, collecting starlight. She didn't look the way I thought the head of a business empire ought to look. I'd expected . . . I wasn't sure. Someone I'd feel good about hating. I knew I couldn't call her out for hoarding information, at least not as long as I wanted to keep my job, but I could have nursed a private hatred on behalf of the lower classes, if nothing else. It was funny how people needed their enemies to look like enemies. What did it matter that Agatha didn't look like elite scum, standing in her garden smock with dirt on her hands?

"You have lovely gardens," I said, somewhat lamely.

"Thank you. Do you garden?"

"I've kept a few houseplants alive."

"An accomplishment. Most people cannot. How do you like the cottage?"

"It's beautiful."

"And the work?"

Here was the opening I couldn't take. Even so, I hesitated before saying, "Absolutely fascinating. Your collection. It's . . . well, the artifacts from Nektopolis alone are incredible."

"It's hard to find a fellow enthusiast."

"Your odds are better than normal, this close to Brixton University," I said.

"I admit I may have stacked those odds in my favor." She winked.

"There are benefits to wealth."

"You help fund the program?" I didn't mean to blurt out the question, as it seemed rude, but perhaps that was just my own financial insecurity talking.

"I do," she said.

"Oh. Well, uh, thank you." It was possible her donations had paid for my education—a prospect I found uncomfortable.

"I should be thanking you. Fiadh has kept me abreast of your progress. She isn't normally so free with her praise."

The compliment overwhelmed my capacity for speech. Agatha seemed to guess this was the case, and spared me the embarrassment of silence. She turned to examine a rose. Its scent permeated the night air, heady and wild. "You are welcome to cut a few flowers for personal use, though be careful of the thorns on the roses. This one has particularly small, fine thorns. Quite painful."

To illustrate her point, she frowned at her bare fingertip as if it hurt her.

The roses reminded me of Gata and Natek.

"If you don't mind me asking about provenance . . ." She didn't protest, so I continued. "There is a particular set of correspondences I've found troubling."

"Troubling?"

"Confusing, I should have said."

Her full attention had not been on me until that moment, I realized as her eyes caught and held mine. They seemed to almost glow in the moonlight. My pulse leapt in response, and a spike of adrenaline coursed through my veins and whispered, *run*. I'd felt that way when my advisor had pinioned me with a similar look during discussions of my dissertation.

"Which?"

"Gata and Natek."

"Gata and Natek," she repeated, though her pronunciation differed from mine, and her words were slightly accented. I filed it away; her pronunciation rang truer. Perhaps she was a scholar after all. "What about it confuses you?"

"It's just shockingly well preserved." Which was true, though not the only reason. "I was curious if you've had it verified for authenticity. Provenance would help, too."

"They are one of my greatest treasures." Her face softened, losing

78

its intensity. "Their authenticity isn't in question. I have read your translations—"

"They are only my rough translations," I interrupted. "For cataloguing purposes."

"—and I am pleased with your work. The footnotes are appreciated."

"Oh." I'd expected reprimands, not compliments. "Um, thank you."

"I studied the Nektopolian language a long time ago. I'm afraid I've forgotten most of it. Revisiting those works has brought me much joy. They are so very raw—a reminder that the past also *felt*."

"Yes." Warmth bubbled up inside me. Hoarder of knowledge though she might be, she understood the allure of my field: touching the lives of those who'd gone before, and for a moment, erasing the veil of time and all it concealed.

"I was very sorry to hear about your former living situation. To have your home invaded without an invitation is deeply upsetting. I hope you feel safer here. Our security is quite good."

"Thank you. I do." Otherwise, I might have added, I would not be walking about the grounds at night.

"I've lived through several such invasions, and each time, I am reminded of how deep our fears run."

"Oh," I said. "I'm sorry."

But not surprised. The rich made themselves targets. She seemed to see this in my face, for she continued, "It is interesting that the theft is not what lingers, but the sense of violation. Or perhaps it is the theft of safety, and our illusion of it, that matters, rather than physical possessions."

"I was just glad my cat wasn't harmed."

"I do love cats," said Agatha. "I have several. They are wary of strangers, however. I doubt you'll see them for some time."

I thought of the silver cat I saw periodically, and wondered how many more I hadn't seen.

"Gata and Natek," I began, circling back. "I don't really know what to make of them. My translations may be deeply inaccurate. Once I have the full scope of their correspondence, however, I am hoping things will seem clearer."

"History is full of strange and inexplicable things. Trust your instincts." She patted me on the arm with a cool hand. The dismissal was gentle, but clear.

"You're welcome to stop by and meet my cat sometime if you like,"

I said, though why I offered was unclear. My employer didn't want to meet my cat. It was the kind of socially awkward comment I thought I'd learned to contain.

Her eyes fixated on me with an iridescent flash.

"Thank you," she said slowly, "for the invitation."

"I met Agatha," I said to Fiadh the next morning.

She was wearing another skirt-and-blouse combination, which reminded me of how she had looked in her camisole, drenched in dappled light. This blouse was a pale gray. The color accentuated her eyes. I, meanwhile, was already sweating in my slacks and button-up from the walk across the lawn, but the house was comfortable. Someone had fixed the AC situation.

"Really," Fiadh said. "How?"

"I took a walk."

"At night?" A hint of alarm crept into her voice. She leaned against the library table and looked down at me.

"It was the only time of day cool enough for a walk. It must be safe if she gardens at night, right?" Panic edged my words as I thought of the break-in.

"What did she say to you?" Fiadh asked—not answering my question.

"We talked about Gata and Natek. And cats."

Her face brightened. I wasn't the only one with a burgeoning obsession.

"What did she say about the letters?"

"She didn't say much exactly, but she alluded to them." *And that you were impressed with my work.* For reasons involving pride, I didn't mention that last bit. Nor did I repeat my question about safety. I was fine. Of course it was safe. Fiadh was just surprised I'd chatted with Agatha at such an unconventional hour.

"Nothing specific?"

"Trust my translation instincts. We talked about history more generally, and Nektopolis. I didn't realize she'd studied the language."

"Yes. She's very well educated. You sound surprised."

"She wasn't what I expected. But I think I liked her, despite . . ." I trailed off. No point bringing up knowledge hoarding again.

"Yes, she has that effect on people." Fiadh smiled to herself more than to me, her lips a quick curve of private amusement.

"She's down to earth—literally. She was gardening."

"Do you know some of her roses have won awards?" Fiadh leaned forward, though I didn't think the motion was conscious. Her blouse hugged her shoulders and I caught a whiff of her delicate perfume. I was spending too much time with her; proximity bred attraction.

"No, I didn't." Feeling bold, I added, "You should show me which ones sometime."

—⁓— —⁓— —⁓—

Collection: Nektopolis
Title: Letter 19
Description: Correspondence; Gata and Natek
Date: TBD
Cataloguer: Clara Eden

Nektaria to her dearest Gata,

It has been too long since I've heard from you. Do not mistake me—I do not hold it against you. We've all had to do whatever we could to survive the madness of the last two governors. I was able to save your rose before the fires[19]. It grows now in my new home, which you've found by means I'd very much like to discover. I searched for you in the rubble and in rumors, and I found nothing. I confess I'd allowed some small measure of doubt to creep in. Not about your survival. That was never in question, my slippery friend, but that you'd decided to cut your losses in their entirety. I feared I'd been too much, too fast, though it has been years since I first wrote to you.

---

19 Translator's note: This suggests a date either in the second century BCE during a brief uprising, or in the second century CE as Rome began her slow decline.

And now I find out you've been hunting me. You might have knocked, you know. We could have had a drink together. Have I not proven, after all this time, my intentions toward you?

I can see you shaking your head, though I know what you look like only from hearsay: a woman of middling height with a piercing stare. But I digress. My intentions are honest enough, for there is honesty in selfishness. I wish to know you.

I've left this reply in a place you'll find eventually. How long from now, I can't be sure, but you left me no return address.

Your Natek

The madness of the last two governors. I turned the phrase over, reordering the words each time. There was a dark period in Nektopolian history, several decades before their ultimate collapse, that could account for this. I rubbed my eyes and wished I had made tea the last time I was up. If this was merely *pseudonymoi*, then my translation couldn't be correct. The timeline didn't add up with the previous letters, or at least, not in a way that accommodated a single mortal lifetime, unless the game was carried out by multiple senders. Was this code? A priesthood or cult that employed the same characters over generations? I scrolled through the documents I'd photographed, then scrolled again.

A document caught my eye as I made a third pass. Another will, this time bestowing a country estate to a widow named Agate.

Agate. Gatalina. Gata. Such striking similarities between the names. Did that mean something?

Collection: Nektopolis
Title: Letter 20
Description: Correspondence; Gata and Natek
Date: TBD
Cataloguer: Clara Eden

Gata, writing to her Natek,

I did not mean to fall silent, but I think you know the cause. Nor are you as innocent in these events as you claim. It was your strategizing that kept out the Romans—what did they offer you to turn you to their side? Or did you grow so weary of Nektarian madness you thought you'd trade it for a Roman strain? All empires are mad. I would have thought you knew that better than most.

I am glad you were able to keep the rose. Its thorns will do what I cannot. May they pierce you deeply.

There is an abandoned temple outside your city, little larger than a roadside shrine. I do not know what gods it served. I will be there the next time the moon is full in Martius if you promise not to search for me. Leave your reply beneath the altar stone and I will receive it.

Gata

Collection: Nektopolis
Title: Letter 21
Description: Correspondence; Gata and Natek
Date: TBD
Cataloguer: Clara Eden

Natek writing to her heart's gleam,

I must apologize. I could not keep my word. And now that I have seen your face—Gata, how can you blame me? You are more than I dreamed, and I have dreamed of you so many times. It is not enough. Your solitude, your hoarded hours—I wish I could respect them. I wish I knew if solitude was what you truly desire. Whatever it is you think I know about you, you are mistaken, and if you ever trust me with such knowledge, I will carry it far beyond the grave.

Here is what I do know: I was satisfied in my work before our paths crossed. Now, nothing satisfies me save the thought I might one day stand before you and confess, with all the aching years as witness, the sincerity of my desire.

Past the shrine stood a grove of oaks. I wandered there after you fled, hating myself for the betrayal in your eyes even as I longed to touch you (again and again and again). Why did you allow me that one brief brush of hand? Did you know how it would torment me? I cupped your cheek in the moment before your stricken eyes turned cold, and I felt you tremble, Gata. No one has ever broken me so swiftly. The fates have played me—I thought you were a puzzle I might solve, when instead you are the kind of trap I've avoided all my life.

Do not mistake me. I've loved plenty, and at times with too much passion. It is a Greek affliction. I have known obsession and heartache and loss. I have known jealousy. I have known contentment and the slow degradation of two mingled lives, or, as has happened on occasion, three. Love is meant to be shared. Never have I felt what I felt beneath those moonlit trees. Never have I been so willing to forsake all oaths. I do not even know you, Gata. Not really. So why did my soul recognize yours?

That grove was full of you. I cannot explain it. I stood and wept and the leaves whispered my name in your voice. Then I wandered, and as I touched the bark of my companions, I saw you again. Not in the flesh.

You wavered like a ghost or a vision in my mind's eye, a woman younger than you were when you were turned, with her hand on the ripening swell of her womb. Gata, the shrine might be abandoned, but the shrine was never why you came here. Those trees hold the fullness of your grief. I stayed until sunrise gilded the dusty leaves and then I took refuge in that crumbling temple, where I wept blood for you until necessity forced me to stop.

As for Rome, her time, too, will come. All empires might be mad, but all empires fall. It doesn't matter who moves the pieces.

Please forgive me.

Nektaria

PS. Keep the horse this message came with. She's one of mine, and she's with foal. You need a faster mount.

—⚯— —⚯— —⚯—

I emerged from the fog of translation with a mighty need for caffeine and high from the thrill of a good novel, except this wasn't a novel. I stumbled to the kitchenette and flicked on the electric kettle, fumbling for a mug and a bag of Irish Breakfast tea—the really good kind—while my mind whirled.

Fiadh needed to see this, I decided as the water boiled rapidly. I needed to establish my sanity, and the easiest way to do that was cross-referencing it against someone else's. When the kettle clicked, I let the steam wreathe my free hand as I poured. The sting of the heat didn't rouse me from my stupor. Gata and Natek. I wondered, again, if this was some sort of elaborate hoax.

I drank the tea scalding hot despite the summer heat, grateful for the cool air coming from the tastefully wrought vents.

Fiadh. I needed to find Fiadh.

Finishing my tea, I called her on the phone she'd provided. It went to voicemail. I hung up and sent her a text: *Can I see you for a sec?*

No answer. I washed my mug and returned to the library.

The silver cat sunned itself on the window seat. I moved slowly so as not to startle it. I recalled Agatha's words about the shy nature of her felines, and the honor its company bestowed upon me filled me with absurd pride. I returned to the pages in front of me and resisted the urge to keep reading, instead making myself go over my work, checking and double-checking words and facts against everything I knew about Nektopolian culture.

When Fiadh finally appeared, my nose was so close to my screen I had to unfold myself slowly, accompanied by complaints from my back and a massive headache.

"I think," said Fiadh, observing me, "that you could use a walk outside."

"But—"

"No arguing."

I shed my shirt, not wanting to ruin it in the heat, and was glad I'd worn a clean tank top beneath, instead of the permanently stained one I'd considered. Fiadh's dark dress did not offer her similar accommodations. She led the way into the garden, but first she grabbed an *actual fucking parasol* from an umbrella stand. My first inclination was to ask what century she was from, but then I ducked beneath it at her nod, and the relief offered by that circle of shade obliterated all else.

"Ready for a rose tour?"

"Sure. Why not." I needed some time to clear my head. This would do.

We strolled over the grounds through walled gardens and topiary mazes and gazebos, all of which sported roses of different varieties. Their names slid by me on metal plaques, and I focused on color and scent as Fiadh's voice washed over their petals. Sharing the parasol required we stand close, and I took over holding the implement, as my height was the greater. Fiadh didn't seem to mind our proximity. If anything, she leaned into me as she explained the breeding practices used by Agatha to increase bloom size and fragrance, and the different fertilizers the flowers preferred. I still hadn't mentioned the letters, but for now, I was content to listen to her voice.

She paused in the shade of a clematis-covered portico. I could have lowered the parasol, now that we were out of the sun. I didn't. She remained so close our hips touched as she indicated a rose with lush, nearly black petals.

"This is her favorite. Be careful of the thorns."

I eyed the stems. Thorns as long as my little finger curved beneath the glossy leaves. The scent was hard to pin down: not the rich, heady rose scent of her other blooms, but . . . wilder. Fiadh touched a bud with the tip of her finger. Her arm brushed mine in the process. My skin shivered at the contact as a peculiar possibility crossed my mind: was Fiadh flirting with me? I was aware of the curves of her body in an electric, almost alchemical way, as if the space between us contained mercury. It seemed to pool and ebb, leaving me short of breath and tasting metal. The bitter iron tang of my pulse beating in my throat mingled with roses, crushed grass, and her perfume. I couldn't think. The prospect of Fiadh's interest had rendered me as senseless as aged papyri.

I lowered the parasol and leaned it against the portico before she could notice my trembling hand. Our fingers brushed.

That was a mistake. Her skin was as soft as the petals surrounding us, and desire punched me in the gut. She glanced up at me through her lashes—slowly, the motion liquid with intent.

Yes. Fiadh was absolutely flirting with me.

"Tell me about the letters," she said. The words were innocent; her tone was not.

"Um."

The letters. That last, incomprehensible missive. My hand, bereft now of the protection offered by the parasol's handle, hung far too close to her thigh. I raised it out of danger, only for my fingers to hover uselessly midair.

"You did want to talk about them, didn't you?" That coy little head tilt of hers snapped something in me. Fuck it. I could flirt, too.

"Well," I began, gently stroking the small of her back, aware this was a step I could not retract and wanting to give her every opportunity to pull away in case I'd misread the signs. "They continue to be compelling."

I saw the hitch in her breath as my thumb traced a line across her spine, crossing once, then twice. She pressed closer to me. There was no mistaking the flush creeping over the modest expanse of chest revealed by her dress, nor the heat between our bodies. I deepened my touch into a caress as I spoke, exploring the dip of her spine, the curve of waist, the arch of hip, the flare of ribs. Her breaths came faster. The sight of her pulse ignited a hunger I was terribly afraid might destroy my career. Then again, there hadn't been any rules against fraternizing with the staff, and Fiadh had instigated this. Hadn't she?

She turned her back to me, and my doubts died as she leaned against my chest, cupping the nape of my neck with a warm hand. Both of my hands rested on her waist, now, and I recited what I could remember from the letters into her ear through this new haze as I ran my fingers over the light cotton of her dress and across her stomach. She plucked a petal with the hand not twisted in my hair. It clung to her fingertips, garnet red.

Maybe we'd gotten too caught up in Natek and Gata. Maybe this was longing transferred, and we were both just romantic enough to be taken in. I didn't care. My lips brushed her hair, then her ear, as my voice dropped to a whisper. Her eyes fluttered closed. I wanted to drag this moment out—Fiadh amongst the roses and the thorns—forever.

The sound of an approaching lawnmower interrupted us. She pulled away, but not before turning her head and grazing my lips with hers, a half smile twisting them, as she whispered, "I suppose you can call me Fi, Clara Eden."

—⁊⁊— —⁊⁊— —⁊⁊—

Sleep did not come easily that night. I replayed my encounter with Fiadh over and over, wondering what it meant. My body ached, craving more of that contact, and nothing I did alleviated it. When I at last dozed off sometime around one o'clock in the morning, I was half mad with desire.

Only dreams brought relief. I drowned in a dark, red, fevered heat, satiety a slow crescendo.

I woke drained and wet. My head felt like a hard-boiled egg, and my limbs moved slowly. Even my neck was sore and stiff. I splashed water on my face and blinked blearily at my reflection in the antique bathroom mirror. Tangled dirty blonde hair. Bloodshot eyes, ringed with purple. A pallor that didn't look healthy. I prodded my lymph nodes. Those seemed fine, but my neck was definitely sore. I also appeared to have gotten scratched by some of the roses on my arms and throat. I remembered the incident: I'd ducked beneath a hanging branch and felt the catch of the thorns on my skin.

Coffee helped. I considered calling in sick, but then Fiadh might think I was avoiding her, and that was the last thing I wanted—though after the dreams I'd had, I wasn't sure I could face her ever again. I forced myself to eat a large bowl of oatmeal topped with fruits and nuts, along with a preposterously large glass of water. As I set the empty glass down on the table, I realized it was a vase. Not that it mattered. A water vessel was a water vessel.

By the time I was showered and ready to go, complete with cover-up beneath my eyes to conceal the shadows, I felt better. The sleeplessness that had plagued me since the break-in must have caught up with me, or perhaps my period was due to start. Bleeding always exhausted me.

I chose my outfit with more care than usual: a soft blue shirt that looked like silk but wasn't, slacks that flattered my ass instead of sagging from too many washes, and loafers that hadn't been scuffed to high heaven and back. I looked acceptable, which was as far as I was going to get without shopping for a new wardrobe.

I paused in front of the mirror, the realization that I could afford a new wardrobe slowly sinking in. Agatha paid me generously. Even with the money I was setting aside for savings and paying off my student loans, the amount I saved on monthly rent alone was probably more than enough to refurbish my meager closet.

Crossing the grounds in the morning heat winded me more than usual. I rested in the shade of a sycamore halfway across the lawn, then continued, my thoughts torn between Fiadh and Natek and Gata. Fiadh and I hadn't really had a chance to discuss the letter. I'd been too distracted by her to focus. Today, though, I'd rein in my impulses long enough to show her the translation. And then . . . then we'd see what happened. A shiver passed over me as I remembered the way her hips felt against my palms.

Fiadh opened the door in the midst of this recollection.

"You look . . ." She paused, frowning. "Kind of terrible. Are you okay?"

So much for the power of concealer.

"Good morning to you, too."

She stepped back, allowing me into the citrus-scented entryway. My pulse skittered. "I didn't sleep well," I confessed after a tight second.

"Oh." Her gaze fell along with her shoulders, and she bit the corner of her lip.

I waited until she looked up at me again, and then gave her a very pointed stare. "I had a hard time falling asleep."

She blushed, comprehension blossoming through her capillaries.

"Well, you don't have to worry about me distracting you today. I have to run some errands for Agatha, so I won't be around until this evening. If you need anything, you'll have to call."

"Are you headed out now?"

"I'll escort you to the library first."

Would I ever be considered trustworthy enough to make that perilous journey on my own? Not that I minded her company. She walked beside me today instead of several steps ahead, her hand periodically grazing mine. I wanted to taste her lips again. That brief, teasing contact burned like an unanswered question.

"I'll be on my patio if you want to stop by when you get back," I said. The words were confident; my delivery was not. She paused outside the library door and reached up to brush my lower lip with her thumb. I closed my eyes involuntarily. When I opened them again, she was smirking.

"Perhaps I will."

—⁓— —⁓— —⁓—

Collection: Nektopolis
Title: Letter 22
Description: Correspondence; Gata and Natek
Date: TBD
Cataloguer: Clara Eden

Natek,

Don't be a fool.

Gata

Collection: Nektopolis
Title: Letter 23
Description: Correspondence; Gata and Natek
Date: TBD
Cataloguer: Clara Eden

Nektaria writing to Galatea,

Of course it is foolish to court you as I have been, with words and broken promises, but forever stretches bleakly on. What risk, really, in risk itself?

Your Nettle

Collection: Nektopolis
Title: Letter 24
Description: Correspondence; Gata and Natek
Date: TBD
Cataloguer: Clara Eden

Natek,

Speak plainly. The risk is greater than you know.

Gata

———※———※———※———

The urge to call Fiadh on her errands nearly overpowered me. I restrained myself. I could show her these letters tonight. Perhaps over a bottle of wine. A burst of nervous excitement at the thought of spending time with her twisted my stomach just as something brushed against my leg. My already buzzed nervous system sparked, startling a squeak from my lips. I glanced down into a pair of bright green eyes: the silver cat.

"Why hello there," I said, reaching a tentative hand down for her to sniff. Her whiskers pricked me as she inspected the offering; then she butted her head against my fingers and accepted a scratch before sauntering off.

I put the letter away, eager to start on the next. The rest of the collection could wait. Natek had bared her soul, and I needed to know Gata's real response, academic rigor be damned.

Get a grip, Clara.

I braced my hands on either side of the documents and took a long breath in and out. Remain detached, I reminded myself. Getting too invested in my material was an inevitable risk for any scholar, but one that had to be monitored. Grow too invested, and I'd run the risk of twisting the translation into what I wanted it to be, rather than what it was.

A wave of light-headedness washed over me. Stars danced in the corner of my vision, and I blinked to clear them. No luck. Nausea curled in lazy ripples in my gut.

What the hell?

Not wanting to disturb my workspace, I moved to the window seat gingerly and collapsed onto the plush cushions. Lying down brought immediate relief. I closed my eyes and concentrated on breathing. The cat jumped up and settled against my stomach, purring.

—w— —w— —w—

"Clara?"

I woke to a hand on my shoulder and a concerned voice repeating my name. The warmth of the cat was gone. I peered up into Fiadh's face.

"I thought you said you were leaving," I said, my voice raspy. I cleared my throat.

"I did. I got back an hour ago and stopped by your place, but you weren't there. Then I saw the lights were still on here."

"Wait, what?" I rubbed my eyes and sat up, feeling much better than I had when I'd dozed off, and saw the reflections of the library lights on the darkened windowpane. Beyond, the last pale blue of sunset glowed on the horizon; the rest of the sky gleamed a velvety purple.

"Oh my god. I didn't—I just—"

"Are you feeling okay?" she asked.

"Better now. I had a dizzy spell earlier, so I lay down, and then the cat was purring and I must have fallen asleep."

"The cat?"

"The silver one. Agatha's."

Fiadh's face blanched, and she sat heavily beside me.

"What?" I asked.

"Tell me your symptoms."

"Just tired and a little nauseated and light-headed, but that nap kicked it out of my system."

"Clara—"Fiadh chewed on her lip hard enough to leave an indent.

I reached for her wrist. "I'm okay. Really. Just concerned I might lose my job for falling asleep in the middle of the workday."

"Don't worry about that. We should go."

"Where?"

Her eyebrows rose in exasperation. "To your house, in case you start feeling sick again."

I didn't argue. She helped me pack my bag, and then we walked out of the house and across the lawn. Nighttime transformed the grass into a silver lake. It reminded me of the cat's fur. I was almost sad to enter my cottage, suggesting we sit outside and enjoy the evening instead, but she insisted.

Mr. Muffin greeted us with a yowl. He darted toward me, his tail twitching with indignation over his late dinner, but froze when he noticed Fiadh.

"This is Mr. Muffin."

"An insulting name," she said, crouching slowly to greet him. His nose twitched as he sniffed her. I turned and set about opening a can of wet food. A special treat would speed him along the path of forgiveness.

My stomach rumbled. Now that I was awake and feeling better, I was starving. Did I have any food ready to eat? I scanned the fridge. A wilting salad. Pickles. Some yogurt. I really needed to take better care of myself.

The fridge door shut. I stared at it in confusion. Fiadh's small hand gripped the handle, preventing me from opening it again.

"But—"

"Sit. I'll order us takeout."

"Do they deliver here?" I asked, picturing a pizza delivery person stepping along the path to the cottage. It seemed anachronous.

"Why wouldn't they? Well, they won't deliver *here,* but they come to the carriage house. I can nip over and pick it up."

I allowed her to lead me to the couch. She placed an order for Thai from a restaurant I'd never been able to afford while I lay back on the cushions and marveled at this turn in events. When I'd pictured us on my couch, it hadn't been a fantasy of her bossing me around and ordering food, but I didn't mind.

"Whatever this is, I hope I didn't give it to you," I said.

"Hmm." She tapped her fingers on the armrest. I leaned my head back against the couch, enjoying the scratch of the wool blanket against my cheek as I studied her. She sat primly, one leg crossed over the other, and I noted a small scar on the smooth moon of her knee. The image of a young Fiadh tripping and skinning her knees as a child, perhaps in gravel, as had often happened to me, stirred a protective yearning in my chest.

I'd take a thorn to the heart, for you.

"Grab my laptop and read the latest installment," I said.

"Or, you could rest."

"I'll rest while you read it. I promise it's worth it."

She rose to fetch the computer. The slightly harried edge to her motions revealed genuine worry. I shivered at the memory of her lips ghosting over mine, the inevitability of attraction washing over me like the rippling waves of my dream. Her eyes reflected the light from the computer screen as she scanned the hastily translated text.

"Well?"

"It's a love letter," she said, looking up.

"I know."

"It's . . ." She trailed off, chewing on the corner of her lower lip. The clean white of her teeth against her flushed lip distracted me, and I didn't press her to finish her thought—instead thinking about what it might feel like to bite her lip myself: the soft give, the sharp intake of her breath, the way her mouth would part for mine.

". . . intimate," she finished. "In a . . . I'm not sure. It almost reminds me of that novel I lent you."

"*The Honey Gatherers?*"

"Yes."

I considered this. The lexicon was different—less euphemistic, direct to the point of violence—but the voice did carry certain similarities. A dark languor, an undercurrent of fierce desire.

Now, nothing satisfies me save the thought I might one day stand before you and confess, with all the aching years as witness, the sincerity of my desire.

No one had ever written anything like that to *me*.

"I just don't know what it means," I said. "And I can't figure out the timeline at all."

"No." She looked away from me. "Time seems somewhat flexible for them."

"Which is impossible," I said.

"Well, yes."

She twisted her hands together. Those hands had tangled themselves in my hair, pulling longing up from the roots.

"Fiadh," I began. But what was I going to say? I want you? Too blunt. Too vulnerable. Too honest.

As if sensing the shift, she shut the laptop and set it on a side table, all briskness once more. "How do you feel now?"

"Hungry."

"I can fix that in a few minutes. Can I get you anything until then? Water?"

"I'm okay."

She looked like she wanted to get me water anyway.

"What fascinating errands did you run?" I asked to keep her close.

"The usual. Documents to pick up and drop off. Groceries."

"Don't you have a personal shopper or something?"

"We do, but Agatha needed a few things not on the list. May I feel your forehead?"

She leaned over at my nod, her breasts brushing my folded knees, and pressed the back of her hand to my head. I held my breath. The sight of her almost on top of me would have made me dizzy even if I had been feeling one hundred percent.

"You don't feel feverish."

"That's something, at least."

She glanced down, and the concern in her gaze warmed to interest. Her eyelids lowered. The memory of the garden floated between us.

"You're sick," she said, in the tone of someone reminding themselves of the facts.

"Or just tired."

She hadn't pulled away yet. Tension thrummed between us, and I shifted, sliding slightly lower on the couch in invitation.

"I'm not kissing you right now," she said.

She wanted to, though. I could tell by the way her eyes kept flicking to my lips, and by the heightened color in her cheeks.

"Fi." Her name came out of me in a pleading rush of air.

"You need to rest."

"I'm resting now."

"You know what I mean," she said, still leaning over me. I wanted to feel her on top of me so badly it hurt. My hand cupped the soft warmth of her thigh just above her knee, the one with the scar, and when I squeezed, she exhaled sharply. The hem of her skirt skimmed my wrist like a caress.

"Haven't you read any fairy tales?" I said. "A kiss might cure me."

That made her laugh, and with the laugh, she regained her composure and straightened. I felt the loss like an eclipse. She softened the rejection with a touch to my cheek.

"Do me a favor, Clara."

"What?"

"Don't let anyone in."

"Metaphorically, or, like, into my house?" Right now, the only person I wanted to let in anywhere was her, and by anywhere, I meant everywhere.

"Into the house."

"You're the only one who's been here since I moved in, except for my friend Mark, who helped me move." I paused, remembering something. "Though I did tell Agatha she could stop by to meet my cat."

Fiadh coughed.

"You okay?" I asked.

"Swallowed wrong," she said, clearing her throat. "You invited Ms. Montague over to see your cat?"

"Something like that. Why, was that unprofessional? I wasn't sure, since we live on the same property, but she said she likes cats . . ." I trailed off and tried to make sense of Fiadh's expression. It didn't match her measured tone. She looked worried again—more so than before. I'd definitely crossed a line, then. A new and dreadfully embarrassing thought occurred to me. "You don't think she thought I was propositioning her, do you?"

That was the last thing I needed: my employer thinking I was vulgar enough to invite her over to meet my pussy. Fiadh scoffed. I relaxed into the cushions.

"I highly doubt it," she said. "Has she stopped by?"

"No."

Her phone buzzed. She glanced down, thumbed the screen, and rose.

"Well, if she does while I'm off to get the food, tell her I say hello."

I closed my eyes as my door shut behind her. I felt like I'd messed something up, but I wasn't sure what.

She returned with fragrant takeout containers. We split the contents, spreading them out on the coffee table and shooing away a curious Mr. Muffin. As we ate, she turned the conversation back to the letters, asking questions about the Roman conquest, Nektopolis's decline, and the historical minutiae of the times. I warmed to the subject, impressed by the keenness of her questions and, admittedly, flattered by her interest. Most people didn't care about history.

"You should sleep," she said, too soon.

I shrugged.

"You look exhausted." Her hand stroked my cheek. I leaned into the touch, a shameless expression of interest, and she brushed my lips with her thumb. I felt the touch everywhere. Her smile suggested she knew precisely what she'd just done, but she was right—I was almost deliriously tired.

"Goodnight, Clara."

CHAPTER FIVE

I Never Stood A Chance

Collection: Nektopolis
Title: Letter 25
Description: Correspondence; Gata and Natek
Date: TBD
Cataloguer: Clara Eden

Gata[20],

You tell me to speak plainly, as if you have ever given me that courtesy. You, who hunt me, just as once I hunted you. I'll tell you what I want, as I have told you before: I want to know you. I want to hunt with you, together, in a world not bound to ink and papyrus.

Do you truly fear discovery so greatly you would turn down the possibility of happiness? Maybe I overestimate myself and what I mean to you, but I do not think you'd write me if you felt you had a choice. I think, Gata, that you hate me a little for this—in the long stretches between your letters, I

---

20 Translator's note: The lack of formal address, here and the almost imperceptible changes to the handwriting, indicate this letter was written with force or haste.

can feel you testing your resolve, longing to sever
this tenuous thing we've woven between us. But you
never do.

So. Do me the same favor in return. Speak plainly,
or not at all.

Natek

—⚏— —⚏— —⚏—

A good night's rest restored me to my usual robust health. Fiadh,
however, looked exhausted.

"Did I give you whatever bug I had?" I asked, catching her elbow
as we walked to the library.

"What? Oh. No, I'm fine."

"When I tried 'I'm fine' you made me sit on the couch and ordered
us Thai."

"That's different. I know exactly what's wrong with me."

"And?"

"And it's that I didn't sleep at all." She snatched her elbow out of
my grasp. "Which is just perfect considering the amount of work I
have to do today."

I let her go, stung. Apparently, sleep deprivation reverted Fiadh
back to the Fiadh of my first acquaintance: prim and snappish.

"What kept you up?"

"Nothing." She pinched the bridge of her nose and let out a sharp
sigh. "I don't mean to be short with you. Something came up with
Agatha, and I had to deal with it, and it took longer than I expected."

I put a tentative hand on her back. When she didn't jerk away, I
rubbed gentle circles across her shoulder, hoping to soothe some of the
tension from her body.

"Did you resolve it at least?" I asked. She leaned against me, letting
her head briefly touch my shoulder.

"I'm not sure."

"Well," I said into her hair, "I still have leftover Thai if you're
hungry later. It could be my turn to take care of you."

I assumed she'd dismiss me out of hand, but she brightened.
"Bring it over after work. I'll show you the carriage house."

99

"And your extensive collection of bodice rippers?"

"Careful, or I'll make you read them to me."

The heat her words sent south shut me up, as she'd no doubt intended.

I got to work.

—m— —m— —m—

Collection: Nektopolis
Title: Letter 26
Description: Correspondence; Gata and Natek
Date: TBD
Cataloguer: Clara Eden

My Dearest Gata,

Your silence has me worried. Do you now wish to prove me wrong? My words cannot truly have come as a surprise.

You're still out there. I'd know if something befell you, for I still sense your stillness, the heavy calm before a battle. My plans and machinations fail in ways no rival but you could conceive. Outbreaks of insanity and hallucinations. Fungal rot in our grain stores. But no sign, ever, of enemy action, and I only know it to be you because I recognize your signature like the breath of scented oil you left behind you in the shrine.

The world shifts. Storms break all around us. The old gods fall to the new, and my work calls me elsewhere. Nektopolis is long gone[21], Nektaria all

---

21 Translator's note: This suggests a date after 150 BCE, when Nektopolis surrendered to Rome, and potentially after the fall of the Western Roman Empire, though the Byzantine Empire did reabsorb the territory by 1025 CE. By then, however, the city-state of Nektopolis was just a memory.

but forgotten, and new opportunities arise in the east.

Come with me.

Yours, Natek

The carriage house's gabled windows and ivy-covered walls watched me as I crossed the lawn. I'd changed into a pair of jeans, though my body had protested. Normally I wriggled into loungewear the minute I got home. I'd considered wearing a pair of joggers until I remembered I might run into Fiadh's mother. I imagined her as an even more tightly wound version of her daughter.

Peepers serenaded from the trees, and a bullfrog croaked from the pond as I knocked on the dark wooden door. The sound echoed in the space beyond. I gazed around the grounds as I waited. Sunset transformed the estate into jewel tones and rich, velvet shadows. The grass here was greener, lusher, more vibrant than any place I'd ever seen before, and the trees reached toward the sky in sweeping grace.

How had I gotten this lucky?

Fiadh answered and waved me in, interrupting my musings. She'd remained in her work clothes, naturally. I held out the Thai container like an offering. *Please,* I imagined myself saying as I knelt before a glittering altar, *forgive my humble peasant's garb, for I am but a poor academic.* The thought amused me enough to get over myself. If Fiadh wanted to remain in her work clothes, that was her prerogative, as jeans were mine.

The carriage house's entryway was decorated in the same style as the main house, and had been tastefully renovated to include multiple apartments without compromising the original charm. There was even a dwarf citrus tree in a pot. Not a speck of dust marred its glossy green leaves. I hoped Agatha paid the housekeeping staff well.

Fiadh took the Thai and gestured for me to follow her through one of the foyer's two doors.

"The other belongs to my mother," she informed me as she turned around. "And security's office is around back."

More potted plants clustered near all the windows of the first

101

floor. Pothos hung from baskets in the kitchen window and tropical plants of all sizes and colors filled other windowsills.

"Plant fan?" I asked.

"What gave you that idea?"

"I'm very observant. Check out this observation: shouldn't you be wearing something more comfortable?"

She glanced at her outfit in surprise. "This is comfortable."

"If you say so. Now, go sit down and I'll heat up dinner."

The living room contained a small plush couch, an equally plush armchair, several floor-to-ceiling bookshelves, and more plants. Cozy. Tidy. Exactly as I had imagined. Fiadh sat on the couch with her stockinged feet tucked beneath her while I rummaged through the kitchen. I found bowls in the second cupboard I tried, and heated the food in the microwave, even covering them with a paper towel to prevent spattering—which I never did at home.

"It's cute," I said, gesturing at her apartment with a bowl as I joined her on the couch.

"Thanks." She brushed a strand of hair behind her ear. I stilled. Another bruise marred her neck. I hadn't left it there, which meant it had been someone else. A surge of jealousy ruined my appetite.

"What?" she asked when she noticed me staring.

"I was admiring your hickey."

She set down her bowl and glared at me. "I do not have a hickey."

"Your neck says otherwise."

"My—" Her hand rose to touch the spot, and she briefly closed her eyes. "It's not a hickey."

"Then what is it? Are you okay?" I ran through all I knew about medical disorders associated with bruising and came up with several terrifying options.

"Yes. I'm fine."

"Fi—"

"Please drop it." Ice slithered into her voice, and the cozy atmosphere circled the drain. I resumed eating, though mechanically. Fiadh's dark brows nearly met as she glowered down at her bowl.

What the fuck?

"If you're worried about . . . you know . . . me, I'm not jealous." This wasn't true, but she didn't need to know that.

"Clara." That glower turned its full force onto me. I tilted away from her. The woman could *glare*. "For the last time. I do not have a hickey, nor will you ever see me with one. Now please *drop it*."

"Okay. Fine. It just looks painful."

Her expression merited radiation warnings. I looked away first. Not a hickey then. Which left injury or illness. She'd said she'd been up all night. Doing what? Had someone hurt her? That stirred something deeper than jealousy. Fiadh wasn't frail, but she was small, and it was too easy to imagine someone overpowering her. I let it go for now. She'd push me away if I didn't—her eyes made that explicitly clear.

"Anyway," I said, forcing my voice to sound casual. "Gata and Natek finally met in the letters."

The glacial cast to her features melted. "Read it to me."

I retrieved my work laptop and settled back down beside her to read the letter aloud. Fiadh closed her eyes to listen.

"And Gata doesn't respond?"

"Not yet." She looked so washed out and exhausted. I wanted to soothe those dark circles away with my fingertips. Instead, I repeated a line from the letter: "Nektopolis long gone."

"What does that tell you?"

"Not much, really. It was a short lived city-state. One hundred and eighty years, to be exact."

"And you are nothing if not exact, Clara Eden, at least when it comes to your scholarship." She cracked an eye open slightly, a corner of her mouth tilting up in a smile.

"Are you suggesting I am less than exact elsewhere?"

"I will leave that up to your interpretation."

"I interpret things all day." The whine in my voice was only half in jest. I quite desperately wanted to know what she thought of me.

She opened both eyes to appraise me fully. "You're not what I expected."

"In what way?"

"You're different from the other researchers I've worked with on Agatha's behalf. Or maybe you're just younger."

"There's still time, then, for me to disappoint." I paused. "You're exactly what I expected."

"Oh?"

"Meticulous."

She laughed. "I need to be. For work."

"Too meticulous. Can you please change into something more comfortable? You're making me nervous."

"I am comfortable," she said. To my surprise, she set her bowl aside and lay down, resting her head in my lap. "See?"

Her hair was soft. I let the strands flow between my fingers, thinking of forest streams and shadows and wondering what kind of shampoo she used. It smelled expensive. I was a "whatever brand is on sale" kind of girl, but feeling Fiadh's hair, I could see why people sprang for more.

"Your hair is ridiculously soft," I told her. My voice was low and rougher than usual.

"Mmm." She leaned into my hand. The motion reminded me of a cat. I half expected her to purr as I ran my nails along her scalp.

She fell asleep in a matter of minutes. I didn't intend to doze off with her. I'd decided to rouse her in an hour and help her to bed, but her cheek was warm against my thigh, my belly was full of good food, and I awoke with a crick in my neck to the quiet of three o'clock in the morning. I didn't need to look at my phone to know the time. Three a.m. had a taste to it I'd become intimately acquainted with during my graduate studies.

Fiadh remained snuggled up against me. Her hair rose and fell with her breath where a dark lock lay across her parted lips. We'd left the kitchen light on, and it cast enough illumination for me to make out the details of her face: small and sharp and utterly lovely. I wanted to press my finger gently into the divot of her upper lip, where, in a single moment of cosmic alignment, I knew it would fit perfectly. Tenderness tightened my throat. My left hand cupped her shoulder. With my right, I tucked the lock of hair that had fallen over her lips behind her ear, careful not to wake her.

I closed my eyes again. It was three in the morning. Moving wasn't an option. My neck could deal with the crick.

My bladder, however, had other plans. I tried ignoring it. As the pressure grew, so did the pain in my neck, and I became aware of a hundred other small bodily irritations. My jeans felt tight. I had an itch on the bottom of one foot. And I really, really had to pee.

Carefully, I eased Fiadh's head off my thigh and stood. She didn't wake. The nearby chair had a light throw tossed over the back; I retrieved the blanket and tucked it around her, wishing I could stay, but unsure of the line.

"Goodnight, Fi," I whispered, and edged out of the room. I used the bathroom, wincing at the sound of the toilet flushing in the silence.

104

"Clara, wait!"

Her shout startled me with one shoe half on and the other still lying on the doormat. I ran back to her side with an awkward hitch in my step and found her sitting bolt upright, her eyes wide and wild.

"Are you okay?"

"You can't go."

"Fi—"

"It's not safe."

"Fi, you had a bad dream or something."

"No, I—" She blinked, seeming to realize where she was. "What time is it?"

"Around three."

"You can't go out there." The panic still clinging to the edges of her voice unsettled me, but I recognized the irrationality of a person recently awoken from a nightmare, and since I wasn't particularly keen on walking home anyway, I gave in.

"Okay. I'm staying. But you're not sleeping on the couch."

She rose, smoothing out her rumpled dress, and grabbed my hand as if afraid I'd flee. I let her lead me up the narrow staircase to the second floor. It was dark—I thought about mentioning the kitchen light we'd left on, but her grip on my fingers dissuaded me—and into a room lit only by starlight. Her pale coverlet was the brightest thing in sight.

"You sure you don't want me to leave? It's not exactly a long walk. I could—"

Fiadh turned and threw her arms around my neck, kissing me hard. Her lips were soft and yielding, a contrast to the force behind them, and my mouth surrendered before my mind had a chance to catch up. I'd been kissed plenty, but not like this. She was liquid metal, kinetic energy, the smooth give of water. We both took a second to catch our breath when she broke away.

"Stay," she said. It was not a request.

I nodded. My heart was a pounding wreckage in my chest, and I stared at her face, which the starlight had transformed into something ethereal and dangerous.

"Clara."

The illusion faded. Fiadh gazed up at me with vulnerability and need clashing in her eyes, and I was helpless to resist.

She pulled her hair over her shoulder and presented me with the

105

back of her dress. The gesture conveyed a thousand things and nothing. Did she only want help undressing? Or did she want more? It was late, we were both tired, and I'd made poor decisions at this hour before.

Her back waited. I undid the delicate button at the top of her collar and slid the zipper down her spine. The fabric unfurled like a white rose to reveal her starlit skin. I brushed my hands along her shoulder blades and felt her shiver. Gooseflesh rose along her arms. I wanted to pull her flush against me, as she'd been in the garden. She slid one bra strap off her shoulder and looked at me, her profile soft in the near-dark. Gently, I undid the clasp of her lace-trimmed bra and slid the straps over her arms, my palms skimming the surface of her biceps, elbows, forearms, and hands, each centimeter perfect.

She stepped away with a slow smile, the dress falling to the ground. I watched her shimmy out of her stockings and stand, wearing only a pair of simple underwear, her curves catching every stray gleam of starlight. The tips of her breasts were dark against her skin. I wanted to kiss the curve of shadow beneath them, and I wanted to stare at her forever. Still sporting that smile, she lifted a nightshirt from her drawer.

I was unable to suppress my small groan of protest as it slunk over her body. Her laugh was light and knowing, and I didn't know what to do with my hands. All I wanted to do was touch her. The nightshirt fell to just below her ass, revealing as much as it covered. It looked like real silk, unlike my shirt. I didn't really give a fuck about the material, but the way the fabric clung to her breasts was mesmerizing. She held my eyes as she walked over to the bed.

"Fi . . ."

She tossed back the light quilt and waited. We'd barely shared one real kiss. This was too soon, too fast, and it was too late—but everything in me screamed *yes*.

I shed my shirt without any of her slow seduction. My bra lacked lace, and I didn't care, and I didn't think she did, either. What my bra did do was unclip in the front. The feel of her eyes on my skin was like warm sunlight on a cold spring day. I left my jeans beside the rest of my clothes on the floor. In the darkness, they became merely another shadow.

I sat at her silent bequest and wondered if there were things that we should say: boundaries to be defined, assurances to exchange. Her sheets were cool against my bare legs. When she slowly straddled me, her eyes at the same level as mine, words died in my mouth.

Her hands found my hair tie and undid my messy bun. My skin was so hypersensitive even the feel of my own hair brushing my shoulders made me shiver. She slid her hands beneath the tangled mass of it and drew my face to hers.

This kiss was gentler than the last, but no less hungry. Her lips were soft and full and pliable, and I drew the lower gently between my teeth, intoxicated by the way it gave. Her hands tightened in my hair and pulled me closer. My hands, freed from awkwardness now that I was thoroughly distracted, stroked the fabric of her nightgown. Beneath the silk, the curve of her waist responded to my touch, trembling, and I resisted the urge to squeeze the soft rise of her hips and tumble her to the mattress—if only because she felt too damn good on top of me. I trailed my fingertips along the hem of the nightshirt. I didn't know Fiadh. I didn't know what she wanted or what she liked, and gentleness was the safest starting ground. I felt her, hot against my stomach as we kissed. The thought of my mouth on that heat made a moan rise to my lips. She heard it, smirking.

The smirk did it. I flipped her, parting her legs as I settled my hips over hers and trapped one of her hands with my own. Her breasts pressed against mine, as soft and full as her mouth, and I buried my face in the curve of her neck.

"Not that side," she whispered in my ear.

Remembering the bruise, I paused.

"Are you sure—"

She arched up into me, center to center, and my question turned into a hiss of breath. I raked my teeth along the other side of her neck, no longer able to be gentle, no longer able to think about anything except the places where our bodies met. Her skin tasted clean and sweet as summer rain. I did have enough wherewithal not to leave a mark. With each kiss, her body rose, and I pressed back, setting a rhythm that increased in time with our ragged breathing. The hollow where her neck met her shoulder made her cry out when I ran my tongue along it, and I repeated the motion, the sound of her rising voice a building crescendo.

Had it not been so late in the night that we'd crossed the border into morning, perhaps we would have taken our time. But her body rocked beneath me, and I rocked harder, my hips finding her rhythm and driving us over the edge in a sudden rush.

"Clara," she said, her voice a strangled whine as her legs tightened around me and her free hand raked down my arm. "Oh, god—"

That undid me. I came hard against her, feeling her slick through both pairs of our ruined underwear, the friction unbearable as she trembled, right there, so close I could feel her nerves singing. I sank my teeth into the muscle of her shoulder, and she screamed as she came.

—·— —·— —·—

I woke to the smell of coffee and the taste of shame. Fiadh sat beside me in her night attire, a large and aromatic mug steaming in her hands.

"Here," she said, holding it out.

I wriggled out of the tangle of sheets and accepted the brew, not meeting her eyes. The memory of last night burned within me in alternating waves of lust and the knowledge that I'd been so eager for her I hadn't even taken off her underwear. In the privacy of my mind, I at least liked to pretend I was a halfway decent lover. Someone who took her time. Someone who teased and listened with eyes, mouth, and ears for what her partner wanted. But last night, all I'd been able to think about was her: her body beneath mine, the heat between her legs, and how good it felt to top her.

"Clara?"

I dared a glance into her eyes. Puzzlement creased her brow. She really did have the most amazing eyebrows: thick and striking, like a slash of oil paint across the canvas of her face.

"Thanks for the coffee," I mumbled. It was good. Strong and rich, no cream, no sugar. She knew how I took it. That surprised me, and the shame intensified. She knew my coffee order. I should have—

"Hey." Fiadh plucked the mug back from my hands and set it on her bedside table. In the morning light, her room unfolded around me, revealing her inner world. It was tidy, which didn't surprise me, but the rest of it did. A massive landscape painting dominated the wall opposite her bed. Mountains rose above a clearing, and a storm gray sky roiled above silvered grass and leaves. The brush strokes were frantic, erratic almost, but the overall effect was soothing. Fingers on my chin forced me to look at her, not the wall. I felt blood flow into my cheeks.

"What's wrong?" she asked.

"I feel like I took advantage of you last night," I said. "You were so tired, and—"

Fiadh's laugh was rich and throaty, and I felt it everywhere. "Clara Eden," she said, her eyes boring into mine. "Who dragged you to my bed last night?" She ran her nails along my jaw. "Who," she continued, "straddled whom?"

She straddled me again now, and the swell of her breasts caught the morning light. Thank all the gods for low-cut sleepwear. I couldn't help myself. I cupped them with my hands, my thumbs sliding over her nipples through the silk.

"But," I began, unsure of what I wanted to say.

"You did nothing I didn't want you to do." She leaned in until her lips brushed my ear. "And I can think of one or two more things I'd like you to do later."

"Fuck," I said, rolling her nipples between my thumbs and forefingers before pulling her roughly against me, her ass filling my hands. She smelled like coffee and perfume and a hint of sex, and I wanted to fucking devour her.

"But first, I have to go to work, and so do you." She slid off me with the contented smile of a woman who knew exactly what she'd just done to her lover and was enjoying every cruel minute of it.

"That," I said, my heart racing, "was exceptionally mean."

—w— —w— —w—

Collection: Nektopolis
Title: Letter 27
Description: Correspondence; Gata and Natek
Date: TBD
Cataloguer: Clara Eden

Natek to Gata,

I leave tomorrow. I do not yet know where my path will take me. Find me, if you can. Or better, join me. My teacher, as you once called her, would welcome you. I respect your secrets. I have not spoken to her of you. But think, Gata—think of what we could have.

At least keep yourself safe. I see your face in dreams.
That will have to be enough.

Your Natek

I stared at the translation, a lump in my throat. The pain, not just in the words but in the handwriting, ate at me. Natek's normally elegant script had bled onto the page in raw syllables. With as much eagerness as caution allowed, careful not to damage the documents, I searched for the next letter.

It was not from Gata.

Collection: Nektopolis
Title: Letter 28
Description: Correspondence; Vezina and Natek (?)
Date: TBD
Cataloguer: Clara Eden

Nightshade,

The time for you to leave your city has come and gone. I will send one of your Sisters to make sure all is well if I do not hear back from you soon. Your acumen is needed elsewhere, my love. I understand you've grown attached to your city, but the seat of power has shifted, and you are too far from the action. You will like Kōnstantinoupolis. You will also like this new assignment. Tomislava is waiting for you with trading contacts farther east and north. Once we control the routes, shortages will be easier to arrange as necessary, and there is blood waiting to spill. We are only safe in orchestrated chaos. Remember that.

I write to bid you hasten your departure, but also to tell you of my sorrow. My beloved Yelena has died. I wear strands of her tail woven in with my hair and I released her spirit to the wind and flames. She danced on the smoke. Her son is strong and swift and sees well in the dark, but he is not his mother. Your mares always are exceptional creatures. Bring your herd. They will help you make a name for yourself.

There is another of your Sisters I would have you take beneath your wing. She is nearly as brilliant as you, but with a mind bent toward discovery instead of conquest. Together you will be formidable. Tomislava has raised her up to now, and I see great potential in the three of you.

Vezina

Vezina—a new name. I jotted it down, along with Tomislava. Names from farther east. But who were they, and how did they fit into Natek's world? Not for the first time, I wondered who had gathered this correspondence. Perhaps the next letter would shed light on things.

Except there were no more letters. I'd reached the end of this drawer of documents, and had not found another.

The long table was perfect for laying out all the documents I'd translated. I assembled the catalogue cards I'd made for myself on notecards to stand in for the letters themselves. Twenty-eight letters in total, not counting the other documents. There had to be more.

Hours passed. My eyes burned from peering at faded script and squinting at my dictionary. Lists of merchandise. A few deeds to properties long since turned to dust. Nothing else about Natek or Gata. I took a short break to rub my temples, closing my eyes against the throb of my headache. They twitched beneath their lids. I was missing something. Objectively, I knew this wasn't fiction. A satisfying ending wasn't guaranteed. It was more likely that the rest of the correspondence had indeed continued, only to be destroyed later. There was a reason statuary and cookware were far more common archeological discoveries than writings. Time wasn't kind to the biodegradable.

On a whim, I checked the cabinet with the creepy cat skull one more time. The drawers all had tight seams, and while I knew it was foolish to look for false bottoms, I couldn't help it. I needed the rest of the correspondence.

The emerald eyes of the skull winked up at me. I lifted it, feeling oddly compelled despite its macabre appearance. Its weight surprised me. I'd expected heft, but this was unmistakably lead.

Dimly, I was aware that darkness beckoned beyond the windows. Even more dimly I felt the stirrings of my stomach, neglected since a light lunch. And most dimly of all, a faint sense of unease. Normally, Fiadh came to see me off the premises before sunset. All those dim signals paled in comparison to the mounting frustration beating behind my breastbone.

There had to be more.

I set the cat skull back down in its drawer and stared into its glittering eyes. Green eyes, like Fiadh's. I was an idiot. Fiadh would know if there were more letters, and if she didn't know, she could ask Agatha. I'd let frustration cloud my judgment.

I bolted out of the library, leaving my possessions scattered over the table. The house was silent. No distant vacuums roared over carpets and polished hardwood. No pots clanged in the kitchen. The only living creature I saw was the silver cat. It darted out of a guest room and raced down the stairs in front of me, pausing to wind between my legs. I scooped it up. Soft silver fur brushed my chin as the cat butted me aggressively, her purr a small engine. At least she hadn't scratched the shit out of me.

"Fi?" I called as I stepped off the landing into the front hall.

No response, but I thought I heard a sound from the gallery and started off in that direction. Some of the house's lights were off, but ambient hall lighting kept the shadows at bay and each painting and sculpture had its own individual lamp, no doubt with bulbs carefully selected so as not to harm the work.

At the far end of the gallery, lit upon a marble plinth, stood the ruins of a statue. The woman's head and arms were gone, but the curve of her spine and the gentle bend of her knees retained some of her character. The cat's purr seemed louder than was natural as I took in the details of the marble figure. Time had worn her down, and a chunk was missing from one bare breast, but the craftsmanship was exquisite. My heart pounded against the cat's warm body. Nothing moved in the gallery. And yet, my pulse tasted coppery in my throat.

I needed to find Fiadh. Setting the cat down, I stared a little wildly around the gallery. The house, which had felt welcoming up until now, seemed to stare back from the painted eyes in the portraits. Many of the portraits were of women—especially a woman with dark hair and darker eyes, painted in different styles and clothing, but similar enough in her features I could tell it was the same person.

I hightailed it out of the room and into the safety of the hallway. No sign of Fiadh. I called her name again, then pulled out my work phone and punched in her number. It rang and rang, then went to voicemail. My breath came too quickly. I willed my body to calm itself; this was not worth having a panic attack over. They were, after all, just letters. It was a miracle so many had survived at all.

I ran back to the library in case Fiadh had arrived while I was gone. Nothing. I paced the room. Still nothing. Fiadh had no doubt been called away on important business and had simply forgotten to tell me, despite the fact that we'd slept together only last night.

Stop, I told myself. I had no claims on her time. She owed me nothing.

Well, not entirely nothing. She was the link between me and my employer, and her absence was unusual.

After what I gathered to be a reasonable amount of time for someone to check their messages, I ceased my pacing and jogged back downstairs, planning to check her apartment in the carriage house. As I breezed down the hall, skin prickling, I noticed the doorway she'd yelled at me for entering. The door stood ajar.

I hesitated. I really, really liked my job. Even though I was freaking myself out over nothing—though at least I *knew* I was being ridiculous—I still understood how lucky I'd been to get this gig. Going down that staircase was a terrible idea.

A low moan, so faint I almost didn't hear it, drifted up those stairs. *Fiadh*. My heart stuttered. What if she'd fallen, and that was why she hadn't answered any of my calls? What if she'd been lying there injured for hours, waiting for someone to come to her aid?

I yanked the door fully open and was about to fly down the narrow stone steps when the moan came again. I recognized *that* moan. It was the same sound she'd made when I'd kissed the back of her neck. Several emotions shot hotly through me. Surprise. Jealousy. And, predictably, anger.

What the hell? Two women in the same day was gross, and Fiadh hadn't struck me as a player. Then again, I remembered the mark on her neck that she'd claimed wasn't a hickey. *Fuck that*. I'd catch her in the act and then see if she tried to deny it.

Careful not to make too much noise, I tiptoed down the stairs. The air smelled like sage, a faintly herbal scent that was at odds with the dark stone. Basements had never bothered me, probably because I spent too much time in university stacks. Dark, winding passageways were par for the course. If this one seemed deeper and darker than made architectural sense, it was just because I was impatient.

The stairs ended in a small landing decorated with a tall ceramic vase. Nektopolian, I noted, because my brain couldn't help it. I teetered on the last step and peered cautiously into the room.

If the house above was elegant without being overstated, the lower level was all opulence. Thick carpets covered the floors, and stylish leather couches trimmed with expensive-looking wood were arranged around a fireplace large enough to roast a cow. The high ceiling— which explained the depth of the stairs—gave the room an airy feel, aided by a glittering chandelier. Shelves with statues and books lined the walls in place of windows, and more doors opened off the main room into darkness. In the center of the room, arranged on one of the couches, was Fiadh.

She was not alone. A woman held her in her lap with her head bent to Fiadh's neck. Fiadh moaned again, ecstatic, helpless, and I clenched my fists to subdue the rising tide of emotion. She'd been down here while I searched for her, making out with—

The woman raised her head as if she'd heard my thoughts. All the air left my body. Agatha Montague straightened where she sat, wiping a smear of blood from her lips. Fiadh lay limply in her arms, more blood beading on her neck.

I knew people were into weird shit. This, though . . . this was more than I was prepared to handle. A shudder of revulsion coursed through me.

I turned to run.

"Clara Eden."

Agatha's voice arrested me mid-stride. I tried to push against the command inherent in my name, but my body refused to obey. I looked over my shoulder. Fiadh's eyelids fluttered as she forced them open, and even from this distance I could see her blown pupils. For a moment, her eyes focused on my face. The glazed ecstasy parted, and she mouthed a single word.

Run.

I wanted to. Gods, I wanted to. I wanted to run and never stop, crossing oceans and continents until I was far enough away that the memory of this room was scrubbed from my mind by sheer obliterating distance.

"Sit down," said Agatha.

I entered the room and slumped into the closest chair. Disobeying wasn't optional, probably because I was too shocked and disgusted to think. My clothes shushed against the leather. The white wood bordering the chair was cool beneath my fingers.

Not wood. Carved ivory. Or maybe . . . bone.

"Didn't Fiadh give you instructions not to enter the lower levels?" said Agatha.

"I . . . the door was open. I heard a noise and thought . . . thought someone was hurt."

"She is fine." Agatha had to help Fiadh sit up, which did not aid her case. Fiadh did not look fine. She looked drugged.

"I didn't mean to interrupt." My voice was unrecognizable. It shook and creaked liked a stand of winter birch.

Agatha tapped her fingers on her crossed arms as she considered me. "This complicates things, doesn't it?"

"What happens between two consenting adults . . ." I began, but I couldn't finish the phrase. Blood still clung to Agatha's lip.

A letter whispered from the archives of my memory.

Your rose survives. I feed it blood, and it seems to its taste, though its thorns have grown. Are thorns wood enough to end us?

Agatha.

Agata.

Gata.

My heartbeat pounded so loudly I could barely hear the conclusions ricocheting around my brain.

"Clara," Fiadh said again, this time sounding more like herself. "You shouldn't have come here."

"I'm gathering that."

"I'm sure we will find a way to get past this." Agatha Montague gave me a smile that aimed to reassure but missed the mark. There was something wrong with her teeth.

"Yes," I managed. "Of course." My mouth formed the words, but my mind was full of a violent buzzing.

"Good. Fiadh, please escort Miss Eden home."

Fiadh stood and smoothed out her dress. The print was a dark

115

brown, tinged with red to suggest a hint of inlaid flowers near the hem. I stood as well. The buzzing intensified. Fiadh walked toward me unsteadily, her jaw clenched with the effort of moving, and I followed on her heels like a marionette. I did not look back at Agatha. I did not want to see the expression on her face—or the blood. When we got to the stairs, I took Fiadh's arm to steady her.

She shook me off.

"What were you *doing*?" she asked in a hissing whisper.

"What were *you* doing?"

She glanced over her shoulder and shook her head, setting off up the stairs. Her movements were slow and sloppy, as if she was drunk. Had Agatha drugged her? What, exactly, had I just witnessed? I eyed the spots of blood on Fiadh's neck and couldn't shake the creeping horror from my veins. The conclusion I'd come to moments before was impossible. Such creatures—I couldn't name them even to myself— didn't exist. Kink was far likelier, and yet, Fiadh swayed like someone suffering from blood loss.

She paused to catch her breath when we reached the top of the stairs. I wanted to step away from her, but she looked so frail.

"We need to get out of the house," she said.

"Okay." I helped her out the front door and onto the starlit lawn. Her hand found mine and clung to it. "Where do you want to go?"

"I . . ." She paused and took a shuddering breath. "We can't go to your place."

"Why not?"

"You . . ." Another breath. "You invited her in."

"What does that—never mind. What about your house?"

She loosed a despairing laugh. "It's too late for that."

"Then where?"

Fiadh cast around the lawn with wild eyes. They settled on my car. "Do you have your keys?"

I did, by some miracle. I fished them out of my pocket and fumbled with the lock button. We tumbled into the seats with cut grass clinging to our shoes. The headlights, when I turned the ignition, illuminated a flash of silver on the freshly mown lawn.

"Just drive," said Fiadh. Her eyes closed as she spoke, and her head lolled. I fished blindly in the backseat and pulled out an emergency water bottle.

"Drink this."

She obeyed. Relieved, I pulled onto the long winding drive, listening to the sound of the tires on asphalt and the rush of the wind. *Just drive, Clara,* I told myself. *Don't think. Just drive. Just . . . drive.*

"Here," she said after ten minutes.

Here was a barren stretch of road surrounded by fields on both sides. I pulled off onto the shoulder.

"What," I said, turning in my seat to face her, "the hell just happened?"

Fiadh looked wan and pale in the moonlight. Her lashes lay against her cheeks, and the blood had begun to dry on her neck. I wished I had my phone for a flashlight so I could examine the wound.

"You might have warned me you were into weird shit," I said.

"It's not what you think."

"I don't know what to think."

"I know," said Fiadh. "You were never supposed to see that."

"What, that you're fucking your boss? I mean it's fine, I guess, I just wish you'd told me."

Yes. Fiadh sleeping with Agatha was preferable to . . . alternatives.

"I'm not—I'm not having an affair with Agatha." She still hadn't opened her eyes. I reached over and grabbed her wrist, feeling for her pulse. It was thready and light. Worry superseded everything else.

"Fi, are you okay? Did she drug you? Do you want me to take you to the hospital?"

She shook her head. The motion reminded me of a drooping sunflower. "No. I just need a minute. And maybe . . . maybe some food."

"We can do food."

"I've got food at home."

"You said we couldn't go there," I reminded her.

"I . . ." She trailed off again. I didn't like the glazed look in her eyes, or the blanched color of her cheeks.

I started the car. I didn't normally eat fast food, mostly because I couldn't afford it, but I knew there was at least one burger joint in town. Fiadh made a small noise of protest as I steered us back onto the road, but she seemed incapable of more.

Neon lights ahead promised calories. She did not argue when I ordered us burgers and fries, perhaps because she seemed to be having a hard time holding up her own head. The teenager at the drive-through handed the greasy bag over with a knowing glance. I wanted to slap him. Neither of us were high—though maybe that would have been

117

better. Then I could write off this whole evening as a bad trip.

I plopped a foil-wrapped burger in Fiadh's lap, her dress be damned, and pulled into a parking spot.

"Eat," I ordered.

She peeled the foil wrapper away from the burger, wrinkled her nose, and took a bite. I ate my burger, too, not that I was hungry. I had the feeling I was going to need the fuel. The smell of fast food mingled with the perfume of night flowers and gasoline wafting through the open windows. I cleaned my hands on a brown napkin and handed one to Fiadh. She wiped grease meticulously off her lips, then sucked down the soda I'd bought her.

"Better?"

"Yes," she said. She did sound better. Stronger. More stable.

"Can we talk now?"

She opened her eyes and looked at me. Anguish twisted her lips. The divot where I'd longed to press my finger had never seemed more prominent.

"Did she force you?" I asked. I'd kill Agatha. It didn't matter that she was my employer, or—

No. I wouldn't go there.

"Never." Fiadh laughed—a bitter, twisted, threadbare thing. "She was after you."

"*Me?*" That made absolutely no sense.

"When you invited her over to see your cat. That was an invitation into your home. Do you remember how tired you were the other day?"

Horror rolled over my horizon in all directions. "Yeah. What does that have to do with this?"

I knew, though. Of course I knew.

Fiadh laughed again, the sound chilling and mirthless. "This is how it always ends," she said, and I sensed the words were more for her than me. Then, she paused. In that silence, I recalled another line from those goddamn letters.

All empires are mad, yes. And all empires fall. It doesn't matter who moves the pieces.

"Agatha . . ." Fiadh pressed her lips together and looked away from me. "Agatha is a vampire."

CHAPTER SIX
Say Anything but the Truth

T ime slowed. I was in a parking lot outside a burger joint, staring at a brick wall, and I was also back in the library, poring over ancient letters.

"Bullshit," I said, because it seemed like the correct response. "That's impossible. You know that's impossible, right? Jesus, what did she drug you with?"

Please let it be drugs.

"There is an anesthetic in her bite."

"You're not making any sense."

"I'm not explaining this well. I know."

"You're not explaining it at all."

She flinched at the scorn in my voice.

"She mostly feeds on donations. That's why she gives so much money to local hospitals and blood banks, but my family has a rare blood type she needs. And . . . I think you might, too."

My stomach gave a warning lurch. The burger might soon be rejoining us if Fiadh kept talking like this.

"Me?"

Her face twisted with misery. "That day in the library, when you fell asleep. Did you have any dreams the night before?"

I'd dreamed of her. Sheet twisting, inebriating dreams. Red dreams.

"Why does that matter?"

"You had a bruise on your neck," she said.

"From a thorn."

"It wasn't a thorn, Clara."

"You're suggesting my employer broke into my house in the middle of the night and . . . what, sucked my *blood*?"

"Yes."

I laughed. It was outrageous. Preposterous. Absolute insanity.

"I asked her not to do it again."

"How generous." I put as much derision into my voice as I could, knowing it was cruel, and needing to hide behind the cruelty.

"And I told her she could feed off me until the cravings pass," Fiadh continued, monotone, inexorable, undeterred by my responses. As my eyes adjusted to the light of the parking lot, I could see the puncture wounds in her neck. The burger lurched. Prosthetics could maybe achieve those marks, but I somehow doubted it.

This was still impossible.

And yet, I'd never seen Agatha in the daylight. Her estate had an underground suite. She'd hired me to translate a correspondence between two women who also seemed to enjoy drinking the blood of humans.

I refused to believe it.

"Fi," I began, committed to denial. "I think I should take you to the hospital."

"Absolutely not."

"You're not . . . you're not making sense. And I think Agatha gave you something. A date rape drug."

Fiadh seized my hand in a painfully tight grip. "No hospitals."

"Fi—"

"I said no."

"Okay!"

She loosened her hold on my hand. My bones creaked gratefully.

"I just need a minute, and I'll be fine. I promise."

I concentrated on the familiar feel of my car's seat and tried to ground myself. *Think, Clara.*

I thought.

I thought some more.

I thought about how much I regretted the burger. If only I hadn't left the library to search for Fiadh, and had remained with my translations and the dead security of history. At least Gata and Natek couldn't eat me.

Gata.

Galatea.

Agata.

Agatha.

Oh, fuck.

"Clara?"

"She's Gata, isn't she?"

Fiadh's hands lay limp in her lap. "Yes."

"And you've known that this whole time."

"I—"

"Are you Natek?"

She laughed that dry, mirthless laugh I was growing to dread. "No."

"Why did she hire me, then?" I seized upon this fragile thread of logic with triumph. "She's Nektopolian. She knows the language. She doesn't need me."

"She's old, Clara. I don't know how old. I'm not sure even she knows. But she hasn't spoken that language in centuries. It's like any other language. If you don't use it—"

"You lose it," I finished. "But why did she decide to have it translated now?"

The subtext to my question was so obviously *why me* that I might have cringed, had I not been so desperately confused.

"She wants the work catalogued and digitalized because that will make it easier for her to move it, if she needs to leave quickly. She hired a conservationist before you, and she's had archivists before that, over the years. It's been hard finding an expert in Nektopolian, though, which is why she funded the program at Brixton."

A long game played well, since here I was. The contract she'd had me sign made sense now, too. No wonder she didn't want anyone looking into her collection or its provenance.

"There was also a near miss a few years back when a grease fire in the kitchen nearly burned down the house. That's when she first started talking about digitalizing documents."

"She didn't want an Alexandria," I said.

"No."

"What happened to Natek, then?"

Fiadh looked at her hands, which the napkins hadn't quite cleansed of fast food residue. "She doesn't talk to me about that sort of thing."

121

I scoffed. "No, she just—"

A glare from Fiadh cut me off. "Think, Clara. What's in her library besides the letters?"

"I don't know, Fi, why don't you tell me?"

"The Sappho. The Byzantine *Alexander Romance*. The illuminated manuscript from that nunnery. Even the codice from Alexandria—I looked into the codice. Some of those works aren't by any known classical writers, but you know what the authors' names sound a lot like?"

My shell-shocked brain struggled to attention, and the answer was so obvious that I almost laughed.

"Natek." It wasn't quite an anagram, more like a code. Each variation of name contained the same five letters for Nektaria, and four for Galatea. Natek and Gata. Their letters frequently mentioned poetry, hence the Sappho. As for the rest . . . *I told you once you'd one day come across my work. I'll write to you. I'll sing to you. I'll paint your face into the histories, and each word, each note, each stroke of brush will be for you.*

"It's all about her," I said. "Or by her. Even that novel you lent me. That's her, too."

"*The Honey Gatherers?*"

"The *N* in *Anonymous* is circled."

We looked at each other, the excitement of revelation flaring between us.

"Are there more letters?" I asked.

She hesitated, but did eventually speak. "Yes. Agatha wanted them held back, though. Because . . ."

"Because they mention that she's a *fucking bloodsucker?*"

"Clara—"

"How can you work with her?"

"My family has been with her a long time."

"How long?"

"I don't have an exact date, but I know it was sometime before the seventh century. We came over from Europe with her during the Civil War. There's a photo of my great-great-great-grandmother in New York City."

Her family. A special blood type. Were they Agatha's goddamn *juice boxes?*

"That's some serious Stockholm syndrome."

"You have no idea what you're talking about."

"I don't?" I took a shuddering breath and stopped myself from shouting. She looked so tired. "Fi, I don't know what to do with this information."

We watched a family of four walk into the restaurant, one of the children asleep in his mother's arms. A desire to call my own mother overwhelmed me, but what could I say to her? *Hi, Mom, so it turns out my new employer is an ancient vampire and if you don't hear from me again it's because she ate me?* No.

And Fiadh. Fiadh, whose family had fed into whatever sick fantasy this was for generations. Letting your boss drink your blood *wasn't normal*. I wanted to deny everything I'd seen. I could still, with enough willpower, chalk up Agatha's bite to prosthetic fangs, and her horrifying habit of sucking the blood from her employees as some kind of sick fetish, but there were too many coincidences. The letters. Her library. *My sore neck.*

"You could run away with me."

"What makes you think I'd leave?"

I stared at her, too stricken to speak.

"She's a good employer. She keeps us safe."

"Safe? Fi, she was *eating you.*"

"If you hadn't interrupted, she would have fed, then given me electrolytes and I would have been fine by the next day."

Her easy acceptance was even more insane than vampires.

"No job is worth that!"

"As if academia didn't suck *you* dry. I have health insurance, a generous salary, a place to live, work I enjoy—"

"Still not worth it."

"And I repeat: you don't know what you're talking about. How is this any different from a blood donation?"

"Listen to yourself! Do you like it? Does it feel good when she—" I flinched at the disdain in Fiadh's eyes and broke off the rest of my tirade. I was shaking. I still wanted to throw up, only now I also wanted to ditch a few organs in the process.

"Would you rather it hurt?" she said into that frigid silence.

Hot and rancid shame filled my mouth. "Of course not."

"I understand that you're in shock and overwhelmed, Clara, but I will thank you not to judge me."

On any other day, I would have covered a smirk at her archaic phrasing. Now, though, I wondered if her manner of speech was a result of living with an ancient, undead monster.

"This is all insane," I said.

"Hardly."

"I can't do this."

"You don't have a choice, now that you know what she is. She'll blacklist you. You'll never work in academia again, or any other field. Remember your contract."

"Better than her draining me."

Fiadh held my gaze with her exhausted one, and a deeply, deeply disturbing possibility occurred to me: If I quit, Agatha would have no more need for me, and there would be nothing stopping her from slurping me down like I'd just done to my soda.

"Oh, fuck," I said, burying my face between my hands. They reeked of fast food. "Oh fuck, oh fuck, oh fuck."

Gentle pressure on my knee interrupted my looming panic attack.

"It is not as dire as it seems, Clara."

"You're the one who basically just told me I'm doomed."

"You're statistically more likely to die literally any other way than from a vampire."

"Wait." A fresh injection of panic hit my bloodstream. "She drank your blood. I saw her. Does that mean—"

"No. I am not going to turn into a vampire. You're thinking of werewolves."

No, I was absolutely not going to think about werewolves, because that would open up a whole new host of horrific possibilities, and I was pretty sure my brain would flatline if I learned any other monsters were real for at least another forty-eight hours.

"You said she could get into my house."

"It's not—okay. I need you to take a deep breath."

Deep breaths weren't the problem. *Vampires were the problem.*

"Look at it this way. If she really wanted to, she could break into your house with a crowbar, not that she would, since it is her house, and she has a key. It's not as if withholding an invitation will keep out a determined vampire. By inviting her, you simply made it easier. It's like . . . you know how cats carry toxoplasma gondii?"

"Toxo-what?"

"It's a parasite. Rodents and other animals infected with it lose their fear of cats, which makes them easier for cats to catch and eat.

Makes humans more reckless, too. Giving permission for a vampire to enter your home has a similar effect, only psychic. It relaxes your mind's defenses, which makes you easier to manipulate."

"Can I revoke permission?"

"Yes."

"Okay. Then I want to do that."

"We'll tell Agatha."

I didn't want to tell Agatha anything. I didn't want to see Agatha ever again, and the mere suggestion renewed my hyperventilation.

"Listen to me." Fiadh, seemingly revived by food, took my hands and squeezed until I calmed enough to hear her above my panicked breath. "Your contract binds you to silence, but—"

My contract. The red ink. The plasma donation I'd made the day before.

I ripped free of Fiadh, opened the car door, and delivered the burger from its acidic prison. Vomit splattered across the asphalt.

"Here." Fiadh handed me the remainder of the water in the bottle from earlier. I washed out my mouth and spat, unwilling to look at the unfortunate mess I'd made of the parking lot.

"Thank you." I felt strangely better after getting ill, as if I'd emptied some of my fear along with my meal.

"Agatha isn't going to kill you. I can't promise she'll never feed on you again, but she takes good care of her people."

"Like fucking beef cattle," I said.

"No. She respects your intellect. It is in both your interests for you to keep working for her."

"How is it in my interest?"

"Besides survival, you like the work, don't you?"

"I did *before*."

"Nothing's changed. Not really. You just know more now."

"Whose side are you even on?"

"This is *precisely* why I didn't want to like you," she said, her voice bursting with frustration.

Before I could process her words, a meow sliced through our argument.

We both jumped. I whipped around in my seat to locate the source of the voice, and discovered the resident silver tabby sitting in the backseat of my car, where I was one hundred percent certain one had not been before.

It meowed again, its eyes fixed on Fiadh.

"I know," she said to the cat. "We're going home soon."

I flung open the car door for a second time and, leaping over the vomit, fled.

—⁓— —⁓— —⁓—

Fiadh found me huddled against a scraggly oak tree on the outskirts of town not far from the burger joint. I knew it was an oak because fallen acorns dug into my seat bones. She sat next to me, unsteady on her legs.

"I don't want to know," I said as she opened her mouth. "However that cat ended up in my car, I don't fucking want to know."

"Okay."

"Okay."

The sound of traffic filled the night, mocking in its normalcy.

"Will you come back with me?" she asked.

I glanced at her. There was a plea in her voice that was echoed in her eyes, and I remembered the sweetness of her sleeping body next to mine. I wanted to be angry with her for not telling me the truth sooner, but I was emotionally spent, and besides—I knew why she hadn't told me. Ignoring for a moment the fact that Agatha had no doubt forbidden it, I wouldn't have believed her.

I still wasn't sure if I believed her.

"Fi," I said, my throat tight and raw from my impromptu expulsion of dinner.

She took my face in her small hands. "I will keep you safe, Clara Eden. Do you believe me?"

Did I? How well did I even know this woman? Her eyes were black and liquid in the darkness, and lights from passing cars reflected off their surface. She couldn't keep me safe. I knew that. But I wasn't sure *she* did, and her fierce belief in the aegis of her body accomplished what her words never could.

"I don't know if I believe you, but I trust you," I said, and tasting the words, knew them to be true.

—⁓— —⁓— —⁓—

Agatha Montague waited for us in the first-floor sitting room.

126

It occurred to me, in a haze I was partially convinced might be delirium, that this experience had just answered the hypothetical question all historians asked themselves: Given the opportunity, I did *not* want to reach through the veil of time and speak to the subject of my research.

The subject of my research had wiped the blood from her mouth by the time we entered the sitting room. Agatha appeared as unassuming as she had when I met her in the garden: a middle-aged woman dressed in clothes that might have been expensive, but looked entirely ordinary in the soft light of the lamps. Slacks. A blouse. Leather shoes. Her tastefully exposed ankles gleamed a light brown in the lamplight.

Unassuming, yes, but unassuming in the way a snow-covered mountainside was unassuming; Agatha Montague was an avalanche-in-waiting.

"How are you feeling?" she asked Fiadh. Concern laced her words, though whether real or feigned I couldn't tell. I wasn't in a condition to judge. *Vampires didn't exist*, my mind tried reminding me. There was another explanation, if only I could clear my head long enough to find it. In the light of those lamps, however, I got my first real look at Agatha Montague. This wasn't a half-lit encounter outside a greenhouse, where shadows lay comfortably across her face. In the light, in that precious, unasked-for light, Agatha Montague's faintly lined face was as ageless and ancient as the sea.

"Clara got me food. Red meat," said Fiadh. Her voice was all that kept me from running.

"Good. I worried. I do hope you were not the one driving."

"I drove." I curled my arm around Fiadh's waist. She leaned into me, and her weight became a counterbalance to my own shaking legs.

"I am glad to hear it. Now, please sit. I'd like to talk to you."

Her eyes met mine as she issued the request—so polite, her tone. But that face. That terrible, ordinary face. I might have passed a hundred faces like that on the street and never paid them heed, only to have them visit me in shifting, intangible nightmare. Her face was too ordinary. Too perfectly frozen, as if caught in amber. I'd observed in our first encounter that she was a handsome woman. Now, I understood the deadly beauty of the fox, its precision as it lunged for the rabbit, the soft plume of its red tail against the snow. My vision split. Through this kaleidoscope, I saw her through my eyes and through the crumbling words of a woman who had once been named Natek, and my heart squeezed with longing and with fear.

We sat, though I kept my arm around Fiadh. She was warm and delicate against me, and I would not let Agatha Montague so much as breathe near her again. I dug my fingernails into the cracks of my conviction and held on to my flickering anger, desperate for its warmth.

"This was an inevitability I was prepared to navigate, due to the nature of the work I've hired you to do for me, though I'd hoped to avoid it for a great while longer. Innocence is precious. This world is darker than you know, and while Fiadh was born into it, I do not willingly drag in outsiders."

I said nothing, because there was nothing I could say.

She continued. "I do not know what Fiadh has told you."

"I told her the truth." Fiadh delivered her words calmly. Only one of us was shaking, and it wasn't her.

"Did she believe it?" asked Agatha.

"Not entirely."

Agatha turned to me.

"Your belief is irrelevant. You signed paperwork that binds you to silence by blood as well as law, and you will not speak of any of this."

Anger sparked against those flinty words.

"The paperwork was about the *work*. Not—not you drugging Fiadh!" It was a feeble, last-ditch attempt at denial.

"Drugging?" Agatha tilted her head, her confusion seemingly genuine. The faintest of frown lines creased her forehead. "Why would I drug Fiadh?"

"So that you could do . . . whatever you were doing when I walked in."

A normal human would have come up with an excuse. I waited for it, hoping for words I could assail with a decade's worth of experience gleaned from listening to pontificating professors.

"I have no need of drugs," she said instead.

"Fi wouldn't—"

"Do not presume to know what Fiadh would do for me."

"You will not touch her again." My voice cracked as I said the words, but I hardened it. Brittle steel was better than nothing.

Agatha was sitting. I was sure of this in the way I was sure of gravity, and yet, suddenly she stood before me, my chin in her hands, and my head was jerked sharply upright to stare into her eyes. A maelstrom gazed back, colorless and all-consuming. Pure fear slid through the ether between my atoms. If her face was ageless, her eyes were like looking into the red light of a dying star.

"Clara Eden," Agatha said in a voice stripped of anything remotely human. "Understand me. You are not in a position to make demands. You are not in a position to do anything but serve, and you *will* serve."

I would. I saw that now, clear as anything. This woman would not be denied.

"Please, Agatha." Fiadh's voice cut through the oppressive weight of Agatha's words. "She's just—"

"Do not interfere, love."

Fiadh fell silent.

"Now." Agatha released me and returned to her seat at a mortal pace, settling into the chair with her hands clasped in her lap. "You have done excellent work on the Nektopolian collection. You will continue. This unfortunate incident changes nothing. I pay generously, and you seem to have found the work rewarding, yes?"

I nodded.

"Then there is no reason for anything to change. We all are what we are. You are a scholar. I am a . . . collector. And Fiadh is what she is, are you not?"

I could not interpret the look that passed between them.

"I revoke my consent," I made myself say, remembering what Fiadh had told me outside the fast food restaurant with the smell of grease clinging to our lips and fingers. It was harder than it should have been to speak.

"Very well."

"So that releases Fi, since she said she was only doing . . . that . . . for me."

Agatha smiled. Her incisors lengthened as her lips curled past amusement and into a snarl, and the breath in my lungs crystalized into particulates of ice. Attempts to draw more sliced through alveoli and bronchi, drowning me in bloody fear. *Oh god. Oh god oh god oh godohgodohgod.*

Fiadh had been telling the truth.

"Child," said the monster sitting calmly in the armchair, "I do not need your consent to kill you. Do not tempt me." In a milder voice, she added, almost tenderly, "Do not waste your talents fighting this."

"I revoke my consent," I said again. The words felt like a talisman, and I needed something to clutch against the dark. "I revoke—"

The quality of the air changed.

129

"Maria, you may leave us."

Maria?

A warm body brushed my leg. I'd forgotten all about the cat. The animal, who had trotted at Fiadh's heels on our way in over the moonlit gravel drive, departed on silent paws.

"Please don't," Fiadh said to Agatha.

"She must understand."

"Agatha—"

I glanced away from Agatha, which felt like turning my back on a panther. Fiadh's face was twisted by the most complicated bouquet of emotions I'd yet seen on those sharp features. Fear, yes, and pained regret, but also something fervid, almost like anticipation, and beneath that the stir of something absolutely feral.

A memory came back to me from that terrible dream: my thighs slick with want, and lips on my neck. I'd chalked it up to flirting with Fiadh in the garden. But now . . . Languor eased the ice in my lungs, warming me. I felt myself rising from the couch and approaching Agatha, though I hadn't made any conscious decision to do so, and the fear that had strangled the very oxygen from my blood cells melted away.

Agata.

Gata.

Words brushed against the back of my throat: old words, written in ink before Rome's fall. Words of want and longing. *I see your face in dreams. That will have to be enough.* How many hours had I spent immersed in those letters, parsing possible meanings from each syllable? Enough that I knew the woman she'd once been: lonely, afraid of contact with her own kind, and violent in her passions. To spend the centuries alone—my own heartbreaks were nothing in comparison. What was my life, really, but a moment in the long, aching years of her undeath?

I knelt, heedless of the catch of protest in Fiadh's voice, and swept my hair off my neck so I could bare that unmarked flesh to Agatha Montague. Her fanged smile was gentle as she looked down at me.

"Ask me," she said.

"Please."

"Please? That is the best you can do?"

Her gentle mockery held no sting.

"When was the last time you tasted someone who spoke your native tongue?" I said, and I didn't recognize my voice or the thoughts

130

that had framed those words.

"Better."

A cool hand brushed the curve of my neck. I shivered at the contact, my overtaxed neurons unsure of what signals to send. My body's supply of cortisol, however, had apparently run out, and endorphins took their place. What fear was left receded entirely. Warmth spread over me. My skin tingled with anticipation, and I heard the breathy edge to my voice. I heard the whisper of papyrus. Nektopolian patterns painted the backs of my eyelids with each blink as she stroked my neck.

Fiadh was saying something. I couldn't understand the words, not with Agatha touching me. I leaned into it like a cat, eager, desperate for more. I would please this woman. I would serve. I would offer up my body and my soul, and mourn I did not have more to give.

The hand withdrew. I whimpered.

"Perhaps another time," Agatha said to me, her voice red velvet. "I did, after all, just eat."

Fiadh caught me as I slumped, horror striking me with the force of a meteor.

—ᵀᴹ— —ᵀᴹ— —ᵀᴹ—

Collection: Nektopolis
Title: Letter 29
Description: Correspondence; Gata and Vezina
Date: TBD
Cataloguer: Clara Eden

Galatea of Illyria,

I extend my offer a final time. I will not ask again. Your lover has come to her senses; you would be wise to follow suit. Lest you think this offer without teeth, may I remind you who holds her leash?
She tells me you feared Rome's legions. I have made their atrocities look tame. Undo what you've done to me, or I will send you her cremains before I add you, too, to the forests of my victory.

Vezina

131

I awoke in a bed with Fiadh beside me, holding me in her arms. Time moved slowly, and nausea twisted my stomach. At my groan, Fiadh woke at once.

"Clara?"

"Ughnn."

She reached for a glass of juice on the bedside and handed it to me.

"It's fresh orange juice. The sweetness will help with shock."

I drank obediently, trying to parse through the vague sense of dread and shame to the cause. Thankfully, I'd finished the drink by the time I remembered, so I had something to throw up when I stumbled to the bathroom. Hard tile bruised my knees with the force of my emesis.

Fiadh rubbed my back as I emptied the contents of my stomach, then wiped my mouth with a wet cloth. I let her mother me. I needed comfort. I needed all the comfort I could get.

I worked for a vampire.

Vampires existed.

I had almost let a vampire—

"Oh my god," I said over and over into the ceramic bowl. The words echoed.

"You're okay," said Fiadh.

Was I, though?

"We're taking the day off. Both of us."

"It's not real," I said.

"I don't have the energy to argue with you."

Agatha could have drained me like Capri Sun. And I'd wanted it. Begged her for it. I leaned back against the bathroom wall, recognizing my location: a guest room in the main estate.

"What the fuck?" I said, clarity at last bringing with it anger.

Fiadh turned her head away, revealing the bruise on her neck.

"What the fuck was that, Fi?"

"Clara—"

I raked my hands through my tangled hair. I felt—I didn't know what I felt. *Terrified,* came the answer, and with it, panic.

"I didn't want that. I didn't fucking want that."

"I'm so sorry." Fiadh's voice was barely a whisper. "You have to understand. Choice doesn't come into it."

"That's—that's so fucked up."

"It's called *thrall*."

I remembered reading that word in the letters I'd translated for the monster who had—who had—my brain spiraled away.

"I don't care what it's called," I said.

"It's a kindness. Blood loss is painful, but with thrall—"

I put all the viciousness I could muster into my next words. "Nothing about that is kind."

Fiadh's face went as slack as if I'd struck her. "But she didn't—"

"She fucked with my *mind*, Fi." My voice broke. Thrall was pure manipulation, and I needed Fiadh to see that. I needed her to acknowledge the crime that had been committed against both of us.

And yet even as I raged, I knew part of that rage was shame: because while last night hadn't been my choice, there had been a freedom in surrendering. To flirt with death, a monster at my throat, had been a comfort and a rush and something darker. My throat tightened. There were some depths I didn't want to know I contained, and I was grateful, grateful to the cringing core of my marrow, that Agatha had shown restraint. I would have given her everything she'd asked for and begged her to take more.

Restraint did not absolve her.

"I know," said Fiadh, surprising me. I'd expected her to make excuses. She was Agatha's employee, and her family had served Agatha for years. Hadn't she excused Agatha already for feeding—*feeding*—on her very blood? I let out a shaking breath, my gorge rising again.

Because of course Fiadh understood. This was her life. I remembered the closed door of her mother's apartment. Had Agatha touched Fiadh's mother the way she touched her daughter? How many fucking generations of that lineage had she manipulated? Preyed upon? *Groomed?* And Fiadh's mother—to leave her daughter to that fate. To pass on the job, knowing, *knowing*, what would happen to her.

Nothing derailed a family like intergenerational trauma.

"Fi," I said, heartbreak thickening my voice. I wanted to weep for her and for me and for the innocence I hadn't known we'd shared until it had been stripped from us by Agatha Montague. She turned away from me and let the rumpled fall of her hair shield her face.

"How can you be okay with this?" I asked her.

133

She shrugged, looking very small on the polished bathroom tile. Nektopolian tile. The familiar patterns taunted me.

"It's complicated. Agatha is . . . she isn't human, Clara. Holding her to human standards doesn't work. I also agreed to this position, and all it entailed. She's never put me under thrall without my consent."

"No, she just groomed you since childhood to accept this as normal."

"She didn't need to let you live," she said, which wasn't a denial.

"Is that supposed to make me feel better?"

"Honestly? Yes."

Her snappish words echoed hollowly. I reached out and parted the curtain of her hair, tucking the thick strands behind her ear so I could see her face. Tears gathered in a pearlescent line along her lower lids. I didn't know what to say. What could I say? Nothing in my rather impressive lexicon had prepared me for this eventuality. I wanted to comfort Fiadh and I wanted her to comfort me, because she was the one person who might understand the sick horror uncurling in my chest, and I wanted to scream at her, because she alone could have warned me about what was coming.

I did neither. We sat on the cold tile, the lingering smell of vomit and bile mingling with the potpourri by the sink, and sank into our separate hells.

"She's wrong," Fiadh said after the silence had stretched past bearing and entered that strange suspension of time that makes the sufferer question if there had ever been words at all, or if they'd been born into that silence, trembling and naked in the cold.

"What?"

"You are in a position to make demands."

Her hand covered mine, and it was warm and real.

"Steaks don't get a choice in how they're cooked, Fi. She can find another scholar to translate her collection. I'm replaceable." I'd always been replaceable. As an adjunct. As a partner. I liked dead languages because those words could never be turned against me.

"Make her need you."

"*How?*"

Her eyes had taken on the shine of fever. She leaned closer, heedless of the smell of sickness, and said, "Find Natek. Barter the information for whatever you want. A release from your contract. Rights to publish some of your work on her collection."

"Natek could be dead."

"Or she could be out there, still waiting for a reply."

"If Agatha wanted to talk to her, don't you think she would have by now?"

"Not necessarily. Not if it put either of them in danger, or if she couldn't forgive Natek. But she's kept everything. You don't keep an entire archive of your ex's things, moving it across continents, paying witches to preserve the unpreservable, unless you still care about them. And . . . and I know for a fact that she still loves her. I didn't think there was any hope for them until we realized Natek never stopped writing to Gata. Agatha didn't share that with me. But if we could reunite them—"

"Why would I want to do anything to make Agatha happy? *Or to bring another vampire anywhere near me?*" I'd sort out the "paying witches to preserve the unpreservable" later, or maybe never.

"Because you'd get to talk to Nektaria."

Anger gusted out and away from my sails, leaving me with the taste of bile on my tongue in a sea of confusion. Nektaria. My Nektaria, whom I'd studied for over a decade, whom I'd devoted so many hours to researching, who had occupied so much of my headspace since that fateful undergraduate lecture when my classics professor casually mentioned the small city-state and its ruler.

"What if it's dangerous?" I asked, stalling for time. "Or what if Agatha just puts me under thrall and gets the information, leaving me with nothing to bargain with?"

In a low voice, almost as if she feared someone might be listening, she said, "Thrall can be broken, Clara."

"What?" I dug my seat bones into the tile and let the pain ground me. Thrall could be broken. This didn't have to happen to me ever again.

Her hand squeezed mine. "She taught me, just in case another vampire tried to put me under the dark."

One monster at a time. I would not follow that statement to its logical conclusion, which no doubt would involve things like other vampires, and instead focused on the bathroom and its human inhabitants.

"And the danger? What if Vezina or whatever is still around?"

"I don't know." She chafed her thumb against the back of my hand. "It could be dangerous. We don't have to do it if you don't feel comfortable. We don't have to do anything."

135

But doing nothing meant living in this fear, powerless, aware that even if I could throw off thrall, I was still a snack. Finding Nektaria wouldn't necessarily change the snack part, but if I could publish? Speak to my research subject? Get real, concrete details about Nektopolis?

"I need to think," I said, leaning away from the toilet. "And brush my teeth."

"I'll help you get home."

Fiadh pulled me to my feet and shakily, my hand clamped around hers like a vise, I took a step toward my uncertain future.

CHAPTER SEVEN
Even Still, Even Now

Collection: Nektopolis
Title: Letter 31, Sappho Fragment 1
Description: Correspondence; Gata and Natek
Date: TBD
Cataloguer: Clara Eden

For Gata, from Nettle

Ποικιλόθρον᾽ ἀθάνατ᾽ Ἀφρόδιτα,
παῖ Δίος, δολόπλοκε, λίσσομαί σε
μή μ᾽ ἄσαισι μήτ᾽ ὀνίαισι λάμνα,
           πότνια, θῦμον.

ἀλλὰ τυίδ᾽ ἔλθ᾽, αἴποτὰ κάτέρωτα
τᾶς ἔμας αὔδως αἴοισα πήλυι
ἔκλυες πάτρος δὲ δόμον λίποισα
           χρύσιον ἦλθες

ἄρμ᾽ ὑποζεύξαισα, κάλοι δέ σ᾽ ἄγον
ὦκεες στροῦθοι περὶ γᾶς μελαίνας
πύκνα δινεῦντες πτέρ᾽ ἀπ᾽ ὠράνω αἴθε-
           -ρος διὰ μέσσω.

137

αἶψα δ᾽ ἐξίκοντο, σὺ δ᾽, ὦ μάκαιρα,
μειδιάσαισ᾽ ἀθανάτῳ προσώπῳ,
ἤρε᾽ ὄττι δηὗτε πέπονθα κὤττι
   δηὗτε κάλημι,

κὤττι μοι μάλιστα θέλω γένεσθαι
μαινόλᾳ θύμῳ, τίνα δηὗτε πείθω
μαῖς ἄγην ἐς σὰν φιλότατα τίς τ, ὦ
   Ψάπφ᾽, ἀδίκηει;

καὶ γὰρ αἰ φεύγει, ταχέως διώξει,
αἰ δὲ δῶρα μὴ δέκετ ἀλλὰ δώσει,
αἰ δὲ μὴ φίλει ταχέως φιλήσει
   κωὐκ ἐθέλοισα

ἔλθε μοι καὶ νῦν, χαλεπᾶν δὲ λῦσον
ἐκ μερίμναν, ὄσσα δέ μοι τέλεσσαι
θῦμος ἰμμέρρει τέλεσον, σὺ δ᾽ αὔτα
   σύμμαχος ἔσσο.[22]

Literal translation: Poem I
Translator: Edwin Marion Cox
Text: The Poems of Sappho (1924)

Immortal Aphrodite of the shimmering throne,
daughter of Zeus, weaver of wiles, I pray thee crush
not my spirit with anguish and distress, O Queen.
But come hither if ever before thou didst hear my
voice afar, and hearken, and leaving the golden
house of thy father, camest with chariot yoked, and
swift birds drew thee, their swift pinions fluttering
over the dark earth, from heaven through mid-
space. Quickly they arrived; and thou blessed one

---

22 Translator's note: The original Greek. While proficient, I do not feel it is my place to
attempt a translation, nor is it what you hired me for. I would be happy to recommend a few if you do not have your own preferences. Anne Carson's translation, *If
not, winter* is particularly accessible to the modern reader. The translation I have
included here is by Edwin Marion Cox.

with immortal countenance smiling didst ask: What now is befallen me and why now I call and what I in my heart's madness, most desire. What fair one now wouldst thou draw to love thee? Who wrongs thee Sappho? For even if she flies she shall soon follow and if she rejects gifts, shall soon offer them and if she loves not shall soon love, however reluctant. Come I pray thee now and release me from cruel cares, and let my heart accomplish all that it desires, and be thou my ally.

I didn't sleep that night. Instead of a French press, I made a pot of double-strength coffee, and sat at my kitchen table with a mug between my hands and my eyes glued to the door. I'd lodged a chair underneath the handle, as if that could stop a vampire.

A vampire.

Were my hands shaking from fear, or caffeine? I couldn't tell. The light from the laptop lit the dark kitchen. I'd turned on all the lights in my cottage at first, but the blackness of the windows even with the curtains drawn felt too much like eyes. With the lights off, I could at least see out—and it would be harder for someone to see in. I should have asked Fiadh if Agatha had night vision, or super strength, or whatever else vampires were supposed to be able to do: climb down walls like a lizard, turn into a bat, trap unsuspecting real estate agents in their Gothic palaces. Agatha didn't strike me as a Dracula, however, and I was no Jonathan Harker.

If Agatha came in to feed on me again, assuming that had really happened, which I was still not willing to accept, I would at least be conscious. I would know. Fiadh had promised to try to teach me how to break thrall, but she hadn't started yet. Instead, I had, like an idiot, found a sharp stick in the garden. I kept it tucked underneath my thigh, though it kept rolling out, since I couldn't seem to stop jiggling my legs. The placebo was better than nothing.

Mr. Muffin periodically emerged from the bedroom to yowl his displeasure. I opened a can of wet food for him in apology, but did not dare follow his twitching tail back into the bedroom. Instead I worked on my book to stay awake.

Words blurred on the screen. Nektaria. Nektopolis. Gender politics of the ancient world. I couldn't use any of the information gleaned from the letters in my book. Agatha was right; no one could ever see them. I wasn't a total idiot: other humans had learned of vampires over the centuries, and yet, they were still relegated to the stuff of legend. That wasn't a coincidence. Whistleblowers no doubt got eaten.

I could use the artifacts, however. That coin with Nektaria's face alone merited a reexamination of her entire rule. The fact that I'd just learned Agatha was immortal, and therefore unlikely to die anytime soon, leaving me free to publish, wasn't relevant at the moment. I needed the mundanity of work if I wanted to stay sane.

But what if I *could* use the artifacts? What if I could offer Agatha something she wanted, assuming Fiadh was right and she did still love Natek, in exchange for publication rights? Anxiety sizzled beneath my skin. *It isn't worth it*, I tried convincing myself, but the counterarguments kept rolling in: *You might as well make the best of the situation, since you can't get out of it, and how incredible would it be to meet Nektaria? Everything is fucked anyway.*

The smell of burning coffee filled the cottage as the clock on the wall ticked toward midnight, then past. I drank more coffee. I paced. I jumped up and down to wake myself up, and when that failed, I pulled a pack of frozen peas from the fridge and pressed my face into it. Cold temporarily roused me.

I would not think of Fiadh. I would not think of the frenzied tumult of our first night together, or how, in retrospect, she might have seduced me to prevent me from leaving her house during Agatha's hunting hours. It hurt too much to consider. Most of all, I would not think of Agatha's teeth, and how, like a viper's, they'd elongated into needle-sharp fangs when she snarled.

I'd always been able to trust my own mind. I had doubts, like anyone, but my mind had never betrayed me before. I didn't even do drugs, save the occasional social joint, and that was rare. But Agatha had turned my thoughts, my emotions, my *body* to her will without effort.

I didn't think I'd ever feel safe again.

The last sludge of coffee hissed at the bottom of the pot as light glimmered on the horizon. I shut off the pot, double-checked that the chair was still lodged securely beneath the doorknob, and curled up on the couch beneath a blanket to catch a few hours of sleep before work.

It was not a good day. I jumped at every sound in the library, turning my chair to face the door, and had sweat through my clothing within the first hour. This left me chilled and clammy in the cool air conditioning, which I treated with hot coffee, which in turn led to more sweating and shivering. Disgusting, all around, but I wasn't in a mood to care. This was the lair of a beast. And I worked here.

The only brief consolation was the box Fiadh brought up from what she called "the basement stacks" and what I interpreted to mean "the vampire's bedroom closet."

Collection: Nektopolis
Title: Letter 30
Description: Correspondence; Gata and Natek
Date: TBD
Cataloguer: Clara Eden

Gatalina writing to Natek,

I will not count the years. They pass so quickly, and each has been an agony. I did receive your letters. Each was a risk—though cleverly hidden indeed. You did tell me, once, I'd find your work amid Alexandria's scrolls. But things grew complicated.

Did you know you were followed? Did you know you were not the only one to see my face, for all that I asked you not to?

I should not write you. You are more of a danger to me than you can know. But your teacher either has told you everything, or nothing at all, so I shall do as you asked and speak plainly. Years of silence have done what even she never could, and forced my hand. I've missed you.

You've spoken of your teacher. I assumed it was a

ploy to draw me out, another one of your taunts, like your devious endearments. I believe this no longer. You've had too many opportunities to set a trap since you discovered me, and you haven't taken them.

Your teacher is the reason I leave no ripples. She is the reason I do not dare walk beside you, or stay in one place for too long, or put down the roots that used to bind me to this earth. I do not cast judgment. As you said to me those years and years ago, there is nothing more terrifying than a woman confident in her own power, and she draws power to her like threads to a spindle. I think of the joy she must have felt in turning you, and it thrills me with hate.

I will tell you her story as I've learned it over the years, first in my travels, then through my network. I can see you frown, here, wondering what I meant by that last word after all my assertions of solitude, and I will not tell you, save to say it is not what you think. You may know some or all of this already.

She was born in Dacia with the name Vezina to the Dacian king Cothelas. They, too, fought the Macedonians, and her father surrendered, offering Vezina in marriage. She refused. What is that saying? Women are the prize of conquest and the price of peace? He disowned her and married another daughter off instead. Vezina loved her Sister, Amalusta. Ask her about that name, if you doubt me. Things did not end well for either of them.

Eventually, her path crossed with a man named Scorylo. Perhaps she had been left for dead. Perhaps he just saw an opportunity, or he, too, had a grievance with the king. He made her his, and by all accounts used her to flay Cothelas's kingdom to the bone—as he, in turn, flayed her. By the time she killed him, she'd been warped into what she is now. This is the story she told me in bits and pieces, when she tried winning me with sympathy. But there is another narrative. In this, the child of a king not known for mercy grows into her father's legacy, blood-drunk on power and more than happy to dismiss the value of a life. In this story, death is her birthright, and she tells herself she is righteous in its deliverance. My parting gift to her was the dissolution of this fantasy.

Do not mistake my tone for pity. Women are misused every minute of every day in this world, and they do not all become monsters. But I can understand, at least, that which drives her. She creates women like us, her Daughters, as she perversely calls them, to break this world in every way she can, for she only feels safe at the head of a legion. But control is always an illusion.

I do not know what she's told you. I do not know the orders she gives her other soldiers. With me, she sought a greater reckoning, one I was uniquely suited to deliver. I refused. One day, I'll tell you the price I paid for freedom. Until then, understand this: she is my antithesis.

I cannot join you. As long as she still hunts me, you are a danger to me, and I to you. Perhaps if you foreswore your oath... but I will not ask that of you. She might intercept this letter. I've waited longer than my heart could bear to send it, and I fear it is still not long enough.

Yours,
Gata

Well, that answered my earlier question about Vezina—turns out she was the bitch responsible for Agatha. On a notepad unrelated to translation, I jotted down the following proper nouns: Dacia, Daughters, Cothelas, Scorylo, and Amalusta. Dacia I knew, as it was a kingdom from antiquity, located in modern-day Eastern Europe. Cothelas, however, was a ruler I could potentially find records on, though there was no guarantee. Kings rose and fell like grass. I'd have even less luck tracking down a warlord, but lists brought me comfort.

The next letter was also from Gata. I recalled the urgent need I'd felt for these very letters only a few days ago with derision. How little I'd understood. The magic was gone now, replaced by the reality of *real* magic, or something close to it, with none of the previous magic's charm. Gata's obvious heartbreak rang hollowly as I worked through the translation. I guessed where the markings had faded or torn, and did not bother with any helpful little footnotes for Ms. Montague, save one at the end of letter thirty-two.

Collection: Nektopolis
Title: Letter 32
Description: Correspondence; Gata and Natek
Date: TBD
Cataloguer: Clara Eden

G to N,

No word from you. I should rejoice, for it means you could not find me, which was my intent, but there is no joy in this victory. I do not know why I write you now. I cannot send it. What I didn't say in my last letter: You asked me once if I was lonely. I have kept a part of myself from you, which is easy enough in writing, and that part was once part of a greater whole. A vast collection of selves and a oneness spanning a time and space far greater than our single lives. I'd never been lonely because I'd never truly been an I. Vezina took that from me. Not entirely—a partial severing. A constant, bleeding wound. Like when you can see the fire on a winter's night but cannot feel its heat. I've prayed for death every dawn since.

And then you happened. The loneliness I've felt without you is new. It has a shape. Your shape. I cannot let you fill it because I cannot let her take you from me, too. But I know you are out there, and you've given me something more insidious than any evil. Hope. As long as you walk this green earth there is hope, and that hope has grown through me like grapevines. The fruit is always your name.

Yours,
G

PS. Gata, you are a poet after all[23].

—⁂— —⁂— —⁂—

The translation work took all day. Fiadh walked me home at the end, well before sunset, and I was tired and twitchy and in desperate need of more answers by the time we settled into the couch with cups of tea—herbal for her, black for me, because I didn't plan on sleeping at night ever again.

"I'm not sure where to begin," she said.

"How many other . . . types of . . ." I trailed off. Monsters? Creatures? *Others*? What word even fit?

"The world is bigger than you think."

Comforting.

"There isn't, like, some sort of directory?"

"The need to categorize everything beneath the sky is human. Other beings are more content to let things be."

"In your best estimation, then," I said in a strained voice, "approximately how many types of *beings* are there?"

"Well, there's the fey, of course."

"Of course. Naturally." *Fucking fuck.*

She raised an eyebrow very slightly at my tone. "And the weres."

---

23 Translator's note: This postscript is written in a different hand. Perhaps Natek's, though while the script is identical to previous letters from Natek in my eye, I cannot say for certain, and it would be difficult to date the ink, given the margin of error in our technology and the time elapsed from the writing.

"Maybe let's not talk about those." I had never gotten on the werewolf bandwagon as a teenager, and I wasn't about to hop on now.

"And the Demonic Orchestra."

"The *what?*" I gripped my mug tightly, grateful for the thick ceramic. A lesser vessel might have shattered. Demons were a step too far for credulity. And yet . . .

"Not orchestra like you're thinking. Like the verb: to orchestrate."

"Does that mean there's a hell?"

"In the sense that once there was a 'hell' dimension, and the Orchestraters came through before losing their way home, yes." I whimpered and took a sip of my tea to hide my face in the steam. Fiadh continued in a gently relentless voice. "And the nature spirits vary from place to place, which makes them hard to classify."

"Then why haven't I ever seen one?"

"You probably have."

"I think I would know if I'd seen a demon or a nature whatever thingy."

"What do you think demons look like, Clara?" she asked. Her tone was still tender, which made the question all the more terrible. I didn't want to know the answer. Especially because I was fairly certain the answer was, "like us."

"Well, I definitely would know if I'd seen a werewolf."

"You've never seen a werewolf. Wolves aren't found in this region anymore. A werecoyote, though, probably, and lots of weredogs. But they look just like people the rest of the time."

Nope, nope, nope.

"What about science? Biology? The laws of physics?" I concentrated on the smell of my tea. Bitter. A hint of bergamot. Earl Grey tea had never let me down before, no matter how insurmountable the obstacle.

"They apply," she said with a shrug of her shoulders. The motion distracted me as it always did. It drew attention to her prim carriage, and I'd very recently seen that primness melt into something far more feral.

"Transfer of mass. Werewolves—or werecoyotes—"

"Any canid."

"That's—okay, I didn't need to know that werechihuahuas existed. Anyway, they can't. Humans have a much greater mass. They can't just lose it and get it back." This was familiar territory: debate. As long as these things remained strictly theoretical, I could handle it.

"I'm not a physicist, and neither are you. What do we really know about the universe?" She moved closer as she spoke, softening the horrifying concept of the unknown with the warmth of her body.

"What about the fey?" I asked.

"Fungal lichenization."

"*What?*" I'd been going to inquire about the type of fey she referred to—tiny little elves? Fairies with wings? The terrifying tricksters of legend?

"A different branch of evolution. Like how lichen are formed. The right alga meets the right fungi, and a lichen is born, only it's the right fungal strain meets the right human genetics." She gestured with the hand not holding her mug of chamomile as she spoke, enthusiasm rising in her voice.

"And where do vampires fit in? Do they really hate werewolves?"

She shook her head disparagingly. "Why do humans always assume that?"

"Hollywood."

"Their hunting doesn't overlap. Weres don't eat humans, usually. There is no reason for a rivalry."

"What about dragons?"

"I've never seen one," she said. "But that doesn't mean anything."

"Mermaids?"

"If they exist, climate change will probably drive them to extinction."

A sobering thought, all things considered.

"Then why are humans the dominant species on the planet?"

There was a pause. Then, quietly, she asked a question that sent gooseflesh over my skin.

"Are you?"

The outer world pressed against the windows, and I felt how I imagined early hunter-gatherers had felt: exposed and vulnerable to predation, half convinced something stalked me down a forest path. Fiadh, perhaps sensing my sudden terror, set down her tea and took my face in her hands. They were hot from the mug, and that simple pleasure kept me from spiraling.

"Nothing has changed, Clara. You merely know more now. Like how people used to believe the sun orbited the Earth, or that Earth alone of all the planets in the universe was capable of supporting life."

147

Still focusing on the sensation of her hands on my face, I asked, "How did you adjust to this?"

"I didn't have to. I grew up in this world." Her eyes brimmed with sympathy.

"You said, after . . . after what happened . . . that she wasn't turning you. I've wanted to ask you what you meant by that."

Fiadh folded her legs beneath her and frowned, as if considering how best to explain. The wrinkle between her eyebrows made my thumb itch to smooth it away. "Different transmission. If a werebeast bites you, you're infected immediately. If a vampire feeds on you, you're just a meal. Turning someone is a process."

My stomach quivered like cold jelly at the thought. I didn't ask what that process entailed.

"If Agatha is turning you, you'll know. And she won't. You're more useful to her as you are."

"A translating juice box," I said.

"I wouldn't have put it like that."

"What about you?"

"She won't turn me, either."

I gazed into Fiadh's face, more human lore rising to the top of my consciousness. "Would you want her to?"

"Absolutely not." Her brows constricted with offense.

"I thought vampire familiars wanted—"

"Don't be bigoted."

"But then what do you get out of this?" Her sigh suggested she didn't want to have this conversation again, but I pressed on. "Why is this job worth it to you, Fi?"

"Because I like it. And she isn't a monster."

I recoiled. "How can you say that, after what she did to me?"

"She's not human. Like I told you before, she doesn't play by our rules. I respect her. By putting you in thrall, she was showing you who was in control."

"That's your justification?" I stood, tea sloshing over the rim of my mug, nausea curling around my throat like smoke.

"Not—Clara, listen to me."

"I'm not sure I want to."

"I know you're scared. I'm not trying to diminish that at all. But Agatha doesn't see things the way we do."

"It doesn't matter how she sees it." I wanted to kick over my coffee table in my hurt and anger. How could Fiadh defend her?

"I know. Clara, that's not what I'm trying to say. I—I know I'm messing this up. I like you. I like you so much. But you're asking me to choose between the life I've built and you, and I'm not ready to make that choice."

My anger sputtered out. I sat in the chair opposite the couch, not willing to resume our earlier intimacy, but no longer hell-bent on heading for the door. She'd said she wasn't ready to make that choice, which meant she might be someday. And she'd said, *I like you so much,* her voice breaking on the words.

"What you need to understand about me," she continued in that soft, quavering voice, "is this is my life, even if it seems strange to you. I've never been put in thrall against my will. I don't know what that feels like, but I can imagine it was awful."

It had felt ruinously easy, and it had felt *wrong* on a level too deep to describe.

"Agatha is like family to me," Fiadh continued. At my expression, which must have conjured up the decidedly sexual moan I'd heard her make, she amended her words. "Not . . . she's a friend. She's been a friend to my family for a long time. She's protected us, and cared for us, and in return we protect and care for her. Yes, occasionally she takes some blood from me, but don't you donate blood to people in need?"

"Not the same."

"Why not?"

"It just isn't."

"I love her, Clara. And I've spoken with her. She's promised never to put you under thrall like that again, unless her life is at stake, or yours."

"And you believe her?" I spat the words. I hated hearing *"I love her"* from Fiadh's lips.

"I do. She swore it on the grave of her first life."

"What is that, some kind of holy oath? Couldn't she have sworn it on her coffin?" My chin quavered dangerously, a herald of tears to come.

"You're being crass."

"No, I don't understand."

"You don't *want* to understand!" She shouted the last words. I'd never heard her shout before.

"Maybe I don't," I said, and though I'd meant to match her shout for shout, the words broke on a sob.

"Fine," she said. Color stained her cheeks and throat.

"Fine."

We both breathed hard as we glared at each other. How could she not see where I was coming from? How could she overlook how *wrong* her relationship was with her employer?

"Did you even want to be with me that night in your apartment?" I asked.

"What?" Real confusion suffused her features. "Of course I did. How could you even ask that?"

"Because it seems like you just used it to—"

"Protect you?" she finished for me.

"Well, yeah. Or protect Agatha."

"If that's what you think of me, then I think I should go," said Fiadh.

My throat worked as I struggled to find the words to express the hopeless hurt compounding my fear. *Please don't go*, I wanted to say, but my words had suddenly dried up. I stood there silent and shaking as she walked to the door with the restrained motions of someone longing to run, then slammed it behind her, but not before I heard the first gasp of her sobs.

—⁂— —⁂— —⁂—

Collection: Nektopolis
Title: Letter 33
Description: Correspondence; Gata and Natek
Date: TBD
Cataloguer: Clara Eden

Gata,

When I received your letter, I did not know what to think. I could not search for you. Not if she was watching. Did you truly think I'd set you traps after all this time? That I sought to know you, not for myself, but for the opportunity to ensnare you?

It explains a great deal. If you could see my hand

150

shaking—I, who've fought in the blood and the dirt of countless campaigns, whose hands have slain kings. I did not know, Gata. I swear this to you. When I recall your letters, I could weep at what I thought was reticence, and now I see plainly as your courage. I am not worthy. The fact that she did not task me with your capture is not a comfort. It means she has another on your tail, or else she hunts you herself.

But time enough has passed. Time, time, and more time. And now, to know you found your way to this gods-forsaken island at the edge of civilization...well[24].

London is a hell. I would have warned you away if I'd known you were coming. Wet and dark and dirty. It rains too often. As for our local brethren, they are little better than the barbarians[25], painting their faces with woad and feeding like beasts. Roman soldiers need only carry spears—the blue-faced fools rush the phalanxes, staking themselves. I've half a mind to learn their language, so that I might train them. Imagine the conflict I could engender! The rain, however, is constant and hateful, and I'd rather remain quartered with the legions than out in that wet, dank darkness.

Your rose survives despite the cursed rain. I feed it blood, and it seems to its taste, though its thorns have grown. Are thorns wood enough to end us? Perhaps this was your plan all along, back when

you thought me her spy: a slow, twisting battle of

---

24 Translator's note: This suggests a missing piece of correspondence, since Gata did not specify her location in the documents I've examined. Alternatively, she could have instructed the messenger to supply this information.

25 Translator's note: Presumably the native (itself a relative term) inhabitants of the Isles.

attrition, until my body feeds its petals, one prick at a time. You needn't be so patient. I'd take a thorn to

the heart, for you. I'd foreswear any oath.

You know where I am. You know how to find me. She is elsewhere—I have this on good authority, though I cannot promise she doesn't have me watched. Come anyway. The two of us will fight. You can fight, daughter of Illyria. You left that out in your replies. It was the Autariatai [26] tribe that has the honor of claiming you, according to my source. My mother was Ardiaioi[27], but I will not hold it against you. I left those loyalties behind long ago.

I have no poet to offer you, but there is a sculptor with a poet's touch in this city of soldiers' tents and half-built villas. I think you'll enjoy her. She's very good—It is almost a waste to consider silencing that chisel.

Until then,
Your Nettle

PS. I was right, long ago, when I said you were impossible. One of the blood, and one of the Otherworld, as they say here. Vezina fears you more than anyone alive. I will not ask why. You will tell me someday, face to face, or you will keep your secrets. I only wish to keep you. Please, Gata. I know no way of assuring you this is no trap, and so I fall to begging. Come to me and release me from this longing[28].

---

26 Translator's note: An ancient Illyrian people found in the pre-Roman Balkans. One of the peoples in the territory that eventually became Nektopolis.

27 Translator's note: Another Illyrian people and frequent enemy of the Autariatai tribes.

28 Translator's note: Possibly a reference to Sappho Fragment 1 ("Prayer to Aphrodite").

I paced my cottage that night filled with furious thoughts, which even in my agitated state I knew was just a cover for fear and confusion. I didn't know how to handle this. I didn't know how to handle anything. Fiadh hadn't denied the accusation. She'd as good as admitted she'd only slept with me to keep me out of harm's way.

What was I supposed to do with that information? How was I supposed to look her in the eyes, knowing that not only had our first time been rushed, but that she potentially hadn't even wanted it? Yes, she was into me, but would she have asked me to stay if Agatha hadn't been on the prowl? Had she been ready to take things to that level? For that matter, had I? Then there was her continued defense of Agatha.

The questions chased themselves around and around my head as I roamed the cottage. Midnight came and went. Then one. Then two. I tried to sleep and gave up almost immediately; lying down felt like too vulnerable a position. I resumed my restless wandering.

An open notebook lay on my desk as I stalked in and out of the office. I reached over to shut it with satisfying violence, then paused. My familiar, tight, impatient script scrawled in neat lines down the page. Notes, speculations, facts—all about Nektopolis and its mysterious founder. A sketch of a weaving pattern with poetic meter mapped against the weave. I had so many unanswered questions. I stroked the slight texture of ink on paper. The fridge hummed in the background, preventing the silence from reigning absolute.

Lying to myself was harder in the indigo space between two and three in the morning. Of course I wanted to find Nektaria. Yes, she was apparently an immortal leech, but she was *Nektaria*. Agatha was only an employer. I couldn't compare the situations, and knew I would spend the rest of my life in regret if I passed up this opportunity, even if the rest of my life might be short. Especially since it might be short.

Someone knocked on my door.

Common sense urged me to stay in my office. If it was Agatha, opening the door would just be an invitation to suck me down like a milkshake. Besides—I didn't think Agatha would knock after recent events.

But I wanted it to be Agatha. I wanted to scream at her, maybe try my hand at a punch or two, perhaps attempt a staking, just to vent some of the hot, boiling confusion bubbling inside me. I refused to allow myself to hope it was Fiadh.

The knock came again.

Fuck it. I crept in socked feet over the cold floorboards and scratchy area rugs until I came to the door and, summoning courage I didn't have, yanked it open.

Fiadh flung herself into my arms. Her hands dug into my back, almost claw-like in the intensity of her grip.

"Fi—" I lifted her legs around my waist and held her. Our cheeks pressed hotly against each other. Hers was damp and sticky, and I knew she'd been crying.

She pulled back to search my eyes. In a small, tremulous voice, she asked, "Can we talk?"

My chest was too tight with emotion to answer, so I set her down and led her into my bedroom. Perhaps the couch would have been safer, but it was well past late and into morning, and the living room windows overlooked the greenhouse. The drawn shades were not nearly enough of a barrier for comfort, whereas my bedroom faced away from the manor and felt, therefore, more secure.

Fiadh sat with her legs folded beneath her on the end of the bed. I positioned myself at the headboard.

"I wanted you," she said, staring at the bedspread. The plain blue cotton duvet wasn't particularly interesting, but perhaps it was better than looking at me. "That part was real, even if I was also trying to protect you."

My eyes closed against the confirmation I'd feared. At least she hadn't danced around the issue.

"That's what we do for the people we care about," she continued, jerking her gaze up sharply to pierce mine. "And I didn't think you'd believe me even if I could have told you that you were in danger."

"You could have just asked me to stay."

She scoffed, her hands twisting together in her lap. "And how do you think that would have ended?"

"I could have slept on the couch."

"I didn't *want* you to sleep on the couch." The frustration in her voice, I realized as I stared back at her, wasn't directed at me. The tightness around her mouth and the anguished knot of her fingers plainly spelled self-loathing. "Maybe you could have lain there next to me without touching me, but I don't think I could. Not with the way you've been looking at me."

My cheeks heated. Subtle, I was not, apparently. Nor did I know how to respond. Would we have ended up in bed regardless?

"You don't—" Her cheeks flamed to match mine, but she pressed on. "You don't have to say anything."

Her fingers were turning a mottled red from the force of her nervous wringing. I reached out and placed my own atop hers to soothe them. "Come here."

"Are you sure?"

I nodded. She crawled into my lap and I leaned back against the headboard, stroking her hair. The warm weight of her body set me immediately at ease. My muscles unclenched. Exhaustion grayed the corners of my vision. It was, after all, very late, and she smelled very good, and I was very susceptible to soft, warm things. I'd started to drowse off when she spoke my name.

"Hmm?"

"What do we do?" she asked.

I considered this. Part of me wanted to reassure her that everything was fine. That part cared more about pleasing others than taking care of myself, though, and that was deceitful in its own way. Instead, I thought about the question. What did I need from her? What could we do to prevent this from festering?

"I can't believe I'm about to say this," I began, playing with her hair, "but maybe we should slow down?"

After a pause, she said, "I agree. I can go."

"Don't be ridiculous. It's late."

She nuzzled more firmly against me and splayed her hand across my chest, right over my heart. "I can do that for you."

"It doesn't have to be glacial or anything," I amended, already regretting my words. "I just think—"

"You don't need to explain, unless you want to." She tapped my sternum thoughtfully. "Besides, there's something rather enticing about the idea of making you wait."

～⁓～ ～⁓～ ～⁓～

Collection: Nektopolis
Title: Letter 34
Description: Correspondence; Gata and Natek

Date: TBD
Cataloguer: Clara Eden

[Transcribed from stylus[29]]

While you are at the London forum, can you pick up more beeswax, and also more wool from the merchant with the blind right eye? You know she is my preference. Silk damask, too. You'll look lovely in more of that red you found last year, if it ever grows warm enough to wear silk this summer.

N

—⁂— —⁂— —⁂—

"Let's backtrack," I said one afternoon in the library. "Gata clearly found the letters she sent to Natek, which means at some point they must have been in the same place."

We'd know for certain once I'd finished the painstaking work of restoring the letters in the second packet. All but two had suffered smoke damage along with the other insults of age. I itched to translate them.

"It seems likely," said Fiadh, not looking up from the book open before her. It was one of the handwritten collections of fairy tales, which she'd suggested might contain lore about Nektaria or Vezina. I was impressed she could read the cramped Latin. Her lips moved slowly as she worked through the page before her.

"But why does she have Natek's *and her own?*" I continued. I couldn't picture the woman who had written those letters leaving them behind. The Natek I'd come to know would have eaten them before losing them in any other way. My vision blurred, and I blinked furiously to clear it. *Stay awake, Clara.* "What are you reading about?"

"Irish folklore," she said. I leaned over to see the page, which had a drawing of what might have been a cat, if a cat and a parsnip ever had the misfortune to reproduce. Her arm slid over her notes as she

---

29 Translator's note: A note made on the tablet itself, suggesting this is a copy of an original document.

adjusted the book to show me. "Nothing useful so far."

I offered up my parsnip theory and earned a smile. "If I come across a crop of parcats, I'll let you know."

"What is the cat supposed to be, anyway?"

"Something to do with witches. What do you think happened with the letters, then?"

"No idea."

On a legal pad beside my laptop was a list of everything I knew about Natek. It wasn't very long. I knew a little of her locations over the years—Nektopolis, London, if the few words I'd been able to read from one of the letters was correct, along with Gaul, though that too was conjecture based on a single reference, and possibly Constantinople—and I suspected her political acumen was behind more than one war. That, at least, had been easy to deduce, thanks to Gata's comments. The battle that led to the final death knell of Nektopolis's stand against the Roman empire was credited to a man who might have been Natek's husband. Simple enough to imagine him as her thrall, communicating her plans to his superiors. Did it rankle her, having to hide behind a puppet? It certainly made her hard to track, which I guessed was the intent.

"Do you know if Agatha is in contact with other . . . people like her?" I asked.

The waning daylight cast Fiadh's face in sharp delineation: her left cheek blazed with light, while the right absorbed all the shadows in the room. Also, I couldn't help noticing that the top two buttons of her blouse were undone—not enough to be scandalous, but more than enough to tease.

"That isn't something I'm allowed to talk about. I'm sorry."

My hand tightened on my pen. I still hadn't seen Agatha since The Incident. My decision to search for Natek didn't mean I'd forgiven my employer. Far from it. Fiadh wanted Agatha to be happy. I just wanted permission to publish my research, and if nothing else, talk to Nektaria before I was eaten.

"So, that's a yes, then? You wouldn't be forbidden from talking about it otherwise."

"Even if there were someone who could help us, and there isn't, it's too dangerous." She pinched the bridge of her nose, then rubbed her temples. At first I thought it was in exasperation. Her posture, however, was hunched in a way that suggested physical, rather than

157

emotional, discomfort.

"Are you okay?"

"Just a headache. I get them."

"Do you want me to rub your shoulders?" I asked. Years spent hunched over books had given me intimate insight into the world of tension headaches.

She looked up in surprise. "Really?"

"Why wouldn't I?"

"No one's ever—" She cut herself off, as if revealing she hadn't been on the receiving end of a massage was something to be embarrassed about. Perhaps it was. I'd received plenty from friends, family, and previous girlfriends. The fact that she hadn't suggested a loneliness that reminded me of Gata. (If I kept Gata mentally separated from Agatha, I could almost handle things.) I stood up carefully. Lack of sleep was making me prone to light-headedness, and I didn't want to pass out.

"Uh, no wonder you have a headache," I said, resting my hands on her shoulders and feeling the tension radiating from her muscles. She was wound as tight as an antique projector reel. At the first squeeze of my fingers, she leaned into the back of the chair with a groan. Knots crunched beneath my thumbs.

"It never occurred to me muscles could be part of the problem," she said as I worked my way down her shoulders.

An odd statement for someone as intelligent as Fiadh, but I let it pass in favor of sliding my hands down the taut bands of unhappy muscle along her spine. She let her head fall against my arm in relief. It would have been so easy to kiss her parted lips, especially since I had to lean farther forward anyway to reach the base of her spine.

"Tsk, tsk," she said, and I snapped my attention away from her lips to her eyes. Beneath her amusement, however, I saw naked want.

"This would be easier if you were lying down," I said, nodding toward the window seat. She cocked a brow, but I found a knot the size of a large marble at that moment, and she sucked in a breath, wincing.

"I was going to protest, but . . ." The longing in her voice had so little to do with lust that I laughed.

"I'll control myself. And with knots like this, you're not going to be able to move. I think we're safe."

"As long as you're sure . . .?"

I patted her shoulder and stepped away from her and toward the window, gesturing with a dramatic wave of my arm for her to follow.

She shook her head and smiled, that rare, bright thing I craved more and more each day.

"In the least erotic way possible, could you take off your shirt?" I asked.

"Whatever gets your hands back on me. In the least erotic way possible, of course." Turning her back to me, she untucked her blouse from her skirt and began undoing the buttons. I'd assumed she'd be wearing a camisole beneath. As she placed the white shirt carefully on the window seat and lay down, however, only her dark green lace bra interrupted that gorgeous expanse of freckled skin. I didn't quite manage to suppress my sharp inhale. She lay with her head cradled on her crossed arms, watching me.

"That's not fair," I said.

"You asked."

"Well, yes, but I'm a known dumb-dumb." *Dumb-dumb? Really, Clara?* Idiot *not a good enough word for you?* Her laugh was worth my embarrassment, though. I straddled her cautiously, not daring to rest my weight on her ass for many reasons, chief among them *not* the chivalrous desire to spare her my weight, but the memory of how her ass had felt against me. Taking it slow would not be possible under those circumstances. I considered asking her to unbutton her skirt so I could start work at her sacrum, but that, too, was playing with knives. This whole situation had turned into a knife-filled quagmire very quickly.

When my hands touched her back, however, and began working the tension out of muscles I hadn't known could *get* knots, I forgot about quagmires. The woman was a wreck. I walked the heels of my palms up and down her spine, leveraging my weight as she melted into the window seat. Once she began to loosen a notch, I worked my way up her neck and into her scalp, then back down to her shoulders, which seemed to hold the worst of the tension. Small sounds of relief escaped her every few breaths.

"How long have you had headaches?" I asked. It took her a moment to respond, and I watched her lashes flutter as she brought herself back from wherever relaxation had taken her.

"As long as I can remember. Even as a kid."

"Migraines?"

"Sometimes. Usually just these, though. Low-grade. Annoying more than anything. Sometimes . . . worse."

159

The knots at the base of her skull certainly felt like the embodiment of "worse." Her hair slipped over my fingers like water.

The glass in the window was rippled with age, and those ripples created intricate patterns of light on her skin. Rainbows bent around my fingers. They dazzled my eyes, which were already bleary from exhaustion, and I let my eyelids fall shut. The world narrowed to the supple feel of her body beneath my palms and the hot, slightly baked smell of the wooden window frame. Such simple luxury.

Eventually the effort of holding myself off her body grew uncomfortable. I settled slowly over her hips, focusing on my breathing and not the exquisite torture of the way she fit against me. She didn't protest. My head drooped forward as I dug an elbow into a knot along her shoulder blade. Her body tensed, then relaxed. I could feel every minute movement she made.

Drowsy heat uncurled along my limbs. It would be so easy to slide my hands beneath her, feeling her breath quicken as I teased her through the thin lace of her bra. It would be so easy to part her thighs with mine.

She shifted her weight, perhaps to accommodate the additional pressure of my body, or perhaps because she knew, damn her, what her ass did to me. I couldn't help it; my hips responded. Her quiet laughter was only slightly muffled by the seat cushion.

"Slow, remember?" she said, arching *slowly* up into me.

"Uh huh," I said intelligently. Fuck, but she felt good. I wanted to bite her shoulder instead of working her trapezius. I wanted—

I stopped myself. Wanting was fine, but if I let myself start down that road right now, I'd derail both the backrub and my resolve. *Want later*, I told myself. Focus returned. Her neck was especially crunchy with tension. My hands sought out the knots and pressed inexorably down.

"Clara?"

I startled. Had I actually dozed off sitting upright? I scrubbed at my eyes with the heels of my palm, hating the grainy, burning sensation that had become part of my new normal, along with the heart palpitations brought on by the caffeine pills I kept on me at all times.

"Does your head feel any better?"

She squirmed until she was fully rotated beneath me. "Are you sleeping, Clara?"

The gentle way she said my name, softening the harsh consonant at its beginning into something quiet, brought a lump to my throat. I knew she wasn't talking about just now.

"A little." The admittance cost me nothing. There wasn't a point in lying when the shocking purple bruises beneath my eyes gave me away.

"Do you want—"

"I'm going to go to the university this weekend," I said, forestalling whatever she was about to offer. Sleeping was not an option. Not yet, anyway.

"Why?" She sounded genuinely confused.

"I want to get some context. Historical context. Brixton has a good collection."

She nodded, considering this. "It might be good for you to get away for a few hours. But be careful."

I tried and failed to keep my eyes on her face. The massage had tousled her hair, and one cheek was red from where she'd lain on it— in the same way her cheek might have been red if she'd buried her face in the cushion to muffle sound. The bra wasn't helping me stay focused, either. The lace gave the illusion of modesty with its cut, but hid nothing.

She flicked my belt buckle to get my attention. "Slow."

"Fuck slow," I said, the pouting note in my voice poorly concealed.

Tapping my belt once, twice, three times, she asked, "Is that how you like it?"

Desire stunned me. At my expression, she laughed, and gestured for me to get off her with an imperious wave of her hand. I searched for a witty reply and came up empty.

"And yes, my head does feel better. Thank you." The touch she gave the back of my wrist was fleeting and gentle, and despite my tongue-tied frustration, I had the presence of mind to be grateful for her restraint. She had to have known I would have done anything she wanted right then. Instead, she'd respected my request.

—⁓— —⁓— —⁓—

Collection: Nektopolis
Title: Letter 35
Description: Correspondence; Gata and Natek
Date: TBD
Cataloguer: Clara Eden

Galatea,

Lest you forget all the names you've worn through the ages.

You asked me, yesterday, if I ever regret this life I've chosen, if I mourn my broken oath. You know the answer. There can be no regret when I have you.

But we haven't had to run, yet. I sense your worry that when the time comes, my loyalties won't hold. Love is irrational, and often full of fear, or so the poets say. If they don't say it, they ought to. I write this to you so that you may reread it when these doubts cloud the knife blade of your mind.

I think of you beneath me, the implicit trust in the tilt of your neck. Do you not see how you've flayed me open, too? Our vulnerabilities—they are what make us whole. And I am wholly yours.

Nektaria

—⟋⟍— —⟋⟍— —⟋⟍—

Walking onto the university campus on a late August morning brought back a decade's worth of memories. The leaves hadn't quite begun to turn, and the day had a hint of heat lurking around its cool, dew-drenched beginnings, but the ivy winding up the brick façades of the building and the sleepy faces of a few early risers—mostly graduate students, I wagered—tugged at the perennial student heart of me. I'd given this up.

Granted, I'd also given up what amounted to a ton of unpaid labor in exchange for a comfortable wage and health insurance, but I still missed mornings like this.

The smell of the university library greeted me with its particular mix of books, unwashed hair, university cleaning products, and beneath those, a slightly musty odor that suggested mold had taken residence beneath the colorless carpets. Once, I'd even found a mushroom growing in the lower stacks. *Home.* I inhaled deeply, which wasn't particularly advisable, given the historical prevalence of respiratory illness on campus. One of those cleaning products *had* to be toxic—either that, or it was the mold.

I strolled the familiar aisles until I came to the third floor, where my dissertation carrel had been located. Now, the warm, scratched wood held the tomes of another scholar. I brushed my fingertips over the spines of the books and wished them well.

An empty carrel by a window caught my attention. I set my things down beside the well-worn chair and gazed out over the green lawn, the dew dazzling my tired eyes as it refracted the morning sun.

Sun. I was safe in the sunlight. Right?

Doubt had no place in my fervent, fevered belief in light. I *needed* to believe in safety, or else I would go completely insane. Perhaps that was what had driven me back here, to the university where I'd poured most of my young adult life in libation at the altar of knowledge.

I spent the next several hours combing the stacks, the list of call numbers I'd researched prior to making the drive gripped in one sweaty hand, keeping myself awake with force of will and stimulants. Byzantine history. Military History. A primer on military strategy from the centuries I estimated Natek most likely to have exerted influence. Nektopolian fragments from before the fall. Each title weighed down my arms with the comforting certainty of the written word.

When I'd finished, my carrel shelf was full. Seeing the line of neatly arranged titles above my laptop filled me with quiet satisfaction. Maybe I couldn't escape the clutches of a vampire—a truth my mind wasn't quite ready to accept, even if my adrenal glands were onboard and primed to pump me full of adrenaline and cortisol—but I knew how to do this.

The library gradually filled with students studying for summer semester finals as morning turned first to afternoon, then evening. I paused every so often to refill my coffee thermos and consume carbohydrates from the strategically located café across the green. By the time shadows stretched across the lawn and the sound of clacking keyboards rose in harmonic chords from the full carrels, I had made a decent start on narrowing the vast expanse of history into something slightly less vast. Nothing I'd read pointed directly to Natek, but I sensed her in the margins. My understanding of military strategy was admittedly deplorable. I contemplated picking up a few volumes on Aegean strategists, or perhaps *The Art of War*, but didn't have it in me to tackle Sun Tzu on . . . how many hours of sleep?

I tried to concentrate on the annotated bibliography open on the desk. Had I really been up for almost twenty-four hours? My stomach ached in that desolate, empty way of deprivation, and the fog swirling in the corners of my vision wasn't promising. The urge to lay my head on the smooth, white paper put sirens to shame. I wasn't a sailor; I was the fucking rock the sirens sang from. I was—

Tired, clearly. But I didn't want to go home. Could I even call my cottage home? Text danced on the page. I needed Fi's reassuring, starched commands, telling me where I was and wasn't allowed to go, or what I should request to eat, or . . . That thought, too, wandered, leaving me alone with the image of Fiadh in my mind's eye. I let myself take that meager comfort.

"Excuse me?"

I jerked awake, paper sticking to my cheek. A young, slightly harassed-looking student with an asymmetrical haircut that might have been trendy if they hadn't radiated disgruntlement stared down at me, and the lights in the stacks had dimmed.

"We're closing soon," said the student.

Right. Technically, the library closed at two a.m. There were ways around this: the deep stacks, for instance, were the university's worst kept secret. The librarians never penetrated those murky depths unless they had something to reshelve, and they never reshelved past one, which meant students with the foresight to slip below could make use of the library until morning—unlike me.

"Oh," I managed to say. "Okay."

"Do you need a reserve slip?"

"I have one." I pulled the crumpled paper from my pocket and laid it on the carrel, indicating my right to leave books helter-skelter on its surface, and blinked spots from my eyesight.

"Are you okay?" Disgruntlement turned to concern on the kid's face. "Do you want me to, um, call someone?"

Fi, I almost said. *Call Fiadh.*

"I'm fine."

The student librarian wandered off, but I felt the glances they shot over their shoulder. I wasn't fine. I was so, so, so far from fine, it might have been a foreign country. I fumbled in my bag for my phone.

Notifications lit up eagerly at my touch, only to be swept away—all save one. My thumbs tapped out a short message. Then I shoved my phone back in my bag, gathered my things, and made a Herculean effort to walk in a straight line out of the library and to my car, where I drove the careful drive of the drunk back to Agatha's estate.

⁓ ⁓ ⁓

"Clara?"

Fiadh's voice came through the door. I unlocked it, my cheeks damp, and stumbled into her arms. She supported me with only the barest suggestion of difficulty. I was, after all, a good head taller and significantly heavier, and should not have dumped my full weight on her smaller frame.

"Thank you for coming," I mumbled into her shoulder.

"When I got your text—" But she didn't finish because I'd started sobbing. Gently, she guided me to my bed, where I collapsed into the fetal position. She kicked off her shoes and curled up next to me, tucking my head against her breast and stroking my back. The whisper of her fingers against my ragged nerves granted a reprieve I sorely needed.

"When was the last time you really slept?" she asked.

I shrugged. Keeping track of the hours I slept wasn't as important as keeping track of when I was awake. The sound of Mr. Muffin's purr punctuated our breaths.

"I *can't* sleep," I said, loading everything into those three words. "Not at night."

"Do you . . ." She paused. "Do you want me to stay?"

The skin beneath her collarbone brushed my lips with each of her inhales, smooth and warm and real. She owed me nothing, and yet she'd done what she could to protect me. I remembered her frustrated *I didn't want to like you*, and understood fully, finally, what she'd meant. It would have been so much easier for her if we'd remained merely cordial. So much less complicated.

In retrospect, I wished I hadn't started to like her, either. If I hadn't, I wouldn't have gone looking for her, and might never have discovered I had a crush on a vampire's assistant.

The full reality of my circumstances broke over me with the crushing finality of acceptance. I worked for a vampire. I couldn't deny

165

it any longer. My body knew what it had experienced on a primal, cellular level, and some ancestral memory from a time when humans were prey for anything with large enough teeth flooded me with certainty. "Please," I said, choking on my sobs.

I woke to sunlight and the smell of coffee, reminding me of another morning.

"Hey, you," said Fiadh as she stroked my forehead. A steaming cup of freshly brewed coffee waited on my bedside table, and the room glowed with yellow light. The rosebush outside my bedroom window nodded against the glass in a breeze, casting shadows over the rumpled coverlet and scratching pleasantly at the screen. A normal, lovely, late summer morning.

"Morning," I mumbled back, feeling drugged from my first full night's sleep in two weeks. The clock on my nightstand was partially obscured by that glorious cup of liquid wakefulness, but I registered the nine on the left and knew Clara had let me sleep in. She'd probably left and come back, doing whatever it was she did for Agatha when the sun rose. Shutting the lid of her coffin?

No. Too gauche.

I expected fear to rill through me with the thought, but instead I merely felt sleepy and content, Fiadh's hand cool on my forehead.

"I know you're confused," Fiadh said in a hushed voice.

"I—"

"Shh." Her fingers pressed against my lips, gently sealing them. "Just know that I'm not going anywhere."

"Because you can't," I said, thinking of Agatha.

"Because I *don't want to*," she corrected, as gently as she'd sealed my lips.

I buried my face deeper into her chest, blocking out the sunlight. If I could just stay right here, everything would turn out okay.

"Today, if you're up for it, there is work to do. But first, I made you breakfast."

Collection: Nektopolis
Title: Letter 36
Description: Correspondence; Gata and Natek
Date: TBD

N,

You should have been a poet, not a soldier. My people have a way of trusting, of living inside one another, that has no mirror elsewhere. We call it the talamü[30]. But your words come close.

I've invited a sailor for dinner. I remember how you like the taste.

G

— ɷɷ — ɷɷ — ɷɷ —

Autumn unfolded around me, the leaves on the rosebushes changing from green to red, and the trees following in a haze of color. A few late rose blooms lingered, their heads bobbing on their long stems as I passed on my walk to and from my cottage, where the ivy blazed a brilliant alizarin crimson and the flower boxes on the windowsills now sported mums instead of elegant summer annuals, courtesy of the grounds staff—who I watched with suspicion from the library window as they tended to the sweeping lawns and fragrant gardens. Were they human? They were rarely present for casual conversation, which I hadn't taken note of previously but now seemed suspect. Yellow jackets hummed on the warmer days, searching for dropped fruit or open beverage containers. I waved them away from my wineglass in the evenings. I still preferred red wine to white—a pity, since drinking it now reminded me of other red, drinkable liquids, but the sun teased rubies from my glass and Mr. Muffin, leashed, joined me on the patio to absorb the fading heat of those rays.

I catalogued for Agatha during the day and pored over my research at night, searching for hidden meanings and hints about what might

---

30 Translator's note: Talamü: As best I can gather, a reconstruction of the Proto-Celtic word for earth, from the Proto-Indo-European *telh* (also a reconstruction) and comparable to the Latin word for earth, *tellus* and the Sanskrit word for bottom, *tala*. Alternative interpretations include "oneness" and "the wholeness of all things," but this is pure speculation.

have happened to Natek and Vezina, or even Agatha herself during the intervening years. On the weekends, I went to the university library. My carrel overflowed with a rotating collection of eclectic titles, some on military strategy, some on history, and a few biographies. Natek was in there, somewhere. My sense of her grew stronger as I scanned the pages, her words repeating in my head.

Will you take a walk with me, one of these years?

I see your face in dreams. That will have to be enough.

Natek was bolder than Gata. More entrenched in Nektopolian society, though after her reign, mostly by way of convenient thrall, or so I'd gathered. I searched for likely men, compiling lists of generals, advisors, philosophers, and strategists. Anyone with influence. Unfortunately, as with most history, their wives were footnotes—if they were mentioned at all.

I had more luck cross-referencing conflicts with the location and time period of Natek's publications. This was guesswork, but Natek's presence coincided with a startling number of conflicts. The Iberian War. The Slavic Revolt of 983. The Battle of Kleidion. The Saxon Rebellion. The Battle of Rozgony. And that was all before the mid-fourteenth century. Granted, Europe was in near constant conflict, so this wasn't proof of correlation, but it was a start. I broke down eventually and checked out a series of tactical manuals recommended by one of the research librarians, which she assured me were the premier texts taught in military institutions around the globe, and which thoroughly covered the tactics used in modern warfare.

I certainly hoped she was right. *The Shrike's Nest: A Historical View on Modern Warfare* by Nathaniel A. Kerr contained eighteen volumes and counting, and I didn't love the way their stark, black covers and silver font dominated my carrel. I shoved the first of them into my bag to bring home with me.

Light reading it was not.

One morning I pulled on a pair of slacks to discover I needed to tighten my belt a notch. I pulled my shirt up in the mirror and stared at my body. I'd lost weight. My hand was warm on my ribs as I placed my palm on my left side, trying to summon some compassion for my flesh. Sudden weight loss wasn't healthy. People would notice soon if I wasn't careful, and then they'd start asking questions. To cope, I stocked up on peanut butter and started wearing makeup to hide the worst of the shadows beneath my eyes and the new hollowness to my cheeks. I knew Fiadh noticed, but she made no comment.

September passed. I looked at my buzzing phone one night to see *1:30 AM October 1* on my lock screen. *Spooky Season Is Nigh*, read a message from the group chat with my university friends, proof that none of us had healthy sleep habits. I typed out a quick reply so they didn't realize I was avoiding them, then stared up at my ceiling. Did Fiadh even have friends? I'd never seen her with anyone else, or heard her talking on the phone with someone who sounded like a friend, versus business. Maybe it was hard to make friends when you were worried your boss might eat them. Maybe she'd meet my friends one day. I entertained that fantasy for a few minutes before my thoughts drifted back, as ever, to Nektaria.

She was out there, somewhere. If I could isolate her tactics, find patterns in history's weave, I could find her.

Light from the greenhouse pricked my curtains. Agatha, gardening. At least that made sense now.

You, though. My gardener. You must miss the sun.

I could think about Agatha through Nektaria's lens. In her words, Agatha became Gata, and Gata was still an artifact to me—Agatha was a person.

Agatha. She'd kept up with their naming conventions. Did that mean anything? Or was it just habit, at this point? More importantly, what name did Natek use now? I opened a note on my phone and started a list of names containing *N, A, T, E,* and *K.*

Katelyn. Aniket. Kaetana. Nakeeta. Taneka. The problem Fiadh and I kept running into, however, was the occasional absence of one of the letters from her aliases. Only the *N* seemed truly constant, which made narrowing down a concrete list of names impossible. Her use of Anonymous was particularly aggravating.

Agatha must have known it was Nektaria through other means. Placement, perhaps, or context clues. Some made sense—notes in the margins of illuminated manuscripts, the decayed shadow of a pressed rose, and Pieria.

My classical education left little doubt that this referenced the roses of Pieria, which grew in the fabled abode of the nine Greek muses on Mount Olympus. To the Greeks, and later poets, the roses represented the highest bloom of art. I closed out of my note and opened up my e-reader app, searching for Anne Carson's translation of Sappho Fragment 55, which scholars speculated lambasted a rival poet.

I hadn't had time to translate the volume of Sappho in Agatha's library. For all I knew, Natek's use of Pieria was in reference to another poem, or perhaps didn't involve Sappho at all. My gut told me otherwise. There was a volume of Sappho in Agatha's library, and Gata and Natek discussed poetry and the Poetess in their letters. *And ate poets. Kobe beef for vampires.*

Carson's translation swam on the screen, overbright in the darkness.

> Dead you will lie and never memory of you
> Will there be nor desire into the aftertime—for you
> do not
> Share in the roses
> Of Pieria, but invisible too in Hades' house
> You will go your way among dim shapes. Having
> been breathed out.

A stinging indictment, but what the hell did that have to do with Nektaria? It was hardly romantic. Gata had written, *I've tasted poetry. Or rather, poets. Complex, like good wine. I will send you one—poet, not poem—and we can compare notes. I dwell far from the roses of Pieria, here in the countryside, though the night birds provide a pleasant chorus of their own. Your collection keeps me company.*

Far from the roses of Pieria . . . But Gata wasn't a poet.

Pieria. Gardener. Roses.

"Fucking cryptic cryptids," I muttered, and opened a new tab.

I think my boss is a vampire, I typed. The search results were supremely unhelpful. *Proof vampires exist*, I tried next, feeling like an idiot. This was not how scholars conducted research.

"Historically, vampires have long been scapegoats for disease," read one result. Well, that made sense. The rest of the search results devolved into speculation, clickbait, and conspiracy theories. I switched to an academic search engine. Sociology. Anthropology. Folklore studies. Nothing suggesting there was any science behind my employer's thirst for blood.

"My family has a rare blood type she needs. And . . . I think you might, too."

My blood type was O negative. Rarer than others, but not unusually rare. Maybe I'd gather up my courage to ask Fiadh what she'd meant by that.

I wished she were here. If I called her, she'd come over, trekking across the moonlit lawn to lie in my bed, and then I'd be tortured by her nearness and my wavering resolve, and not the constant cycling of theories and questions that otherwise kept me up. That, and the constant fear I'd hear the creak of my door and the soft scrape of Agatha's shoe on the carpet.

My pillow swallowed my groan of frustration. How had this become my life?

───※─── ───※─── ───※───

"Teach me," I asked Fiadh over her lunch break.

"Teach you what?" She looked up from a slim illustrated volume of what looked to be botany, its pages filled with watercolor drawings. The open page showed a pale green lichen dotted with red stalk-like structures. I hadn't seen the book before.

"How to break thrall."

"It's a process." She turned the page. Another lichen, this one coral-shaped. "This isn't the place to try it."

"Can you at least explain it?"

"Clara—"

"What are you looking at?" I plucked the book gently from her hands. *An Illustrated Guide to Schwendener's Theory of Lichenization*, by Ira Atken. My eyes automatically picked out the anagram in the last name: Natek. "Lichens?"

"Look at the first page."

I carefully flipped open to the beginning. On the once-white paper, someone had written, in red-inked English, "For G, with hope."

"Natek?" I asked.

"That was my assumption. Does the handwriting match?"

"It's hard to tell in the English alphabet. I'd have to do a closer comparison. Please, Fi."

She looked up at me with those viridian eyes, and I experienced a different kind of thrall.

"Okay," she said. "But not here."

I followed her, not outside, as I'd thought, but up a flight of stairs I hadn't known existed to a room at the top of the turret. A small door opened onto a balcony tucked into the shelter of the manor wall on three sides, and shaded from the direct blaze of the sun. Below, the

171

gardens bloomed. We sat on the tiled floor, cross-legged, facing each other in the breeze.

"Why here?" I asked.

"You need to feel safe. This is safe."

"We're very high up in the air."

"Trust me." She scowled, and I couldn't help smiling at the way her smooth brow puckered between her eyebrows. *Though she be but little she is fierce*, Shakespeare had written in *A Midsummer's Night Dream*. Perhaps he'd known someone like Fi.

"Can I ask you something?" I said, asking her something. I hated when people started questions with that phrase, but here I was, on a balcony, trying to learn how to escape a vampire's will, and everything felt tenuous.

"Of course."

"Why are you helping me?"

Hurt twisted her mouth. "Clara—"

"Not—I just mean, you work for Agatha. Would she be upset that you're doing this?" I tried to keep my tone as mild as possible so as not to hurt her further.

"Agatha wants you to stay on working for her. She'd understand." Her teeth were very white against the red of her lips. "But I'm not going to tell her. You have a right to your privacy so long as it doesn't put her at risk, and this doesn't."

"Thank you."

"Besides." The hurt shifted into something sly. "The only one you should be swooning over is me."

I blushed despite myself and lightly swatted her knee. "You have never seen me swoon."

"Are you suggesting I couldn't make you?" The sultry shift in her tone took me off guard, and I stared at her mouth, unable to think of a comeback. Her lips curved in a self-satisfied smile. "Good."

"Unfair," I said.

"Hardly. Now, to start, think of an object or a person. It can be anything."

The switch from sultry to professorial did nothing to cool me down. If anything, it made things worse. I searched her face, noting that the sly look hadn't left her eyes. Did she know her haughty professorial vibe was my Achilles's heel?

"Anything?"

"A banana, a childhood toy, a friend—something you know really well. What it looks like. Feels like. Smells like. Tastes like."

She absolutely had me figured out. The way she lingered on the last sentence left no doubt. I forced myself to concentrate. What did I know that well?

"Can you tell me what I'm supposed to do with it?"

"Close your eyes and hold that object in your mind."

I closed my eyes and pictured Mr. Muffin.

"Think about what it smells like." Warm cat fur and the slightly fishy odor of his breath. "Feels like." Soft, muscular, warm. "Tastes like." I'd certainly swallowed enough cat hair to attest to its texture, if not taste. I would *not* think about how she tasted. "Sounds like." His meows. His purrs. Fiadh's voice. "Looks like." Mr. Muffin, curled up on a windowsill. Fiadh, asleep beside me, the pillow between us dislodged in the night and my arm around her waist, light creeping over the rise of her hip while I pretended to still be sleeping. Fiadh's body, curled into the curve of my own. The smell of her shampoo, lingering on my pillow on the nights she wasn't there.

"Think of as many details as you can about your object."

The way she tilted her head when she listened. The smell of her skin. The quick, certain way she walked. How, in her presence, the sharp edges of the world no longer cut me quite as deeply. The way she watched me when she thought I wasn't looking, as if she was afraid I'd vanish.

"That's it," she said.

"That's it?" I opened my eyes and met hers. The small balcony held us, and for a moment I pretended we were far away, just two people sitting in the early autumn air.

"Practice holding that object in your mind, first when you're alone and calm, and then when you're stressed. The more stressed you are, the better. You need to be able to call it up immediately, so that it feels natural to reach for it; otherwise it won't work."

"How will that break thrall?"

"It's a touchstone. If you can focus on that instead, you'll stand a chance."

A chance. It was better than nothing. "But how does thrall work?"

"Like, scientifically?"

"Yeah."

"I'm not sure. Pheromones, maybe. Thrall activates the pleasure center of the brain. You associate the good feeling with the vampire, which makes it easier for them to feed. It's a kindness, really."

I disagreed with that last statement, but kept my thoughts to myself.

"Have you ever had to break thrall?" I asked.

"Not outside of training. We should get back to work." She stood up. I followed suit, hoping she might linger, but she headed for the door without looking back—a lecturer walking offstage. Pleasant frustration rippled through my body.

—◊— —◊— —◊—

She did not sleep in my bed that night. Without speaking of it, we both seemed to know there wouldn't be any sleeping if she stayed. Not that I was sleeping without her.

Another restless night. Another French press. Another hour of typing frantically, as if analyzing the surviving fragments of Nektopolian poetry in light of Nektaria's gender reveal might fix something in my real life. Muffin had given up on regular bedtimes, and was curled up in my lap. He fit in the space between my thighs and my desk, but barely. Whenever I moved too much a pair of claws sank into my skin in warning.

"...when seen through this lens, we must reconsider the gender politics of the time, bearing in mind biases both old and new. Nektopolis had no concept of feminism as we know it today, but neither can we prove they entertained the same gender biases, or that those biases presented in similar fashions."

My fingers tapped the keys lightly as I paused to consider the wording of the next lines.

Something yipped outside. A fox, probably, but I jumped in my seat, disturbing my poor cat, who evacuated my lap. I strained my ears. Another yip—definitely an animal, and moving farther away. Nothing to worry about. I wouldn't think about werefoxes.

I tried to turn my concentration back to the screen. No luck. Fiadh had suggested I try to call my object up at random, I remembered. I tried now, aided by the lingering scratches on my legs from Muffin's rapid exit. Fiadh's face floated into my mind instead, as had happened on the balcony.

Every bit of vampire media I'd ever consumed had failed to

account for this conflict, instead romanticizing the erasure of willpower and consent. I understood the intent—that kind of media allowed the consumer to imagine giving into their darkest desires. *It isn't your fault you want this*, fictional thrall reassured. The reality wasn't so black and white. Agatha was a predator. To forget that was to forget to breathe, yet Fiadh was right. Of all the things she could have done to show me who held the power in our relationship, this was the kindest. She hadn't drunk my blood (that time). She hadn't broken my skin. She hadn't decided to cut her losses and end me right there. Humans pulled worse power moves every day.

I couldn't muster any gratitude.

If only I had someone else I could talk to. Had the previous archivist known the truth about our employer? Had it mattered to them? Were they even still alive?

I could look them up. This possibility hadn't occurred to me before, but it was simple. I'd ask Fiadh for their name tomorrow.

"Why do you want to know?" Fiadh looked up from her phone as she escorted me to the library.

"Professional curiosity. Unless Agatha drained them?"

She shot me a glare. Her hair was up today, pinned in place and shining darkly. "Marisa Delmonte is very much alive," she said, disapprovingly. I tucked the name away for reference.

"Did she know?"

"About what?"

"About Agatha," I asked.

"Of course not."

"She didn't even suspect?"

"If she did, she didn't say anything to me."

"How long did she work here for?"

"Fifteen years? Maybe sixteen?"

That was a long time to work for a vampire without suspicion. Then again, if she rarely saw Agatha, she'd have no reason to suspect anything was amiss.

The first thing I did after work was look up the name. Marisa Delmonte had published a few papers, but nothing of particularly scholarly note. Nor did she pop up on a search for currently active academics. On a whim, I dove into the Brixton University alumni network.

Marisa Delmonte did turn up a result there. I squinted at the slightly grainy photograph, a feeling of foreboding stealing over me. Something about that young, severe face looked familiar. Below the photograph, in the search result, it read: Marisa (Delmonte) Bertucci.

I knew her as Professor Bertucci—my PhD advisor and the chair of my department at Brixton. Professor Bertucci, who, if she'd seen Agatha's collection, especially the coin, would have known full well there was more supporting evidence for Nektaria than was known to current scholarship, and had said nothing all these years. Could say nothing. Maybe she didn't know anything about the undead, but she knew a hell of a lot more about Nektopolis than she'd let on in her lectures.

Anger boiled up in me, unexpected in its heat. Anger at Agatha, and anger at Bertucci, who'd held so much back, and who, I now suspected, had been the one to recommend me to Agatha as a possible replacement.

She picked up on the third ring. "Hello?"

"Sorry for calling you so late," I said, not feeling particularly apologetic. It was only eight o'clock, and no one had forced her to take my call.

"Is everything okay?" Her familiar, gravelly voice stoked my anger even further, coupled with an overwhelming urge to burst into tears.

"You used to work for Agatha Montague."

There was a long pause on the line. I heard the intake of her breath, then a long exhale. "Yes."

"Did you pass on my CV to her?"

"Clara—"

"I need to know."

"I did. I thought, given your interests and her needs, it would be a good fit, though I was sad to lose you from the department. With luck, we'll get you back one day."

"You've seen her collection."

Another pause. "I have."

"All of it?"

"Whatever was in the library, yes."

"You could have warned me."

"About what?" She sounded genuinely confused. I tried to evaluate

176

her sincerity, wishing I could see her face.

"All of it. Nektaria. The sheer scope of materials." Unspoken: *the fact that Agatha snacks on her employees.*

"Are you unsatisfied with the work?"

"No, but—she shouldn't have sole access to those artifacts. It isn't right."

"Of course it isn't right. The Earl of Elgin intended to decorate his private home with the Parthenon marbles. National treasures sit in the museums of their former colonizers. You are well versed in the complexities of provenance. One day, the Montague collection will come to light. Honestly, it gives me hope—what else will turn up in time?"

"How did you handle keeping it secret?" I asked, some of my anger evaporating.

"It was difficult. But I would rather know, wouldn't you? Knowledge for knowledge's sake."

I considered this. Would I rather return to a world where I hadn't held a coin with Nektaria's face in my hands, or read a thousand-year exchange between two women named Gata and Natek?

"Knowledge for knowledge's sake," I repeated. "I guess."

"You want to publish your findings," she said with the tone of someone coming to an understanding.

"I can't publish anything from—"

"No, you can't. And that is frustrating." Sympathy soothed away the last of my rage.

"Weren't you frustrated?"

"It drove me crazy at times. But Clara, listen to me. You've been given a once-in-a-lifetime opportunity. Find a way to come to terms with the rest."

"How did you?" I asked, wondering if she knew what, exactly, "the rest" entailed.

"By restoring the work to the best of my ability, so that posterity would one day have a chance to experience it."

"But I'm more than a conservator."

"Then do what you do best. Write toward a future when your contract expires."

"Speaking of the contract."

She waited, and I couldn't tell if I was imagining the tension on the line.

"Did you find it . . . odd?" I continued. "Or anything about Agatha odd?"

"It's a good job, Clara. Don't overthink things." Her tone sharpened. Was that a warning, as in, *Don't look into your employer because she'll eat you?* Or did she simply wish me to make the most of what she saw as a "once-in-a-lifetime opportunity"? Either way, I knew her, and knew I wasn't going to get any more out of her than that. I thanked her for the chance to express my frustration, told her a little bit about how the job was going, in vague terms, and bid her goodnight.

On the bright side, I told myself, at least Bertucci was still alive.

—⫘— —⫘— —⫘—

Collection: Nektopolis
Title: Letter 37
Description: Correspondence; Gata and Natek
Date: TBD
Cataloguer: Clara Eden

Gata, writing Nektaria,

I burned your letters. Not all of them. I couldn't. Instead I held my hand over the flame until the flesh melted instead of your words. I told you the names of others were indelible. I cannot burn yours out of me. Nor can I fully blame you for your betrayal. You did not know. In all our years together, six hundred by our best count, I never told you. I couldn't. Not all of it.

She stole my daughter, Nettle. She used that precious life against me, keeping her someplace I never found, until the years of her life ran out in a dark hole. I do not know if I can tell this story even now. That pain has not faded. I cannot let it. Pain is all I have left of her.

I served Vezina for one hundred years. Then I waited another ten, just to be sure there was no chance

178

that my baby still lived. Vezina sent me locks of her hair as a reminder, but she refused to tell me of my daughter's death. I do not know if she lived to twenty or fifty-five. I do not know if she cried for me in her sleep. She was only twelve years old when we were separated.

Fey cannot easily be put under thrall. I do not know why. When Vezina turned me, she tried. I was too stunned and weak to fight. She handed my daughter off to one of her soldiers and I screamed until my throat bled as the horse faded into the night. I could do nothing. We are so vulnerable in those first few days. So powerless. I had never been powerless before. Always I had the talamü.

Understand, I had never felt alone. She does not know I am muted by the change, an ignorance I have taken great pains to preserve. I work through others. You know some of this. You've seen me protect my people, and you know what I am. You've felt the talamü in my kiss, and I took you while the great trees whispered around us, my name the only word you knew. I will remember you like that, Nettle, your body against the forest greens, the rush of belonging tart and perfect on my tongue. I will remember everything.

I am not like you. I have not had many partners, nor have I wanted them. It is too difficult. I cannot fully join with a lover of my own people, and the disconnect is agony. The occasional mortal sufficed when I couldn't bear the loneliness. Never one of us. But by all the empires we've seen rise and fall, Nektaria, I love you. I was whole with you. I was content in my singularity. You made me happy. That is not an emotion I expect to feel again.

I wish more than anything you could have met my

child. Now I will carry both your ghosts.

My daughter was not a changeling like me. If she had been, I would have known she lived. We could have spoken. Shared the talamü. Instead Vezina used her like a goad. For her sake, I sowed famine in years that should have had good harvests in order to turn the people against their rulers. I brought fever dreams and visions to those Vezina needed moved to action. I rent the earth and tore the roots of trees I'd known as friends. I remember each command, though some are blessedly fading. I remember the choking fear of failure. My daughter. My beloved, brown-eyed daughter. The fear in her eyes when they took her away and her certainty that I would save her are branded within my breast. I pray you never fail at something so utterly completely.

I ramble. I do not know how to tell this story, and the pieces cut me as I reassemble them.

Vezina knew I hated her. It pained her. She desires love and loyalty above all else, and so she kept me close. We shared tents and caves and castles. I learned her nightmares, learned to soothe them, and learned to give her worse dreams. I studied her fears. On the third day of the one hundred and twelfth year of this second life, after years of research and study, I cursed Vezina with the cruelest thing I knew.

I gave her perfect memory. Perfect, verdant memory, clear as the sky after a storm. Impossible to repress. Impossible to escape. Every terrible thing that ever happened to her and every terrible thing she'd ever done, forever emblazoned on the backs of her eyelids.

We are not made to remember. We forget out of

necessity. We cannot carry everything and remain ourselves. I knew time would drive her mad, and I vowed to live to see it.

I have. And dear heart, I regret what I cannot undo. She was never good, but I made her worse. You love her. That means something must remain within the monster. For your sake, though I did not yet know you, and for the sake of the lives she's taken, I made a second vow: to thwart her where and how I could. Rot only ever spreads, Nektaria. It cannot be cured, only burned or severed. She and I are both rotten in our own ways. One day I will burn us both.

I loved you. I still do. But for the space of those blessed years I forgot that I let her make me into all I stood against, and I cannot let that happen twice. Better that I'd killed my precious child myself. At least then I could have held her one last time.

You will not hear from me again. I am not a poet. Not like you. But every time you hear the crack of thunder or the splintering of stone, know it is my heart breaking. Take care of yourself.

Love,
Gata

—⚏— —⚏— —⚏—

Fiadh and I met up Saturdays and Sundays to continue our work, either at the carriage house, my cottage, or the library. These were also the nights she reliably spent asleep beside me, and therefore the only nights I was guaranteed a good night's rest. To say I looked forward to them was the kind of understatement made by someone unwilling to admit the depth of their addiction. I'd been right to slow things down. I knew that, and so did she, but those nights felt like they belonged outside of that arrangement, and were both torturous for their chastity and my greatest solace.

"We haven't been able to narrow down a single location not mentioned in the letters," I said, setting down my notepad with disgust.

"We've narrowed—"

"Sorry, forgot to add *definitively* to that sentence. We haven't been able to narrow anything down *definitively*. And the restoration is taking *forever*."

"Let's go for a walk."

"What?" I looked up at her. She stared back, evenly.

"Let's take a walk. You're getting too in your head."

I opened my mouth to argue, but she was already headed for the door to her apartment, pulling a light jacket on over her dress. Outside, the sun warmed the air, but the shadows warned of the changing season, and the light breeze carried an edge of frost. The gardens still flourished. The changing leaves were almost as spectacular as summer's blooms, and late-season flowers still held on to their petals. Fiadh touched a plump rosehip as we passed a hedge.

"Do you have a favorite flower?"

I considered her question, eyeing a cluster of purple asters. "I like a lot of flowers."

"Choose one."

"Violets."

She stopped, brows raised in surprise. "Really?"

"Something wrong with violets?" I asked with feigned offense. I understood her confusion, especially standing as we were, surrounded by Agatha's splendid garden.

"Not at all. Just not what I would have guessed, for you."

"What was your guess?" I hoped she couldn't guess from my face how the idea of her thinking about my favorite flower made me feel.

"Something more dramatic. Like roses, or orchids."

"I like wildflowers." I shrugged, letting the motion bring my hand closer to hers. "Are you saying I'm dramatic?"

"You like things with history."

"Your evasion was noted. For your information, violets are like cheeseburgers for pollinators. Crucial in the spring."

"Cheeseburgers?

"A very important source of fast calories." I recalled the burger I'd bought her after she'd been drained, and forced myself to push the memory aside. "And violets are small and pretty. I like that."

Too late, I realized those words also applied to Fiadh. She didn't blush, but her pupils expanded despite the sunshine. I hurriedly added, "What's yours?"

"You don't have a guess?" she asked.

I considered the roses around us. No, Fiadh might have thorns, but I didn't think roses were the answer. "Foxglove?"

"Good guess, but peonies."

"Why peonies?"

"Why not peonies?" She released the rose hip. "I like the way they smell."

"Not the way roses smell?"

"Can you keep a secret, Clara Eden?"

I looked down at her as the wind stirred her hair, blowing it gently around her face. Almost, I brushed a lock behind her ear. "Yes."

She rose on her tiptoes to whisper in my ear, "I don't particularly like roses."

"Blasphemy," I said, shivering with the sensation of her lips against my skin.

"I find them interesting," she continued, stepping away, "but they're not my favorite. Too sharp."

Do you have thorns, Gata? Or are you all petal and supple stem?

"You don't like sharp things?" I challenged.

"I prefer to be the only one with claws." The look she sent my way went straight through me. The Greeks had the right of it; lust hit like an arrow. She gave a soft laugh and tugged me onward by the sleeve.

Moments like this, Fiadh walking just ahead of me, the wind teasing autumnal notes from the leaves and the sky blue and bright above us, a happiness unlike anything I'd ever felt swelled within me.

Impulsively, I took a jogging step to catch up with her, linking my arm through hers. The shy smile she tried to hide behind her curtain of hair hummed along my nerve endings. We walked in silence, the air between us ripe with autumn, and I let myself imagine a world without past or future—only Fiadh's fingers around the curve of my arm.

The greenhouse loomed into view as we followed a winding path over the grounds. A wheelbarrow sat outside the door, piled with empty plastic plant trays.

I pulled away from Fiadh and stumbled back, half expecting Agatha to appear with a trowel and her ordinary face, her smile hiding viper's fangs.

"Clara?" Fiadh frowned, looking around for the cause of my

reaction.

"It's nothing." I linked our arms together again, but the magic was broken.

—⁊⁊— —⁊⁊— —⁊⁊—

Collection: Nektopolis
Title: Letter 38
Description: Correspondence; Gata and Natek
Date: TBD
Cataloguer: Clara Eden

Gatalina,

Beloved, I am broken. I've left London. Without you it is unbearable. You always did like this island more than I. May there be less rain wherever you have run to, and more blessed heat. I miss our years in Hispania. The sun warmed the stones well into the dark hours, warm against my palms as I pushed your blood-warmed body against the city walls, and it was easy to imagine its light as we walked its streets and forests. I would have liked to see what colors Helios teased from your hair. Moonlight, like everything I feel when it comes to you, was never enough.

I've settled temporarily in southern Gallia, where I have commissioned a sculpture while I watch the rise of the Franks. I'll leave it in the courtyard here, so that you may know my heart is always yours, and so that you might find me should you change your mind. The sketch is on the back of this hide.

Thank you for your letter. I wish that I could hold you. I did not know. I would never have tried to make peace between you and Vezina if I had. Please believe that. I have made very few tactical mistakes in my life, and this is the greatest and most

184

damning. Forgive me, if you can. If you cannot, know that I suffer as your hand must have suffered in the flame, but without our accelerated healing. Know that if you come to me, whenever that may be, I will leave her service in an instant. I am yours, Gata. I am yours, and I cannot see a future where that ever changes. Until then, she's sworn that she won't hunt or harm you so long as I remain loyal. I do not trust her entirely. But at least I can find out your daughter's fate.

You say I will not hear from you again. I cannot make that same promise. I'll write to you. I'll sing of you. I'll paint your face into the histories, and each word, each note, each stroke of brush will be for you, so that you remember me—even in another time.

I betrayed your trust. I know you, and I know how careful you are. How cautious. How unforgiving.

But know, too, that I've only ever loved you in all the years of this long life.

Come home.

Your Nettle

—◊— —◊— —◊—

November passed with days in Agatha's library and nights spent by the fire in my cottage, wrapped up in a wool blanket with Fiadh while she read me scenes from her eclectic collection of romance novels. Some we suspected were by Natek; others were by known authors with online presences and photos of themselves in sunlight. Mr. Muffin took to her presence instantly, purring as he butted his fat head against her hand, and she seemed to know instinctively where to scratch him. Best of all, she cooked, and my house smelled lived-in and loved.

It wasn't that I couldn't cook; I just couldn't cook like Fiadh. I loved watching her as she busied herself in my small kitchen, the copper pots and pans clinking on the stove, accompanied by the sweet, low sound of her voice as she hummed, while I sat in a chair pulled in from the living room and went over the day's findings on Natek.

The first snow fell early. We ran outside like children, our lips cool as we kissed beneath the falling flakes, and sat bundled in a down quilt by the pond to watch the snow melt into the black water. When I thought of Fiadh, I could understand how Gata could breed and cultivate a strain of roses for another person and guard that cultivar through the centuries. War, drought, disease, persecution—through it all, Gata had kept Natek's rose alive, and it sounded like, based on the letters we had and conjecture from the sources we suspected were Natek, so had her lover.

My hand tightened on my mug of tea so fiercely it spilled across my lap. I hardly noticed.

"Fi," I said, frozen in place. She turned from the stove, where a savory soup was simmering, and wrinkled her forehead in concern.

"What's wrong?" she asked.

"I'm an idiot." Hot tea dripped down my wrists and into my lap.

"Care to elaborate?" She set down the spoon she was using to stir the soup and tossed me a towel.

"Hang on." Wiping off the tea, I darted to my bedside table, where I'd left volume one of *The Shrike's Nest*. I'd been using it to fall asleep at night. The writing style was engaging, but the content was dense, and as it turned out, I had no head whatsoever for military strategy. Last night's chapter had compared the tactics used in the Wars of the Roses to current civil conflicts, and how they often made way for new regimes entirely.

"Look at the author." I waved the book in front of Fiadh's face a little too enthusiastically. She steadied it with a hand to my wrist, eyes widening as she read.

"Nathaniel A. Kerr."

"Yes. And I think—" I rummaged around for a pad of paper and scribbled down the name, jotting *Nektaria* beneath it. Six letters remained after I crossed out all the letters from Nektaria. I rearranged them in several different configurations, dismissing each in turn until I had two likely variations: Earl, NH and Lear, NH. Could it really be this simple? Were the leftover letters in the previous anagrams all directions to her location at the time?

I migrated from the kitchen to the living room, where my personal laptop lay on the coffee table. Fiadh followed.

"Earl and Lear are both real towns," I said, staring at a map. "One's farther north than the other. I might be pulling this out of my ass, but—"

"Clara." Fiadh had her phone out and was staring at the screen. I leaned in to see what had captured her attention. An article headline dominated the top half of her screen: "Local Earl Estate Wins *American Rose Digest's* Best New Cultivar of the Year Award for 'Cynane.'"

"Cynane," said Fiadh. "Why is that name familiar?"

"Alexander the Great's half-sister. Natek knew her. She's mentioned in the letters." My pulse tripped over itself in excitement. "She was killed in battle after his empire collapsed. The regent for Alexander's successor, Philip Arrhidaeus, was threatened by her plans to marry her daughter to Philip. He sent his brother with an army to kill her."

"You're an encyclopedia, Clara."

"But why name this variety after her now?" I wanted to pace, but Mr. Muffin had jumped into my lap. "There's a message there. I just don't know what it is. Unless—"

"Unless?" Fiadh prompted.

My mind churned through possibilities. Cynane had urged her husband to make a bid for the throne, for which Alexander had him killed. She'd then refused to be married off again, and after Alexander's death, she arranged for her daughter to marry the recently crowned King of Macedon, Philip Arrhidaeus, the elder half-brother of Alexander and a man who was reputed to have an intellectual disability—which would have left her daughter, Adea, as the real power. This threatened the regent, Perdiccas, who wished to retain his position. Perdiccas sent his brother, who'd been a close friend of Cynane at court, to either cow her or kill her. Cynane underestimated the bonds of their friendship. While she verbally lashed her old companion from horseback before their armies, lecturing him on loyalty, he'd cut her down mid-speech.

Was Natek expressing regret that she hadn't helped Cynane? That didn't bear any relevance to her relationship with Agatha, as far as I could tell. Fiadh waited for me to come to my conclusion with poorly concealed excitement, clearly trying to be patient. Cynane hadn't quite been betrayed. She was, after all riding at the head of her own army. But she'd underestimated how far her opponent was willing to go for power—something the *Shrike* manuals cautioned constantly against.

"White could be a call for a truce," I said, slowly, referencing the color of the roses in the photos. "And Cynane . . . I'm not sure what that reference means. Betrayal, maybe? The price of pride? Never assume your friends won't kill you for ambition?"

"But it means *something*. It's too specific not to," said Fiadh.

"Yeah." I willed my brain to make connections. "It could . . . it could also be a warning."

"How so?"

"I'm not sure, exactly." My head throbbed as I yanked open door after door of stored memories, searching for the reason for my unease. "A new rose variety seems like a big leap. She hasn't done that before, that we've found."

"Or it's an incredibly romantic gesture. Roses take a long time to breed. If it's a warning, there can't be much urgency."

She had a point, but I still couldn't shake the link between Cynane and betrayal.

"Does Agatha subscribe to *American Rose Digest*?" I asked.

"I will check." She opened up a new tab on her phone and scrolled. "She's a major contributor. But how could Natek know that?"

"Maybe she doesn't. Maybe she's guessing. Unless . . ." I did a few searches of my own. "Hang on. 1902. Look at this."

She leaned in to look at my screen. A grainy photocopy of an old magazine filled my screen, and I zoomed in on an illustration. "Recipient of the Rose of the Year Award: 'Pieria,'" I read. "It doesn't say anything about the grower, though."

"Natek would have left a signature," said Fiadh.

"Which means it might have been Agatha." It was the first possible evidence I'd seen of Agatha reaching out to Natek in all the years of their separation, and 1902 was recent, in the scope of their relationship. If it truly was Agatha's submission, this was further confirmation of her continued feelings. Had she left other, subtler signs I'd missed?

We held each other's eyes, exhilaration sparking from iris to iris.

"You did it," she said. "You found Natek."

"We can't be sure of that. It could be coincidence, but New Hampshire is only a few hours from here. We can check."

"What, drive there?" Her enthusiasm dimmed. "That isn't safe."

"I don't think Natek is going to hurt us. Not if we tell her why we're there. We can call the estate and pretend we're just interested in the rose. Say we're botanists or something. She'll never know."

"Clara—"

"If I'm wrong and we tell Agatha, she'll know what we're doing, and she might stop me. You said she was lonely. We know she still loves Natek, *ipso facto*, my position, but if she's too prideful or afraid to re-establish contact, she isn't going to like our plan. We could ascertain if it is safe, or at least tell her definitively where Natek is."

"But Vezina—"

"Do you really think Natek would betray Agatha by telling Vezina about their correspondence?"

"Maybe." Fiadh fidgeted. "We don't know her. We only know what she's written, and this could be a trap."

"Do you really believe that?" I asked. I knew my excitement was clouding my judgment, but this was my only leverage against Agatha. I couldn't lose it.

"I don't know what I believe."

"Please, Fiadh. We can call ahead. Ask them whatever you want. Just . . . don't tell Agatha yet."

She stared at me for what felt like a very long time.

"Fine," she said at last. I heard the doubt in her voice, but didn't cave. "I don't like this, but fine. As long as you promise to follow my lead."

"I promise."

Sitting there, enveloped in warmth, I could almost believe luck was on our side.

CHAPTER EIGHT
In the Roses of Pieria

Collection: Nektopolis
Title: Letter 39
Description: Correspondence; Gata and Natek
Date: TBD
Cataloguer: Clara Eden

Beloved,

Please come home. Your anger is justified, but the years have done what your fury never could. I've seen ships wrecked against more shores than I can count, and each spar is lodged between my ribs when I think of you.

And I always think of you.

She told me she would forgive my defection and welcome you into the family if I could get you to the bargaining table. I thought—I thought I could save you. Free us from running. I underestimated how very badly she wants you.

Love, why? Why, with all the soldiers at her command, has she been hunting you for two millenia? What

190

have you not told me?

Forgive me, I do not mean to blame you. I betrayed you. My intentions matter little. I am comforted that at least I bought you time to flee. Each fading scar from that day is a reminder of you. I trace them like I used to trace the beloved bones of your body as night tilted toward dawn. I admit I've freshened them a few times to keep the memory.

I do not deserve your forgiveness. I beg it anyway.

Natek, writing to Gata

—— —— ——

Mark agreed to feed Mr. Muffin on the condition I come to his holiday party in December and, in general, stop acting like I'd fallen off the face of the earth. I agreed, and promised I would also bring the woman I was seeing.

I knew something was going on, he texted me. I felt guilty for letting him think that was the reason. I wasn't the type to vanish over a relationship, but since I couldn't tell him what was really happening, I had no choice but to let the lie stand. At least it saved me an explanation.

"Where are you telling Agatha you're going?" I asked her as I tossed my bag into the backseat. We'd decided to take my car, which, while less nice than Fiadh's, handled better in the snow.

She flushed. "Just a weekend getaway. She'll be fine without me for two days, and I gave her the name of the bed and breakfast, in case something goes wrong."

A getaway, like for a couple? I'd process that later.

The crisp morning rolled before us, the sky a hard, clear blue and the clouds still pink with sunrise. Leafless trees stood sentinel along the drive, a few curled, sere leaves still clinging to branches here and there. Patches of grass retained their greenery, for true cold hadn't come yet with its scythe, and puffs of steam rose from the mouths of the cows in a roadside pasture as they browsed on the remaining forage.

Earl was six hours away in the mountains. An easy drive. Fiadh had booked us a bed and breakfast for the night, paid for, of course, by Agatha, and the prospect of spending time with her away from the house alternatingly thrilled and unsettled me. We'd taken things slowly long enough. Was I ready to give her more?

We chatted off and on as morning turned to day and the first wisps of clouds appeared on the horizon. She asked me about my family. I told her about my strained relationship with my mother, whom I loved and who loved me, but who worried about my future. Or at least, had worried up until I told her my new salary. Fiadh, in turn, told me stories about growing up on the estate, playing hide-and-seek with the groundskeeper's twins and reading books in the library under her mother's watchful eye.

"What would you do," I asked eventually, "if you could live forever?"

She turned in her seat to study me. "I suppose it would depend on the circumstances. Do you mean like Agatha?"

"Sure, why not?"

"Read," she said at once, in the tone of someone who had pondered the question many times. "And learn to make really good cheese, the kind that takes years to cure."

"Cheese?"

"Why not? I'd plant trees, too. Whole forests. I like the idea of watching something play out over time."

"Does Agatha have any forests?"

"Yes," said Fiadh. "Somewhere in Europe, I think. Oh, and I'd learn to draw."

"I'm still stuck on the cheese."

"You would be." She swiped my cheek playfully with her thumb. "What about you? And you can't answer, 'read every book ever written.'"

"That's not fair."

"You're allowed more than one hobby if you're immortal."

Unbidden, the memory of Fiadh's sheer nightshirt brought heat to my cheeks. When the blush faded, the heat remained, pooling in my stomach. Given eternity, yes—I'd probably have a lot of sex. But I wasn't going to say that aloud.

"Depends on if you're immortal, too," I said, buying myself time.

"Let's say I am."

"Then I suppose I'd make you read to me."

"Clever workaround. And what, exactly, would you want me to read?"

I turned, risking removing my eyes from the road, and shot her a

192

loaded glance. This time, she was the one who blushed.

"But that still counts as reading," she said. "Try again."

Truthfully, given the prospect of eternity, my mind shied. I'd thought about it before in terms of books and study, but now that I knew it was possible, my brain refused to frame it in terms of personal significance. I didn't want to want it, maybe. Or maybe it was merely that the idea of forever was fucking terrifying.

"I'd nap," I said eventually. "Catch up on all the sleep I missed as a mortal. And then ..."

Immortality didn't guarantee immunity from death if one was a vampire. They could still be killed. Presumably. I hoped. One would need to protect oneself as Agatha had done, gathering a few loyal servants and amassing a fortune small enough to avoid too much notice, but enough to ensure security. It would be work. More work, perhaps, than simply living as I lived now. I tried to imagine planning for a retirement that lasted indefinitely, and failed. I thought, too, of the world at large. Would I meddle, like Natek, twisting the world to my purposes? Or retreat, like Agatha? Fiadh's comment about mermaids and climate change came back to me. Maybe I'd target oil executives, sucking them dry the way they'd sucked the Earth's blood from her veins.

"I'd collect books, too," I continued. *Like Agatha.* I didn't want to be like Agatha in any way, but her library was a testimony to what could be accomplished outside the bounds of a mortal lifetime. "And I'd write."

Fiadh didn't tell me this was, once again, not a hobby. Instead, she asked, "What would you write?"

"Histories. I'd look for patterns. Links. Things only a long perspective can provide. And hidden histories. The pets would be hard, though."

"There are long-lived animals."

"I was thinking of cats," I said. "And maybe I'd learn to knit."

We lapsed into a comfortable silence, listening to the sound of the tires on the road and the wind whistling past the windows. Clouds gathered in thicker bands on the horizon, no longer white but an iron gray.

"Did you happen to check the weather?" I asked.

"Sunny for the most part." She peered up at the sky, her legs tucked beneath her and her brows furrowed. "That does look dark, though."

"I feel like weather forecasters are getting less accurate."

"Right?" Her frown deepened as she stared at the sky.

"I've got all-wheel drive, though," I reminded her. "We'll be fine."

She dozed off shortly after, her dark head resting against the window, her breath fogging the glass. I reached into the backseat and grabbed my jacket, draping it over her one-handed. She snuggled into it, and I smiled, my chest too full to breathe. Like this, she reminded me of my cat napping in the sunlight, all feline contentment and smooth, sun-warmed fur. I wanted to stroke her hair but refrained, lest I wake her. Outside, the trees sped by, their trunks gray and purple in the gathering gloom. I loved days like this, with the sky lowering and the air still. Heat poured over my hands from the dash vents, warming my knuckles.

I turned over what I knew about our search while Fiadh slept. Why would Natek have referenced Cynane, with all of history to draw on?

I've had many teachers. Alexander. Cynane. And the one who made me what I am.

The line floated back to me. Nektaria had known Cynane at court. Who knew how many stories she'd told to Gata about her life? All I had to go on were their letters. They weren't enough.

A white rose, and a rose the deep, red-black of the last drop of heart's blood. Not that I'd ever seen the last drop of heart's blood. For all I knew, it was the same red as the rest. I hoped never to find out. I discarded color symbolism quickly, not because I thought it unlikely, but because the meanings had changed too many times over the years for me to pinpoint with any accuracy which meaning Natek intended. White could mean fire, or it could mean virginal, though the latter seemed unlikely.

And why now? That was what really perplexed me. This was the problem with scholarship. Documents were leaves, dropped by the changing seasons, but they only revealed so much about the forest.

Fiadh woke as the first flakes of snow spiraled past the windshield. She stretched, the soft cashmere of her sweater clinging to her body and distracting me from the road. The car hit the rumble strip, and I corrected, blushing.

"Nice cat nap?" I asked.

She smiled that slow smile of hers and rested her hand on my thigh. "Snow."

"Yeah."

"It's pretty."

The flurries danced over the faded grass and gravel on the side of the highway, then thickened into more serious flakes. I turned on the wipers.

"Clara?"

"Hmm?"

"You're gorgeous."

I glanced over at her, and the open admiration in her drowsy eyes warmed me faster than a hot mug of tea.

"You're not too bad yourself."

She swatted my shoulder gently, then linked her arm through mine on the center console and leaned against me.

—⧆— —⧆— —⧆—

The cozy atmosphere devolved into white-knuckled determination as the car labored up the mountain roads, unplowed snow squeaking beneath the tires as the line of traffic wove back and forth up the slippery incline. The wipers beat as fast as the snow allowed, and both Fiadh and I squinted into the white. All we had to go by were the faint taillights ahead of us, which, after watching two cars drive off the road, wasn't as reassuring as it could have been.

"How much farther?" I asked her. The GPS had failed us, as the signal couldn't penetrate the cloud cover nor, apparently, was there consistent cell coverage here, and we were relying on patchy updates from the occasional signal flash.

"We're nearly at the estate, I think."

"Thank god. What about the bed and breakfast?"

"That's another six miles."

We didn't exchange looks, because that would have been suicide, but the potency of the silence suggested we were both thinking the same thing: risk getting trapped at the estate in a blizzard, or struggle onward to our hotel and wait out the storm, but risk driving off the road.

"Hotel," I said after a moment. "Plows will be out by tomorrow."

"Okay. Then we need to look for Old Oak Lane. It should be somewhere on the left in the next few miles."

Most of the road signs were too blasted with snow to read, but we could pretend we'd see it for now. Fiadh had already gotten out of the car once to wipe snow from a sign, though she'd had to bring the snow brush, since she was too short to reach.

"The estate should be just up here."

I thought I could make out a turn and a mailbox, but in the whiteout, I wasn't certain. The tires slipped and skidded as the car struggled uphill, and my molars felt like they might crack with the force of my clenched jaw. Ahead, the road surged on, ever upward. There were no more taillights. We were alone in the cold and neither of us had brought snow boots.

The tires slipped again. The car fishtailed. Fiadh held on to my leg and the handle above her door, her feet braced against the floor. I tried to straighten us out. The tires spun, churning the snow to ice beneath them.

"We're not going to make it up the hill," I said, realizing the truth as the car slid dangerously backward.

"What do we do?" Panic tinged Fiadh's voice. I'd never heard that note before, and my heart clenched. Nothing would happen to Fiadh on my watch. I couldn't protect her from the uncanny, but I was a born and bred New Englander, and I knew how to handle a snowstorm. Sometimes, the only way to handle whiteout conditions was to accept defeat.

"We go to the estate."

"How? We can't turn around here!"

"Backwards till we can."

Her nails dug into my leg as I let the car slide the way it wanted, my blood thundering through my veins with adrenaline. Slowly, as gradually as I dared, I let us descend, my eyes straining for oncoming headlights and my neck aching from craning over my shoulder. At the first side street, I turned. The tires gripped the snow. I felt the change and let out a breath of relief; off the incline, the car handled well.

I pulled out and drove carefully down the mountain road, the white all-encompassing and hypnotizing, the flakes hurling themselves earthward.

"That's it," Fiadh said, leaning forward to point at the faint indication of another turn. I took it. Like Agatha's estate, the long drive curled through trees and landscaped grounds—or at least, I imagined they were landscaped, since I couldn't see them. Our tracks were the only ones on the road.

196

"I thought we were going to end up in a ditch." Fiadh's voice shook. I wanted to hold her hand, but needed to keep both of mine on the wheel.

"You and me both. We're here, though. At least, I hope this is it."

"Look."

I squinted. A house emerged in a gray blur from the snow, larger than Agatha's, and more austere. Not quite Gothic enough to justify a gargoyle or two, but far from cozy.

"Who are we meeting again?"

"A man named Brandon. He's the groundskeeper. He said to call when we get here, but I don't have service. The grounds cottages are usually easy to find, though. Yes—keep going past here. I think . . . I think it's that building there."

How she could tell, I didn't know. It took me another moment to make it out: the building was squat compared to its companion, and as a gust of wind briefly cleared my vision, I saw lights on in the windows. They were warm and inviting, and I sighed.

"Are you all right?"

"I want to be in there," I said. My whole body ached from the tension of driving in the snow, and the thought of shelter and maybe something to drink overwhelmed me.

"Park here."

I obeyed. We sat, breathing in tandem as another gust of wind rattled the car.

"I swear this wasn't in the forecast."

"I believe you," I said. All the same, despite my relief at arriving, there was something unsettling about the circumstances. I didn't love the idea of being trapped here when night fell. I'd seen too many movies to doubt how that would end.

"Can . . . any of the other . . . beings . . . control the weather?" I asked.

"It would take a lot of water manipulation even for the fey." She took my hand and held it between hers. "But follow my lead, whatever happens."

I nodded. The lure of the golden light warred with the animal instinct to remain safely in the car. Perhaps getting stuck in a ditch would have been preferable. Tow truck drivers were human. Or at least, I assumed they were. Down that road lay madness.

"Does all this seem too easy?" I asked.

Fiadh pondered this as snow mounted on the windshield. "I don't know." Her voice sounded calm, but the hand holding mine was clammy with stress.

"What if it isn't Natek? What if this is a trap?"

"Then all the more reason to follow my lead." The squeeze she gave my hand was reassuring, clamminess aside.

"Have you ever staked a vampire?"

Her laugh dispelled some of my growing fear.

"I don't think anyone's staked a vampire in centuries."

"Does it work?"

"I suppose in theory, but it would work best if you had a long wooden spear and threw javelin in high school. By the time you're close enough to stake one, they can put you under thrall."

"Then how do you kill one?"

"We don't. We're not here to kill anyone, Clara. Vampires are people too. We'll talk to them."

Vampires were not people, but I let that one go. "And if they don't listen?"

She pulled a hand away from mine and held it up to the light. I didn't know what I was supposed to see. I'd turned her hand over in mine many times, noting the patterns in her palm and the pinprick scars at the base of her wrist, the silver ring she wore . . .

The scars. I stared. Two points of white against the cream of her wrist, framing the blue vein.

"Are those . . .?"

"It's a precaution. Any vampire who sees these marks will understand I belong to another, and am off-limits."

"Who enforces those rules?"

"The vampire who leaves the mark. You haven't seen Agatha angry, but I have. Don't worry."

A knock on my window startled us. Someone stood outside, bundled up in a jacket and hat. I rolled the window down a crack and felt snow sting my cheeks.

"Are you lost?" the person asked.

"We had an appointment with Brandon," I said, trying to sound confident.

"Please call me Bran. You must be Fiadh."

"Clara, actually. This is Fiadh." I tilted my head to indicate my companion.

"Then come in and get out of this hellish weather," said Bran, stepping back so I could open the door.

Lacking an obvious avenue of escape, I did what was expected of me, and stepped out into the storm.

The air was cold, but not unbearably so, and tasted heavy and damp. I breathed it in along with several flakes. Fiadh rounded the car and came to stand at my side. She gave me a minute nod of encouragement. This was why we were here. Whatever danger lay ahead, we would face it together, no matter how supremely unprepared I felt at the prospect.

Bran led the way into the grounds cottage. Snow crunched beneath my shoes and blew down the front of my shirt. A storm like this should have been on the news. Already at least four inches were on the ground, maybe six. Enough to track into the warmth of the cottage and collect on the jute mat.

Inside, exposed beams and warm, cream-colored walls brightened the space. I kicked snow off my shoes as I took it in: wide, open kitchen; chalet-style living room; large window on the back side of the cottage looking out over the grounds. A very, very nice groundskeeper cottage.

"Please, take a seat by the fire," said Bran. Now that we were out of the blizzard, I could see his face, which glowed as warmly as the lamps, his light brown skin reddened from the cold. Smile lines crinkled around his eyes.

I rounded the corner into the living room proper and was hit with a breath of warm air and woodsmoke. Leather armchairs huddled around the hearth, and Fiadh and I sank into them. I refrained from wrapping the tartan wool blanket draped over the back around my shoulders, but it was a close thing.

"Can I get you something to drink? Tea? Coffee? Something stronger?" Bran had shed his jacket and hat and, without them, had lost some of his bulk. He was a slender man, well-muscled beneath his flannel shirt, but lacking the burliness I'd come to associate with groundskeepers after Agatha's estate. His skin glowed a warm brown, and his dark hair and brown eyes fit into his surroundings as if he'd been made for them. Everything about him radiated warmth. Despite myself, I relaxed.

"Coffee would be wonderful," I said.

"I'll put the kettle on, then."

He puttered in the kitchen while I exchanged a glance with Fiadh. She wore her slight frown again, and when I raised an eyebrow, she shook her head. Whatever was on her mind wasn't worth sharing yet.

A bookshelf on a nearby wall caught my attention. Books on flora, fauna, and fungi of New England lined the shelves, some new, most old. A legacy of previous occupants perhaps. My fingers itched to touch their spines. The smells of smoke, leather, and pine permeated the air. After the crackle of burning wood was punctuated by the whistle of a kettle, the aroma of freshly ground coffee joined them. Fiadh and I waited quietly, listening to the clink of mugs and spoons. Nothing out of the ordinary glimmered a warning from my surroundings. I didn't relax, but my heart didn't go into overdrive, either.

"Cream? Sugar?" Bran called from the kitchen.

"Cream, please," said Fiadh.

"Black is fine," I said.

"I still don't understand how you can drink black coffee." She pitched her voice low enough that Bran couldn't hear.

"And I don't understand how you could dilute it." I pulled a face, and she smiled. The cold had pinked her cheeks, and they glowed in the firelight.

"Here you are," Bran said as he brought out two glazed ceramic mugs. Mine featured acorns worked subtly into the rim. I couldn't make out the shapes on Fiadh's. The coffee was rich and hot and sweet, and I drank it quickly, eager for the slip of heat down my throat. Bran settled into a third armchair and leaned forward, elbows on knees, hands clasped loosely in front of him.

"Do you often get storms like this?" Fiadh asked. "I didn't see it on the weather."

"I should have warned you," he said with an apologetic shrug. His voice was as warm and rich as the coffee. "We get localized storms like this in the mountains. It will blow over soon, and no doubt melt by the weekend. Winter hasn't really set in yet."

"Sure felt like winter," I said with a shudder.

He smiled. "When the trees start cracking as the sap freezes, then it's winter."

I shuddered again. "No thank you."

"We appreciate your hospitality, and your willingness to answer our questions," said Fiadh.

"It's no trouble. Roses are my specialty; I'm happy to help. And this cultivar in particular is fascinating. Its roots are very old, or so I've been told."

"You said on the phone there is a greenhouse?" Fiadh asked.

"Yes. Let's give the weather a few minutes, and then I'd be delighted to take you to see it."

"Wonderful." She took a dainty sip of her coffee, then continued. "What can you tell us about the rose? Clara, as I mentioned, is a scholar, and she's tracing the roots of certain cultivars for her research."

"Ah." I'd never seen someone personify the expression "beam" before, but Bran positively beamed as he turned to me. "Well, the cultivar is a mutation from one of our oldest varieties: 'Pieria.'"

I tried not to let shock show in my face. *Pieria.* That had to be the original rose developed for Natek by Gata.

"Can you tell us a little bit about where these two cultivars originated?" Fiadh asked, doing a better job of masking her emotions.

"'Pieria' is Mediterranean. She's quite old. I can't tell you exactly how old—that's your specialty, I assume—but there are records of it from the Byzantian era."

This was it. This was the right flower; certainty filled me like the coffee, buzzing along every capillary.

"As for 'Cynane,' she's a more recent development. 'Pieria,' despite the strength of her roots, doesn't take well to grafts or hybridization. 'Cynane' is the first successful variation."

"And the person who developed it? Was that you?"

"Before my time, unfortunately. But I dug through our records after your call, and while I cannot divulge the name—" He winced apologetically. "—I can attest to the provenance."

Provenance. Just like the art world.

"We understand." Fiadh gave him her politest smile. "Though of course any information you *can* give us would be appreciated."

"A botanist is only as good as his word."

"Not his soil?" she countered.

"His word, you could say, is a soil of sorts. Plant lies, grow lies. I make a habit of the truth. Now, the most remarkable aspect of both 'Pieria' and 'Cynane,' aside from the color, is the fragrance. It is rich and floral, of course, but with undertones of iron."

Well, it would, wouldn't it, if it was fed blood. I kept my expression as neutral as possible, lest my distaste for "undertones of iron" show through.

"Metallic? That's very unusual, isn't it?" said Fiadh.

"Mineral, rather than metallic. And barely detectable. I doubt

201

you'll notice, to be frank, unless you're a rose connoisseur."

We confessed we were not connoisseurs, merely interested in the history.

"What prompted entering it into a rose show?" I asked.

"It was felt the time had come for 'Cynane' to reach a wider audience. She has a bit of a siren's call. You'll see."

Little did he know.

"The estate is lovely," I said to change the subject before I gave us away. "Has it been in one family for a long time?"

He waved away my fascination, ignoring my question entirely, which was good, considering I could barely even see the rest of the estate. "Now, when we get to the greenhouse, I'll show you how to properly scent a rose . . ."

Fiadh and I managed to feign interest in the botanical aspects of roses for another half hour. It wasn't difficult; Bran, like most people truly passionate about their calling, explained things with enough loving detail to stir my curiosity, but I was nonetheless relieved when he glanced over my shoulder at the window, and pronounced the weather settled enough for a trek to the greenhouses.

—⚞— —⚞— —⚞—

The snow had faded to a few flurries, and the long glass buildings rose from the grounds, frosted with drifts along their steep roofs. Steam fogged the glass. I followed in the path cleared by Bran's boots, wondering what to expect. Tidy, orderly lines of cultivars, no doubt.

In this, I was correct. Huge ceramic pots held rosebush after rosebush, and the overpowering smell of so many flowers made it impossible to even consider noting undertones. My head swam as I gazed around.

Few petals littered the concrete floor. The place was as immaculate as any museum, and cleaner than most, if I was honest. We walked past white roses, red roses, orange roses, purple roses, pink roses, creamy yellow roses, and all the possible shades and hues between. I touched a few of the heavier heads as we passed, and Fiadh brushed the tip of her finger against a small white teacup rose blossom. In the distance, the far wall of the greenhouse faded into the white of the sky beyond.

"Here we are," said Bran. We were near the middle, and I knew at once which rose he meant. Natek's rose was not as large as some of the other bushes, nor were its blooms as luscious, but the thorns were long and vicious, and the color of those petals was unmistakable: red as seen by moonlight. Red as only this flower could be. *Pieria.* I leaned in and inhaled.

"It smells like roses," I admitted.

Fiadh, however, wrinkled her nose.

"Do you taste it? It comes at the back of the throat," said Bran.

"I do." Her nostrils flared again. "What is in the fertilizer?"

"My custom blend of compost."

"It's . . ." Her eyes widened, then narrowed nearly to slits, and she turned toward him slowly. I'd been testing the point of a thorn against my finger, and her reaction startled me; the thorn pricked my skin.

Bran watched Fiadh with mild interest. He hadn't worn a hat, and his hair curled in the humid air. Drops of melting snow glittered in a sudden ray of weak sunshine. The light haloed him, and the smell of roses settled into my lungs with a sense of permanence. The halo around Bran intensified until he seemed to stand in a pool of it, sunlight catching on water droplets and a faint haze of dust, or maybe pollen.

"Fuck," said Fiadh.

I breathed in more roses. Insects fluttered high up near the glass, their brightly colored wings glinting. Had there been butterflies before? I hadn't noticed. I heard, too, the sound of running water, and wondered if a fountain lay deeper in the heart of the garden. For it was a garden. Climbing roses vined above my head, and moss grew over the hard gray floor as I watched, its minuscule fronds unfurling. A bird chattered. I followed the sound until my eyes found the trees growing in the distance. Their leaves brushed the snowy ceiling, green and golden as midsummer.

"There are trees," I said in awe.

"Would you like to see them?"

I looked at Bran. His eyes burned gold, too, and the halo of golden dust followed him as he moved.

"Yes."

"Clara—" said Fiadh, urgency in her tone.

Fiadh should come too, I decided, and grabbed hold of her hand. Her small fingers clung to mine. We had to walk more carefully, now that the rows were gone. Bran picked his way over hillocks of grass and moss, pausing to stroke a rosebush now and then. They bent their stems in his direction as if he were made of sunlight. Green shadows flitted over his skin, which was still brown, but dappled, too, and with more hues than before. I could have watched his skin for hours.

"Clara," Fiadh said again, but her voice sounded far away, and her hand slipped from mine.

Animals moved in the shadows between the plants. I caught glimpses of green eyes, and yellow, and black. Bran kept an even pace, pausing when I wanted to admire the astonishing perfection of a single leaf. I never wanted to leave this garden, and said so aloud.

"I feel that way too," he said. "The modern world is so demanding."

"Yes."

The moss beneath my feet was softer than my mattress at home. Gradually, I noticed the roots snaking through it, narrow at first, and then growing until they were as thick as my arms, then my thighs.

The oak tree welcomed me with a susurrus of leaf on leaf. Its bark was old and gnarled, and acorns littered the floor, for all that the leaves were still green. I tilted my head back to take it in. Light hummed through me.

"Have a seat," Bran suggested.

A smooth hollow at the base seemed a good spot, and I settled into it with my back against the trunk, cushioned by years and years and years of loam. Bran's golden eyes met mine, and he smiled his warm smile.

"Rest, Clara Eden."

"Where's Fiadh?" I asked through a yawn.

"She'll be along shortly."

I closed my eyes to better hear the sounds of the forest and the water and the birds, and when I slept, I dreamed of summer.

CHAPTER NINE
Another Unpleasant Surprise

woke with a headache and a dry, tacky tongue. My limbs still clung to the soporific embrace of sleep, warm and heavy on the moss as I shifted. Consciousness stirred uneasily. Moss? Cool leather touched my cheek, not moss, and it was winter. I remembered arriving at the estate in the middle of a snowstorm. I remembered walking through a sunlit forest and following the sound of water running beneath the ferns. I remembered Fiadh's hand slipping from my own. With that last memory came the sick, frigid rush of fear.

My eyes snapped open. I lay on a couch in a dark room, lit by a few soft lamps and a fire, and someone had draped a blanket over me— Fiadh? I looked around for her, sitting up as I did so, and met the eyes of the person lounging across from me in an armchair.

She wasn't Fi. My heart battered my ribcage and up into my throat, heavy with the tang of iron. *This* was how I'd imagined vampires might look, on the few occasions I'd given them any thought at all outside of Hollywood renditions, prior to my current employment: tall and cold and lovely. She wore a dark wool jacket over a white blouse, which plunged over her collarbones and down the shadows along her chest, caressing a curve of breast and accenting the black of her hair where it fell over her shoulders. But cleavage was nothing compared to her face, which bore traces of Eastern European ancestry and sported the kind of beauty normally restricted to high fashion magazines— striking rather than conventional, and utterly arresting even without the ice cores of her eyes. Those eyes sent the hairs on my body into pained alertness, summoning primordial instincts of which Agatha had merely brushed the surface. *Predator*, my body screamed. I would have been more comfortable sharing a room with a leopard, or a cave bear, or some saber-toothed menace of an age long past.

"How are you feeling?"

Ice flaked from that voice. Agatha, I realized through the pounding of my panic, made the occasional pretense toward humanity. This woman hadn't been human in several millennia, and it showed. I opened my mouth to speak, though what I was going to say, I didn't know. A squeak came out: high and hissing through my strangled breath.

"Fi," I managed after several more attempts. "Where is Fi?"

"Fi?" The familiar syllable ground over the woman's tongue, inexorable as a glacier.

I nodded. My body shook. I tucked my knees to my chest, noting the dirt on the scuffed fabric. Had I been drugged? Put under thrall? Where had the forest come from, and where had it gone? Because I wanted to go back to the warmth beneath those branches, despite the danger I was beginning to suspect lurked there. At least that death might come unawares, whereas this one seemed destined to hurt.

"Your companion did not see fit to join us." The woman folded her hands in her lap. She had strong hands—elegant, yes, but with a faint network of scars beneath the silver jewelry glimmering at her wrists. They winked in the candlelight.

"Is she okay?"

"I see no reason why she shouldn't be, unless an accident has befallen her elsewhere."

Was that a threat? I had no idea, and her tone gave nothing away. I pressed my back against the couch, trying to put a few inches of distance between us and too afraid to run.

"Bran said she would be here." Hadn't he said something like that? The memories were hazy and bright with gold. Why had I let my guard down? We should never have accepted food and drink, but we'd been cold and shaken by the unexpected weather. He'd drugged us. Maybe Fi had made it to the car and escaped before the drug took hold of her, too. I hoped so. She could go for help.

"Why were you asking questions about my roses?"

My teeth chattered with each sharp breath. I needed to calm down, but I also needed to relieve myself as my bowels joined the agony of fright. My stomach cramped painfully.

"They look like a cultivar created by my employer," I said. Obfuscation didn't cross my mind until after the words were out of my mouth, and even then, I couldn't care. Lies, I sensed, were useless here.

Surprise broke the frost of the woman's features as her lips rounded to accommodate a sharp inhale.

"Gata," she said, testing the name. "I'd hoped, but—"

Light blossomed beneath the glacial chill of her skin, a living flush that must have owed its existence to someone else's blood. With it came a thought.

"Are you Nektaria?"

"Nektaria." She savored the name just as she'd lingered over Gata. "It's been a very long time since I've heard that name from mortal lips."

Relief punched a hole in my panic, and a sharp sob tore from my throat. Natek. We'd found Natek. She wasn't going to eat me— probably—and soon I'd be able to bargain with Agatha and I could sleep without the fear of teeth at my throat. This was Natek. Natek, whose heartache I'd translated and whose sharp humor had made me feel, briefly, seen. If the years had changed her into this, who was I to judge? Who was I to guess at the burdens of immortality?

"Gata sent me. Well, not exactly—I've been translating your letters."

"Translating?"

"Yes. Digitalizing, too, in case of an accident."

"Why does she need you to translate her own correspondence?" A fair question, and one that had made less and less sense to me once I learned of her identity. Why not pay me to teach her the language? Wouldn't Natek's words sound better in her native tongue?

Fiadh had solved that mystery for me. *Memory is painful,* she'd said. *And memory lives in language. A translation is . . . easier.* I didn't feel comfortable explaining that right now, however.

"Well, she's forgotten most of her Nektopolian, which is why she hired me, but she wouldn't have hired me if she had forgotten about you."

"No," said Natek. "I suppose she wouldn't have."

"You've been reaching out to her all these years. She's kept so much of you, even if she never responded. We thought the rose might be another message."

Also I wrote my dissertation on you, I didn't add.

Natek chuckled. The sound carried edges of melt, but still chilled me to hear. "Providence so often disguises itself as coincidence."

"I have to let her know you're alive," I said.

"She knows."

"Still, she'll want to know if it's safe to see you. I can drive back in a few hours, now that the weather has calmed down." I looked around for a window, but the curtains were all drawn, and no light shone through. Night must have fallen. "She'll be . . ."

Natek watched me as I searched for the right word. I didn't know how Agatha would react to news that Natek lived within a day's drive. Did she really already know? There were no copies of the *Shrike* manuals in her library. I didn't know how *I* would feel in her position, and guessing at her feelings as I'd been doing was folly, I realized now—a gnat positing theories about whales.

"She'll be suspicious," said Natek. "She always was."

"Why didn't you go to her?"

Those pinpricks of pupil found mine, full of a cold best described in degrees Kelvin. The cold of deep space and oceanic abysses. "I did not know where to find her. Gata has always been good at hiding. It is what has kept her alive."

Yes, that echoed the letters.

"What happened between you two?" I asked, unable to contain my curiosity. "The letters—"

"The details of my private correspondence are just that, little translator: private. Be grateful she hasn't destroyed the evidence."

My curiosity vanished with the threat, for I had no doubt that *I* was the evidence in that scenario.

"But I will humor you, since you have come this far. We encountered ideological differences, and she could not get over them."

"About Vezina?"

"What do you know about Vezina?" Natek's tone sharpened, the modulation noticeable for the lack of inflection in her previous speech.

"Just that Gata was afraid of her, and did not want to join her."

"She did fear Vezina, and with good reason." Natek unclasped her hands and leaned toward me. "But Gata never played by the rules."

"And you?"

She smiled. "I made the game."

Ages echoed through her words. I was aware once more I was

in the presence of a predator, and stilled in my seat, hardly daring to breathe. *I've had many teachers. Alexander. Cynane. And the one who made me what I am.* Who better than they to teach the ways of warfare and manipulation? Was that what she'd meant, when she'd named the second cultivar? A reminder that she was skilled in both war and politics, and that Gata was safe with her? Or, more disturbingly, was it a threat? We hadn't considered that possibility.

"So," she continued, that horrible smile still on her lips. "Let us write Gata a letter."

"A letter?" I said.

"A letter, written in Nektopolian, with your translation accompanying it."

"I . . ." Relief suffused my limbs. I could do that. "Yes."

Granted, we both knew I would do as she commanded, whether through thrall or violence. I'd learned my lesson with Agatha. Resistance wasn't feasible, no matter what Fiadh had told me about throwing off thrall. Resistance also wasn't logical—this was why we'd come. I'd just hoped to get the hell out of here under the guise of delivering the message myself. I needed to find Fiadh.

"Let me fetch paper."

She rose, giving me the chance to observe the way she moved: graceful as a martial artist, her balance perfect, her form radiating readiness even as her eyelids hooded laconically. A desk, neoclassical in its design, yielded up a pad of yellow legal paper from a drawer.

I stared at the anachronism. A vampire, clutching a legal pad. She handed it over with an imperious tilt of her wrist. I accepted the paper and the fountain pen that followed. The pen felt cool to the touch, and had been carved from a white material that felt like ivory. I recalled the furniture in Agatha's basement and tried not to think about bones.

"What do you want to say?" I asked, testing the nib. Black ink. Not red.

She considered this for a long time. I waited, listening to the sound of my breathing and noticing that she, too, breathed, her chest rising. Vampire biology wasn't important right now. I'd ask Fiadh later.

"It's been a millennium, has it not?" Natek frowned as she spoke. "What does one say after a millennium?"

"You could say that," I suggested, not daring to meet her eyes. "Something like, 'I don't know what to say to you, after these lost centuries of time.'"

209

"Poetic," said Natek. "Fitting. Yes, we shall start there."

I copied down the words in English, planning to make the translation once we'd finished the draft, and glanced up. Her eyes looked past me without seeing. I waited again. When nothing else appeared forthcoming, I experimented with clearing my throat. Silence.

"Maybe mention the rose?" I said.

"Yes."

More of that dreadful silence. Perhaps time passed differently for her kind.

"Um, 'Your rose has kept me company,' maybe?"

"No. 'Your rose lives, while all others burn to ash.'"

I copied this down, too, morbid though it was. She continued.

"And end . . . end with, 'I've kept your translator for insurance, lest your anger still burns hot. Meet me at . . .'" This pause felt more potent than the others. At last, she gave me an address. I wrote it down, then examined the letter we'd drafted.

> Dearest Gata,
>
> I don't know what to say to you after these lost centuries of time. Your rose lives, while all others burn to ash. Come to me. I've kept your translator for insurance, lest your anger still burn hot.
>
> Yours,
>
> Natek

"I did not say 'Dearest,'" said the vampire.

"It is the form you used in your letters, at first. She's been reading my translations. Shouldn't this . . ." I trailed off before I dared to suggest to Natek that I might better know how to write a letter than she.

"Adjust my words as you see fit. As I've said, it's been some time."

I squinted in the dim light at my shaky writing. Something about the words rang false. Thinking was difficult under the current circumstances, but I summoned up the single-minded focus I'd relied on as a student during exam time, when each moment was precious, no matter how loud or distracting the background noise.

Dearest Gata,

I don't know what to say to you after these lost centuries of time. Your rose lives, while all others burn to ash. Come to me. I have your translator—I offered you poets and sculptors, once. Shall we drink her words together?

Yours still,

Natek

Joking about my own consumption brought the taste of bile to the back of my throat, but the words had come to me with the certainty I'd learned to recognize as insight. I scrawled the address of the estate beneath the place Natek would sign.

"Show me."

I offered up the pad. Her eyes skimmed the page faster than even the most prodigious human reader, and she nodded.

"I'll need to make the translation. And if you'd like to copy it out—"

"You will make the copies."

Almost, I asked for nicer paper. The idea of resuming the correspondence I'd spent months laboring to understand on a *legal pad* left me feeling like I was helping Natek commit a sacrilege of sorts, but perhaps the medium had never mattered to them. I clenched my teeth against the injustice, and then, because I was a fool a thousand times over, said, "Do you by chance have any stationery?"

Natek stared. "Stationery?"

"Something nicer to write on. To show your regard."

"Paper. To show my regard." She huffed. "Paper is transient. Paper is the pulp of dead forests. Paper—" She cut herself off with a slash of one hand. "I will have finer paper sent to you here, along with food and water. Will you need anything else?"

"Fiadh," I said at once.

She left without acknowledging my request, shutting the door behind her. I listened for the turn of a lock. Nothing. I could run—

Unbidden, I imagined how my corpse might look, drained as white and bloodless as the snow. No. I would not run, not while cooperating still seemed like the more viable of the two options. With luck, I might survive long enough in the cold without a coat to come across another car or house, but the odds were much better that Natek would hunt me down first, or that I might freeze to death in the mountains.

Though Fiadh had escaped. I chewed on the hard end of the pen before remembering it might be human bone. Fiadh understood vampires. She would have known how—and where—to hide. The shadows of the small sitting room mocked me as they flickered in the friendly firelight.

How long would it take Fiadh to get help? How much time had elapsed? My phone had been taken from my pocket, and there was no way to know how long I'd been asleep. They could be on their way back even now. Or Natek could be lying, and Fiadh remained locked away somewhere else on the estate. But that didn't track with what I knew about Natek. She wouldn't want to damage something that belonged to Gata, and Fiadh had said she bore Agatha's mark.

My spiraling thoughts were interrupted by a knock on the door, then the faint creak of its hinges as Bran slid into the room. His eyes flashed that fey gold again as the light hit them, almost like a wild animal's, and another conclusion clicked into place: Bran wasn't human. Or at least, I couldn't be entirely sure he was human, and the hazy memory of my previous interaction with him couldn't be trusted.

"Paper, water, and food," he said, approaching cautiously.

I realized I'd scrambled as far away from him as the couch allowed, and made myself sit still.

"I'm not hungry."

He set the brown cloth bag down on the nearest side table and plucked a sheaf of cream-colored stationery from beneath his arm. This I snatched, crinkling a corner. One of the pages fluttered to the ground and landed half beneath the couch. I left it there.

"You should eat, or at least drink," he said in his calm voice.

"So you can drug me again?"

He gave a small shrug and said, his tone almost apologetic, "I can drug you at any time, Clara. Food will give you strength, and you are thirsty."

I was thirsty. Terribly thirsty, in fact, and my mouth tasted acrid with fear, but I wouldn't admit it to him.

"What are you?"

"Always so polite, your kind." The apologetic note left his voice. "I am someone to whom your continued survival is immaterial. I can be kind to you, or I can be cruel. The choice is yours."

My momentary defiance wilted. "If I take—" I waved at the sack of food and water. "—will I be back in the forest?"

"Would you like to be?" He tilted his head in that way of his, more bird than man, and the question seemed genuine.

I almost said yes. I'd felt safe in the forest, and I wanted to feel safe again even more than I wanted water or Fiadh.

"I have to translate this for Natek."

His brows creased, the skin velvety where they met. After a pause, he said, "You'd best focus, then."

"What do you mean you can drug me at any time?"

He held his hand out to the nearest lamp, palm down. I blinked, thinking the light had dazzled my eyes as dust motes swirled in the beam of lamplight. The dust intensified. There had been dust in the greenhouse, I remembered now. Gold and glittering. Almost like . . . spores.

Fungal lichenization, Fiadh had said of the fey. A hundred stories full of warnings not to eat or drink in fairyland shrieked their messages too late.

"I cannot touch food or drink without leaving trace, not without extreme precaution. A precaution," he added, correctly interpreting my jerk, "I did not take with you. It will be a very small dose. You won't notice."

And you won't ever find your way home again, warned the fairy tales. That, however, had been true since I had set foot inside Agatha's estate. I just hadn't heard the door shut behind me.

"Where is Fiadh?" I asked instead of continuing this vein of conversation.

"Your friend has a higher tolerance than you do."

A non-answer. "But where is she?"

He shrugged and tapped the sack. "Really, you should at least drink."

"Wait," I called after him as he turned to leave.

The look he tossed over his shoulder was the sympathy the shepherd gives the lamb, caring even as he lifts the knife. He waited until it became clear I had no words to follow my plea, then left me to my drugged food and crumpled paper.

213

The antique neoclassical writing desk from which Natek had retrieved the legal pad occupied one of the walls. I settled into the equally antique chair and got to work.

—⁓— —⁓— —⁓—

Natek returned too soon. I'd finished the translation, but I wasn't ready for my heart to once more palpitate with panic. She swept in with those Antarctic eyes fixed on the letter in my hand, stopping close enough for me to smell the coppery scent clinging to her skin. Blood, I realized. I didn't know if I'd missed that smell before or if she'd fed while she was away.

"May I leave now?" I asked, knowing it was futile.

Natek touched my cheek with a warm hand. Her skin wasn't as pale as it had been previously, either. *Fiadh's blood?* No. She wouldn't. Natek wouldn't, and I had to believe that for now if I had any hope of staying sane.

"I think you know the answer to that, little one."

I did.

"With luck, we'll receive a reply before nightfall tomorrow."

Her hand dropped, but I remained frozen, too petrified to move. Her presence flooded my nostrils with terror. In letters, Natek was wry, occasionally passionate, and nothing like this creature. I much preferred the former.

I watched as she signed her name, shaping the letters in Nektopolian script as if the motion cramped her hand, and then she left me alone with the legal pad and the first draft of our missive. I stared at the imprint of her fading signature on the yellow lines, where she'd pressed hard into the stationary. It matched the handwriting from the correspondence, though it was clear that hand had been filtered by the years.

Natek and Gata, soon to be reunited at last. I should have felt relieved. I could claim credit, and . . . Dread warred with exhaustion. This wasn't at all how I'd pictured things playing out. I forced myself to stand and explore a closed door on the far side of the room, hoping it was a bathroom. In this, at least, I was lucky.

When I'd finished venting my fear into the sewer, I added more logs to the fire, curled up on the couch beneath a wool blanket, and emptied one of the two water canteens provided. Tears arrived soon after, as if all they'd needed to start was lubrication. I sobbed with fear and nerves and the uncertainty of my continued survival, wiping at my cheeks with the scratchy weave of the blanket until they stung and my abdominals ached with effort.

"Come back for me," I whispered into my hands.

I'd wasted so much time on fear, not fully understanding what fear was. Now, as a captive, I saw that I'd held Fiadh at arm's length when I could have held her close. Screw slowing things down. Feeling exceptionally sorry for myself, I cried some more.

Eventually, wrung out and sniffling, hunger claimed me, and I remembered the brown sack had also contained a sandwich. I fished it out and examined it more closely: some sort of thinly sliced mushrooms on rustic bread, along with greenhouse-grown tomatoes and arugula, doused in a mustard sauce. It smelled incredible, and if the mushrooms were a little too on the nose, I was too bitter to care. I licked the parchment paper wrapping it when I'd finished.

Satiated, I tucked the blanket up to my chin and let my eyes glaze as I watched the flames.

Sunlight filtered through the curtains when I woke. Daylight. The implications brought me awake faster than espresso. In daylight, I was safe from vampires. I grabbed the blanket for warmth and stumbled toward the door, glad I'd fallen asleep with my shoes on and forgetting I'd decided to cooperate, and turned the handle. It opened easily. Beyond, the hallway, with its paintings and vases and pleasant floral carpet, carried no menace.

I'd taken three steps toward what I guessed was the outer door before the buzzing started. There was no gradual rise, rather the angry, instantaneous rage of a kicked hornet's nest, or a disturbed hive of ground wasps. A sawing, vicious sound that promised pain. Instinct got me back inside the room in time to shut the door right before a wall of black and gold bodies swarmed me, and I shoved the blanket into the crevice at the bottom. A few exoskeletons crunched beneath my fingers, and one stung me through the cloth. I scrambled away from the door in case any found their way in around the frame, fumbling for the legal pad and swinging it at the solitary wasp who managed to infiltrate my defenses. Its body fell to the floor long enough for me to stomp it into goo.

I locked myself in the bathroom in case more got through, jamming the cracks around the door frame full of paper towel while I hyperventilated. I'd never liked wasps. Bees at least sacrificed themselves for the hive, dying after delivering their sting. Wasps and their ilk could sting again and again, and as a child, I'd made the unpleasant discovery that they could also *bite*. Dying by exsanguination was far preferable.

My breathing filled the tiled bathroom with ragged echoes. I perched on the toilet, pad clutched before me as a shield, and waited for the hellish boil of insects to die down outside. The buzzing faded gradually, periodically rising in bursts as if they had zoomed back to verify I hadn't attempted another escape.

Fat chance. I wasn't ever leaving this bathroom again. Fey, vampires . . . did there have to also be wasps?

I turned on the tap and splashed cold water on my face to dispel the dried sweat of fear. My reflection gazed back, wild-eyed and stupid, so *fucking stupid* for thinking she could just hop in a car and track down a vampire without consequences.

Someone knocked. I ducked behind the toilet before realizing how feeble a hiding spot it proved.

"Clara?"

Bran. I abandoned my hiding spot and opened the door a crack, just in case the wasps had accompanied him. A few wads of paper towel fell around me.

"It's okay," he said. "I've brought you breakfast."

"Are the bees still there?"

"They won't bother you."

"Not what I asked."

"There are no bees in this room."

"Or wasps? Or yellow jackets, or hornets, or anything that might be semantically similar to them?"

Bran laughed his disarming, musical laugh. "There is nothing in this room that can sting you."

"How can I trust you?" I asked, crossing my arms over my chest and scanning the air around him through the crevice.

"I don't lie."

"I've read enough fairy tales to know your people have a loose relationship with truth." The handle of the door creaked under my grip.

"And yours have a loose relationship with birth control. Come out and have some breakfast since I see you ate dinner. There's coffee, too."

I opened the door a little wider, prepared to slam it at the first hint of buzzing. Bran stood there holding a mug before him like an

216

offering. My shoulders slumped in relief. I decided not to dwell on how quickly he'd just gone from "mushroom monster" to "not a wasp" in my mind.

"Thank you," I said, accepting the coffee.

"As I told you—I can be cruel or kind. The choice is entirely yours."

Too shaken by the wasps to be wary of him, I sat back down on the couch and opened the breakfast parcel: a fat blueberry-studded muffin and an apple. The muffin was still warm. I bit into it, expecting him to leave as quickly as he had the evening before, but he lingered, studying me.

"Any sign of my friend?" I asked him.

"No. Which is . . . unusual."

"Why?"

"She inhaled me. I should be able to track her, once I've spread."

The tart flavor of the hot blueberries soured in my mouth. I didn't like the way that sounded at all. "What do you mean by 'spread'?"

"A temporary mycelial matrix. It isn't permanent in most cases—you needn't worry."

"So why can't you track her?" I asked, refusing to analyze *in most cases*. Bran wasn't a vampire. In the scheme of things, he was safer to be around, but that was only relative. He was still dangerous, and, it occurred to me, the comparative ease I felt around him could be the result of those goddamn spores. I'd read somewhere once that there could be up to ten thousand fungal spores in each cubic meter of air.

"Nature is fickle. Not every seed sprouts. But I wouldn't recommend you try leaving this room again without an escort."

I shuddered, my skin crawling as I recalled that boiling mass of winged black. "You don't need to worry."

He gave me that warm, reassuring smile. "I am not worried. If you die, I will make compost from your body. You won't be wasted."

I laughed; it carried a manic edge. Bran recoiled slightly. Perhaps he wasn't used to hysteria. Were the fey ever hysterical? I wondered how much of his human side remained. Fiadh had explained the process of lichenization, but not much about the end result. Another giggle escaped. I clamped my jaw shut on the sound, resulting in a choking snort. I felt like a piece of cheap furniture, bound to come apart at the joints at the first sign of strain. I couldn't handle this. I had to handle this.

"Is that what is in your special compost?" I asked when I was

217

coherent. I needed to keep him talking, in case he mentioned anything that might help me get out of here alive. "Natek's leftovers?"

"Occasionally." This fact didn't seem to bother him, judging by his nonchalance. I decided to change tactics, and the subject.

"When I was . . . well, you know. Were those trees real?"

At the mention of trees, his expression flickered. "Why so curious, Clara?"

The golden light of that forest flooded me in memory. I answered truthfully. "It was beautiful."

The expression on his face now was entirely familiar. His grief cut me in its suddenness. Natek had been human once. Had Bran?

"They are beautiful," he agreed.

"Were they real?"

"They were, they are, and they will be again." The phrase had the rote quality of prayer. His attention slid from me to the door, and this time, when I called out for him to wait, I had words to follow. *Keep him talking, Clara,* I told myself. It was the only defense I had.

"Is that why you work with vampires?"

His eyes narrowed, losing some of their warmth as they flashed that feral gold. "Elaborate."

"I was just thinking that you both live a long time, and together you could, I don't know, buy up land or something. For . . . trees."

I realized I'd made a mistake when his face shuttered and he took a step toward the door. "The wasps are but one of several preventive measures around the estate. We do not, as a rule, allow humans about unescorted."

Watching him go, I felt the sting of missed connection, and something almost like rejection. Stockholm syndrome had apparently set in quickly.

The day passed. I slept some more, lassitude taking the place of fear, though I dreamt of swarms of insects and golden light, and woke to move aimlessly about the room. I counted the squares in the carpet. I opened drawers. Nothing of use presented itself to me, and the activity didn't take my mind off my predicament. Natek might dispose of me once I'd served my purpose. I couldn't rely on my usefulness to Agatha to keep me alive, and what if Agatha didn't respond? Better not to be here if that happened. One of the windows overlooked a narrow ledge that couldn't possibly support a human's weight. I examined it anyway, trying to convince myself that with the right distribution of mass I could inch my way along the brick façade to the nearest slope of roof. And then what? Jump? The ground lay several stories below. I abandoned that avenue of possible escape. The only other exit lay through the door I'd tried already.

There was no version of escape where I lived. Better to lie on the couch and trace the cracks in the ancient plaster ceiling. I'd felt this lassitude in hospital waiting rooms, one of the few places where the illusion of control could be entirely stripped away in a socially acceptable manner. In the face of helplessness, my body slid into a dazed state somewhere between wakefulness and dreaming. I wondered, fuzzily, if I was still drugged, but didn't see a way to do anything about it.

The sound of a meow roused me from one such interval. I pushed back the blanket and craned my head over the back of the couch to see the window, convinced I'd misheard.

A pair of black ears just barely crested the windowsill. I hadn't misheard—a fucking cat was balanced on the ledge I'd stared at mere hours before, teetering over open air. I leapt to my feet, kicking off the blanket, and fumbled at the window latch. It gave with a groan. A blast of frigid air blew into the room, along with a massive housecat. I shut the window before anything thought I was trying to "go about unescorted" and turned to appraise my unexpected companion. The cat crouched on the carpet, fur ruffled and green eyes large in its wide face. A white spot on its chest was the only deviation from the rich black of its fur, though a few dead leaves clung to its ruff from the gutter, and judging by the way it crouched in displeasure, the climb hadn't been pleasant.

"Hey, pretty kitty," I said in my best cat-lady voice. "What are you doing so high up?"

The cat blinked its green eyes in response.

"This isn't a good place for cats," I continued, holding out my hand. "Everything here wants to eat things like us."

Slowly, the cat stalked forward to sniff my outstretched hand. Its whiskers brushed my fingers, reminding me of my own cat, who was no doubt getting lonely in my absence despite Mark. Tears burned my eyes, and I blinked them away. Muffin would be okay. Even if something happened to me, he'd be okay.

"I have a pretty kitty like you," I said to the cat before me. "A little smaller, and not quite so brave."

The cat blinked again. Carefully, I stroked the large head, scratching beneath the chin when the cat leaned into my touch. I wanted to hug the animal to me for creature comfort, but knew from experience that most animals found the gesture claustrophobic from strangers—and occasionally their own people.

"Clara," meowed the cat.

I twitched. My mind fumbled for an explanation, and I decided I'd misheard. The cat had simply meowed and I was exhausted and high on fungi. *Fung-hi.* I filed the pun away for later, staring at my guest. Cats couldn't speak. This was simply fact.

Except it wasn't entirely a cat anymore: fur retracted, the follicles slurping the black strands back beneath pale skin. The toes spidered into fingers. The skull expanded, and for a deeply traumatizing moment, I thought the eyes might pop out as the planes of the zygomatic bones adjusted the shape of the sockets. They didn't. Instead, the skull rounded, and the hair that had receded elsewhere grew in a black torrent to hang around the creature's face. I scuttled backward on my rear. The feline spine arched and elongated with a series of horrible cracks, the thigh bones stretched like taffy, and smooth, hairless skin cupped the delicate sweep of ribs.

A woman crouched naked before me, leaves in her black hair, and her green eyes wild with worry.

"Fi?" I sputtered the single syllable of her name into the space between us.

"You're alive," she said, throwing herself into my lap and knocking me off balance. We landed on the rug. I smelled snow in her hair, and dirt, and the unmistakable musk of leaves. I rubbed my hands over her freezing skin while my brain tried to process what had just taken place.

"You're naked," I said when I was sure I could form the words. She raised her head from my shoulder. Scratches marred one cheek. I touched a finger gently to the fresh scabs. Thorns? Claws? "Let me get you a blanket."

She refused to let go of me, so I stood, lifting her, and wrapped the woolen blanket around her shoulders, wondering if the salt from my dried tears would rub off on her skin. This small act of caretaking grounded me in preparation for what had to come next.

"Also," I continued, feeling hysteria bubbling back up, "what the actual *fuck* was that?"

"We don't have time for me to explain right now. I have to get you out of here." She released me and began pulling me toward the door. I grabbed her wrist before she could touch the doorknob.

"We can't go that way. It's trapped to hell and back by killer wasps."

"Wasps—what are you talking about?"

I explained about the wasps, and about what Bran had said about the rest of the estate.

"Bran." She hissed his name, very much like the cat I'd mistaken her for a moment ago. An exciting possibility occurred to me: surely it was just the mushroom spore in the food making me see things. Fiadh had never been a cat. "I should have known the minute we went into his house, but I was so—"

"Fiadh," I said, pulling her farther away from the door and its wrathful guardians, "I need you to explain to me how you got in here, and I need you to do it now, using small words, because I've had a bit of a day."

She bit her lip and looked away from me, and it registered, as it did occasionally, just how much smaller she was than I. Small enough to carry easily. Small enough, maybe, to balance on that ledge, though why she'd chosen to do it naked I'd worry about later. I'd imagined the cat. Now, I tried to imagine the wind plucking at her as she climbed, threatening to toss her to her death with every gust or slip of frozen hand. A nearly suicidal venture.

"You came back for me," I said, momentarily forgetting about the nightmarish cracking of spine I'd hallucinated.

"I never left you." Her glare warmed me more than the fire. "Did you—Clara Eden, how *dare* you."

"I thought maybe you'd gone for help—"

"And leave you behind? Would you have left me?"

"I—"

"I know I haven't earned your highest esteem, but I'd thought—"

"Who even *says* things like that?" I interrupted. "*Highest esteem.*"

"People who hang around immortals. Don't interrupt me while I'm yelling at you." Despite her words, neither of us had raised our voices higher than a loud whisper.

"Please. Lecture on."

She'd come back for me.

"And wipe that grin off your face. This is hardly the time—"

I took her face between my hands and kissed her. She made a squeak of enraged protest before melting into me. Her lips were cold and chapped, and I kissed warmth back into them as best I could. She pulled away too soon, wearing a somber expression. The relief of reunion faded.

"I have to get you out of here."

"It's impossible. But Natek sent Agatha a letter—" I broke off at the pure horror on her face. "What?"

"This isn't Natek."

"But—"

And then I remembered where I'd seen our captor's handwriting before. It *had* been in the correspondence I'd translated, but not in Natek's letters. In fact, I'd only seen it in two letters, but I'd devoted an inordinate amount of time to the second's translation. *The forests of my victory.*

"Oh my god," I said, terror reclaiming its stranglehold on my throat. "Fi, it's Vezina."

CHAPTER TEN
Time Doesn't Heal All Wounds

Collection: Nektopolis
Title: Letter 40
Description: Correspondence; Cynane and Natek
Date: TBD
Cataloguer: Clara Eden

Cynane, writing to her blood Sister Nektaria,[31]

I've bade this messenger find you even if it takes him the rest of his life, a life that will be shorter if he fails. Do what you will with him.

Your defection has broken our eldest Sister's heart, and mine. Will you not even tell us why? She does not sleep. She paces all throughout the daylight hours, and I cannot soothe her, and neither can our other Sisters. None of us have ever seen her so distraught. I know she'd bargain with you, were you to extend the olive branch.

At least promise you will write. I cannot bear the thought you'll never ride with me again. You gave

---

31   Translator's note: Miscellaneous correspondence???

me my name when my first ceased to fit. Do you not remember? You said it would mark us kin for always, because she'd been like a Sister to you, too, and she had given you your name[32] when Alexander made you a general. Did you intend always to end so soon? At least draw up a truce with her over whatever quarrel has divided you so that I might see you again. I miss you. There is only so much reading a body can do to distract oneself from such an absence.

Your Sister,
Cynane

I stood, lifting a couch cushion and staring at the cavity beneath. Springs. No room for a person, even a small person, to hide. I moved next to the bathroom.

"What are you doing?" Fi asked.

"Looking for a place for you to hide in case they come back."

"That's not important—"

"It's important to me. Can you fit in here?"

She followed me into the bathroom and peered into the linen cupboard. The upper shelves were all full of towels, but when I moved a stack, I discovered a reasonable amount of space. She could cram into any of them with my help, and with some rearranging, could even hide behind a narrow stack of towels.

"Yes. I can fit. Now I need you to tell me exactly what you said in your letter to Agatha."

"The rough draft is on that pad of paper on the desk." I adjusted the towels for easy concealment, then motioned for her to join me with the paper in the bathroom and locked the door. I turned on the sink for good measure. It would make it hard for me to hear someone entering the outer room, but I doubted I would be able to hear Bran anyway, and the water might at least drown out our voices.

"Shit," Fiadh said when she'd finished reading.

---

32 Translator's note: It occurs to me, and I have confirmed this through research, that the proto-Indo-European root *nek* means "night" as well as "death."

"Yeah."

"It's a trap."

"I know. Now. I know that now." I scrubbed my face with the heels of my palms. Of course it was a trap. The whole setup had been a trap, and I'd fallen right into it. The Natek I'd come to know through letters would never have let me write a letter for her. I should have known. I should have at least *questioned*—

"Stop," said Fiadh.

"Stop what?"

"Blaming yourself. I can tell you're doing it, and we don't have time. She's a powerful vampire, and you're a human. She would have compelled you if you hadn't cooperated. It's even possible she did, and you didn't know. When we practiced breaking thrall, I didn't have someone like *her* in mind."

"But—"

"What's done is done. We have to stop Agatha from coming here."

"She'll write back, won't she, before she comes?"

"I don't know. She might. But I'm missing, and she'll come for me if nothing else."

"Are you sure? You're merely another human, too."

I regretted the words the minute they left my tongue. Silence fell between us, as tight and hot as a boil.

"Clara," she began.

I held up a hand to stop her. "Don't. I can't. I take back what I said earlier. I don't want to know. I need you to be *normal*."

She recoiled as if I'd punched her in the throat.

"I didn't mean—" But I had meant it, and we both knew it. "Fi."

"I'm not normal."

"I meant I'm overwhelmed—"

"Why do you think I haven't told you? Why do you think I've never let you meet my mother, or called you out on your frankly xenophobic comments, or, or—"

"Fi, please, just let me—"

"There's never going to be a good time. You know that, right? You're never going to be ready to hear this, or want to hear this, because I'm a fucking freak to you, and I'm an idiot for thinking this could end any other way."

"You're not a freak."

"*I* know that."

225

"I do too." I clasped her hands between mine and held on tightly. "And I'm sorry for the things I've said. I'm sorry I'm an idiot and that we're going to die. You should have left me and gotten the hell out of here."

"Shut up. We're not dying, and your self-pity is repulsive." She scowled even as her hands clung to mine. "We need a plan."

"Could we go out the way you came in?" I asked.

"You'll fall. I barely made it. I searched every window I could reach looking for you, and this one is particularly poorly situated."

"We could make a rope out of towels," I said, hope sparking in my chest. "And rappel down."

"That's actually brilliant." She assessed the towels, and I saw her counting under her breath. "We could tear them in half to make more lengths."

"You need shoes."

"I'll wrap my feet in a towel once we're down," she said, dismissing my concern. "And I know where I left my shoes."

"Why did you take them off?"

"Start getting the towels down. You're taller."

I obeyed, letting the evasion slide. If we survived this, I'd find the strength to ask her what she was without hurting her with my response. Until then, she was probably right—there wasn't time for her to explain. The image of her spine lengthening would haunt me, whether it was real or not, and I was going to hold on to my fung-hi theory until we were out of here.

Tearing the towels wasn't easy. They were newer than the furniture, and still retained the strength of the fiber. Fi huffed with frustration as she strained to make headway against the hem.

"Isn't there anything sharp in here?" she asked.

There wasn't. I'd looked. Fi scanned the bathroom with quick, darting eyes.

"A screw. We need a screw to unpick the hemline."

I tackled the nearest cabinet with a fingernail until I'd loosened a screw from the hinge. Fiadh shredded her hem with surprising speed, then passed the towel to me to tear before moving on to the next. Desperation lent me the strength to rip the cotton down the center. Vezina or Bran could return at any moment, and that knowledge eclipsed the burning in my hands.

Our rope was an ugly, mangled line of white and blue, secured with knots I hoped would hold. We bound one end to the couch, moving the bulky piece of furniture against the window as quietly as possible, and let the other end drop. It fell short of the ground, as we'd known it would—from our vantage point several stories up, it wasn't possible to tell by exactly how much. It would have to be enough.

"I'll go first," said Fi. "I'm lighter, and if the rope doesn't hold me, it won't hold you."

"Then—"

"And it will be easier for you to haul me back up than for me to lift you. Try to place your feet where I do. I'll pause at that ledge halfway down, then you follow."

Clothed only in the blanket, which she'd knotted over one shoulder, she crawled onto the window ledge and dropped out of my sight. I leaned out to follow her progress. My head spun at the sheerness of the fall. But the alternative was someone even other vampires feared, so when Fiadh reached the halfway point I scooted out on the sill and turned, facing the wall, and clutched the towels until my knuckles bleached in the pale light of the overcast day. The brick was old and dark with age, more brown than red, and the toes of my boots jammed in the cracks between them as I took my first step. *Breathe*, I told myself. All I had to do was keep breathing.

One step at a time. One arm at a time. Pass one hand under the other. Don't look down.

"Clara!"

Fiadh's shout broke my concentration. I looked down to where she stood, her face contorted with fear. At first, I didn't understand the cause of her concern. Then I saw the ivy.

Winter should have frozen its growth. This ivy, however, sped toward me, unfurling leaves and tendrils as it roared up the walls in a tangle of dark green. It parted around Fiadh like a tide. When it reached me, however, the stems twined around my limbs, binding me to the wall before I could react. Brick scraped my skin. A vine snaked across my stomach. Another plunged into my hair.

I hadn't realized I was screaming until Fiadh placed her hand over my mouth, her lips making words I couldn't hear over my voice.

"—I've got you," she was saying. She clawed at the vines, but as fast as she tore at them, more grew, and I smelled a sharp, fungal odor each time a stem snapped. Biting pains pricked my skin. My head had been bound to one side, one eye blocked by a pointed leaf, but I could

227

see my right arm. Blood trickled down that wrist. The pain intensified. Something *moved* beneath a burgeoning bruise.

"Fi," I screamed, flailing against my bonds. "It's—it's digging into me."

She'd wrapped the towel rope around her waist and was using both hands to try to free me, but she paused at my scream and tugged on the vine burrowing into my arm. Elsewhere, vines slid under my clothes and dove into me like I was water. Lights flickered in the corners of my eyes as the pain seared, and my screams intensified until I could barely distinguish any other sounds. It hurt. It hurt so fucking much. I was going to die on this wall with ivy growing through my organs, and there was nothing either of us could do to stop it. Fiadh repeated my name over and over, tears streaking her face as she tried to free me with increasing desperation.

"What did I tell you about trying to leave the room?" said a voice from far below in the break between one scream and another. I couldn't look down, but I knew it was Bran.

"Make it stop," Fiadh shouted. "Make it stop hurting her."

"The more you fight, the more it fights back."

Fiadh ceased her frantic scrabbling. The pain eased very slightly. I hung, panting with agony, and wished the vines would let me fall to my death.

"Stay there," Bran said. "I'll be right up."

"I'm so sorry, Clara," Fiadh said as she pressed herself against me. Vines shifted between us.

"Run," I managed to get out between gasps.

"No."

The pain was an obliteration. I wanted to argue. I wanted to tell her to save herself, to run and hide until another chance came to rescue me, to go to Agatha, but I couldn't speak. She kissed the parts of my face not covered by insidious growth and repeated my name. Briefly, blissfully, I blacked out.

"Grab hold of her," Bran said an eternity later, this time from the window we'd left open. Fiadh gripped me as best she could. With a ripple, the vines retracted, tendrils reversing their journey into my body with a sickening wriggle. It hurt less than when Fiadh had tugged, but only marginally. Consciousness flickered again. I felt Fiadh secure the towel around me, and felt the strain on the cloth as I was lifted, but it was as if I watched Bran lift my body through the window and onto the couch, punctured in a thousand places and white with shock, while I hovered on the wind. The slam of the window brought me back to myself.

"—sick bastard." Fiadh crouched over me, feral in her blanket dress, her hair snarled by vines and sap, and cursed Bran out in a voice that was more hiss and growl than her usual crisp annunciation.

"I did warn her," said Bran. "Which begs the question: what, exactly, are you?"

"The last thing you're going to see, you—"

"Calm yourself."

She spat at him. Actually *spat* at him. Fiadh. Prim, neat, precise Fiadh. He wiped her spit from his face with the back of his hand and—licked it. I gagged. His eyes flashed golden as he stilled.

"Cat Síth," he said, working his mouth as if savoring the taste. "Which of your nine lives did you use to escape me?"

She flung herself at him. He stopped her with a hand to her chest, but she got a few scratches in.

"Fi," I said, struggling to sit up. "Stop."

"Listen to your friend, kitten."

Fiadh took a step away from him and curled back around me, shaking with rage.

"I'm okay," I told her. I wasn't, but I was afraid of what he might do to her.

"Clara," said Bran, crouching down to bring his face to the level of mine. "That was exceptionally foolish."

"I had to try."

He smiled, almost sadly. "I suppose you did. I hope you've finished satisfying your curiosity."

"Yes."

"Get it out of her," said Fiadh. "All of your poison."

"Her wounds won't become infected. As for the rest, it will work its way out over time."

"As if I can trust the word of a fey who serves one of the blood."

His eyes narrowed to golden slits. "I do not serve."

Fiadh laughed. The sound was cold and mocking. "Neither do I then."

"Fi." They both ignored me, glaring at each other. "*Fi.* It doesn't matter."

The defeat in my voice softened her posture. She stroked my hair. Her next words were calm, but no less vicious. "Agatha will burn what's left of your forest and pour salt on your barrows."

"Perhaps."

"Or you could help us, and—"

"Do not make empty promises. Will you stay here, or must I bind you? I'm sure I can find a collar to fit."

I braced myself for another uncharacteristic outburst. Fiadh merely said, albeit with a tight jaw, "I will stay."

"If you run again . . ." He trailed off, but his eyes fell on me, and I read the unspoken threat.

I can be kind or cruel. The choice is yours.

— — —

Fiadh sponged my wounds with one of the washcloths we hadn't shredded for our rope. Her touch was gentle, but the warm water and soap stung, and the memory of watching—*feeling*—the plant growing into my skin was worse than both.

"You should have run," I said.

"Lift your arm."

I obeyed, and she tended to whatever was making my armpit ache with a grim expression.

"Why does Vezina even still care about Gata?"

"You should rest while you can," she said.

"I'd rather talk. It's distracting me."

"And I need to concentrate so that I don't hurt you."

"Please, Fi."

She shot me a quelling look, but relented. "I know a little."

"More than in the letters?"

She nodded and tugged at something. I swallowed a gag at the pain.

"Their feud shaped Agatha's life in some ways. And I think it shaped Vezina's, too. Opposite forces. Hold really still for a second." I did, and regretted it. "Some types of hatred fade with time. Others grow."

"I wish we'd figured out more about who Vezina was before we got in the car," I said.

"I don't. I've seen—Agatha's shared a little with me. Nothing that would have helped us, or I would have told you. Vezina's history is dark, and it is harder to forget the darkness than the light." She rinsed my blood from the cloth and applied more soap.

"You should clean your hands," I said. Fiadh's hands were sliced and scratched from the climb and the vines, and some of the wounds looked deep.

"I will take care of my hands after I've finished with you." The warm cloth returned to tenderly dabbing my skin.

"I hate that I'm going to die with unanswered questions. Do you know how frustrating that is?"

"You're not going to die, Clara."

"I don't see Vezina keeping us around. You've seen the way she treats her human guests."

Fiadh paused in her ministrations and settled on the edge of the tub, her brows contracting in concentration.

"What I don't understand is Bran," she said. "I wouldn't have thought someone like Vezina would work with them, or, more precisely, I can't see any of the fey wanting to work with someone like her."

"Why wouldn't they work with her?"

"They usually have different priorities. The fungal half only needs the human half for any fey to manifest, after which they tend to ignore human society except when they need to intervene to protect their host trees, and vampires need humans for food and are therefore invested in our daily lives, but less so in our overall welfare. Counterintuitive, I know, since we're a food source, but they promote population growth, which has come at the expense of the environment. Some, like Agatha, recognize that destabilizing the environment is now putting the food chain at risk, but most don't care."

"Why do the Cat Síth work with vampires, then?"

She jerked her gaze back to mine. "If we get out of here alive, I'll tell you."

"I just told you how I feel about dying with unanswered questions."

"Then live."

"Okay, then what are the usual motivations for interspecies partnerships?" I asked.

"Protection, usually. Mutually beneficial relationships. Agatha protects my family, and we protect her, for instance, which is the short answer to your question."

"What about the fey? Do they work with anyone?"

"They're . . . hard to understand, and there are different branches and species within the fey, depending on what animal the fungus binds

231

with. Usually they work with other fey species. That's why Bran doesn't make sense. He's working *for* her. You saw the way he reacted when I suggested it."

Suggested was a mild word for how she'd phrased it, but I let it pass.

"Do you think we can use that?" I asked.

She rinsed the cloth again and tended to my other leg. "It's all we have so far."

We lapsed into silence. My skin throbbed from its myriad punctures, and I sank into the comfort of the distraction that pain offered. Natek probably wasn't even alive. Everything had been for nothing, and now we'd die. What I'd give for a boring, soul-sucking day of adjunct work now.

Not much, said a small part of my frazzled brain. I ignored it.

"Why couldn't he bind you with his creepy mushroom dust?" I asked eventually. "That doesn't make sense either."

"You should rest."

"Fi," I began, reaching out to touch her face. Her expression tightened as she prepared to deflect again, but all I said was, "Thank you for coming back for me."

She kissed my palm in answer. "Sleep. I'm going to look around the room."

—⚡— —⚡— —⚡—

"Clara."

I jolted out of a doze to find Fiadh crouched beside me, clutching several faded envelopes.

"What—"

"Read them."

Sitting up, I carefully withdrew a letter. It was written in English, and I recognized the slant of the handwriting as Natek's, in case the signature wasn't clue enough.

Collection: Nektopolis
Title: Letter 41
Description: Correspondence; Cynane and Natek
Date: 10/14/1996
Cataloguer: Clara Eden

October 14, 1996

Sweet Cynane,

Of course you may complain to me if it helps prevent rash action. You know I am a vault. What goes in does not come out. (Yes, I did set you up for a joke, there. You're welcome.)

More seriously, you can't make the science happen. Each failure brings you closer. You didn't tell me what the project was, so I can't offer you concrete advice—nor would I insult you in that way, since you are the expert, Doctor. All I can do is remind you that you've been here before, and each time you crack the (genetic?) code. And if you don't crack it, that is an answer too. The boss doesn't always get what she wants. You're not ready to give up yet though, or you wouldn't be bitching.

On second thought, I do have one piece of advice: don't blow up the lab. As cathartic as that would be in the moment, think of the cleanup involved.

Your loving Sister,
Nat

"Well," I said, putting the letter down, "at least we can be pretty sure this is Natek's house."

"Then why is Vezina here?" asked Fiadh.

"I wish I fucking knew." I did, however, have a sneaking suspicion that it had something to do with Bran. I thought about saying, *Maybe we shouldn't have called ahead*, but calling ahead had been Fiadh's idea, and I wasn't going to put any of the blame for this on her shoulders. Not when I'd begged her to keep this quiet from Agatha.

I expected Vezina to return the moment she found out Bran had caught Fiadh, but the sun set and the door remained shut. Bran didn't bring me food as he'd done before, but at least we had water from the taps—not that I trusted it entirely.

"You could leave and snoop around the rest of the house," I suggested. Unspoken: *The house won't bother you, since you're not human.*

"What if he comes back when I'm gone?" she countered.

"What if we both die?"

"There's dying, and there's dying. I won't have you tortured on my account. Rest." She smoothed my hair back from my forehead. I lay in her lap, staring up at her, and trying not to feel the fleeting preciousness of these moments, without success.

"Cynane again," I said, picking up our earlier conversation.

"It does seem to keep coming back to that. This must be her office when she visits, or something."

"Do you think the rose is named for her?"

Fiadh wrapped and unwrapped a lock of my hair around her finger. "If it is, I don't know why. This isn't *the* Cynane. It can't be."

"No," I said. "Or at least, I don't think so. Too many people would have seen her die. Natek would have mentioned it in the letters. It might have been a common name, for all we know. But it is a big coincidence."

"I don't like it."

"Tell me more about the Cat Síth," I asked, hoping to smooth some of the lines from her forehead.

"Clara—"

"Something small."

"Fine. We come from Ireland."

"And?"

"And that's something small." Her lips curled at the edges as she tried to keep a stern tone.

"Are there a lot of you?"

"No."

"Were there ever a lot of you?"

She tapped my forehead in a gentle reprimand. "You're pushy, aren't you?"

"I'm professionally curious."

"I don't think there were ever a lot, but probably more than there are now."

"And the cat part of Cat Síth. Is that . . . literal?"

"Why don't you tell *me* something about *you*."

"I promised to bring you to a holiday party. Guess you lucked out." I tried to smile.

"Why do you say that? I would have gone."

"Would you? Consorting with mortals?"

"I would have worn a nice dress," she said, narrowing her eyes. "Something with a low neckline, maybe."

Desire whispered around the edges of the pain, and I felt my cheeks and throat redden, as she'd meant them to.

"I didn't realize you owned anything that wouldn't pass muster in a convent."

"I didn't realize you were into sexy nuns, Clara Eden. Though with that last name—" She squealed in surprise as I nipped at her bare side, which was exposed by the blanket.

"I've always considered myself more of the apple," I said when I'd used up my meager energy.

"What a cliché."

We lapsed into silence.

"Is it painful?" I asked eventually, memorizing the bow of her lips as I changed the subject.

"What?"

"Being . . ." I struggled to form the next word, my childhood stutter throwing up a ghost of a block, as it did occasionally under great duress. Finally, a few breaths later, I managed, ". . . drained."

Her eyes were pine-dark with empathy as they gazed back into mine, and full of a bitterness I understood all too well.

"No," she said. "It isn't."

"Well that's something."

"It is." Her hand in my hair soothed away the meaning behind our words, and I let my eyes close, choosing to believe her.

—⁓— —⁓— —⁓—

In my dreams, trees whispered my name in a language I knew instinctively my waking brain would not understand. I swayed with them. A Sapphic fragment skittered around my soul like a dry, dead leaf. Lost words. Dead words. Lovely even in their bones.

Now Eros shakes my soul, a wind on the mountain overwhelming the oaks.

That, too, was in no language I had ever understood, though I had heard it often. My limbs reached for the sky and knocked against my neighbors. My roots tangled with their beloved roots, twisting, speaking, seeking. Together we nurtured the seedlings unfurling toward the sun and the old, old trees in their restful decline.

In my dreams, Bran stood before me. His voice pulsed and sparked. I listened with ears that were not ears, and spoke with a mouth that was not a mouth, and the forest bathed me in its memories while small, warm bodies nested in the hollows of my breathing bark.

—⁓— —⁓— —⁓—

Fiadh woke me with an urgent shake as the door opened. I sat up as quickly as I could, breaking open some of my wounds, and leaned into Fiadh for creature comfort as the sharp pain subsided into something only mildly less sharp. Memories of my dreams jarred me fully awake.

Vezina swept into the room, followed by Bran, who bore a tray of bread, cheese, and fruit, along with several jars of preserves.

"Natek," I said in greeting, forestalling Fiadh and trying to signal the plan my sleeping mind had conjured with a squeeze. "Have you received a reply?"

Vezina ignored me, instead sitting in the same chair she'd used last time and fixing that abyssal gaze on Fiadh.

"I did not realize she'd sent her toy," Vezina said. "Show me your wrist."

Fiadh held out her arm with a blank face, but I could feel her tremble of rage against my body. Vezina leaned forward to examine the faint scars. Faster than either of us could react, she seized Fiadh's hand and pierced the skin with her teeth, licking up a drop of blood.

"It's been a long time since I shared even that much with Gata," said Vezina. It wasn't an explanation. Fiadh's trembling intensified, and I sensed her outrage and her fear. "She'll forgive me."

"Will she be here soon?" I asked. I wanted to throw a couch at her face. Or stake her through her dead heart.

"Her reply was unspecific. She ended with a phrase I require you to translate." Vezina pulled a folded piece of paper from her breast pocket and handed it to me. Her skin was cold; I tried not to wonder if that indicated hunger. My working theory on vampire homeostasis suggested the more recent the feeding, the warmer the stolen blood in their veins, but none of that was peer-reviewed.

The single line of text was in Vezina's handwriting, not Agatha's. I longed for the entire missive, as it would have given us information vital to our survival.

"Without context," I began, thinking as quickly as I could, "it's hard to say. If I had the rest of her response—"

"You will translate this now."

Behind her, Bran shook his head minutely, and despite Fiadh's cautions about confusing him with anything human, I took the motion as a warning not to press the issue.

"I'll need a moment."

She waited, as still as one of the statues in Agatha's gallery. I stared at the words. Fear made translating difficult, and Agatha's Nektopolian was rudimentary. It took several minutes for me to make sense of her jumbled tenses.

"She . . . she says, I think, 'I do not want to be remembered in another time.'"

"That doesn't make sense," said Vezina.

"This word, here—it could also mean mules, instead."

Vezina repeated the words, touching the ink with the tip of her finger. I remained as still as possible, lest she brush my skin with hers again.

"She never knew the true agony of memory." An emotion that might have been anything rippled across her ageless face. Fiadh's ankle pressed against mine, no doubt urging me to be quiet. That was easy. Had Agatha wanted to speak in code, she would have used one of the lines known only to them. This was a line so similar to one I'd translated for her that it had to be intentional. I just didn't know what she was trying to tell me.

Vezina stood, still staring at the words I'd translated for her. I did not repeat my question, nor did Fiadh, who had remained silent the entire exchange. I watched Vezina leave, bracing myself for the moment when she might turn back and decide to drain us both, but the door shut behind her—leaving us alone with Bran. Bran, whom I'd dreamed.

"Some of her wounds will need antibiotics," said Fiadh the

moment the door latch clicked.

"And where do you think her kind get antibiotics, kitten? She won't become infected. The spore will not allow it, and we are more effective than penicillin."

"Thank you," I said. Fiadh opened her mouth to argue, then seemed to register my thanks. Her eyes darted to mine again.

"Yes," she said slowly. "Thank you."

"Eat. The preserves are from the estate, and the bread is from my kitchen," said Bran.

It smelled the way bread smelled in stories, warm and rich and *home* in a loaf, and since I was already in fairyland, I reached for a slice.

"That tree in my vision. The big one." I bit into the bread without adding any of the cheese or preserves and momentarily lost my sense of time. *This* was bread.

"Yes?" he said. Was I imagining the knowing glint in his eyes?

"What kind of tree was it?"

"You saw one of the Great Trees?" Surprise filled Fiadh's voice, and Bran's eyes crinkled with satisfaction at her reaction.

"What's a Great Tree?"

"Are you aware, Clara, of how lichen are formed?" asked Bran.

I shook my head. Fiadh had explained this to me already, but perhaps he would reveal something new. Studying how different cultures addressed the same questions was part of my job. The answers revealed just as much about the speaker.

"An alga and a fungi come together to create something new. Such is my own history. The Great Trees housed our first mycelium, before we joined with the Animalia. The Great Forests are long dead, but we carry their memory. You would call them . . . oaks."

"I hope you see them grow again someday." I even meant it, though I also hoped a few thousand small, sharp objects penetrated his body in the interim. Keeping my breathing steady throughout all this subterfuge was making my head feel light. At least the pain of my injuries gave me something to concentrate on.

"I admit I'm surprised you were allowed so close." He studied me. "Perhaps you have the makings of a changeling."

I did not ask what he meant by that. I needed to maintain some semblance of sanity, and I didn't like the sudden stillness in the way Fiadh held herself.

"The rose," I said, choosing my words carefully. "Did Natek breed the new variety for any specific reason that she might have mentioned to you?"

He held my gaze. Did he know that I knew Vezina wasn't Natek? Did he care?

"Not that she shared with me." My hopes fell, though I hadn't realized there had been any depths left for them to plunge. He didn't drop my eyes as he added, "But I know the name was important to her."

"I see." My brain churned at the implications. He *was* trying to tell me something, but I didn't know what.

"Try the honey, too," he said, as if he hadn't mentioned anything of note. "I'll bring some clothes by later for you, kitten. Try not to shred them."

"I would appreciate that," said Fiadh. Only when the door shut behind him did she add, "you fuck-faced fucker."

"I think he tried to tell us something," I said, still staring at the door.

"We can't trust anything he says."

"No, but we can't discount it either. We knew there was something about the name we were missing." I lapsed into silence, and Fiadh let me think without interruption. *Cynane.* Fiadh's small hand rested in mine. I stroked the backs of her knuckles as I thought, worrying the gentle ridges of bone over and over. The answer kept to the shadows, always darting out of reach of my searchlight.

"If he was trying to help," said Fiadh after several minutes of furious thought on both our parts, "*why*? What's the incentive for him?"

"Maybe he doesn't like working for Vezina. Can the fey be put under thrall?"

"Not usually." She frowned. "They're too deeply rooted. Too . . . plural. Someone as powerful as Vezina might be able to hold them for a little while at most. What I don't understand is why she'd bother."

"What do you mean?"

"We know she sows chaos. That's what your research revealed, yes? And the fey—they are the antithesis of everything she stands for, unless it's a natural disaster."

Antithesis. Gata had used that word in one of her letters. *She is my antithesis,* she'd written of Vezina. I turned the word over hoping for more answers. Nothing came.

"Then why?" I asked. "There has to be a reason."

"There are bad apples in every orchard. Did Agatha really quote *that* line of Sappho in her response?"

"Yes."

Her eyes grew distant as she thought, seeing past me. At last, she said, "It's a message for me."

"What does it mean? That she doesn't want to see Natek?"

"I don't think so." Uncertainty laced her voice. "I think it has to do with something she gave me, once."

"What was it?"

"A . . . memory."

"Fi, come on," I said, frustrated by the odd phrasing. You didn't give someone a memory. You shared it. "I need more than that. A memory of what?"

"Of something Agatha did to Vezina a long time ago." Her eyes grew distant again, and then she closed them, rubbing her temples as if she had a headache. "Something she regrets."

I waited for more.

Fiadh winced and wrinkled her brow in concentration. "I don't understand why it's relevant."

"But *what is it?*"

"Unless . . ." She opened her eyes, and the finality in her expression dragged cold fingers down my spine. "This is about revenge. Vezina isn't going to negotiate. If Agatha comes here, Vezina will kill her, and us."

We'd suspected that already, but the confirmation made it real.

"You can still warn her," I said. "There's time."

"Bran took away the rope."

"You got in here without a rope."

Fiadh spread one of the preserves and a soft cheese over a slice of bread and settled back onto the couch, her shoulders slumping. "It's . . . not that simple."

"You can turn into a cat," I said, trying to sound nonchalant as I faced the truth. "It's actually kind of cool."

"I can turn into a cat eight times over my life. If I turn a ninth time, I can't turn back."

"That—how many times have you turned?"

She held my gaze.

"Did you . . ." I swallowed around the ashes of my meal. "Did you use your eighth life up for *me?*"

"It was my choice. And it was my seventh, not my eighth. I still have one left."

"Fi—"

"This is why I didn't want to tell you. I—"

I took the bread out of her hands and set it back on the tray, entwining our fingers together. She stared furiously at her lap. I, meanwhile, sank through the depths of what she'd done like a lead line, fathom after fathom after fathom.

"I love you." My voice cracked on the words, but I meant them with every bruised, ivy-punctured part of my being. I loved her. She deserved to know that, before the end. She deserved so much more than this. A mewl escaped her throat, and her voice was every bit as ragged and as fierce as my own when she spoke.

"I would have given you my ninth, if it meant I could have saved you."

I pulled her into me. We stayed like that, silent, listening to each other breathe and sharing the warmth of our bodies for what little time we had left.

—⁓⁓— —⁓⁓— —⁓⁓—

Another morning came and went. I watched the sunrise while Fiadh slept on, wondering if it would be my last. There was almost heat to the light, more heat than usual this time of year, and I turned my face up to embrace it, remembering lying on the summer grass with Fiadh.

I'd dreamed about my parents. Who would tell them I'd gone missing? How long would it take my mother to realize even more time had passed than usual between our sporadic calls? My father would notice, first, and ask her if she'd heard from me. They'd contact Mark. He'd . . . Well, he knew where I lived and worked. He'd contact someone at the Montague estate, then the police.

I pictured the headlines: "Elusive investor and two staff go missing right before the holidays." There'd be a search. Would anyone think to look in the library? At least the Sappho and the other rare, presumed-lost works would end up in the hands of the academy.

I felt oddly calm about my impending demise. It helped, I suppose, that Fiadh had promised it would be painless—which I was still choosing to believe was the truth—but there was also a kind of relief in knowing there was nothing I could do to stop it. For the next ten hours of daylight, I was freer from responsibility than I'd been in decades. No deadlines. No piles of work. No obligations or expectations. A real vacation.

Of course, the serenity also could have been the spores. Some fungi could alter the brains of their hosts to make them more amenable. Did I care, though, or was it a kindness to be free from fear in these last hours?

"You're smiling," said a sleepy Fiadh. Her eyelids fluttered as she looked up through them, squinting against the light.

"I'm being morbid."

"Tell me?"

I explained my reasoning while her eyes opened fully. By the time I'd finished, she was frowning.

"What?" I said. "It is like a vacation, in a weird way."

"You do know that's unhealthy, yes?"

"You're one to talk about work-life balance."

"I'm happy with my schedule," she said. "I might not get much time off in a row, but I receive other benefits, and I enjoy my work."

"I didn't say I didn't enjoy—"

"You just described your impending death as the first chance you've had in years to relax, Clara. I would *never* make that comparison."

Fighting on what was most likely our last day alive wasn't part of that vacation plan. "I just mean I feel at peace with it. That's all."

"Well, don't." She sat up, her blanket slipping off her naked shoulders. God, but she was beautiful. "What's that poem?"

"Rage, rage against the dying of the light?" I offered immediately.

"Yes."

"Dylan Thomas. He—"

"I want you to rage, not *relax*," she said, cutting off my poetry trivia. "And, if we do get out of this, we need to have a serious talk about your priorities."

"I prioritize what's important," I said.

"Academics." She brushed her hair back from her face with a disapproving motion. "Agatha is the same way. Most of my job is reminding her to rest."

"She's a vampire."

"Vampires also need sleep. They're not actually dead, you know."

I waved away the inevitable explanation of viral cancers and blood and whatever else she was going to say to spoil my morning.

"Maybe Bran will bring us coffee."

"Coffee?"

"You said prioritize something besides work. Currently," I said, leaning in to kiss her neck, "that includes coffee."

Her reluctant laugh warmed me.

—※— —※— —※—

Bran brought more than coffee; he also had a folded bundle of cloth in his arms. "I believe these will fit," he said, offering the bundle to Fiadh. She accepted it with a bemused expression. The items fell apart into two distinctly different pieces of clothing: a checkered, somewhat ragged flannel bathrobe, and what was unmistakably a cocktail dress. There was also a pair of wool socks that looked several sizes too large, but no shoes.

"Thank you," said Fiadh, looking anything but grateful.

"I'd bring you more towels, to bathe, but you destroyed the last set, and good linens don't come cheap."

"Bran," I said, drinking the rich cup of coffee with the same calmness I'd woken up with. "Is it too much to ask for you to bring us a rose cutting?"

"A rose?"

"The one we came to see. Two, really—the white and the black."

He pondered my question with an unblinking, and highly unsettling, stare. "Why?"

"I'd like to know what my composted body will feed," I said.

He gave me a little smile. "A cutting won't do. Get dressed, and I will take you to the greenhouse."

My shock must have registered on my face. Fiadh's certainly did.

"The next time you try to run I might be less inclined to stop the safeguards," he said. "Do we have an understanding?"

Both Fiadh and I nodded, and she shimmied into the dress without shame. I didn't know if the fey engaged in intercourse with other species, but Bran didn't give her a second glance. I, however, couldn't look away. The dress was simple, black and full-length on her frame, instead of the usual cocktail cut, but the neckline took a narrow plunge, and the back was open to the dimples of her hips, exposing the gentle lines of her shoulder blades and the dip of her spine. The fraying robe and frumpy socks didn't take away from the effect. Even

243

in a poorly fitting dress she was nothing short of stunning.

"Is this how she likes her meals?" Fiadh asked Bran with a sneer.

"Occasionally," he said, unfazed.

I couldn't blame Vezina. Fiadh looked absolutely good enough to eat, even with her hair still tangled from sap.

We followed Bran out of the room, clutching our coffees, and down the estate hallways and stairs. The décor matched the classic cut of Vezina's suit jacket, all elegance and austerity, and dust hovered only around Bran. Rich, dark wood framed the doorways, and while the effect was somber, it was still lovely—until I imagined the horrors that might be waiting behind the wood paneling for "unaccompanied humans."

Of course I considered running. The moment we stepped out of the front door and into the cold—Fiadh wearing only socks in the snow—a burst of adrenaline shook my system, and I wavered on the front step, my limbs tensing in anticipation of the command to flee. But Fiadh shook her head and mouthed, *not yet,* and so I reined myself in and set one foot in front of the other through the snow.

Snow blanketed the grounds. It would have been beautiful if it wasn't my prison. I let the glancing sunlight blind me as I traced the shape of topiary shrubs and stone walls hidden beneath the blue-white lumps. Steam fogged the glass of the greenhouse, giving the panes a frosted appearance, but inside the air was warm and redolent with the scent of plants and earth. Fiadh walked beside me, the robe trailing on the ground. Had it been velvet, she could have been a queen. Bran did not spore. I kept a hand at the collar of my shirt just in case, ready to pull the cloth over my nose and mouth in the hopes that might save me.

The black roses shone redly in the sunlight as we approached. Their fragrance mingled with the scents of other roses and flowers, but I thought I could differentiate the subtle aroma that set that rose apart.

We stood before the sprawling bush, careful of its thorns. I stared at the lush heads and the tight buds, noting the dark green of the foliage and the hints of purple in the new stems. It was a monstrous, gorgeous plant, worthy of a love affair that spanned millennia, and it was also just a plant. No inspiration hit me as I'd hoped it would. Nothing leapt out: no secret binary code in the number of thorns or petals, no scented missive from Natek, wherever she might be.

And where in all the hells *was* Natek?

Fiadh reached out a hand to a low branch and let a thorn hook the fragile skin of her hand until a small bead of blood welled. I waited, wondering if she knew some magic, or if magic existed. She just stood there, though, her face pensive and somber and the thorn kissing her knuckles like a royal subject. What a tableau we must have made, had there been anyone to see.

The rose was only a rose. Its thorns were only thorns. The message it carried was simple and heartbreaking and of absolutely no use to me: *I love you, I remember you, please come home.* Beside it, hidden by the dark petals, grew a smaller rose.

"Cynane,'" said Bran, noticing my gaze. "A subtle flower. Easy to overlook, but breathe it in."

I crouched by the potted plant and buried my face in the lush petals. They kissed my cheeks, cool and smooth. The scent resembled "Pieria," but was softer, rounder, an aromatic bouquet worthy of a sommelier. It smelled like home.

I still hear it in Cynane's sweet, rough voice.

Natek's words came back to me with sudden clarity. The poem— Fragment One, a poem that I, as a besotted teenager, had memorized. A poem that had reminded Natek of Gata in its final stanzas. I murmured it into the petals, wondering how it had sounded sung, and whether Natek and Gata hummed it to themselves the way I might have hummed a song on the radio that reminded me of a lover. But it was the last verse that mattered. Carson's translation spilled off my tongue.

> Come to me now: loose me from hard
> care and all my heart longs
> to accomplish, accomplish. You
> be my ally

Was this meant to be an overture of allyship? A promise to take Vezina down together, as well as an aching cry for all that had been lost? Or did it have something to do with the Cynane named in the letters? I brushed my fingers against the leaves, thinking fast. It was difficult. The spore was definitely making me sluggish and docile, but I pushed against it. Poetry played too large a role in their correspondence to rule out a hidden message. *Be my ally.* Conviction stirred. It fit too well.

"She didn't know about Cynane, did she?" I asked Bran quietly, withdrawing from the rose. I did not specify the she in question. He'd know who I meant: Vezina.

Bran turned from the finger pruning he was inflicting on a nearby rosebush and met my eyes. They did not flash gold, this time, but remained brown and deceptively human as he appraised me.

"No," he said, and that single syllable changed everything.

Fiadh's gasp cut me as it must have cut her throat, so sharp were its edges. We'd walked right up to Natek's front door and revealed her betrayal to Vezina. Bran, Vezina's agent, must have contacted her while I was drugged, and now Agatha was on her way, walking right into a trap we'd unwittingly helped Vezina set. I wanted to throw up. Instead of reuniting her with her old lover, I'd led her into the jaws of her enemy.

"But you helped Natek," said Fiadh, recovering more quickly than I. "You helped her, and you didn't tell Vezina about the rose."

"And he also told Vezina we were here," I said.

He twirled a brown leaf between his fingers. Dirt clung to his hands. He was a gardener, like Agatha. Fey. He'd helped Natek. He'd also obeyed Vezina. This could mean Vezina had some sort of leverage over him that superseded his morality, whatever that morality might look like. Time stretched, and the sunlit morning wavered in and out of linear time and into fairyland.

"My reasons are my own," he said at length.

Fuck it, and fuck him. I didn't have time for anger. We had everything to lose, and so I asked, "Would you help us? For the right reason?"

"Perhaps." He considered me. Fiadh's breath hitched as his eyes blazed golden with interest. The leaf crumpled in his closed fist. "There is one bargain you could make."

"She doesn't know what she's asking," Fiadh said. Her voice was frantic. Bran, however, smiled a smile that had never been human.

"No one ever truly does."

"What's the price?" I said.

"Your body and soul."

I felt the blood leave my face. "That's a little steep."

"Are you in a position to bargain?"

Fiadh put herself between me and Bran. "She isn't doing this."

He turned those blazing eyes on her, and whatever he read in her expression dimmed that light.

"Very well."

246

CHAPTER ELEVEN
Sappho, with What Eyes?

Collection: Nektopolis
Title: Letter 42
Description: Correspondence; Cynane and Natek
Date: 8/3/2005
Cataloguer: Clara Eden

August 3, 2005

Cynane,

The first time her horse died she disappeared into the mountains for three days and came back covered in pitch. Some deaths are harder than others. She tolerates the loss of human lives far better, which I know you've observed before this. This isn't to say she doesn't grieve, but that she doesn't show it, just as she does not accept comfort from any human hand. I will tell you a secret: this is why I still give her horses, even though she has no practical need. Dogs hurt her too much. Their lives are too short, and they are too easy to love. Occasionally I gift her mules, though she has an aesthetic objection I've never fully understood, which is a pity considering their longevity. Parrots, too. There was a time she

247

kept elephants, but that was years and years ago, and the laws are too restrictive these days. Would that she had settled in Texas. Her fondness for crocodiles could have been indulged as well. She had one named Habibi who lived to be one hundred and seventy two. After his death, I rarely saw her without Habibi's hide. She wore it over her shoulder until it disintegrated with age. This was when we were in Egypt. He walked beside her on a golden leash, and was useful for disposing of bodies. Ask her about him, sometime.

She does mourn Tomislava, as do I. I know what she meant to you, and I know what you meant to her: everything. She raised you with such love, fauntkin. I never heard her speak your name without a softening around her mouth and eyes, and you know Tomi. She wasn't soft. She called you daughter, Cynane, and she would have split the earth in two for you. (As would I, but I am not the one you miss.) We made a mighty triad.

I cannot offer you words of comfort. There are none. Death is an abyss, and you will grow, in time, to contain it, but the abyss remains. Cherish it. The larger the loss, the greater the love. Pain is sometimes all we have left of a person.
Stay in the house as long as you need. Work can wait. Your laboratory assistants will run things in your absence, as I know you do not tolerate incompetence. Take time. Breathe in the gardens. Weep, if it helps. I will be there shortly, unless you'd rather grieve alone.

All my love,
Nat

Sunlight followed us back into the estate. Bran led the way not to our cell, but to a room high on the east side of the manor house overlooking the mountains. It was spare, with only an antique stick of furniture and an old telescope, but what set it apart from the other rooms was the glass. Glass walls, glass ceiling. Slate floor. Hauling the slate up these stairs must have been a nightmare.

"Why are we in an observatory?" asked Fiadh.

"The view of the east." He gazed out over the forested slopes, his expression neutral.

Fiadh scoffed and began to pace. Her hem whispered over the slate each time she turned.

"If I may, I'd like to show you something," he said to me. I nodded. A haze of gold shimmered around him, but this time I knew what to expect. I closed my eyes. When I opened them, the world had changed.

We stood in the middle of a forest vaster and wilder than any I'd before seen. Sunlight stabbed through the canopy in rays. Thick trunks sheltered moss and small brown mammals, and in the distance a bear lumbered about on its business. Squirrels leapt overhead.

"The forests of this continent once stretched across her Eastern coast. Trees flourished, and so did we, for we are bound to their roots through the mycelium. So it was everywhere. We grew in Europe. Africa. Asia. Oceania. But gradually, the Great Trees fell to your axes or to the diseases you brought with you from across the seas. We adapted. What other choice was there?

"The Irish know our world as the Otherworld, but each of your cultures has its own mythos. Some call it the spirit world, for we remember the dead. We are the dead as we are the living. We transcend. I am a man named Bran, and I am also thousands of years of memory, something both and more.

"Now imagine if someone created an antifungal that could wipe out those memories, shriveling hyphae and destroying our fruiting bodies where they crested earth or skin. Imagine if that person came to you and said, 'Work for me, or I will wipe out your civilization.' What would you do?"

Fiadh had stopped pacing. She watched Bran with an expression of dawning understanding.

"Who could do such a thing?" he continued. "Someone who has done it before. Someone who has painted your history red. Vezina, I'm afraid, was especially fond of crucifixion."

The forest shifted, and we were on a dusty stone road lined with olive trees and crosses. A hooded figure drank from the living corpses in the bright moonlight, pressing her mouth to the vein in a woman's thigh. A shudder of revulsion pulsed through me.

"But her best known work," he continued, "was in Dacia, now Romania, the land where she'd been born several empires past."

The Roman road rippled and vanished, and now the reek of rotting corpses rose like fog from a field of stakes, upon which men, women, and even a few children groaned and died. Flies rose in black swarms, wings glittering in the moonlight as they parted before a figure I now recognized as Vezina. She rested a hand on the head of a man still in the throes of death. A spike pierced him from rectum to stomach. My own stomach lurched at the grisly tableau. Bran's voice shattered the spectacle and returned me to the observatory.

"And so I knew, when she came to me with a poison strong enough to erase my people, that she was capable of the act. Tell me, kitten, what would you do for those you love?"

"She has a way to kill the Mother?" Horror roughened Fiadh's voice.

We were back in the woods, now, but the image of the staked man's face lingered.

"She does."

Fiadh flinched.

"Natek," I urged him. "How does she fit into this? Where is she?"

"She is Vezina's general, and she forfeited her soul to protect the only person that woman has ever truly loved in two thousand years."

Gata.

"Until she realized what Vezina planned to do," said Fiadh.

He nodded. I looked between them, confused.

"What did she plan to do?" I asked.

"It is nearly impossible for fey to be turned," said Bran. "I say nearly, because it has happened at least once."

My mind churned. Agatha in her garden. The oak trees all over the property. The botany books and the handwritten journals and the mushrooms I'd found sprinkled across the estate, but especially at the base of the oaks, and in the university library of a campus also dominated by oak trees. The way her garden burgeoned with an almost unnatural life. The cryptic lines from her letters.

Agatha was fey.

Before I could concentrate on this revelation, another question surfaced. Agatha drank from Fiadh because she possessed a special blood type. Fiadh, a Cat Síth, which translated simply into "fairy cat." Was Fiadh fey, too?

"The fungicide would not kill her body," he continued, unaware of my turmoil, "though shock might, even with a vampire's strength. But it would cut her off from the mycelium, and I cannot guess at how much of who she is now would survive."

"What is the method of delivery?" I regretted asking it immediately, for in his gaze, I read a truth as dark as blood, though I could not see the shape of it clearly.

Fiadh closed her eyes. "I see," she said. "Has it happened already?"

"You will know when it does."

"And Natek?" she asked, rubbing her wrist.

Bran gestured at the room. "She does not know Vezina is aware of her betrayal. I do not know where she is right now, but were we Vezina, we would have sent her far away. Unless, of course, we wanted her here to witness. There are no other Daughters of the Blood in attendance."

I noted the shift in pronoun. Did it mean anything? Language hid as much as it revealed.

"Why are you telling us this?" asked Fiadh.

"Think, kitten. What could you possibly do with the information?"

"Who—" I broke off my inquiry into the Daughters of the Blood as I understood why we were in this room. A glass room, facing east. Even I, who had no love for Agatha, shuddered. Like binding someone to a rock in the rising tide, it would be an agonizing wait for death. First the sky would lighten from velvet black to gray, then purple, then the reds and oranges of sunrise as the horizon line burned gold, gilded by impending death, until at last the eye of the sun crested the ridges and burned away the second life of the blood. Much like crucifixion or impalement, in its own way.

In the event it failed and Agatha escaped, either Fiadh or I would carry a fungicide in our blood designed to finish the job. I didn't ask how Vezina would ensure that Agatha drank; she no doubt had that all figured out.

—٭— —٭— —٭—

Fiadh woke me hours later with a whisper. I stirred, untangling myself from her limbs and the blanket, and raised my head. She was staring at the window, and as I watched, a pair of headlights lit the ceiling. Someone was here.

"Agatha?" I asked.

She slid from my arms and padded to the window, opening it to lean out for a better view. I cringed before remembering she wasn't human, and so the vines wouldn't attack her.

"The trees are in the way. I can't—I can't see." She remained hanging out the window, the winter wind blowing her hair off her neck. Moonlight lit her pale skin. "But I don't think I recognize the car."

Relief and disappointment chased each other around my stomach. I didn't want Agatha to fall for Vezina's trap, but I also wanted, desperately, for all this to be over. The sound of a car door shutting drifted in.

"Wait—" Fiadh's tone lifted in alarm. I wrapped the blanket around my shoulders and joined her at the window, careful to stay within the safety of the walls. I could still see. A woman stood on the distant drive, looking up at the house. For a wild moment, I thought it might be Natek, but then she moved, and I recognized the careful motions of Agatha Montague, for all that she was bundled into a parka.

Across the snow-covered lawn, Agatha raised her head. She was too far away for me to make out her expression. All I could see of her face was a partial oval before she started walking toward the manor.

"What is she doing?" Fiadh said, her voice high and panicked. "She knows this is a trap."

I kept staring at the spot I'd last seen Agatha, though not for the same reason. Wind stirred little whirlwinds of snow across the lawn. "Fi, she's here for you."

Fiadh's "oh" was part exhale, part pain. Something I didn't want to admit was love filled her eyes. "She shouldn't have."

"She absolutely should," I said, pulling Fiadh away from the window.

"We have to do something."

"Go," I suggested, pointing at the door. "Tell her Vezina's plan. The house won't harm you."

"I already told you I wouldn't leave you."

"Well we can't do anything from here." I chewed on the inside of my lip. "Fi, go. I'll be fine. Bran isn't going to hurt me, and this could be our only chance to get out. You have to go." I took her by the shoulders and knelt very slightly, putting our eyes on the same level. "I hate it, but I'm right. You're the only one of us who can leave this room."

"No."

"Fi—"

"*No.*"

"I'm right," I repeated, holding her gaze. "I'm right, and you know I'm right."

Her cheeks reddened with what I suspected was a suppressed scream. But she nodded slowly, her shoulders shaking, even as she said, "I can't do this."

I crushed my lips against hers hard enough to bruise, and she kissed me back just as desperately, her tongue claiming my mouth and her arms wrapping around my neck. I memorized the way her body felt: her hips cresting mine when she stood on her tiptoes, her breasts beneath my own, the warmth of her arms against the nape of my neck.

We broke the kiss at the same time. She searched my face with her green, green eyes, then turned and stepped out the door.

―※― ―※― ―※―

As it turned out, the catatonic state of total and utter helplessness that had accompanied my first day as a captive had been a blessing—and one I did not receive twice. Waiting in that room for Fiadh to return made my skin crawl with anxious terror. My mind conjured gruesome outcomes: Agatha and Fiadh impaled in the entryway; Agatha crying over Fiadh's dead body, Vezina standing over them both with a cruel smile; Vezina, her teeth buried in Fiadh's neck, draining her, turning her, poisoning her, stealing her away from me forever.

Without a phone, I had no way of keeping track of time besides the moon, which barely seemed to move in the sky. I paced. I came up with idiotic plans. I punched the couch cushions to relieve some of the adrenaline, until finally I slid to the floor at the base of the door and listened to the silence beyond.

A scream punctuated the stillness of the house. I leapt to my feet and turned the handle of the door without a thought for the wasps. I knew that scream. I knew it, and nothing this house could throw at me was going to prevent me from getting to Fiadh.

My feet pounded on the wooden floors, only slightly muffled by the thin carpets, and I rounded corners and bolted up stairs as I

253

followed the direction I thought her voice had come from. *Up*, my intuition told me. Up to the room on the east side of the house, where Vezina planned to let Agatha burn.

I'd managed two flights of stairs before it occurred to me through my ragged breathing and the staccato pounding of my heart that nothing was chasing me. No wasps swarmed around my face. No plants sent out creepers from the dead wood of the walls and floor. I was a human unescorted, and the house had turned a blind eye. I paused on a landing to listen. Nothing. I waited.

A thud came from the distance, and I set off running again. Portraits and paintings hung sentinel. The eyes of the portraits marked my progress, but if they were more than paint, they didn't let on. At least my legs hadn't totally lost their conditioning, though I hadn't been jogging as frequently. Something about knowing monsters existed had made the idea of running alone less appealing.

I rounded another corner and halted, panting, as I recognized the flight of stairs ahead. This was the landing beneath the glass room. Voices, muffled by the floor, sounded dimly within. I crept forward, looking over my shoulder to make sure no one was coming to assist Vezina. She seemed like the sort to have an army at her beck and call, for all that I hadn't seen or heard any evidence of others besides Bran. Sweat dripped in icy rills down my back. I had no weapon—nothing with which to fend off an ancient vampire save my bare hands. I scanned my surroundings with wild eyes. Paintings. Carpet. No convenient umbrella stand or ancient sword. My palms itched. Something. Anything. There had to be *something* I could use.

The heavy gilt frame of the last painting in the hall caught my attention. I yanked it off the wall, too afraid to admire the landscape etched in shadow and blue within as I positioned it diagonally to the ground, and stomped on the corner. The frame cracked. I froze, waiting for someone to come rushing to see the cause of the noise, but the murmurs continued above me. Sick with adrenaline, I pried the frame apart until I had a two-foot piece of gilded crown molding in my hand. As stakes went, it wasn't much, but it was a hell of a lot better than nothing. I had no hope of taking on Vezina myself, but perhaps I could distract her long enough for Agatha to do whatever it was vampires did to extinguish each other's endless lives.

I mounted the stairs as quietly as I could. The element of surprise might be all I had going for me, and I didn't want to squander it.

Mercifully, the steps barely squeaked. I placed one foot in front of the other, sweat making the stake slippery in my hand, and pressed my ear to the door.

"... and as I've told you before, *Vezina*, I find your methods abhorrent. Your work in Germany—"

A low laugh interrupted Agatha. "Germany was not my work. They did that all on their own, though I admit, I enjoyed the benefits. You give me too much credit."

"Stalin, then."

"He did have great hair," said Vezina.

"Mass graves hardly yield a feast."

"But who would notice a disappearance or twenty? Easy to blame it on the state. Truly, it was a glorious time. You should have joined me when you had the chance, Gatalina."

"Do not speak my name to me after all you've done."

"All *I've* done?" Vezina's words turned into a snarl. "I gave you this life. It was you who threw—"

"You kill—"

"*You knew the price.*"

"No one should have to pay that price." Agatha's voice now matched Vezina's snarl for snarl. My nerves sang with fear. "Or have you forgotten Amalusta?"

"Where did you hear that name?" Footsteps accompanied each word, slow and measured, and it was easy to picture Vezina approaching Agatha in a shroud of menace. The ridges of the broken frame dug into my palms.

"You used to cry it in your sleep. I've forgotten much, but not that. No other name ever crossed your lips. Just Amalusta. It means chamomile, does it not? I took such comfort in knowing those flowers would never soothe you." There was a pause, in which I strained to hear some hint of life from Fiadh. "I tried to find out about her after, for reasons you of all people would understand. But she was already dead. A short, bitter little life—not at all like yours."

"But rather like your daughter's."

As an academic, I'd read enough closing arguments to know one when I heard it. Even without context—and honestly, I didn't care about their personal vendettas—I could tell Vezina's words had hit on an irrevocable truth. I half expected Agatha to lunge at her, shrieking.

"You wield cruelty so casually you forget yourself," she said, scornful instead of wounded.

"I've never forgotten anything. You made sure of that."

Another silence. I imagined them circling each other. If they started fighting, maybe I could slip into the room, grab Fiadh, and get out while they were distracted. My muscles trembled with adrenaline.

"Does Natek know what you have planned for me?" Agatha's voice remained impassive, but there was a forced quality to her calm now. Refusing to rise to Vezina's bait was costing her. I still hadn't heard anything from Fiadh. What if she wasn't even in the room? I put my hand on the door handle, noting the array of locks on this side of the door. How had Vezina convinced Agatha to walk into this room? More importantly, why had Fiadh screamed?

"Ask the sun, Gatalina."

A chain jingled. Shuffling sounds followed the words, muffled by the door, and I could only guess at what was taking place beyond it.

"Spoiler alert," said a voice near my ear. "She knows now."

I scrambled back against the wall and brandished my stake before me. In the darkness, lit only intermittently by low, incandescent wall sconces, a woman leaned against the opposite wall. A braid hung over her shoulder, black against the green of her thick chamois shirt, and a smile sharp enough to scratch a diamond split her narrow face. Mediterranean features. Nose and lips rendered in lush angles. I'd seen that face in the paintings in Agatha's gallery.

"Nektaria," I whispered.

She nodded, holding a finger to her lips, as if I needed a reminder to be quiet. Snow melted where it still clung to her black-booted ankles, and she smelled like gasoline and ice. Natek. Nektaria. Fear was the only emotion I could touch, but a shadow of awe still managed to flutter beneath it.

The sound of something striking flesh penetrated the wood. Natek pushed off from the wall at the moment of impact. I was glad of the dark. I couldn't see much of her eyes, but what I could see resembled a chemical fire. She strode past me, shouldered open the door, and stalked into the moonlit scene with the murderous grace of a comet. I teetered on the last step, staring.

Vezina and Agatha stood face to face, Agatha no longer wearing her parka, and Vezina surpassing her in every way: height, beauty, presence. Yet Vezina trembled almost imperceptibly, and Agatha, a bright red line across her cheek, stood still.

Both turned as the door swung inward. Agatha's face stiffened in the manner of someone clamping down on their initial reaction with every facial muscle at their disposal. Vezina's mouth twisted.

"You're home early."

"Forgot my wallet," said Natek.

The light overtone of the exchange didn't fool me. Rage burned beneath both their words. I shrank closer to the door as a fear so strong I nearly pissed myself clawed up my body.

Vezina managed a bored affect, and perhaps after twenty plus centuries I, too, would be able to school my face and tone no matter the circumstances.

I searched the room for Fiadh. Bright slate floor. Stars glittering past the panes of glass. A lumpy shadow against the far wall. I stumbled forward, keeping close to the windows and trusting my captor was too busy dealing with Natek to care about a walking juice box. Fiadh lay still, her robe covering all but one socked foot as I crumpled beside her. The hair lying across her face barely stirred where it fell over her nose and mouth.

"Fi?" I put my hand on her cheek, willing her eyes to open. Her skin was cold.

Panic lunged against my ribs in the shape of my heart. I fumbled for her pulse, my fingers skipping around as I searched for her jugular vein. Nothing. I pressed into her skin, my fingers leaving a blue shadow. *There.* Faint, and thready, but there. She was alive. I cupped her face with my hands and stroked her cheeks with my thumbs, running through my limited knowledge of first aid. Bits of the vampires' conversation registered distantly.

"... sound like a Hollywood villain, Vezina."

"Well, I've waited a long time for this."

Something sticky met my fingers. I withdrew my hands and saw black blood glistening on one set of ring and pinky fingers in the light. Carefully, I felt the hidden side of her neck for what I knew I'd find: two punctures, close together, approximately the spacing of a bite.

"No," I said. "No, no, no, no, no, no, *no.*" I held her to me and tried to keep her warm with my body, rocking back and forth with her limp form pressed to my chest. "Fi," I moaned, over and over and over. Blood ran down from the wounds and pooled in her collarbone. How much blood could a person lose and survive?

"... burn with her ..."

The drama in the background faded. I heard their voices as murmurs, nothing more or less than the sound of the wind picking up outside the tower. I was type O negative. If I could get her to a hospital, I could provide all the blood she needed, as long as she had enough time. Shaking, I gathered her more securely in my arms and stood. She wasn't heavy, but even a light human still weighed a considerable amount. That didn't matter. I'd carry her to the car, and—

The keys. Where were the keys? My pockets had been emptied, and if Fiadh had pocketed them, her clothes were somewhere unbeknownst to me, and useless. Maybe Agatha had left the keys in her SUV. Anything was better than being up here. I took a step toward the door. The hot, metallic smell of blood was so strong I could taste it.

The house groaned. I halted, as did the horrible tableau. The groan came again, high and eerie, and I blinked dust out of my eyes. Golden dust.

"Fuck," I said.

"Gata, behind—"

Wood erupted from the door frame, interrupting Natek's shout, and several splinters lodged in my skin as thick branches of something bioluminescent and fleshy reached into the room. For a wild, panicked second I thought they were vines, but as they branched, I put the data together: fungi.

Vezina stood backlit in chartreuse by this abominable sight, unconcerned as the fruiting bodies branched again and again, coating the windows and walls and ceiling in a glowing, lacy network. A sharp, earthy smell joined the smell of blood. Spores drifted down like ash. I could hear the faint rush of water as the growth accelerated, along with an organic creaking and popping. I'd seen coral fungi in the woods and around the Brixton U campus; this was similar. Yet despite the monstrous display, nothing leapt to destroy us. The three vampires stood a little to one side of my path to the door. If I could just—

Agatha screamed and swiped at her face. Natek reached for her, trying to stop her as she gouged the flesh around her eyes with her nails, and then she, too, recoiled as if she'd just seen the thing that lurked at the bottom of the well of nightmare. I waited for the spore to do the same to me. *It won't be real*, I told myself. *None of it is real.* Nothing much happened, except that the bioluminescence glowed brighter, and we were standing in a meadow. Fiadh lay limply in my arms.

Natek shouted in a foreign language and drew a knife from her belt, crouching as she faced off with an invisible opponent somewhere in the grass. Agatha continued to claw at her eyes, though now something seemed to also be gnawing on her leg, for she kept kicking and removing her hands long enough to beat the air, eventually falling in a continuous, writhing scream to the ground. Vezina watched with an expression on her lips that wasn't quite a smile, nor was it satisfaction. It wanted to be; it made the right shape, but the eyes told the lie. I looked at her face, with its ageless, ancient bones, and I didn't understand.

"You thought you'd die together, Nat? United once again, holding each other as you fall into the blessed light?"

She raised her hand to the dust and let it swirl around her fingers as she studied the effects of the spore. "Two millennia you were my general. Why did you have to come home early? Tomorrow would have taught you the lesson well enough." She knelt to stare into Agatha's bleeding face, and her voice hushed in the manner of one speaking entirely to oneself. "And you. All this time, and you do not even know. I thought you might have guessed, once or twice, but this is better. Cleaner. Your daughter's mine, Gatalina. Mine as she was never yours."

I didn't dare move, lest I attract her attention, but she didn't seem to care if I heard her, and besides—the words didn't make sense. Agatha's daughter was dead.

Natek chose that moment to swing her blade, striking glass and fungi. The glass held. Bulletproof, maybe. The fungi, however, sighed open, fleshy and bluing around the edges of the wound. Vezina stepped back from the gaping crevice.

"I forgave you once, Nektaria. I cannot bring myself to extend that grace a second time." She walked toward the door, stepping around severed bits of dimming fungi. At the door, she paused and looked back. Her gaze swept over me, then to Fiadh in my arms, and dismissed us. When she spoke again, it was still to herself.

"I thought I would have more to say. I've rehearsed speeches for years and years and years. But . . . perhaps it will be quiet now."

The lock clicked behind her as she exited, followed by the metallic slam of deadbolts driving home.

Natek was now sawing at her forearm. Blood, thick and dark, squirted from the wound. Vezina had been right. They'd kill themselves or each other long before sunrise. Worse, we were trapped in here with them. The imaginary grass rippled in an imaginary breeze. This couldn't be the end. I hugged Fiadh as tightly as I could and futilely willed my life force into her body.

I'll do anything, I prayed to whatever might be passing by. *At least let her live. Please, let her live.* I'd sell my soul to gods, devils—

"Bran," I screamed, scuttling Fiadh and myself against the door frame in the hope it might offer some faint protection.

The fungi nearest me pulsed, the bioluminescence changing from yellow to green. I shouted Bran's name again and reached for my stake, which I'd dropped, to prod at the nearest fleshy branch.

A boot crushed my wrist against the slate. The stake tumbled from my fingers. Natek loomed over me, knife dripping with her own blood, and her arm open to the bone—which had apparently stopped the blade from severing her arm completely. She stared down at me, seeing who knew what, and ground her heel into my pinned wrist. It made a popping sound, and white-hot pain lanced up my arm and into my shoulder and neck. I beat at Natek's foot with my other hand, but her boot was laced up past her ankle, which was all I could reach in my current prone position, and I made no impact against the leather. She snarled something in that same, foreign tongue.

The words sank into my terror slowly. Nektopolian wasn't spoken aloud—who was there to speak it?—and unlike Latin or many other ancient languages, had too few practitioners to justify learning the old pronunciations. I had learned some, of course, but what I'd learned was obviously wrong. Natek repeated the question again. Translating spoken Nektopolian would have been difficult even under ideal circumstances. These were further from ideal than I'd ever imagined, but as I fought against the grinding pain in my wrist, I did my best. *Where is she?* Natek had asked.

"I don't know who you're talking about," I said in Nektopolian, no doubt butchering the pronunciation.

"Gata."

"She's here. She's right here, behind you." Or at least, I hoped that's what I said. The pain was clouding my brain.

She shouted the next word so loudly the windows shook. *Liar*, maybe? The cords in her neck stood out, as prominent as steel cables in the moonlight. Her knife reflected silver light where it wasn't stained with blood.

"Please—"

A vine snaked around her torso and yanked her off me. I snatched my wrist to my chest and cradled it. Was it broken? I didn't want to prod it, but if it was broken, how I was going to carry Fiadh? More vines wound around Natek's torso and legs, and unlike the ivy that had trapped me, these were covered in thorns and small, ridged leaves. I couldn't tell their color in the dark. She struggled. A few vines snapped; the remainder grew a coat of bark as they thickened. On the other side of the room, vines wound around Agatha, pinning her hands to her sides. The chain on her ankle already prevented her from moving too far, and she looked like a freshly caught fish flopping on the deck.

A heady scent filled the room. Natek quieted, and several buds sprouted on the thicket of growth now caging her. The scent intensified as they unfurled. Bran had heard me after all.

His barefoot shape wavered into focus, not quite real even by the standards of this imaginary landscape.

"Help us," I said. "I'll do it. I'll do whatever it is."

"Do you know what you'd be giving up?"

"I don't care." Was it sympathy that flashed across his face as my voice broke?

"Your soul will join with the mycelium, and together you will become something new, half in this world, half in the Otherworld, a thing of beauty and power and history. A changeling. Fey, as you call us."

I didn't have a choice. If he released Natek, she'd kill me, and Fiadh was half dead already. She'd used up a life to come to my aid. I'd do the same thing for her twice over.

"When would you collect?" I asked over her head.

"At a time of my choosing. The time may come soon. It may be when you are old. But when it does, you will submit willingly."

"And you'll help us get out?"

"Yes. I cannot guarantee Vezina will not stop me. She holds a knife to my hyphae, and I cannot let her poison the Mother. My death is nothing. I am not an individual. But my people? That, I cannot risk, and I have drawn heavily on the groundwater over the last few days. You will have to help me help you."

Groundwater? Fungi, I remembered dizzily, used water to grow. Some types could break through asphalt, so high was the PSI of the water pressure they generated. I'd seen that in a documentary somewhere.

"How do I help?"

"I will guide you. Eat this, and the deal is struck," said Bran, cupping his hand. A small mushroom sprouted from his lifeline. It looked like a morel, wrinkly and almond shaped. He plucked it from his palm and held it out to me. I took the mushroom before I lost my nerve, and popped it into my mouth, trying as hard as I could not to think about where it had grown. The flavor was earthy and nutty at once, much like any other mushroom I'd eaten.

"What about Fiadh?"

"You do not need me for that." He nodded toward Agatha. She, too, had stopped struggling, but unlike Natek, who slumped in her bonds, her eyes regained their focus. When I looked back at Bran to ask what she could do, he was gone.

"Agatha," I shouted, "it's Fiadh!"

Agatha's face was a ruin. Flesh hung in strips, and she'd managed to tear . . . I looked away. I'd never seen that much exposed eyeball.

"She needs a transfusion." Her voice rasped, no doubt from all that screaming. "Bring her to me."

"How?"

"There isn't time for explanations. If her brain has shut down—"

That was all I needed to hear. I crouched and placed my good arm around Fiadh's waist, raising her enough to lodge my damaged one underneath her legs. Each step sent jolts of agony through my wrist. Agatha's eyes softened as much as they could, given their state, as she looked up at Fiadh's limp form. Then she wriggled into a sitting position. Her eye . . . bounced.

"Keep her close. You're going to need to hold her up after I've taken your blood, and you won't have much strength."

"When you—"

"Your blood type is compatible, both to her and me. She needs a transfusion. Nothing else matters, Clara."

Nothing else mattered.

"You have my consent," I said, before she could put me under thrall. If I did this, I'd do it clean. I wouldn't let her put me under the dark. *Picture Fiadh*, I told myself. *Like you practiced.*

"Lean her against me. I can't hold her with these vines, but I can help brace you both."

I leaned my bundle against Agatha's chest. One of the vines binding her arms budded a new branch, which snaked around Fiadh's body to create a crude sling. *Thank you, Bran.* Or possibly Agatha herself. Fiadh's chest barely seemed to rise and fall.

"Your neck is the easiest to reach," Agatha said, not commenting on the vine.

This close to her, the thick scent of gore hit my nostrils with renewed intensity. Those were inside smells. They were not supposed to leave the body. Fear blanketed my senses as I remembered the last time Agatha's lips had hovered over my neck. A whimper escaped my throat. I'd promised myself this would never happen again.

Fangs brushed the tender skin above my carotid artery. A slight prick. A pause. Numbness spread, and then she bit deep, and my body tensed as every nerve signaled me to fight. Fiadh had been right; thrall was a kindness. Agatha's throat worked against my shoulder as she swallowed. I clutched the precious burden nestled between us and held as still as I would for any other blood donation.

It didn't hurt, precisely; the local anesthetic in her saliva was doing its job. But the rapid loss of blood was making me light-headed, queasy, and cold. How much did Fiadh need? Moonlight lit the glass tower, illuminating the grisly scene within. Fiadh's legs felt so light across my lap. I shouldn't have pushed her to leave our room. We should have stayed there, she and I, until the undead worked things out amongst themselves. Better yet, we should have stayed at Agatha's estate and never come here. So many shoulds.

Agatha withdrew her fangs, licking the wound when she finished with a tongue that didn't feel entirely human. I shuddered at the sensation even as it eased the pain.

"Thank you, Clara," she said with quiet sincerity as she pulled away. I swayed, Fiadh's body suddenly heavy as the blood loss caught up with me. Agatha's skin glowed with health even in the dark as my blood coursed through her veins.

"Now what?" I asked.

"Can you lift her closer to me? I'll need her neck, and I don't dare tell you to cut the vines. I am not . . . fully stable yet."

"What happened to her?" I asked. Fiadh's head lolled on my shoulder as I adjusted her, and her hair smelled like winter leaves.

"Vezina."

Hatred coiled around my spine. I'd kill her. The fact that I was weak and human was irrelevant. I'd find a way to separate Vezina from her component parts. I'd stake her. I'd—

Fiadh stirred in my grasp very slightly, turning her head.

"Fi?"

"Don't," she wheezed, pain etched into each breath. Blood loss caused chest pain, I remembered from somewhere, and I ached for the woman in my arms.

"You'll be okay," I told her as my arms began to shake. The vine around Fiadh's waist was doing most of the work holding her, now, and another vine curled around her legs as if it was aware of my waning strength.

"Don't," she said again, hoarser this time. Her eyelids fluttered in panic. I didn't understand; don't *what?*

Agatha bent her head to Fiadh's neck. Fiadh twisted, a frail, boneless, lolling motion, hardly able to hold up her own head. "It won't take long," I said, hoping to soothe her. Then, looking to Agatha, I added, "Right?"

"No. Hold still, love," said Agatha in a voice as sweet and heavy as a summer morning. I felt the pull of thrall as she lowered her head again, and shivered just outside the glow of its warmth.

Fiadh's hand found my shirt and clawed it weakly. Her eyes were wide open, now, and she stared at me in that darkness with the desperation of the gallows.

"Wait," I said. Kneeling this close to Agatha gave me an unfortunately clear view of her damaged eye, which swiveled to appraise me.

Short on blood, sleep, and sanity, I pushed my brain into the hinterlands of consciousness, to the place where I'd spent so much of my academic life, forcing sense from my scattered thoughts and hurling them at the work at hand. It was a hot, buzzing place, and sometimes I felt the presence of the other scholars laboring beneath the same burden: creating new knowledge from the old. Sometimes I believed in a collective intellectual consciousness that transcended time and space, a hive of minds harvesting the nectar of knowledge. Then I'd read an inane opinion in one of the scholarly journals I subscribed to and the romanticism would perish. My skin hurt. So did my wrist. *Focus, Clara.* Why had Vezina sucked Fiadh half dry? Fuel for the fight to come? As an insult? Or—

"She's a Trojan horse." I looked to Natek, the strategist, but she was blinking and shaking her head like a wet dog, the spores clearly still having an effect, though at least she was no longer trying to sever her limbs. "Vezina poisoned her."

CHAPTER TWELVE
Fragment the Past for Safekeeping

Collection: Nektopolis
Title: Letter 43
Description: Correspondence; Cynane and Natek
Date: 3/16/2015
Cataloguer: Clara Eden

March 16, 2015

Et tu, Cynane? You know I played no direct role in that debacle. Caesar did that to himself. Yet every year since that frankly hilarious play came out (yes, the Bard intended it to be a tragedy, but he did not know the man like I did) I wonder how I might have twisted that to our purposes. This is not an exercise in regret. It's a strategy game: examine every move from every angle and imagine new iterations of outcomes.

Which brings me to your letter. I am not at all surprised you've had a breakthrough, or that you need a break. When was the last time you left your lab, duckling? You need a drink or a fuck or both. Get thee to a brothel, to keep with the

Shakespearean theme. Go see a movie. Ride the subway and intimidate would-be predators. I know how you enjoy that.

As for how to tell her of your project's current limitations, you needn't worry so much. She will not think less of you, and, as your loving Sister and her general, I will be blunt: you worry too much about her opinion. The pedestal you've put her on is made of sand, as I have told you before. She isn't Tomi.

Bite the bullet (a delightful phrase, one of my favorites from the last two centuries) and send her the results along with the parameters of their use. And yes—you may of course send your test subject my way. I will look after him, though, and I AM prying, Sis, it would be helpful to know exactly what you are doing. I do not love that Vezina has clearly told you to keep this from me. Perhaps she couched it as "keep it secret from the rest of your Sisters" but there is little she doesn't tell me, and never without reason. Rarely have those reasons been enjoyable.

Also let me know about any containment your subject might need. You know I don't spend that much time at the estate, and security is limited. Are they one of the Blood? Another species? Anything but a were-chihuahua is welcome. The last time I encountered one she ate an entire basket of my laundry and I had to take her to a veterinarian. Gorgeous woman, though.

How are you, besides overworked? I'm going to Paris to destabilize a conference this spring. You should come with me. You spend too much time alone in that lab for your own good, and that's only gotten worse since Tomi died. Ask Vezina for some time off. If Paris isn't to your taste, make her take you somewhere. She could use a break as well, and she loves spoiling you.

Do you need me present when your guinea pig arrives? If so, I'll rearrange my schedule. The bike needs a tune-up but she's ready for the road.

Love,
Nat

"Poison will not have lasting effects on me. She doesn't have much time, Clara. If we must force her—"

"This one will." Perhaps the conviction in my voice persuaded her to listen, for she gave me her full attention.

"How do you know this?"

"Bran told me. It's a fungicide." Agatha didn't know who Bran was, of course, but she lifted her head farther away from Fiadh's neck. I added what explanation I could, given the situation. "He's her fey hostage."

"Ah," said Agatha, glancing at the walls. Her lips were still red with my blood as she pursed them in thought. "Another Oak."

Bran had mentioned oaks—something, something, trees and mycelium and lichenization. I didn't care. If Agatha couldn't help Fiadh—

"Natek could perform the transfusion, couldn't she?" Fiadh's hold on my shirt slackened. Relief and resignation shaped the gesture, and her fingers trailed limply down my chest to settle where they would, palm up and open.

"It will take her too long to recover, and Fi doesn't have that much time."

"Will biting her infect you?"

"I have to break her skin with my teeth. No doubt Vezina accounted for transfer through mucous membrane."

"Then how do we save her?" Wildly, I tried to calculate how long it would take an ambulance to get here. I didn't even know where the nearest hospital was located. Would Fiadh make it? How much vital damage had already been done? How much blood had Vezina taken?

Agatha shrugged her shoulders, and the vines fell away from one arm. Free, she raised a hand to Fiadh's face and stroked her clammy cheek, then her tangled hair. Fiadh's eyes flickered behind their closed lids. I hated how small she looked. How empty—as if her soul had

267

already started its separation from flesh, and without it, her body had lost substance. Agatha murmured something in a language I didn't understand and in a register too low for me to hear. Then she said, "Hold her still, Clara Eden."

Agatha punctured Fiadh's neck over the bruised, raw wound left by Vezina. Her lips revealed the sharp points of her canines as she sank them into the pale, bruised skin. Thrall pulsed from her, radiating comfort. Fiadh stirred in mute protest; Agatha did not stop. The sound of her feeding raked against my spine: a quiet, liquid sound that, had I heard it anywhere, under any circumstances, would have nudged my adrenal gland.

I hadn't thought about the mechanics of a vampiric transfusion. The physiology was all wrong. How could Agatha pump blood back into Fiadh? It wasn't possible. It—

Agatha shuddered, and I smelled hot, rich copper. Her jaw stretched wide, teeth sunk into the column of Fiad's neck, and formed a seal with her lips like a leech. I whimpered. It was so fundamentally *wrong*. Each surge of blood coursed through Agatha like milk poured from a jug, a *glug glug glug* so innocuous it guaranteed I'd never drink anything poured from a container again. And yet, as I clutched Fiadh, breathless and repulsed, she warmed beneath the thin dress. Color might have returned to her cheeks. In the moonlight, I couldn't tell, but her breathing eased its painful rasp. Relief loosed a gasp from my lips.

Agatha shuddered again. This convulsion must have jostled her lips, for blood spilled onto the floor before she latched on once more. Another convulsion rocked her moments later, and she grabbed onto me with her freed hand for support. Was it the poison? Natek stirred in her bonds a few feet away, her expression focusing for longer stretches of time. What would it mean for Agatha to have the fey side of her nature scoured clean? And Fiadh—was she at risk? Or was this fungicide targeted specifically for Agatha's fungal spore line? I turned the questions over and over, my heart thudding sickly with worry. The smell of blood fully permeated the room, now, and mingled with the roses.

The meadow faded back to slate tile as Agatha released Fiadh into my arms with a gasp and fell slack against the thick vines. They supported her. Gently, I lowered Fiadh to the floor and sat down beside her, cradling her head in my lap. Her pulse no longer flickered against my fingers, but beat at regular intervals. My lower lip trembled as relieved tears fell down my cheeks and splashed onto her face. I wiped them away.

Coughs wracked Agatha. I didn't want to look away from Fiadh, but the sound was viscous, liquid; the sound of someone drowning in their own blood. She hacked something up onto the smooth slate floor. I caught it out of my peripheral vision and looked away.

"Gata?" Natek's voice wavered.

Agatha didn't respond. *Couldn't* respond, because she was bent double, shaking hard enough to rattle bones. Natek straightened, fighting off the remaining stupefying effects of the spore and fumbling to reach her knife with her bound hands.

"Clara?"

I looked down. Fiadh blinked blearily back up at me.

"Hey, you," I said.

"Where's Vezina?"

"Gone for now." After locking us into a death trap, I didn't mention. "How do you feel?"

She pulled a face and tried to sit up. I put a hand on her shoulder.

"Not yet. Take a minute."

"Agatha?"

"Alive and ... well." The last was a bit of an exaggeration. Something slimy coated Agatha's front and dribbled from her chin. It was like the poison was turning her inside out. Another horrific cough rent the air.

"Agatha?" Fiadh managed to sit up despite my attempts to encourage her to stay supine. I supported her back, rubbing circles to encourage blood flow. "What—"

The black-blue of night had lightened to a dark gray, which meant sunrise was only an hour or less away. In this light, I saw understanding dawn on Fiadh's features with muted clarity. She didn't say anything. Shock worked itself through the twist of her mouth, followed by grief, and superseded at last by a gratitude so profound I had to avert my gaze.

I stared at my hands instead. My wrist had swollen, and the skin felt hot and tight.

"Gata," Natek said again. She'd gotten a hand on her knife, and now she sawed through the vines, shedding white and black blossoms. They gathered at her feet. With a growl, she burst free of the remaining tendrils and crossed the floor to Agatha in three long strides.

I'd always pictured Natek as the taller of the two, but as starlight framed them against the glass I saw they were of a height—only a few inches taller than Fiadh. People were smaller, once upon a time, and girls often underfed. Agatha looked it now. How could I ever have feared that frail, broken creature?

Natek gathered Agatha to her chest and rocked back and forth, her head bowed low over her lover's, and the sound she made should have rent time. Fraught tenderness filled that high, keening note. I felt it vibrate through the hollows of my lungs, my heart, the thrumming highways of my veins. This was someone who'd first learnt grief from the wailing laments of women two thousand years dead. Tears flowed once more down my cheeks. My soul had made those same sounds when I'd seen Fiadh's bloodless face. Natek rocked, and as she rocked, she keened to the rhythm of their bodies. We watched this spectacle of reunion silently. Beside me, Fiadh's cheeks were bright with tears.

Agatha coughed twice more, and each time, Natek hunched as if the pain were hers. *There can be no regret when I have you,* she had written. Fiadh fumbled for my hand and held on tightly. I didn't know what she was thinking, but for my part, while I couldn't forget our predicament, I remembered the longing I'd felt in their words and knew that at least something had come out of this debacle. Agatha turned her head into Natek's chest and buried her face in the bloodstained shirt. Natek kissed her forehead, heedless of the gore.

As I watched, Agatha reached up to Natek's neck and drew their foreheads together. Natek spoke in a low, swift language that might have been Nektopolian or Greek or Russian. I couldn't make out individual words, and it was still too dark for me to see their expressions plainly unless I was directly in front of them, let alone read lips. I was grateful. This moment between them was too intimate. Too *old*. I could taste the years like dust at the back of my throat. I tasted, too, my own regret. I'd misjudged Agatha, because monster or not, she'd just saved Fiadh's life at the expense of her own.

The sky was a light gray when Natek helped Agatha sit up on her own. Agatha's face had partially healed, and the wound in Natek's forearm had knit together over the bone, though muscle and sinew still gleamed wetly.

"Gatalina." Natek said Agatha's old name like a prayer as she touched Agatha's cheek, seemingly heedless of the wounds disfiguring them both. Her hand cupped the bloodied curve of jaw, and the eyes—macabre as they were in their current state—in that ruined face looked up at Natek with such longing I forgot, for a moment, who and where I was. No one had ever looked at me that way.

"Nettle," said Agatha, her voice rough from screaming and thick with emotion. "Nettle, I—"

"Shhh, love." Natek gathered Agatha in her arms, and the way Agatha tucked her head beneath Natek's chin and melted into that embrace said more than any words even the prolific Natek could have mustered. My ragged breathing sounded loud in that sudden stillness, as if time had made an exception for them, and I realized I'd unconsciously tried to quiet my pained breaths.

"We need to go," Natek said, breaking the spell. Agatha pulled away reluctantly. Her eyes were now distant and lost. "We'll deal with this. I promise."

"I . . ." Agatha trailed off. Fiadh leapt up from my side, stumbled, and managed to make it to Agatha before collapsing to her knees and prostrating herself before her. Agatha lightly touched her hair.

"I'm so sorry," said Fiadh. "She drained me so you'd have to turn me if you wanted me to live or finish me off out of mercy, and she jabbed me with a syringe, and I am so, so sorry—"

"Do not be." Agatha's voice was a whisper. "Do not be sorry, love. Come."

She lifted Fiadh's chin, and Fiadh rose to a crouch. "But—"

"You are worth it."

"The shock could have killed you."

"Yes." Agatha smiled, and though it was wan, it was real. "You'll note, however, that I am still among the living—as it were."

"Something none of us will be for long if we don't move." Natek stood and helped Agatha up. Despite the urgency in her words, she again brought her hand to Agatha's cheek and held it there.

You are a feast, and I am starving.

"Right." Agatha ended the moment with an averted gaze and briskly dusted herself off as if she'd merely gotten soil on her slacks and sweater, instead of blood and spore and other, unmentionable substances. "Set her wrist while I get out of this?"

"This" was the manacle chaining her to the floor. The steel links whispered as she appraised the cuff. I, meanwhile, flinched. How had

271

she even noticed my swollen wrist? She'd been out of her mind on fungal hallucinogens. This was not the best time for first aid.

Natek gestured for me to rise and approach. I held tighter to Fiadh. Her hands had been gentle when she touched Agatha, but I remembered the heel of her boot grinding into my bones.

"Now," said Alexander's general-turned-ruler-in-her-own-right, though the command was kind. Nektaria. In the flesh. I shivered, the reality starting to set in with the pain. *Nektaria*. Struggling to my feet, blood loss heavy in my limbs, I laid my wrist in the hand of the subject of my life's work and closed my eyes while she probed the injury. Nektaria—living, breathing Nektaria, touching my skin.

"Dislocated, not broken. Am I correct in remembering this was my boot?" Her cool hands moved up and down the damaged area, clinical without being cold. She'd probably set thousands of minor injuries on the battlefield.

"Yes," I admitted.

"An unfortunate misunderstanding." She set my wrist back into place without so much as a *one, two, three*. I squeaked. Fiadh gripped my other hand as the pain seared, then lessened.

"Give me the tie from your robe," she said to Fiadh. Fiadh complied, and Natek wrapped it around my wrist like a sports bandage. The pressure instantly eased some of the ache.

"What's your plan?" Agatha asked Natek. Her cuff clinked open onto the slate.

"Get out of this room first. The door is locked, no?"

I confirmed that I'd heard Vezina lock us in.

"Once we've managed that, we get as far away from here as we can and regroup." She pulled a ring of small metal tools from her pocket and began working the door locks. Quick fingers probed and paused. The door swung open. Vines had torn the deadbolts from the wood and busted open padlocks. *Thank you, Bran.*

"Should you fake your deaths? Lock the door behind us again and . . . light a little fire or something?" I asked, trying to be helpful.

"I forget humans believe vampires turn to ash when the sun touches us," Natek said without looking away from the hallway beyond.

"Then what does happen?"

"Something much worse. Our skin sloughs off. The sun deactivates several important enzymes, disintegrating our essential matter. Like an acid bath. Ash would be much neater. Come. We run, and we fight

272

only if we have to."

"She has an Oak," Agatha said.

"Yes," said Natek, the word heavy.

I looked to Fiadh for clarification.

"It's . . ." She paused, and I could tell it was a struggle to coordinate her thoughts. She needed rest and fluids. "Like Bran was saying. The fey lines are named for their mycorrhizal relationships with trees. Each is a family, of sorts. Or a clan. But also part of a greater organism."

As I'd suspected. "What line was Agatha?"

"An Oak."

"Is that why the poison worked on her, but not you?" I asked. She gave me a sideways glance. Natek and Agatha continued to discuss our options before the door. "Cat Síth. Fairy cat. It's a simple translation," I said.

"I told you I would explain everything if we got out of here."

". . . navigating Bran will be difficult," Natek was saying. "I don't want to have to kill him."

If Natek killed Bran, I wouldn't have to worry about my debt. However, I wasn't optimistic they could take on Bran, let alone Vezina, in their current state, and I was exhausted and feeling the beginnings of a panic hangover from nearly losing Fiadh. All I wanted was to be curled up in my own bed with Fi and Mr. Muffin and nobody chasing us.

"He'll just retreat into mycelium until he finds a suitable new host," Agatha said.

Fiadh squeezed my hand meaningfully. I shivered at the implication. She was reminding me of the danger she thought I'd escaped.

"Fair enough." Natek motioned for us to follow her as she spoke. "Move quietly."

Fiadh clung to me in silence. Agatha and Natek descended the stairs, the latter supporting the former. I hesitated. Maybe I'd gotten lucky on my mad flight to find Fiadh, and now the house would strike, sending vines and wasps and giant mushrooms to hold me hostage.

"Come on," said Fiadh. I took a step and winced in anticipation of retaliation. Only the creak of floorboards sounded in response.

Natek moved silently ahead, her body coiled, one arm held slightly out to her side to keep Agatha behind her, the other on her knife. Carpet shushed beneath my feet as I followed. I was not a vampire, nor a Cat Sìth, and my booted feet made noise.

Natek stopped us at every corner and sometimes halfway down a hall or a flight of stairs. Each time nothing leapt out to destroy us, her frown deepened. The quiet was a cocked fist waiting to strike.

In that tension, I wondered how tinted the windows of a car needed to be to protect a vampire from the sun, because the odds of us getting out before sunrise looked slimmer and slimmer. Agatha's SUV presumably had some sort of protection—assuming we could make it in time. As for my car, I had the sinking feeling I wasn't going to see it again.

A flutter of movement from an open door caught Natek's attention. She crouched, light on the balls of her feet, then shook her head.

"Curtain."

I peered into the room as we passed. Sure enough, a green curtain fluttered in the draft of a heat vent, each fold of cloth an emerald glow illuminated by the lightening sky. The vent held my attention. Possibilities gestated in those dark ducts. Where were the wasps? Did they live in the walls and HVAC system, content to ignore the other occupants of the house unless triggered?

A tug on my arm: Fiadh, urging me on with grave determination. Her eyes matched the curtain. The little details I'd consciously and unconsciously been gathering about her over the months suddenly mattered terribly. As her socked feet pressed into the carpet runner, I knew her toes turned ever so slightly outward. Beneath her robe, a constellation of freckles mapped the space between her shoulder blades, and strands of her hair clung to the clotting wounds on her neck. I felt each detail like a wound of its own. I was a bullet-riddled tin can, and the wind sang over the holes she'd left behind.

Portraits watched our progress. All were of women, I noted, unable to help myself—an artifact was an artifact, even under duress. Oil paint. Egg tempura. Gouache. The faint light from the windows and occasional lamp lit each medium differently. Oil reflected the light; gouache drank it in. The touches of style behind the brush, however, were remarkably consistent, which intensified the effect of painted scrutiny—especially under the current circumstances. *Were* we being watched?

I'd be a fool to believe otherwise.

The front doors came into view from the half landing of the last staircase. I touched the wood of the handrail, which was so smooth it felt soft beneath my fingertips, and, crucially, helped balance my wavering steps. Gray daylight cast shadows over a high ceiling decorated with murals I couldn't make out. A table with a vase of flowers—not roses, for a pleasant change, but dried hydrangeas—and two benches on either side of the door were all that populated the vast foyer. Vezina and Bran were nowhere in sight.

There stood the doors, waiting. All we had to do was follow the path of the carpet runner down the widening staircase to the exit. I took a step forward.

"Something's wrong," said Natek, throwing up a hand in warning.

"I know." Agatha halted beside her and adopted the same wary posture. "Perhaps she wants us trapped outside—it wouldn't take much. Sunrise is a few minutes away."

"It's not that. Listen."

We listened. I didn't hear anything, but Agatha and Fiadh tensed.

"What?" I asked Fiadh.

"It's—"

Then I heard it. A low rumbling, growing louder all the time. I ducked, expecting to see the wasps swarming around a corner, but the sound wasn't quite right for wasps. More like how I thought an earthquake might sound.

"Run?" Agatha asked Natek.

"Run."

We pelted down the staircase, Natek and Agatha with grace, Fiadh and I with the fatigued shamble of sleepwalkers. Overhead, an unlit chandelier tinkled as the crystal pendants swayed. I put on a burst of speed with strength I was certain came at the expense of several years of my life, towing Fiadh along with me. Three stairs left. Two. My skin prickling with sick anticipation, as if I'd spiked a fever, I set my foot on the last step.

Like a bell, I expected the house to clang in warning, but our feet sank into carpet without fanfare. Ten feet, maybe fifteen, lay between us and the doors. Fiadh lengthened her stride with a growl just as Natek turned the knob of one of the large doors and yanked it open. Wan light fell over the snow, the half-lit world hazy with shadows. The

SUV was parked just twenty yards away. Agatha's footprints were still visible in the snow as dark blue shadows within the gray.

The first shoot exploded from the earth, sending snow spraying across the lawn. It thickened as it grew at impossible speed, putting out branches and leaves and thorns. More shoots tore the snow, a fine mist of soil settling over the white quilt of the ground in the split-second we'd paused in the doorway.

"Back," Natek shouted as a thick whip of growth erupted from between the flagstones. I hadn't known there had been flagstones beneath the snow, but the force of the briars sent the stones tenting skyward. One cracked with a teeth-shattering snap.

Fiadh and I scrabbled backward into the dubious safety of the manor as the briars thickened into a hedge worthy of any Sleeping Beauty, long, wicked thorns snarling in thickets not even a squirrel could have squeezed through. Several such thorns punched through panes of glass in the foyer, and the sound of wood against wood suggested the front door would need serious repair once this was over. A tendril of purple-green branch penetrated one of the broken panes of glass. I watched, transfixed, as it put out a small, tight bud. I knew what color it would be in the lamplight long before it unfurled, just as I knew the smell that would waft over us when it bloomed: deeply fragrant, with a hint of iron.

The rumbling continued long after the leaves had blotted out the weak winter morning sunlight, the roses continuing their awful pursuit of the sky.

"I take it she knows we survived," said Natek, ripping lengths of cloth from her shirt with inhuman ease. The toned, bronze skin of her stomach shone in the light of the chandelier—which was new. There hadn't been light before.

"Here." A length of cloth soared through the air toward each of us. I held mine, confused, until I saw Agatha and Natek wrap theirs around noses and mouths.

"It won't keep spore out for long, but it's better than nothing. Fiadh, Clara—stay out of the way."

More lights flickered on as Fiadh and I backed away from the stairs and behind the table with the flowers. The rich colors of the walls and elegant mahogany furnishings shed their nighttime shadows, their elegance at odds with the profusion of unnatural growth. Natek and Agatha stood shoulder to shoulder, Natek with her braid and bloodstained chamois shirt illuminated by the soft lighting, and Agatha, hair half down from its neat twist, most of her eyelid grown back, and a set to her lips I'd felt through thousand-year-old ink. Had they been human, they might have exuded grim determination. But they were not human, and the gleam in Natek's eye could have been the light, or it could have been war incarnate.

"What a waste of a sunrise," said a voice from the top of the stairs.

"Prick your finger on a spindle recently?" asked Natek.

I wasn't the only one who'd made the connection to that fairy tale, apparently.

"Your absorption of the era's humor is commendable." Vezina's voice flowed down the banister, clear and cold. Their banter was worse than hurled insults. There was such familiarity in the easy spill of syllables, such unconscious fondness amid the fury.

We'd been so close to escape. So close to hugging my cat to my chest in the safety of my little kitchen, with the kettle building up steam and the friendly gleam of copper pots on their rack.

"Would you rather I quote the *Facetiae*? I recall how much you loved the one about the friar."

The *Facetiae*, my mind supplied encyclopedically, was one of the oldest printed joke books, dating from the Middle Ages.

"Emphatically no."

"Well, a friar—"

"*Nat.*" Vezina's voice cracked like the flagstone.

"You lied to me," said Natek in answer. "You lied to me about the one thing you knew mattered above all else. You swore that if I returned, you'd end this mad pursuit. There was no statute of limitations on that promise."

"A promise to an oath breaker means nothing."

"Two millennia of service."

"*And yet you stand there with my enemy.*"

Beside me, Fiadh shivered. I shared the feeling. Even Natek flinched before pressing on. In the light, I could see her clearly: lean as a cheetah, with the same long, loping gait. A hunter. A pursuer. And yet she held herself as one cornered, putting the shield of her body between Vezina and Agatha, one hand on her knife and the other splayed at her side as if that would be enough to keep Agatha safe.

"You're a strategist. What do you think the odds are of me taking you up on that offer?"

"Negligible." Natek bared her teeth in a feral smile. "But negotiation precedes escalation."

In the pause before Vezina answered, another window shattered under the *Rosaceaen* assault. "Not always."

"Just let Gata go. For me. Kill me after if it suits you. I've had more than my fill of time."

And the humans, I wanted to shout. *Let them go too! Right now, in fact!*

"There is too much blood between us for that." Vezina's voice softened as if she wanted Natek to understand. "Too much blood. You know why I summoned you here, though may I remind you I specified *this* evening, not last."

"I do not require an invitation to my own house."

"You betrayed me again. There are consequences."

Agatha pushed past Natek, gently moving that sheltering hand, and stood before Vezina. The fifteen feet or so between us and them wasn't enough to shield me from that look. If Vezina hated Agatha, it was nothing to Agatha's own hate.

"You stole me from my family. You made me flood our fields and parch our forests, and when I tried to make you understand the *consequences*, you turned my daughter into a blade and held her to my throat."

"I offered you immortality."

"*I already had it.*"

"How was I to know? I'll ask you one more time. If you can undo what you've done to me, I will spare Natek." I saw Vezina close the gap between herself and Agatha. They stood a mere foot apart, Vezina all cold beauty, and Agatha real and warm and rumpled. Vezina looked to her with a hope that eclipsed the hope of the road-weary penitent. Agatha might have been the sun, in that moment, and she green leaves. A perfect opportunity for Bran to pop up and take Vezina out.

No such luck. Agatha reached a hand slowly up toward Vezina's face. Natek stirred behind her, ready, but only Vezina's lips moved.

"You painted the past with technicolor, and I see it all: the bright blues of Crete, the cinnabar red of China, and the gleaming white of a chalk cliff. It never stops. I might have healed without you. I might, given time, have turned away from the path you hated, but you ensured the worst of me would—"

"Is that what you tell yourself? That without me, you mightn't have stayed a monster?"

Vezina shifted, leaning her body toward Agatha. "*Memory* is a monster."

"Yes," said Agatha. Satisfaction curled around the single syllable. Her fingers brushed Vezina's cheekbone, and an agonized flinch shuddered through the taller woman's body. I thought at first that Agatha had done something, and then I remembered the poison. There was nothing Agatha *could* do. Except speak. "Tell me, Vezina, how have you been all these years?"

Agatha's finger trailed off that prominence of cheek and returned to her side, where it joined its brethren in a fist. "I haven't been able to do more than counter your moves, and poorly, at that, but I have taken such comfort in imagining the screams that fill your daylight hours. It is the only comfort you've left me. Life is long, Vezina of Dacia, and memory is longer. I hope you live forever."

Vezina didn't flinch at this torrent, but there was a stillness to her body that suggested a flinch had been repressed. She resembled Natek in this.

"One of my Daughters is a brilliant scientist." Vezina spoke evenly, countering Agatha's passionate tone with the cultured, correct voice of a politician. "She's long sought a cure for me—even performed a lobotomy in the forties, which was informative, though not effective, as there are few studies on brains like ours. Perhaps you received the press release with her findings. I know you're a *Sanguine Scientist* subscriber.

"Our cellular resilience is part of the problem. We tried antifungals, thinking they might hold the key, but the fungus was gone. It did what you meant it to do to my neocortex before my body killed it. While studying the mechanisms, however, my Daughter discovered something very interesting about our cells: they are viral, as you know, a viral cancer with certain distinctive features, including an elasticity that in laboratory settings can be mimicked by a mycovirus. I'll skip over the molecular biology in the interest of time and summarize.

"I have the means to destroy your people, cripple your mycelium, and bring blight to your trees. The infection will spread, destroying the lichenization process, and slowly becoming endemic, until you forget the deep truths you are so fond of flaunting and return to your separate parts."

Agatha flung herself forward, halted only by Natek's swift grip from behind. Her momentum was all grief. I could almost see it shudder

279

through her body and into Vezina, catapulted by Natek's arrest.

This, then, was what Bran was afraid of triggering. I couldn't blame him. Hearing Vezina spell it out made it sound even worse than Bran's cursory explanation.

Metal rang as Vezina withdrew a sword I hadn't noticed—and kept drawing, and kept drawing, until nearly four feet of steel glimmered beneath the chandelier. It had been hidden from my view by the angle of her body, its hilt invisible where it reared above her far shoulder.

"Fuck," said Fiadh.

Vezina's profile was to us, and I saw her lips pull up in a ferocious grin. She raised the sword above her head in a horizontal line I recognized vaguely from a fighting manual I'd helped a friend translate early in my PhD. Her arms flexed beneath her white blouse, muscles shifting to accommodate the weight. Natek's knife hand sprang to attention, readying for attack. A knife against a longsword.

Vezina descended the last step. Confidence pooled around her like a shadow.

"Agatha's unarmed," said Fiadh.

"Natek—"

"—isn't enough. Not against her. We have to do something."

"Fi—"

"We have to do something," she repeated, squirming out of my grasp to look into my face. "You don't have to care about Agatha, but we don't leave alive if she dies."

"Bran—" But she cut me off before I could confess the bargain I'd made.

"She came here knowing it could be a trap, Clara, but that *we* were here, and she came alone."

"*And she is a vampire.* Natek was right—we need to stay out of the way so that we don't get in the way. Unless you have a gun?"

"Bullets won't work."

"Oh. Great. Good to know."

Please listen to me, I willed her. I knew if she ventured onto that battlefield, I would follow because I loved her, not because I was brave.

The sound of Vezina's sword striking Natek's long knife grated on my ears. In that lingering shriek, I experienced a moment of suspended stillness, of a silence disturbed only by the bloody drum of my heart. Was this it? Was this the moment before the fall? What had I done with my life? I'd never finished my book on Nektaria. I'd never owned a dog. I'd never gotten around to buying that whole new wardrobe, getting tenure at a prestigious university, or holding my future child. Had I wanted a child? I'd never get to make that decision now. All possibilities narrowed to this point.

Where the fuck was Bran?

As my bubble of suspension slowly popped—even that act a jelled, glutinous violence—I remembered lying on the lawn in the heat of summer with Fiadh on her elbows beside me. I remembered how good even winter sunlight felt on my face in the mornings when I stood before the window with a cup of coffee. I remembered crickets. I remembered the soft weight of my cat, who had now gone several days without food, as Mark would have assumed I'd returned, and the whole-body comfort of his purr, and I remembered the thrill of an idea coming together after weeks of research. It would have to be enough. It *was* enough. Outside, the sun was rising past the snarl of roses, and while I might never finish my book, I'd *met* Nektaria. And Fiadh. I had Fiadh, who was too ready to die to protect the people she loved.

I couldn't let that happen.

CHAPTER THIRTEEN
One More Bite

"The satisfaction of an impalement with the efficiency of cold, hard steel," Natek was saying as Vezina sized her up. A bright ring of sound, too fast to follow. My breathing whistled in my ears as my throat constricted with tight panic. Another pane of glass shattered. Rose canes forced their way in like they were elbowing their way through a crowd, all right angles and long, reaching fingers. Sap scented the air as the glass sliced through the outermost layer of bark. Had Agatha been able to call up forces of nature as powerful as Bran seemed capable of summoning? I hadn't seen it, but that meant nothing. It sure as hell would have been convenient right about now.

More clashes.

Natek's attack, unrelenting as it was, didn't penetrate Vezina's guard. How could it? The knife measured a fifth of the longsword's length.

Agatha broke off a thick cane and joined Natek. The narrowing stair, however, prevented her from circling behind and pinning Vezina between them. Tactically, Vezina couldn't have asked for a better position. One sweep of her sword covered the entirety of her step from railing to railing. She yielded another step.

"She wants to knock them down the stairs once they're high enough," said Fiadh.

I didn't respond. There wasn't time. Vezina lunged, sword raised, but instead of taking Natek and Agatha down in one cut, as I suspected she'd intended—planned for—Natek flung herself forward at the same instant and grabbed Vezina around the knees. They tumbled down the stairs, longsword flying, and landed in a roll Vezina converted to a crouch, one hand pressed to the ground, her head flung back to appraise her enemy. Natek caught herself on Agatha's ankle.

Vezina couldn't have been more than four feet away from us. My breath burned my throat as I panted in terrified anticipation. Her gaze fell on me. *Juice box,* those eyes said. A warm, soft feeling started settling over me, calming my distressed regulatory system.

Agatha pounced, leaping from the third step with the cane held above her head. The tip should have pierced Vezina through the chest, but Vezina knocked it aside with her forearm. Natek kicked the longsword farther away from Vezina on her way to assist. That, however, proved to be a mistake—it cost Natek a precious second. Vezina sprang, bypassing Agatha's guard and colliding with her body. They went down in a tangle of limbs.

The gurgle of air leaving Agatha's throat rose above the scuffling sounds of bodies writhing over tile. Agatha twisted, and Vezina was briefly on top of her.

Natek stabbed her in the kidney. Vezina snapped at the air with her teeth and released Agatha, who coughed and rolled to her feet, massaging her throat. Natek withdrew her knife from Vezina's body and turned to shield her lover.

"She nearly snapped my hyoid," rasped Agatha. "I'll need a second."

Natek nodded and settled deeper into a guard stance.

Vezina, organ damage notwithstanding, had seized her moment and retrieved her longsword. She approached with easy, casual strides, hair fully loose and blowing around her shoulders as she moved. The harsh beauty of her features matched her blade.

Natek readied herself.

And then the front door cracked in half. Thorns cascaded in, rubbing against each other in a chorus of scrapes and creaks. Tendrils twined up the staircase, and a root punched through the floor, sending stone dust and shrapnel skittering across the foyer. The motion of accelerated growth whispered like wind through the unfurling leaves. Roses watched: eyeless, red-black.

Fiadh and I ducked beneath the table, edging away from the viridian advance. Agatha, on the other hand, reached out and caressed the nearest thorn. A line from a letter drifted half-formed into my head.

283

Sharp enough to end us.

The thicket snarled into the chandelier, dangling blossoms over our heads and branching downward as the room shrank to an oval of thorn-free space, trapping us around Vezina and the stairs. Leaves rustled all throughout the hall, filling it with the susurrus of summer, the fragrance of the blossoms choking in its intensity.

"There is so much I wanted to tell you," Natek said to Agatha as the rose wall slowed its perfidious growth and Vezina focused on hacking herself clear. "I wrote—"

"I read them."

"All of them?" Natek turned her head to Agatha, showing me her profile. Vezina sauntered closer in the background.

"All I could find. You rely too much on metaphor."

"I'll accept notes."

Agatha looked at Natek through guarded brows and asked, "Did you know about the fungicide?"

I listened through my labored breathing. I wanted—needed—to know the ending of this story.

"I tried to get in touch with you as soon as I found out." Natek spoke swiftly and quickly, no doubt aware of Vezina's slow advance. "I've been signaling for months. Gata—"

She broke off. Vezina had closed the distance, but I didn't think that was why she'd stopped. I knew the sound of someone choking on their heart.

Vezina brought her sword down with a shriek of severed air. Natek parried. Her shoulders absorbed the impact with the wiry strength of a mule, and the knife didn't waver beneath the strain.

Agatha had broken off a thicker rose cane and held it like a bo staff, blood seeping from where thorns punctured her hands.

Vezina reset. Agatha advanced and raised her staff, her spine determined.

The sword sliced cleanly through it. Agatha ducked, but there was no way she'd move in time to avoid serious damage, and I went rigid with horror.

But Natek must have anticipated this. Her knife caught the sword barely an inch from Agatha's face, cutting her cheek and saving her life (assuming decapitation could kill her, which I wasn't sure about at all). Vezina whipped the sword away from Natek's guard with compressed fury. Natek, unbalanced, moved in time to save her own life, but not her shoulder. Vezina drove the blade deep and withdrew just as quickly. Blood pumped in thick, black gouts out of the wound. Was there an artery, there? Could a vampire bleed out?

"You should have fed," said Vezina. Natek, undeterred, swapped her knife to her left hand and attempted to stand. Thorns reached for Natek's arms and bound her legs, heedless of the suppressed grunt of pain as a cane scraped past her wound. The scent of crushed rose petals was overwhelming. I wanted to scream at Bran to stop, to save us like he'd promised, but he'd only ever promised to save me and Fiadh—not Agatha or Natek.

Fiadh rushed forward.

"Fuck." I stumbled after her. Thorns ensnared Fiadh the moment she reached Natek, winding around her body in a cocoon and pulling her into the wall.

I dove, clawing at the vines, which grew slick with my blood. The outer canes were covered not only with long, vicious thorns, but smaller serrated ones, too. Fiadh reached toward me. I had just enough presence of mind within my panic to notice that the canes holding her captive had their thorns pointing outward, not in, sparing her vegetal exsanguination. Her fingers tightened around mine. I met her terror-wide eyes.

"She's safe in there."

Bran's voice came from behind me and all around. Fiadh didn't seem to have heard.

A cane shot like a bar across my chest and hauled me backward. I fought, wriggling out only to be snared by another, and another, and—

The sword sliced through the roses and I was hauled out of their grasp by a cold hand. I hadn't seen what had happened between Agatha and Vezina, but it was immediately clear it hadn't been good for our side. Agatha clutched her bleeding abdomen while Natek shouted.

Vezina dragged me into the center of the remaining space, one hand holding a sword designed for two with horrifying ease, and the other wrapped in my collar. The cloth tore a little, but held. I could see the reflection of my terrified eyes in the blade.

I flailed. She twisted my collar, choking me, but I fought harder. Animal panic exploded in my chest. She couldn't kill me in front of Fiadh. She just couldn't.

Warmth pulsed through my body in slow waves of calm. My adrenal glands gave one last little squirt of adrenaline, then quieted, and I hung, shuddering, in Vezina's grip. She turned me so that my back lay flush against her, my neck exposed. Pain faded. My breathing slowed. I heard Fiadh scream my name and couldn't understand why. I only wanted to close my eyes and sleep.

Teeth pricked my neck with a pleasant sensation, like pressing a fingertip against the edge of something sharp until it itched. I blinked slowly.

"*Clara!*" Bran's voice. My eyes focused at the distant sound of my name, and I met my own blown pupils in the bloody steel of her raised blade.

No, murmured the animal of my subconscious. I blinked slowly, the riptide of lassitude faltering.

Vezina drank deeply, and warmth returned. Roses wafted sweetly. All was as it should be.

No.

Spots floated over my vision along with the sense that something wasn't right. I moved, trying to turn my head. Every part of me shook with longing to surrender to the dark and sleep.

Fiadh, saying, "Focus on an object."

Fiadh in the sunlight. Fiadh on the grass. Fiadh.

Thrall promised oblivion. There was such comfort in surrender. All I had to do was obey. And really, what did I have to live for? Wouldn't it be easier to let it all go?

Fiadh. Think of Fiadh.

Bran's reflection studied me from the sword where my own had been seconds before.

"Get ready."

His words broke through the remaining grip of thrall. I could see the roses. I could see the gleaming thorns.

Peace faded from my system and pain flooded in. A predator had me by the throat, and it *hurt*. I opened my mouth to scream.

Vezina raised her blade higher. In the newly reflected view, I saw what Bran had done. A massive thorn had erupted from the thickest cane behind her, tapering to a slender curved point, and it rose at least fifteen inches into the air with purpled newness: a fang, a claw, a rhinoceros horn. I remained slack in Vezina's grip, bearing the pain, thinking.

Thinking was difficult. I hadn't had a whole lot of blood left to begin with, and the rising tightness in my chest constricted my ability to breathe. I knew on a primal level that I didn't have much time left.

"Now," said Bran.

I jerked my head forward and away from her, hearing my flesh tear against her fangs, and then slammed my head back into hers with the weight of my whole body. There was a blinding crack. My skull felt like it had split.

But we were falling.

Hot, sharp agony stabbed through my shoulder blade. I screamed. My head felt like it might split anew with the sound. My vision sparked and faded out, then back in.

Vezina convulsed beneath me. The motion tossed me off her body, and I crumpled to the petal-strewn floor. Cool tile met my cheek. I lay there, stunned and bleeding, while people shouted all around me. The perspective confused my vision for several blinks, but raising my head wasn't an option. I squinted in an effort to bring things into clarity.

Vezina's body lay cradled by rough-barked canes before me. The chest arched oddly. I couldn't—I couldn't make myself understand.

"Gatalina," said Vezina in a wheezing rasp. Agatha stood over her, the longsword in her hands, now. Blood glistened darkly on the tip of the thorn rising perversely from Vezina's chest.

Agatha didn't respond. Her face was blank as she stared at her enemy, as blank and smooth as crisp linen. Vezina laughed wetly. The laughter had a surprised, almost delighted edge to it. She should have been dead. Any mortal human would certainly have been, and I did not want to think about the ruin of her ruptured chest. One of her outflung arms rested close to my face and I could see the tremors running underneath her skin.

"Well done, Gatalina."

"This is your orchestration."

Another laugh. It was just as terrible as the first. Each syllable bathed in the blood pooling in her mouth before emerging. Some of the blood had dripped onto her nearby hand. A drop slipped into the curve of her nailbed and beaded there, almost pearlescent in the odd lighting.

"I've waited. A long time. For this." The pauses between the words grew longer.

"For death?" asked Agatha, face still blank.

Death. Had I killed . . .? My shoulder throbbed fearsomely. The ground beneath me was wet and warm.

"To tell you. What I took from you."

Agatha said nothing. I admired her for that. I would not have shown such restraint.

"She's quite like you. Relentless," said Vezina.

The change came over Agatha's face slowly. A crease in the linen. A ripple of doubt. I tried to rise, mostly to get away from them, but the pain in my shoulder sent a barbed lance down my arm.

"The smell of her hair. I remember that perfectly. Thanks to you. I remember. When I. First held her. Was she eleven? So small for her age."

"She's dead," said Agatha, voice tightening. "She's dead, and when you're dead, she'll have peace."

That horrible gurgling again. "I think. She'll be quite. Upset. Actually."

"End it," shouted Natek. "Cut off her damn head, Gata!"

"You killed her," said Agatha, ignoring Natek. "She's dead."

Vezina rose, pulling herself slowly off the thorn until she was partially upright. Revenge lit her up from within like a bomb. I longed to crawl away from the blast zone. I longed for my bed and my cat and the soft, quiet rustlings of my cottage. My mind balked at my reality, trying to slip its leash. There was a fuzzy quality to the edges of my surroundings.

Was I dying?

What an abstract thought, death. Conservation of energy. The immeasurable weight of the soul.

My eyes refocused on the drama before me with difficulty. Time didn't seem to be working properly. I'd . . . had I . . . Blood dripped from the rose canes supporting Vezina in hard plinks where it hit the slate and hushed plops where it landed on petals. I'd killed flies before. Once, a squirrel on the road.

Vezina coughed an arcing vermillion spray into Agatha's face, leaving bright spatters over the drier blood of previous injuries. Agatha didn't flinch. Her eyes, though, were shattered geodes, the emotions written in them volcanic. Her enemy tried to speak. Vezina's lips parted and her throat worked, thick with blood, but a shudder rippled over her body and she slid back onto the thorn.

"Vezina!" Agatha dropped the sword and shook Vezina by the shoulders, which had to hurt like hell. "Answer me!"

Vezina made yet another horrible sound. It wasn't quite a word.

Agatha shouted her name again, all composure gone. Her eyes were wilder than they'd been in the tower room with spore infecting her lungs.

Stillness stole over Vezina's body. Agatha shrieked, almost on top of her in her urgency. "What did you do to my daughter?" she asked over and over, her voice a bridge collapsing in rush hour, the silence of an empty crib, a worry stone kept in a pocket for two thousand years.

"Cynane," said the corpse, in the same way a chess player might have said, "checkmate."

Natek, who had freed herself from the roses, picked up the sword and severed Vezina's head from her body. It rolled down the canes to land inches from my face. Her eyes met mine. They were dead, of course. Unseeing. But I *felt* seen. Those cores of ice saw me, and the mockery was nothing to the relief. Her mouth slackened into a strange, almost wistful smile.

"Fiadh!" Agatha's desperation penetrated the bubble of shock surrounding me. I pushed through the pain and wormed my way into a sitting position in time to see Fiadh in her prison of thorns twist, her body an inversion, an assault on my ocular nerves as the laws of physics made a feline exception.

She leapt, her black coat abyssal in the morning gloom and untouched by the chandelier, and landed on Vezina's body. Her eyes burned a livid green. With a growl, she dug her claws into Vezina's headless breast and let out a long, wailing caterwaul, her back arched and her hair on end. The cry went on and on. I felt—I wasn't sure. Something. A shimmer or a breeze.

A shudder of rose petals fell like ash around us, spinning on eddies of sound. Fiadh's cry ended with a cough, as if she might have a hairball, followed by a spitting hiss. Agatha scooped her up and clutched her to her chest. Fiadh tucked her head beneath Agatha's chin and yowled.

CHAPTER FOURTEEN

Forty Years in the Wilderness for You

Vezina cooled among the thorns, her head lolling to the side
and her chest thrust grotesquely toward the ceiling, giving the
hedge the look of a shrike's nest. Maybe I'd appreciate the poetic
justice later. Right now, it was all I could do to stand. Blood seeped
down my back. I could feel it pooling at my waistband. My shoulder
didn't hurt anymore. The area buzzed with panicked numbness instead,
and I recognized the signs of shock.

I stumbled toward Agatha and Natek as best I could, tripping on
a cane. Natek closed the remaining distance and caught me, looping
her arm under my good shoulder and supporting me the remainder of
the way. Agatha clutched Fiadh tightly. When I reached out my hand,
she shook her head.

"She may bite."

"I don't care, I—"

"Can barely walk, let alone carry a cat. We need to get to the
back door and hope it isn't blocked, too. It will take us too long to cut
through this." Natek kept me clamped to her side as she spoke. I was
grateful; my legs had turned in their resignation letters.

"Where is the back door?" asked Agatha.

"Past the kitchen." I felt her tense and look around. "Bran?"

A slight shape emerged from a door at the top of the stairs. He
descended the stairs slowly. When he reached us, his face ran with
sweat.

"Go," he said. "The ground isn't stable. Took too much water.

290

Sinkhole imminent." A pathway began to clear through the thicket to the door.

"You could come with us," said Natek. "They'll come looking, and you shouldn't be here."

"They will find nothing." He gestured at the body, and as I watched, white fungal threads spread over the corpse. "Go. I've bought you time and shade, but the sun rises."

Natek stuck out her hand, and Bran took it. It wasn't quite a handshake, more like a clasp. Then he turned to Agatha.

"Even a stump may be nursed back to life by its neighbors."

She nodded.

"Until we meet again," Bran's voice whispered in my ear.

"Do not move."

I obeyed Natek's calm voice. The room was unfamiliar—somewhere in Agatha's basement labyrinth—but soothing. A firm cot supported my aching body, and I noted the IV in my arm and the medical supplies arranged on the counter. This was all I could see while lying face down, except for the floor, which was black marble infused with rippling gold. Drowsiness suggested the IV bag contained more than mere fluids, coupled with the fact that I could barely feel the pat of gauze on my skin as Natek sponged blood off my shoulder.

"Deep," she said, sounding impressed. "You are lucky nothing is permanently damaged. The bone is bruised, but it isn't fractured."

"What . . ." I tried to say. My mouth might have been full of the gauze on my shoulder for all its clarity.

"Morphine. Or something like it," said Natek. "I've dressed more battle wounds than there are stars, kid. Try to relax. This won't kill you."

When I next surfaced from that drugged haze, it was to the sensation of a blanket being draped around my shoulders. When had I sat up?

"Fiadh?" I asked.

"Recovering. It isn't easy to consume a soul, especially that one. It will take her time to return."

I absorbed this information slowly. "A . . . soul?"

"Do you not . . ." Natek broke off and crouched to look me in the eyes. "It is not my place to explain. None of this is my place really."

She looked around the little room. I followed her gaze, and the room's purpose finally clicked: the medical equipment, the cot, the cardboard box of collection bags, the sterile cleanliness—this was a blood donation room. How very civil.

"I want to see her."

"You sure?" Her rich voice cut through the painkiller. "I'd recommend resting. You're low on just about everything: blood, electrolytes, fluids—"

"Please. I have to know she's safe." A torrent of words surged into my throat. "I can't—I can't handle any of this without her. I don't want to handle any of this without her. She's my—we never got a chance to *be* anything—please show me where she is."

"If the alternative is your blood pressure this elevated," said Natek, lifting the blanket off my wounded shoulder and frowning, "then I'll take you. Let it be known this is Against Medical Advice." A hint of humor tinged her voice. "I did get a medical degree once, though we mostly used leeches back then. There's an obvious joke there. Don't make it."

I hadn't been going to. What had she meant by *consume a soul*? I longed for the internet and my phone, which, like my car, I wasn't going to see again. An uncomfortable vibration rang through my mind, like the bells in that Edgar Allen Poe poem—*To the swinging and the ringing/ of the bells, bells, bells*—of knowledge learned and discarded, but not entirely forgotten. Cat Síth. Where had I heard that term prior to Fiadh's confession?

"She's physically stable. The blood loss affects her less in that form. You are the only one with a hole in your physical body." Her arm had healed entirely, as if she'd never sliced it down to the bone. As an aside, she added, "You will regret walking."

I swung my legs over the side of the cot and yelped as my shoulder erupted. Natek fiddled with the drip on the IV bag, and the pain diminished a few percentage points, which still left me well within the margin of acceptable error for excruciating. Natek reached into a drawer, sliding across the floor on the wheeled stool like my childhood pediatrician, and pulled out a length of bandaging material, which she wrapped around my arm and over my uninjured shoulder to make a sling. It helped, marginally. Or at least, it helped until I tried to leverage myself off the table. My scream cut off as the intake of breath expanded my lungs. Lungs, which were housed inside ribs, which had all launched themselves at my shoulder with murderous intent. Natek made a noise between a scoff and a laugh.

"Children," she said under her breath. "They never listen."

Gingerly, I experimented with skidding my socked feet over the black and gold floor while holding the IV pole in my good hand. Better. I didn't turn to look at Natek because I didn't think turning my head was a good idea so, instead, I asked, "Which way?"

"Follow me." At the door, however, she paused. Her shoulders tightened beneath her shirt, which was still the same blood-soaked green chamois. "Tell me, archivist, did Agatha set you the task of finding me?'"

Maybe I should have lied to spare her feelings, I reflected, but I wanted to see Fiadh. I didn't particularly care about anything else. And anyway, Agatha wasn't the sort who would send two lackeys without a hope of defending themselves to find her ex-lover. The lie would reflect badly upon her. "No."

"Then why?"

"Leverage." It was easy to admit this now that I didn't care. Leverage wouldn't matter if something had happened to Fiadh. "And misguided altruism."

"Fair enough."

"Cynane," I said. "Did you know she was Agatha's daughter?"

"That child is no longer hers in any way that matters. I would have chosen death for Gata before I told her the truth about Cynane, because the truth will lead her to throw herself on the spear Vezina's been sharpening for more than two millennia. And neither of them will ever forgive me."

With that, she held the door open for me and led me down a high-ceilinged curving hallway lit with soft, recessed lighting. Shelves inlaid into the white walls contained sculptures, pottery, and other unmistakably ancient objects. Of course Agatha had an even more private "private collection." Natek walked swiftly, and I fell behind, panting with pain and the surprising exertion it took to slide one foot in front of the other. Sweat beaded at my temples. The wheels of the IV stand clacked over the grout seams.

"Here." Natek opened a door into the room where I'd discovered Agatha feeding on Fiadh, with the leather couches and the suspiciously white inlays. Agatha sat in an armchair, resting her forehead on two fingers in the universal symbol of "I have a massive headache, leave me alone," a cat carrier at her feet. A low yowl emerged from the carrier. It was one of those plastic airline ones, large enough for a decent-sized dog with narrow slits in the sides for ventilation. I limped toward it, heedless of Agatha, and knelt gracelessly to look inside.

Green eyes burned in a black face, and the cat hissed when it saw me. When *she* saw me.

"Fi," I said. I reached out to open the door, but a hand clamped tightly around my wrist, which at least wasn't the one Natek had stepped on.

"Do not disturb her."

"What if she changes back?"

"She is a danger to herself right now. And to you." Agatha's weary voice contained little inflection. "She is in there at her own request, and we will respect her wishes."

I stared at the frightened animal in the cage and stifled a sob. Fiadh let out another warning yowl.

"Why doesn't she know me? Last time—"

"She does not know herself right now."

"Gata," Natek began.

Agatha held up a hand. "Get her back to bed. She should not be up and walking."

"But Fi—" I said.

"That is not Fiadh," Agatha snapped. "That is a repository, and if you wish to see Fiadh again, the things inside need to sort themselves out."

This was intolerable. I wanted answers, not half truths. "A repository for *what?*"

"Souls," said Agatha, like this was the most normal thing in the world. "That is the nature of the Cat Síth, to steal the souls of the dying, but she must store the soul properly before she returns to us."

"She has Vezina's soul?" Cold, murky water filled my chest as the horror of that notion bubbled up my throat. Vezina's soul was an oil spill in a reservoir. It would pollute everything it touched.

"Let us hope so. Too many things depend on it. And Clara, in the future, please clear any research trips of this nature with me beforehand."

"But what—what do you mean by *soul?*"

"Ψυχάριον εἶ, βαστάζον νεκρόν[33]," said Natek under her breath.

"Perhaps *the* metaphysical question." Agatha's tone was bitter, but she'd glanced up at last, and relented upon seeing my face. "I'd wondered if she'd explained this to you. Since it appears not, and because there is nothing I can do about the other problems at hand until Fiadh returns to me"—here she paused and flicked her gaze toward Natek—"I will explain what I can.

"Think of the soul as a collection of every memory you have of your life, suspended in the ineffable. Dark matter, perhaps. The space between atoms. What the Cat Síth call the soul may not be the same thing as the religious definition, for memories are not immortal, but it is the best term we have. The essence of life's influence on a person. A neural map laid out in lacework.

"Fiadh's mind is more spacious than yours, more elastic, like a house with a certain number of vacant rooms. The ninth is reserved for herself. She's taken Vezina's memories, and we need them. What she made cannot be allowed to exist. It will destroy my people as it has destroyed me. I am left with this." She gestured at her body. "A singular entity. Without access to the *talamü*, Clara, I am . . . I am an *I* where once I was both *I* and *We*. It cannot be neatly translated—a thing you are, perhaps, uniquely suited to understand. When Vezina turned me, all those lifetimes ago, I lost the ability to work directly through the mycelium—as you saw the Oak who calls themselves Bran work—but she did not sever the connection. I could still sense the world beneath and beyond, and I could still communicate with the *talamü*. Now . . ."

She made a helpless, fluttering gesture. Natek twitched, as if she longed to go to her side, but the walls between them were still high and bristling with armed defenders. She remained leaning against the arm of a couch.

"Now all I have left of myself lies here"—she tapped her chest—"and within Fiadh."

"She has your soul?" I asked, staring at Fiadh's mad, green eyes.

"Cat Síth must be in their true form to fully absorb a soul, and only at the moment of the body's death, but she can store memories in unoccupied rooms whilst bipedal. I have given her those memories I cannot bear to lose, and she has carried them for me, as her mother and her mother's mother and her mother's mother's mother before

---

33 *You are a little soul, carrying a corpse.* Epictetus, 50-120 AD

her carried them."

"And it doesn't hurt her to have . . . all that?"

Agatha held my gaze. Her eyes were so deceptively human when she wanted them to be. "The things we carry change us. Sometimes change hurts."

Fiadh's claws gouged tracks in the carrier, leaving gray plastic shavings clinging to her fur as she arched her back. So this was what Fiadh truly did for Agatha. She was a memory lockbox.

"That's . . ." Highly unethical, and disconcerting in its implications. More importantly, Fiadh had just used up her eighth life. How many other souls did she contain? How many deaths had she seen? "That isn't scientifically possible."

"What your scientists don't know about this world could fill it twice over," said Natek. "Disease was magic, once. Don't place too much emphasis on the how of things. Agatha, we must discuss our options. They'll realize something's wrong in a few more days. Cynane knows about that safe house, and if she can track down Bran, she'll know the rest. We should not assume Bran was able to cover our tracks—I trained her."

Agatha's eyes tightened. Natek saw it, too, for again she twitched in the manner of someone longing to give comfort.

"I will not leave my home." The hands in Agatha's lap held very, very still. "Not this time. I ran from *Vezina*. I will not run from the remnants of her cult."

"Gata—"

"*I will not run.*"

"Seeing her will only bring you pain." Natek stepped forward now, raising me to my feet by my good arm and pivoting me onto a couch without breaking eye contact with Agatha. I clutched my IV pole as the cool leather met the backs of my calves. I hadn't noticed I was wearing a hospital gown until that moment, which, given the state of Natek's clothing, was probably more sanitary. The loose fabric reminded me of the oversized robe Fiadh had trailed around the manor. Would she want a robe or a blanket when she changed?

"Pain is all you've ever brought me. Who named her?"

Natek didn't flinch. "I did. It was not unusual for Vezina to return with children after a raid, and we provided for them until they were of an age to turn. She had fifteen sunlit years with us. I cannot account for anything before."

"She already had a name."

Natek dropped to crouch on her haunches before Agatha, her face tilted upward and her hands taking gentle hold of hers. I wanted to hold Fiadh's hands like that. I wanted to hold Fiadh.

"And I am so, so sorry."

Agatha did begin to shake now. I lay down on the couch, bad shoulder up, head on the smooth leather arm, and curled like a child in the backseat of a car listening to her parents debate a serious issue in hushed voices in the front seat, night flashing by in the rays of passing headlights. I was still so tired. My mind, however, had always been restless, and it parsed through letters and memories as I listened to this ancient tragedy and waited for Fiadh to digest a monster and return to me.

"Natek—" Agatha's voice broke. "Did you know?"

Natek bowed her head to kiss Agatha's hands before answering. "I guessed. Vezina was always so careful with her and, in later years, insistent that I be the one to watch over her. Punishment. She wanted me to figure it out, and she knows I can't help but see the patterns. But I never asked. I was afraid of what she might do to Cynane if she thought she could use her as leverage against me."

"That is not her name. Her name is—" Here, Agatha broke off. "Her name is . . ."

She had never named her daughter in her letters. For a moment, I marveled that after all this time those precious few years of this child's life with Agatha still mattered this much to her, but I didn't have children. I couldn't know what it felt like to lose a life I'd made with my own body.

The couch leather was cool, but the air temperature down here was warmer than upstairs, and I didn't chill. When the shock of all this wore off, what would I be left with? Who was Clara Eden in the wake of vampires, ancient grudges, and planned genocides? What had *I* lost?

"The name will come to you," Natek said instantly. "Do not despair, Gatalina."

Two middle-aged women crouched over a cat carrier. Two immortals in despair over time's ravages of memory. It was like one of those visual tricks—candlestick, or two faces? And what was I? Scholar out of her depth, or killer?

Quietly, so as not to draw attention to myself, I tilted my head over the side of the couch and threw up. This was safe, since I hadn't eaten anything in hours and hours, and only a little bile dribbled down my chin. I wiped my face clean on my smock. Neither Agatha nor Natek seemed to have noticed.

"Everything from that time is part of the *talamü*. I can't—I don't—Nat, I cannot bear this." Agatha wept, and the tears were blood. Natek brushed them away with her sleeves.

"We will find a way to undo what she's done. I swear it. I'll swear it by all the gods we ever worshipped. If you want to make a stand here, we'll make a stand. I'll talk to the Daughters. This was only ever Vezina's crusade, and she made it Cynane's out of spite, but I can make Cynane see reason. Vezina sought *you* out. The responsibility of her death lies on her and her alone."

Agatha did look up at me, then, and Natek's eyes followed.

"At least get her a blanket if you're going to leave her there," said Agatha. Natek rose to obey, picking up the blanket I'd dropped from my shoulders by Fiadh's crate and tucking it around me, careful not to jostle my shoulder. Agatha considered me. Faint tracks of bloody tears stained her cheeks.

"They can't trace anything back to her," said Natek, gesturing at me. "She's not even responsible—she was under thrall."

Shivering fear rippled over my skin. *They can't trace anything back to her.* They? Who, except the ominously named and probably revenge-prone Daughters of the Blood?

"You've never been able to lie to me. A risk, no matter how small, is still a risk, and risks should be taken seriously. We did not stay to watch Bran clean. Are you done trying to coddle me? You never used to." Agatha stared up from the chair with an expression I couldn't parse. Resentment? Scorn?

"I wouldn't dream—"

"No, why dream when you can do? I may be lesser, now, but I am still capable of reason."

"Gata." Natek looked as though Agatha had struck her. She opened her mouth again, but paused, reading something I couldn't in the other woman's face. "Maybe I am coddling you."

A quick smile seared Gata's lips. "You are."

"Well, then." Natek settled back on her heels and crossed her arms. "The unvarnished truth. We did not, as you say, stay to watch Bran clean, as I thought it smarter to get to safety. You were injured—yes, I consider severance an injury, do not argue that point—and I was tired. Present vulnerability outweighed future. A head start might have been the only advantage we had. We cannot therefore assume anything about what may have happened after. Operating as if the enemy knows your secrets is the best way to avoid unpleasant surprises.

"In this case, the enemy is my family. I know many of their secrets, and they mine. I must assume they understand how I think. The worst-case scenario is therefore one in which my sisters know I was involved, you were involved, and that the archivist delivered the death blow. They would hunt us down for far less."

The double horror of committing murder and being hunted for that murder by vampires broke me out of the remnants of my dissociative state.

"I didn't know it was a trap," I said, digging my toes into the slight gap in the cushions for emotional security. This was, strictly speaking, not entirely true, but I had not expected the magnitude of the trap.

"This is not your fault." Agatha had the tone of someone trying to be gentle with a child while really frustrated by the interruption. "Fiadh should have known better. I should have paid more attention to her preoccupation with you, but I thought it harmless, and was even pleased for her. It is always these little unexpected details."

"Most battle plans fall apart before the first shot is fired," added Natek.

"She wanted you to be happy," I said to Agatha, indignant on Fiadh's behalf.

"And you?" Agatha asked me. "What did you want, Clara?"

What risk now, in asking?

"Publication rights to a book on Nektaria using some of your documents and artifacts in exchange for information on her whereabouts, and the opportunity to talk to Nektaria herself."

"Bold of you to assume she wanted to see me," said Natek.

"I read your letters," I said. I was tired and sore and, for the moment, unafraid. "And she's paying me to translate them so she can read them again, and to digitalize them so they'll never be lost. She gave Fiadh memories of you to hold because they are too painful. Her library is full of your work. It was an educated guess."

Both of them stared at me. I stared back, increasingly aware of the possibility I was going to get my way simply because Agatha didn't want to look her lover in the eye.

With a delicate clearing of her throat, Agatha broke the stalemate.

"Which artifacts were you thinking of?"

CHAPTER FIFTEEN
Seven Souls Deep

The first thing Fiadh wanted to do when she transitioned back to the form I knew best was bathe.

Agatha's bathroom was exactly as decadent as I'd expected without bordering on garish. The tub was arguably a small pool, set into a raised dais and surrounded by more of that black-gold tile, though here the darker tile was the accent, and the walls and floor glittered in gold and white marble. Fiadh's bare feet padded over a central mosaic of a stylized geometric flower. There were no mirrors.

"Is it true vampires don't show up in mirrors?" I asked as Fiadh turned the tap on the tub, then crossed to the shower with a gesture indicating she wanted to rinse off before her bath.

"If you'd worn the same face for over two thousand years, would you want to see it?"

I couldn't argue with that, so I tasked myself with searching for towels. I found them in the vanity: plush, black cotton, too sturdy and well-constructed for us to ever have torn them into ropes even if there was a window.

"Is the tub full?" Fiadh leaned her head out of the shower, delineated by glass walls, and I stopped staring at the bathroom fixtures.

"Almost."

"Good enough."

I held a towel open for her, more to touch her than to dry her in between one body of water and another, and she stepped in, water droplets beading on her skin. Her wet black hair clung to the sides of her neck and her lips were flushed from the hot water. She was lovely.

"Are you coming in with me?"

"I'll put my feet in, but . . ." I shrugged, and hissed with pain. Damn shoulder.

"Clara—"

"It's fine. Hurts, but it's fine." My eyes dropped to the puddle forming around her feet, distorting the lines of the tile. I'd given myself a sponge bath the day before and would have to settle for another today, as soaking my wounds wasn't advisable.

Steam rose from the water. She let the towel fall and mounted the steps, hesitating a moment with only her toes submerged to test the temperature. A few bruises blued her skin. I had my own collection of bruises and punctures, including the marks from the ivy, but I wasn't interested in my body. I'd seen Fiadh undressed before, but not quite like this. Not . . . I wasn't sure what this emotion was, precisely, but it warmed me like the steam off the water with a surprising innocence. She was lovely, yes, and the line of her leg in the water and the tilt of her hips was sensual, but I didn't want her with the usual intensity. This feeling didn't leave room for anything else.

I watched the water where it met her skin as she slid into the tub; the soft electric light turned her as gold as the walls. *Tenderness.* Maybe it was tenderness I was feeling, but if so, it was a new kind of tenderness, tightened by the remembrance of near-loss. I stripped out of my own clothes and settled myself on the edge with my legs in the water and a washcloth folded neatly at my side before I could start crying.

"There's a ledge," she said, patting a spot beneath the water. I inched over and lowered myself gingerly in with one arm until I'd sunk up to my waist, careful not to wet the bandaging around my other shoulder.

"Are you okay?" I asked. Such an inadequate question. Fiadh closed her eyes and sank. I understood the urge. The pressure of water on my ears would have calmed the mad tumbling in my mind.

"No," she said when she resurfaced. A redness that had not been present a moment ago rimmed her eyes. "I told you I'd tell you about the Cat Síth when we got out."

"You don't have to, if you aren't up for it. Agatha told me a little."

She settled across from me, and it was a mark of the size of the tub that our knees barely touched. "What did she tell you?"

I repeated what Agatha had said. She listened, and the water flushed her skin into a semblance of good health.

"I carry some of Agatha's memories, as I told you: the ones that hurt the most, and the ones she cannot bear to either carry or forget. Most of those memories are about Natek. She would deny it, if you asked her. Natek betrayed her, even though it was partially unwitting, which I didn't know until the letters, and Vezina posed too great a threat for Agatha to risk seeing her again. Both her life and Natek's were in jeopardy, and while I don't know why she didn't just tell Natek everything, since she had a few hundred years to think about it, she didn't, and then it was too late.

"She was so lonely. No fey that she'd heard of, which meant no Oak fey for certain since their cultural memories are long, had ever been successfully turned. She was still one of them, but she described it to me once as feeling muted, like trying to talk on the phone to someone who wasn't standing near the mouthpiece, when you were used to being in the same room. I don't know how Vezina captured Agatha. She's never told me, and I've never seen that memory. Though . . ."

She paused, and I suspected she was thinking the same thing as I: now that she had Vezina's memories, she could find out.

"Anyway. Meeting my ancestor helped, because she could escape some of those memories, and because she had company again after losing Natek. Ancarat—that's my ancestor—formed an alliance in exchange for Agatha's promise to protect her bloodline. They were starting to hunt witches again, and that included us."

"Wouldn't it be too risky to offload memories like that? What if something happened, and the memory died too?" I asked.

"It's happened. But she keeps a record of every memory we hold. Using the techniques we've taught her, she can recall them on her own with time. It is difficult but not impossible. More than twenty-six hundred years of memories, and those of Natek still pain her more than almost anything else, except—"

"—the death of her daughter," I finished for her.

"Yes." She raised her hand to stare at the two small scars on her wrist. "I didn't want to put you in danger. I thought I'd calculated the risks, and I could keep you safe. I didn't think Vezina would be there."

Her voice cracked. I pressed my calf to hers, hoping it conveyed my understanding.

"Her soul," I began, wanting to get Fiadh off the topic of self-

302

blame. "It can't, like, take over you, can it?"

"No." Her hand moved over the surface of the water, creating ripples. She watched its slow passage. "She's dead. All I have are her memories. There's just . . . so many of them. The first hours of absorbing a soul are like a really, really bad film reel, but jumbled, and without context. I tasted your blood through her."

"Awkward," I said, laughing uncomfortably. Her answering smile was mostly grimace. I busied myself hunting around the edge of the bath for soap, and was relieved when the dispenser I found smelled of peonies, not roses. Peonies. Fiadh's favorite flower.

"My mother used that soap."

I looked up to find Fiadh watching me with eyes a little less haunted than before.

"It smells nice," I said. "Turn around and I'll scrub your back."

I rubbed the washcloth over her shoulders, careful not to get too close to the bruised, scabbed wounds on her neck. The cloth slid smoothly over her skin. I'd always liked the way soap lathered, and I created swirling patterns of foam across her ribs, not wanting to stop.

"Vezina is my sixth," she said.

"That sounds a little crowded."

"I'd kill to evict a few," she said with fervor. "Except my mother."

"I didn't know your mother . . . isn't with us anymore." Funny, how hard it was to just say dead.

"She's still with us. Just . . . do you know the silver cat you like?"

"Yes . . . ?"

"That's my mom."

I couldn't see her face and was glad she couldn't see mine. "But her soul—"

"The last change occurs at the moment of death. One last life, only without the memories. She loves me, but she doesn't know me as her daughter."

"That sounds . . ."

"It's nice, actually. She was a big comfort while I was mourning, and I had my mom's memories. That's a lot more than most people get."

I moved to soaping her arms and asked, "How old were you?"

"When my mom died? Fifteen. But I took my first soul when I was ten."

I stopped scrubbing. Ten was so young. I hadn't seen my first dead

303

body until Vezina. "Who was it?"

"Someone who didn't like Agatha very much." She turned to face me and I let the washcloth float on the surface. "There's something else I have to tell you."

"Okay . . ." I didn't like this. Nobody ever followed up that statement with, *I paid off all your student loans,*" or, *"they ran out of slices of cake except for this last piece, which I saved for you.*

"I've been thinking about some of our conversations—the ones about the sacrifices we make for work and family—and you might be right."

"How so?" I asked warily.

"About giving too much of myself to Agatha. I'm not quitting or anything, especially now, but I want . . . I want to have more to offer you. I have hardly anything to give you that's *mine.*"

"You're enough, Fi."

"That's not the point. I want more for me, too. I've spent so much time trying to keep myself separate from the other souls, terrified, and what's the point if all I do is work?"

"If the work matters to you—"

"It does, but I want other things to matter, too. I don't even know how to knit."

"Knitting? Really? That tops your list of regrets?" I teased.

She flicked water at me. "I am merely saying maybe we should do something together that isn't related to any of this."

"Fiadh Halloran," I said, feigning shock, "are you asking me out on a date?"

"Would that be okay?"

Such vulnerability in that question.

"Yes," I said, pulling her to me. "I'd love that."

What I should have said, however, was *I have something I need to tell you, too.*

Some other time. It might be years before Bran came for me. Plenty of opportunities to raise the specter of my choices later, when we'd had time to rest and recover.

Agatha called a meeting on the sixth day of our convalescence. A fire burned in the hearth, proof of her superior ventilation system, and

Natek leaned against the mantel. She was a master of the pose, a leopard at ease. Today she wore ordinary jeans and a sweater instead of clothes clearly borrowed from Agatha, and the gray knit shawl-neck looked as if it had come off the men's rack of some upscale designer boutique.

Agatha sat in her usual chair with Fiadh's mother purring in her lap, looking hollowed out and tired. I wondered how their reunion was going behind closed doors, and how she was coping with the loss of half her self.

"It seems we're in the clear, for now," said Agatha when Fiadh and I sat down.

Natek spoke up from the hearth. "I was able to return to another of my safe houses. Nobody knows about this one—it is an option for us if the worst occurs, though I assume you have your own . . .?"

This was directed at Agatha, not at me or Fiadh.

"Yes."

"I will give you the address to another one just in case. Especially you two." We nodded in understanding. "They are not stocked with human food—though I suppose technically . . . well. They are not stocked with food suitable for *you*. Bring what you can, and in the worst-case scenario, prepare for a few days of hunger. We're out of imminent danger for now. As long as you stay on the property, I believe we're safe."

The rest of the short meeting consisted of establishing the new contingencies and rules of life on the estate until we could be certain the danger had passed. Fiadh and I could otherwise return to life as normal.

"Natek?" I asked when Agatha signified the end to the required gathering.

"Nat or Natalie. Don't make me feel older than I already do, kid."

"Sorry. It's just—I've studied your life and legacy for most of my career." The way she said "kid" was filled with such affection I knew it had to be a practiced tactic since she didn't know me well enough or under normal enough circumstances to have formed any opinion of me whatsoever, aside from *scared shitless*, but it still filled me with unexpected warmth. With that one word, she became the cool big sister everyone wanted.

"My deepest apologies. I should have left more of a legacy." She smiled, indicating the joke was intentional and I had her permission to laugh. "This is why Agatha hired you. I am sorry, by the way, about your apartment. You hit a few too many of my search engine flags, and I was in a hurry. Had to make it look like a burglary. Didn't find anything, though, which just goes to show the importance of follow-up."

"I was wondering . . . What?" *Nektaria* had broken into my home? *You know what,* I told myself, *who cares? At least she didn't interrogate me.* I'd process this later, like so many other issues. I struggled with my next words. Each felt hard and sharp in my throat. "I was wondering if I could ask you a few questions."

She put a hand on my good shoulder and gave me a gentle squeeze. Her face had a browned, weather-beaten beauty, and while her skin was smooth from constant regeneration, it was easy to imagine it pocked with battle scars. "I'll tell you what I remember, which may not be much. That was a long time ago even for me."

I bit my lip to contain my grin, but it broke free anyway. Amid the horror of the recent past this, at least, was brilliant.

"Just, um, let me know a time that works well for you."

Fiadh, who had overheard part of this conversation, raised an eyebrow at me, no doubt amused by my poorly concealed eagerness. Natek glanced around the room, then back to me.

"Now's good. Rule number one of spycraft: take information where and when you can."

I grabbed my new phone, which Fiadh had ordered the moment she was conscious and near a computer, and opened the voice recorder app, then the notes app, where I'd typed up a few questions last night during a bout of wakefulness. As she settled into a chair, suggesting with a look that I follow suit, I experienced a moment of dissociation. I saw myself nestling into the cushions with my phone at the ready, face alight with the prospect of answers to questions that had long been lost to history. This was my dream, had been my dream for so long, and I was giddy with it despite everything.

The bunker cradled us in the earth's bones. It felt a little like being back in the deepest university library stacks. Abruptly and incongruously, I wondered if I had left one job for another much the same. The pay was higher, but so were the risks. Commensuration undermined the perceived gains. The pursuit of knowledge always seemed to have a price, and in stepping away from academia I'd re-created the same circumstances in the private sector. The lesser of two evils was still evil.

But so what if I had recreated the power structures I'd navigated my entire adult life? Society didn't value knowledge that didn't lead to financial gain. Compromises needed to be made. No alternatives existed that I was aware of; this was the way it was.

I pressed record and asked my first question.

EPILOGUE

Mark and his girlfriend, Lydia, arrived at my cottage for the party first. Since I couldn't leave the grounds, Fiadh had suggested to Agatha and Natek that I be permitted to invite a select few friends over the holidays instead.

"I can't tell you what a relief it is not to have to host something this year," Lydia said as she hugged me. "And your place is *adorable*."

She gazed around my cottage with parted lips, appreciation emanating from her along with the smell of her signature shampoo. I associated the scent with Mark, and often forgot until we were all together that Mark smelled like cucumber only because he'd held Lydia when her hair was still wet and at its peak fragrance. I wondered if I ever smelled like Fiadh to other people, or she like me. Thoughts of her certainly clung to me like perfume.

"Clara." The way Mark said my name suggested it wasn't the first time he'd tried to get my attention.

"Hey," I said.

"C'mere." He held his arms wide. I didn't need to be attracted to men to appreciate the beauty of a good bear hug. His muscular arms had been there for me many times over the years, along with the comforting, soft bulk of his middle. He also smelled like cucumber. Tears pricked the corners of my eyes, and I blinked rapidly to get rid of them before he released me and I had to come up with an excuse. I couldn't tell Mark or Lydia that they'd come very close to celebrating the holidays without me, both this year and all the years to come, any more than I could tell them that I worked for a vampire.

He gave me one last squeeze and released me. "So this is where you've been hiding."

"Can you blame her?" Lydia trailed her hand over the wool throw on the back of the nearest chair. The cottage did look lovely. The early sunset meant I'd already lit a few candles and a small fire in the hearth, and the glow, combined with the fairy lights and fresh pine garlands, softened the world's sharp edges. Natek—Nat—knew how to throw a party. She'd arranged the food and décor, muttering about how everything was better back when orgies were socially acceptable. Mulled wine steeped in a crockpot in the kitchen, and some sort of cheese pastry warmed in the oven, sending tantalizing aromas into the air. The lighting was strategic and elegant in its simplicity. Even the music was perfectly suited, though I'd never heard the piano arrangements before, nor could I pick out the almost familiar melodies.

"Where's your girl?" Mark asked.

"Getting dressed at her place." I gestured at my own clothes, which consisted of a wool blazer over my nicest black denim, and a leather ankle boot with only slightly frayed laces. I'd ordered a new shirt for the occasion: a creamy blouse that barely tiptoed over the line into femininity—specifically in the neckline, which, I'd realized when it arrived, didn't even offer a buttonhole until my sternum. I'd considered sending it back until I glanced in the mirror. The woman glaring back at me with her tousled blonde hair and irritated expression looked *hot*. I'd turned, admiring the cut, and decided that owning one item that showed a little cleavage wouldn't kill me.

"You look smoking," Patrice affirmed not long after, sweeping me up into a tight hug before holding me at arm's length. "Take me to your office, Professor."

"She's shameless." Daphne shook her head at her girlfriend and proffered up a casserole dish with several more tinfoil-covered dishes stacked on top, almost obscuring her face. "And so am I. I made your favorites."

She bumped Patrice's hip with her own, nudging her out of the way, and leaned in to kiss me on the cheek. I grinned and told her, "*You're* my favorite. Set them anywhere you can find room in the kitchen, and let me take some of the ones on top."

Daphne avoided my attempts to help and piloted into the kitchen with her oversized load, oohing appreciatively at the smells emanating from the oven.

"I tried helping her out of the car," Patrice said with a shrug. "Girl's independent."

"I carry trays heavier than this at work every day," the independent girl in question called out from the kitchen.

Mark and Lydia greeted the newcomers with warmth, and I offered them drinks and some snacks, full of a strange yearning to be with these people despite already sharing the room. I'd missed my friends more than I realized, and yet now that they were here, I felt the weight of what I couldn't tell them. Idly, I checked my new phone to see if there was a text from Fiadh. Nothing. Several more friends arrived. I stowed the bottles of wine they brought in the kitchen and remembered the cheese in the oven with a jolt.

I didn't hear the knock on the door over the pleasant hubbub of friendly chatter. Mark, who was in the middle of relating a funny story about a student he'd caught asleep in his class, broke off, looked over my shoulder, and then gave me a delighted grin.

Fiadh had stepped into the living room. She surveyed the small crowd, searching for me. My movement attracted her attention, but not before the elegant sweep of her hair in its twist and the candlelight warming her cheeks stole my breath. She rarely wore her hair fully up like this. It shone smoothly around the long clip, each strand neatly in place, and the neatness made me want to loose the clip and bury my hands in it. It was the dress, however, that was devastating.

The dress she'd worn at Vezina's hadn't fit. This one did. The floor-length fabric, which I'd thought was black but realized as she drew closer was a dark, dark green, clung to her hips and chest and nipped in at her waist as if designed to draw first the eye to her curves, and then the hand. I'd always been an absolute idiot over a certain kind of girl in a certain kind of dress—the kind of dress that drew attention without claiming it, as if to say, "what I contain is beautiful enough." The Edwardian scoop of neckline swooped over the rise of her breasts, still somewhat modest, but teasingly so. I didn't get to her shoes. I couldn't look away from the rest of her, or the amused quirk of her eyebrow, or the color slowly rising to her cheeks as I continued to stare. A set of emerald studs in her ears accentuated the green of her eyes, as did her makeup. She often wore mascara to work—but that was it. Now, with her lips a deep blush rose and her eyes even sultrier than usual, she was nothing short of stunning. And she'd done all this for me.

"Hi," she said when she reached my side. Her tone was teasing, but the faint flush across her chest let me know she'd been affected by my obvious admiration. She straightened my jacket lapels and smoothed them down, and now it was my turn to blush beneath the unmistakable hunger in her eyes as she noticed the open blouse only an inch from her fingers. Her hands paused their tidying of my jacket.

"Hi," I said intelligently. "Um, this is my friend Mark."

The look she gave me before she turned to Mark with an innocent smile undid me. I'd seen her look at me with desire before, but never with the blaze of pure want now shining from beneath her smoky eyelids. My body shivered with longing. I slid my arm around her and bit back a groan at the way her waist felt beneath my hand. She shifted closer to me under the guise of shaking hands with Mark, resting her other palm on the small of my back. Hidden beneath my jacket, the little circles she drew with her fingertips sent ripples over my skin. I thanked the universe at large for the fact that my friends had refused to relinquish the ridiculous tradition of dressing up for our winter holiday party. Mark's grin didn't fade as he engaged Fiadh in polite conversation. Did she live nearby, what was her role on the estate, was I at least working hard because otherwise he'd up and die of jealousy, and so on. Fiadh eventually turned the tables and got him talking about his research.

Lydia, Patrice, and Daphne descended during this conversation, and I couldn't wipe the smile from my face as Fiadh charmed my friends with her quiet humor.

"Do you want something to drink?" I asked her as the conversation shifted away from us. "Nat seems to have raided the estate bar. I don't think anything in the kitchen costs less than a kidney."

"I am a little thirsty." She looked up at me from beneath her lashes and I couldn't help digging my fingers into her waist. Had she intended the innuendo? Either way, it had worked. "Though a liver would have been a more apt comparison."

"Do they sell livers on the black market?" I asked, trying not to let my hand wander anywhere too inappropriate for a relaxed gathering.

"They sell everything." She slid a finger beneath my bra strap and gave it a gentle snap. My spine arched in response, as she'd no doubt intended.

"You look so fucking gorgeous," I said, whispering into her ear as I guided her to the makeshift bar. We were somewhat out of sight from the rest of the gathering here, surrounded by glittering bottles

311

and tempting morsels of food. She tangled a hand in my loose hair and pulled my mouth to hers.

My lips parted for her instantly, inviting, offering, and she kissed me deeply in reply. When her tongue brushed mine with a slow sensuality that put the rest of the world on hold, I slid my arms fully around her.

A cheer broke us apart. I looked over my shoulder to find my friends watching us with delighted expressions, and my face flamed.

"Merlot is fine." She said this with a prim clearing of her throat, as if she hadn't kissed me with such deliberate invitation to do more.

I poured her a glass. The red liquid splashed and swirled around the sides, clinging for a moment before dripping down. Fiadh lifted the bottle from my suddenly shaking hands and set both bottle and glass on the counter.

"I should have asked for white," she said, kissing the inside of my wrist as she clasped my hands in hers.

A month wasn't long enough to forget the blood we'd seen and lost. I thought I might be ill, my head swimming and heart pounding until Fiadh placed her palm over my heart. The heat from her skin and the steady pressure slowed the rising tide of panic and bought me enough time to rebuild the levees. With a shuddering breath, I was myself again.

"Where did you even get this dress?" I asked to distract myself.

"It's Agatha's. I had it tailored, naturally."

"Naturally."

"I also had to replace quite a bit of material. Vintage does have its drawbacks."

"I like it."

"I know." She touched my cheek and steered me back toward my guests, who seemed to have forgiven me for dropping off the face of the earth, and who welcomed Fiadh into their conversations gladly. I could tell by the stiffness of her posture that she wasn't entirely relaxed in the presence of strangers, but her laughter was genuine. It was a start—both to our mutual resolve to have a better work-life balance, and, perhaps, to a shared life.

The party wound down around ten thirty, which was already past what

I considered to be a reasonable bedtime, but wasn't as late as we used to linger. I loved being in my thirties. Bedtime was sacred to all of us but Mark. Daphne insisted on helping with the cleanup, but eventually she and Patrice departed with threats about what would happen if I didn't return the casserole dish.

"Take it with you! I have some Tupperware."

"No. I want a reason to see you again." With a hug and peck on the cheek, she waltzed out, girlfriend in tow, and Fiadh and I were alone in the glowing light of the décor. Music played quietly.

Fiadh put the last glass to dry on the drying rack and turned to face me, leaning back against the counter. I locked the door and closed the distance between us, walking slowly, intoxicated by the blush rising on her face and chest as I took her in. This openness between us was new and lovely and everything I'd ever wanted.

I stopped barely out of reach. She let out a tiny growl of frustration, sounding just like a cat. Unlike a cat, her eyes trailed down my chest and lingered. I slipped out of my jacket as sensuously as I could manage without looking like an idiot, folded it neatly, and rested it on the granite. Fiadh's chest rose and fell faster, and I regretted teasing her for reading bodice rippers. I saw the appeal now.

"That's a new shirt."

"Do you have my wardrobe memorized?" I took a step closer. If she reached out, she could grab my belt and force proximity. She didn't. Instead, she settled deeper into her posture and waited with a faintly arrogant tilt to her chin.

"As a matter of fact, yes."

"I'm flattered." I braced my hands on either side of her, our bodies now mere inches apart, and watched her pupils dilate.

"You don't own that many clothes."

"Speaking of . . ." I whispered the words into her ear and was rewarded with a shiver. "This dress is killing me."

She tried to catch my lips with her own, but I was quicker. I kissed her ear, nipping at the earlobe and running my tongue across its curves and ridges. She gasped. I'd never get tired of hearing that sound, and I couldn't contain my little groan of satisfaction. I knew how the sound would vibrate through her body.

Fiadh's second gasp turned into a plea. Bracing myself with one hand, I trailed the other across her chest as I'd fantasized about doing all night, following the hem and pausing to draw a line down over lips and collarbones and skimming over the valley of her cleavage.

She did grab my belt then, tugging me close and yanking my shirt out from my pants. The nails she dragged down my stomach temporarily paralyzed me with naked lust. When she did it again, I abandoned my courtship of her earlobe and kissed the base of her neck. Her skin tasted too damn good. I hoisted her onto the counter for a better angle and buried my face in the perfumed bliss between her breasts, her legs locked around me in folds of fabric.

I teased her with my tongue until she shook and strained to press against me, something I denied her until I couldn't. The heat of her against my stomach might as well have been her mouth on me for how much it turned me on. I raked my nails up and down her legs beneath her dress, loving the sound of my whimpered name filling the kitchen.

"Clara Eden," she said, though talking was clearly a struggle, "take me to bed right now."

I carried her, not out of chivalry, but because the slickness of her underwear against my belt buckle was possibly the hottest thing I'd ever felt.

The knock on the door woke us hours later. I stared into Fiadh's eyes, sharing the same, jumpy terror, my fingertip leaving a slight indent in her lip as we waited. The knock came again.

"It's probably just Agatha or Nat," Fiadh said, pulling away.

"Yeah." She was right. Maybe there'd been a new development. I threw on a sweater and a nearby pair of pants.

Mr. Muffin crouched in the tiny foyer, ears and whiskers pricked forward, his tail bristling. I paused. He'd never looked at the door like that before. My hand hung suspended between me and the doorknob like the Ghost of Christmas Yet to Come, unsure of what to do next.

"Clara Eden." The voice from beyond the door reminded me of another night, and a man knocking on the window of my car with the false promise of safety.

It was too soon. I hadn't even told Fiadh.

"Is that Bran?" Fiadh asked, reaching for the knob.

"Fi, no—" I lunged to try and stop her, but she'd already opened the door.

Bran stood on my doorstep, bundled in a faded down jacket and snow-blasted hat and scarf. He looked absolutely wretched. Purple circles underscored his eyes, and blue tinged his mouth. Fiadh stepped back to let him in and to shut out the cold. Snow was already mounding on the mat. All I could do was stand there and let it happen.

"Are you all right?" she asked him. "Agatha and Nat are at the manor house."

"I'm not here for them."

She frowned, turning to me. The hand of fate lay heavy on my back, shepherding me ever forward. I was glad, after all, that I hadn't told her. There were things you simply could not prepare for, which wrecked you irrevocably and without restraint. What had Nat written?

I've seen ships wrecked against more shores than I can count, and each spar is lodged between my ribs when I think of you. And I always think of you.

"No." Fiadh's head whipped from Bran to me, and anguish gilded her eyelashes in the lamplight. "You didn't."

I had to save you, I almost said, but instinct stopped me. That could too easily turn to blame. "There was no other choice I could live with."

Protest bloomed and died in her eyes. Fiadh understood impossible choices better than anyone I'd ever met. I held out my hand. It had been worth it, even if only for this short while.

She threw her arms around my neck. I held her tightly, breathing in the smell of her hair like it was the last breath of air in the room. Her hands dug into my back in fistfuls of cloth and skin. My own hands were no more innocent. One tangled in her hair, cradling her head, and the other was tightly wrapped around her waist, as if I could pull her into me if only I held on long enough.

"I'm so sorry," I said to her, over and over and over again. "I'm so sorry, Fi."

Bran staggered. He caught himself against the wall long enough to look me dead in the eye. Then his eyes closed, and spore erupted from every pore of his body, staining his shirt and filling the foyer with a golden fog. Within it, he stumbled again. Skin hung from his bones in folds, ripples and eddies of suddenly flaccid tissue. The water pressure needed to propel the spores had to come from somewhere. His body had obliged. White tendrils of hyphae spread across the empty skin.

"Fiadh." I exhaled her name.

She tilted her head back to search my face, her eyes flicking between mine, wild and green and perfect. I had to draw breath to speak the next words. I had to draw breath, and once I did, there would be no return.

"Fiadh, I love you."

She brought our lips together with the urgency of a crashing wave, all softness and teeth, her mouth warm and sweet and—in that moment, in that beating, despairing moment—mine in a way nothing would ever be truly mine again. Fiadh. My bold, bright light. I kissed her to the rhythm of my thoughts as the body of what had once been a person decomposed in my foyer, and the body that had once been wholly mine opened invisible arms.

I love you.

I love you.

We love you.

ACKNOWLEDGMENTS

A few years ago, while recovering from a concussion (which necessitated keeping my eyes on the ground lest I topple over), I noticed just how many mushrooms grew in the nearby woods and fields. I started photographing them, then learning about them. This book is the inevitable result.

Thank you to everyone who has listened to me monologue about the mycelium. Thanks, also, to the following: my publisher, Bywater Books (especially Salem West); my cover designer, friend, and mentor, Ann McMan; my editor, the insanely talented Kit Haggard, who at one point said to me, "It is my job, but also my enormous pleasure, to help you write the gayest, sexiest, most academic, most fucked-up li'l vampire book I can"; Shauntel (SD) Simper, who saved this book from itself; my parents, who have always supported my writing; my students, who inspire and amaze me; my Patreon patrons, who were exceptionally patient with me this year; my wife, who is the most precious thing in the world to me; and you, dear reader, for continuing to journey with me.

My preferred translation of the fragments of Sappho is Anne Carson's *If not, winter*, Vintage; reprint edition, 2003. I have referenced a few lines of her work here, as well as translations by Edwin Marion Cox, from his excellent book, *The Translations of Sappho*, William and Norgate, London, 1924. I highly recommend both. Nektopolis is an entirely made-up polity. I took some liberties with history in its conception (and throughout), though I did try to stick to the historical record whenever possible.

To head off some questions for those of you who may have thrown the book across the room after reading the last page: yes, there is a planned sequel, and no, that was not intentional. This book was supposed to be a novella, not a duology. On that note, Samara and Jenn, I am (not) sorry for blowing up our novella project and forcing you to write incredible novels.

ABOUT THE AUTHOR

Anna Burke is the award-winning author of *Compass Rose, Sea Wolf, Thorn, Nottingham, Spindrift,* and *Night Tide.* She holds an MFA from and teaches Creative Writing at Emerson College. When she is not writing fiction, she is an overly ambitious gardener and teacher. She and her wife live with their spoiled pets in Massachusetts.

For more updates and writing-related news and bonus material, please follow her across social media or consider joining her on Patreon.

Twitter | @annaburkeauthor
Instagram | @annaburkeauthor
Facebook | facebook.com/annaburkeauthor/
Patreon | patreon.com/annaburkeauthor

At Bywater Books, we're committed to bringing the best
of contemporary literature to an expanding community of
readers. Our editorial team is dedicated to finding and developing
outstanding writers who create books you won't want to put down.
For more information about Bywater Books, our authors,
and our titles, please visit our website.

www.bywaterbooks.com

CPSIA information can be obtained
at www.ICGtesting.com
Printed in the USA
JSHW081006140723
44758JS00002B/2